DAKEN DORF

LATEN DORF

CRYSTAL
MOUNTAINS

Pool of
Reckoning

LON

AZURA KAH

Jamoor
600 SOARS AFTER
THE PRIMENGEER

RAINBOW RIVER

MISTY
CROSSING

FRAGRANT
FIELDS

SONGBIRD
HAVEN

IC RIVER

GreeHee and The Star of Knowing
Original Art by Jane Starr Weils

GreeHee

The Journey of Five

by
Michele Avanti

Limited
First Edition

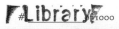

Tales of Tamoor
Book One

Loni and GreeHee
Original Art by Jane Starr Weils

GreeHee

The Journey of Five

by
Michele Avanti

Tales of Tamoor
Book One

A Limited First Edition

GreeHee Publishing
Reno   Myrtle Creek

GreeHee Publishing
125 Susan Street, Myrtle Creek, OR 97457
www.GreeHee.com

Library of Congress Cataloging-in-Pubication Data

Avanti, Michele A
      GreeHee The Journey of Five,   Tales of Tamoor Book
One: An adolescent dragon discovers self-worth when fate and the
unlikely friendship of a fairy, guides him to fulfill an ancient prophecy.

Library of Congress Control Number: 2006925606

ISBN: 978-0-9779590-0-6

GreeHee Publishing
Reno   Myrtle Creek

Hardback,
Limited First Edition August 2006

Cover Art by Jane Starr Weils, www.janestarrweils.com
Cover Design & Test Design by Michele Avanti
Consulting Editors: Diane & Gary Dunham, ETC Publishing, Reno, NV
        Michelene Bell, In Light Times, Las Vegas, NV

Printed in Korea

Table of Contents

Language of Tamoor

1 pinch	1 inch
1 leet	1 foot
1 yont	1 mile
1 tithe	1 second
1 elide	1 minute
1 sene	1 hour
1 beedite	1 day
1 leedite	1 week
1 moontide	1 month
1 soar	1 year
1 linglorn	500 years
1 tont	1 ton

Tortorsall: An impenetrable material made from giant tortoises by the giants of Narsor

Begee: A creature half giant and half gnome

Terrotac: A lower form of dragon. Reptilian beast that flies but cannot breathe fire and is slightly smaller than a full grown dragon.

Carron: A breed of aggressive bird-like creatures between five and six leets high.

Sawtooth: Tiger-like animal four times the size of a Carron.

Characters in order of Appearance

GreeHee: Adolescent dragon, thirteen soars, son of Tereem the Terrible

Tereem: One of the most vicious dragons in Tamoor

Loni: Youngest fairy in the line of Oberlon

Beauty: The enchantment band given to female fairies at birth

Eulool: The wizard of fairies

Potemkin: A Commander in King Narsor's army

King Narsor: King of the giants

Yorkin: A male fairy, Loni's older brother

Sarolla: A young giant, Loni's chambermaid in Narsor

Liz: A Begee in the library of King Narsor

Draydel: The last wizard of the Giants, whose magic ended the Primengeer

Nadeckador: King of the Giants during the first Primengeer.

Maduk: A troll, a part of Tana

Felleen: A dragon, a part of Tana

Beastera: A bird-beast predecessor of Carrons, a part of Tana

Destoor: Deceased Prince of King Narsor

Maltor: General of the Carron forces

Bartet: A Carron Captain

Jarteen: A Carron Admiral

Paychente: A Carron doctor

Baskooto: A Carron Chef

Potsote:	A Carron Corporal
Gento:	A Carron Corporal
Tarktor:	Architect of King Narsor's castle
Beetrea:	Deceased Queen of King Narsor
Starina:	Blue Roan speaking horse - Starina Ronella or Starry
Bravort:	A Carron Colonel
Rant:	A Carron corporal
Petri:	A Carron sergeant
Tana:	A being composed of three who seeks to rule Tamoor
Tyron:	The strongest giant in Potemkin's troop
Pazard:	A giant, Master Pastry and Saucier Chef
Bertrand:	Chief Chef in Narsor's Castle
Lovely:	Female giant who protects Draydel's chambers.
Bounder:	Sawtooth, younger brother
Milkoor:	Rookie Carron scout
King Allielt:	Fairy King of Oberlon, Father to Loni and Yorkin
Marleenah:	Queen of Oberlon, Mother to Loni and Yorkin
Maggin:	Loni's oldest sister
Boldor:	Unicorn
Hydous:	A crow
Doder:	A crow
Goran:	A giant and uncle to Potemkin
Majesic:	Merlin Elder Unicorn

Preface

In early 1981, a unicorn visited my studio and asked me to paint his picture.

I told him I would do so if he would tell me a story. So he did and from his story came the book you now hold.

Tales of Tamoor Book One, is the first in a series of five books that takes place in a time before men. In a land of dragons, fairies, giants, wizards, unicorns and many other creatures with whom you may not be familiar.

This story is much more than a tale of friendship, coming of age and self-discovery. It is more than a mystery and an amazing adventure. It is a world of many secrets, a reflection of earth, a bridge to unite people through the wisdom of real power...

"To your heart be true, this is your test,
For when you are, you are your best."

Michele Avanti

Acknowledgements

The unseen guidance of Spirit directs us all and to this greater power, I stand in awe and gratitude. Through It, I have met many wonderful souls who have influenced, supported, suggested and enthusiastically guided me through the adventure of publishing this first book of the Tales of Tamoor.

I know I will not recall every name, but I want to say, if you are reading this, and have been there for me, in even the smallest way, I am grateful.

To my husband Joseph, thank you for your wisdom, love, editing, and support through the long, late hours.

My beloved nephews, Michael Lopez and Mathew Lopez, your childhood smiles, your eager ears and your wondrous questions launched this adventure.

My dear friend, Michelene Bell, editor and enthusiastic ear, thank you.

My inspiriting artist friends, Ann Rothan and Russell Rothan, it was your excitement that thrust me forward to complete this volume.

ETC Publishing, Diane and Gary Dunham, I owe a debt of gratitude for all your support, encouragement and friendship.

My brothers Tony Avanti, Peter Avanti and sister Annemarie Avanti, always ready to listen through tears of joy or sorrow, thank you.

And my fabulous clients and friends who read, reviewed or supported my efforts: Orin Anderson, Bruce Chernin, Diane Zulim, Deb Blyth, Tom & Jamie Plunkett, Don & Ellen Scott, Rob & Cindy Robertson, Marta Fisher, Vicky Visconti-Tilly, Antonella Sisto, Rich Andrews, Carmen Miceli, Susan Gorrow, I will be ever grateful.

Jane Starr Weils, the brilliant artist that brought GreeHee and Loni to life, thank you for your laughter and dedication.

And finally to my best friends, who cannot read but have been there protecting, unconditionally loving and watching; Bo bo, Shogun, Homer, Pepper, Sousa, Jags, Gump, Pumpkin and yes, even Miss Luna - thank you!

Dedicated
In Loving Gratitude

To the two men who inspired me,

My father, Michael Avanti,
his enthusiasm for life,
sense of humor, integrity
and fantastic storytelling

Rebezar Tarzs,
who taught me everything
I know about the Inner Worlds,
how to see, hear, know and be.

Loni and GreeHee
Original Art by Jane Starr Weils

Chapter 1

THE JOURNEY BEGINS

GreeHee looked in the mirror and snarled. Barring his teeth, he blew tiny smoke rings through his wide nostrils. He studied his face. What is the secret of fierceness? He must become so terrifying that he scared himself. "I must!" he repeated out loud.

Stomping and snarling, he left the jeweled mirror and headed for the forest. At the entrance of the cave, he stopped, threw back his shoulders, screwed his face into a scowl, and stomped out into the afternoon sun.

As he approached the dense evergreen forest, he conjured up the presence of his fierce father Tereem. He began to mimic Tereem's walk, languid yet emphatic, rippling each muscle through to the tip of his tail before taking another stride. He moved towards a shrub, imagining it to be a grubby dwarf guarding his cache of jewels and gold. Pretending to be Tereem, GreeHee stared down at the 'dwarf' commanding in his deepest rumbling voice, "Vermin, die!" Then with a blast of fire the shrub burst into flames. GreeHee imagined the dwarf screaming and running off.

A flicker of white seemed to jump from one tree to another. There again. What would his father do? "Out with you, you trespassing bit of white or I shall burn down all the trees around you!" GreeHee roared, mimicking his father perfectly.

Nothing happened. The young dragon blew hot black smoke through the trees. The sound of choking began. Soon a small white fairy creature coughed and choked before him. No more than four leets high, whitish-blue in color, with big blue eyes, it wore a small gold crown on its golden head.

GreeHee's eyes widened. He asked in his own voice; "Who are you?"

"My name is Loni," replied the creature, coughing, "I am, the youngest of the fairy princesses of the line of Ooden from the kingdom of Oberlon by the great Crystal River."

The smoke began to clear. Sure Tereem would eat this fairy and add the crown to the treasure pile. Of course this is what he must do to make father proud of him. He bit his upper lip in determination, thinking, I can do it, I can eat this fairy.

As he began to move, Loni spoke. "Please, Mr. Dragon, I didn't mean to trespass in your forest. I was kidnapped from my home several leedites ago. I finally got away from the ogre who trapped me. I was only trying to get back home."

The fairy began to sob, then hopefully she continued; "If you would take me home, my father would be very grateful. He would reward you with gold and jewels."

Ah, she seemed so helpless! And the more he looked at her the more he liked her. But no, the dragon-art. What would his father do? Of course, Tereem would look upon the fairy's request as an open invitation to kill all her family and take home all the treasure. Yes, this is what he must do. Go there and return before father got home. GreeHee will show Tereem what kind of dragon he had for a son. GreeHee's chest swelled.

"How far away is your kingdom?" he asked.

Brightening a bit, the fairy answered, "I think it's been ten beedites since the ogre captured me."

GreeHee considered when his father would return. He'd have plenty of time. And father would be so proud! A smile crept over GreeHee's face.

"Yes, I will take you," he said. "But you must direct me. I have never flown beyond these mountains."

Big blue eyes sparkling, Loni said, "Yes, I'll direct you! It will be my pleasure." Beaming she continued, "My father will be so glad to meet you. Uh, may I ask your name?"

"GreeHee. Now, hop onto my back and we'll get started."

The sky was clear and the wind brisk as it caressed his face. The mountainous forests stretched out below. The river Ryon gleamed purple in the distance and the sweeping Plains of Sasso stretched across the horizon in gentle hues of cream and brown.

"GreeHee, this is fun! I love seeing the world from here. The freedom that I feel is awesome!" exclaimed the fairy.

"Yes, I know what you mean. I like the feeling of power when I fly. I can see for hundreds of yonts, nothing can escape my vision. It makes me feel I can control everything below simply because I am above it."

"GreeHee, I'm so glad you found me. I really like you!"

He swallowed hard, electricity ran down his spine. No one had ever spoken to him like this before. It felt nice yet; he knew he would destroy her and her family to prove himself. He felt like a rock hit the pit of his stomach.

No don't think about it. Easier to look at the big clouds and smell the wind.

After senes of silence, Loni's grip loosened.

"Loni, are you asleep?"

The fairy moved a little. "Oh yes, GreeHee, I'm very tired. Could we stop for a while?"

"Yes. I could stand a bit to eat at any rate."

GreeHee landed in a large meadow near some fruit trees and Loni dismounted.

"I'm going to find some food. I'll be back in a little while, rest yourself."

"Yes, this place is perfect."

Loni relaxed on the soft grass and fell into an enchanted sleep. A gentle blue light surrounded her and the haunting sound of fairy pipes whispered in her ears. She became aware of Eulool, the ancient fairy counsel, as he stood before her, dressed in a deep purple robe of velvet, meticulously embroidered with the Scrolls of Ooden in silver threads encrusted with jewels. In his right hand he held the staff of Wizen, a magnificent pearl staff glittering with fairy images emitting colors of blue and gold. Atop the staff stood a winged unicorn with a fairy woman on its back. Eulool's face was stern. The white hair of his whiskers flowed down the front of his robe.

"Come, child," he said, "You are in danger and must do as I say. I have something for you." Out of his robe he pulled a small shining five-pointed star and set it dancing in his hand. Loni stood mesmerized by its beauty. As it danced it sang a sweet low sound and gave off a blue light.

"The one who takes you home has a great and wonderful heart. He is blind but has earned the right to see; yet he must request it. Take the Star of Knowing and keep it. When the dragon asks, the star will hum and you must give it to him at that moment or it will fade and the opportunity may not come again for a multitude of linglorns." Eulool's image disappeared.

Loni woke up squinting and blinking. The dream had been so strong that the actual world around her seemed blurred. What had she done with the Star of Knowing?

GreeHee landed nearby greeting her. "Did you sleep well?"

Nodding in response, she noticed the star in her enchantment band, the ring of fairies that each female in the family of Ooden was given as a child. She rose and moved toward the dragon with joy and relief in her heart. Loni floated in and out of the trees eating a little fruit, glad for the protection of Eulool, and smiling at the star of blue on her finger.

GreeHee noticed her smile and he smiled too. A light happiness filled him though he didn't like the undercurrent that must follow. He forced it into a dark corner of his mind along with his father and began to enjoy himself for the first time in his life.

Once again in the air, Loni began to sing:

> Oh Fairies of Ood, the truth have told,
> A tale for all the young to know
> Of two hearts fond, that love and grow
> Together through the times of Shoald
> Through pain, through war,
> Though blood be shed
> The friendship of fairies we shan't forget
> To help our friends near death we'll tread
> Forever a friendship till death we pledge.
> The friendship is greatest when both shall be
> Dependent on the inner lead
> To stand against Tana with Friends abreast
> Both truth and fear shall be their test
> And through the traps of Wizards' Web
> This friendship great shall weave a thread
> Of Freedom, of Wisdom, Of Dawn and Song,
> In truth a friendship to gift us all!

She sang and sang in her tiny voice with every string of her heart. Even GreeHee hummed along, the tune making a home in his mind.

After awhile Loni stopped and said, "You know, GreeHee, I think that our friendship will one beedite be as great as the friendship we sing about--

"GreeHee we must stop! Please there is some terrible danger before us! Please we must stop!"

"Where? Why? How do you know?" GreeHee began looking at Loni. She glowed in a red light, eyes fixed, mouth gaping. He followed her stare.

Four purple and black Terrotacs approached, their teeth barred, sickening yellow glint in their penetrating eyes. GreeHee shouted, " Loni, hang on! I'm not as powerful as those filthy beasts, but I'm faster."

The vicious terros! GreeHee flew into a death spin almost, perpendicular to the ground. The first terro could not follow. The other three did.

Reaching the height of the great Marmosa trees, he flew in and out beneath their branches. His stomach rumbled. His nostrils grew heavy with the stench of beast boron meat, the staple menu of terros.

GreeHee landed in the middle of a tight thicket of Marmosa trees. "We're safe for the moment," he said. "The terros are too large to move between these trees and tearing them down is too dangerous because Marmosa sap can make a terro very sick. It could even kill them."

"Really?" Loni said, eyes wide.

"My father told me that the Maap Seres rid themselves of the vicious terros by poisoning them with Marmosa sap. He said they mixed it into the borons' food and when the terros ate them, they died."

"That was really smart!" said Loni.

"Yes and after a while the terros began to die off. Then the last of them moved here to the Plains of Sasso. If only I had remembered that before! We could have flown further south and avoided this mess."

"GreeHee, don't be so hard on yourself, we'll find some way out of here."

"Yes, you're right, Loni. But it's going to be tricky getting out of this mess. Those beasts are drooling at the thought of a nice juicy young dragon. I'm a great delicacy to them. But they won't get a bite without a fight. At any rate, I know four is more than I can handle." GreeHee frowned, angry that he had not simply eaten the fairy and stayed home where he would be enjoying his comfortable cave, practicing smoke rings and eating dinner. Oh why did he care about growing up and making his father proud of him anyway? "What a mess! What a mess!"

"Oh, GreeHee, don't worry, the sun will be setting soon and we'll think of something." Loni said. After a moment she began to smile. "GreeHee, I have an idea."

Chapter 2

THE STAR OF KNOWING

When the sky filled with light, GreeHee and Loni prepared the final part of her plan.

"Are you ready, GreeHee? The sun's almost up. They'll be checking soon."

"Yes," he said his upper lip twitching. It was a good idea but a nasty, messy way to have to get out of this awful situation. What if it didn't work? How long would it take a terro to get sick on marmosa sap? What if it took a sene? Or worse, a beedite? What if these weren't marmosa trees at all? No, they were. But what if marmosa sap didn't make terros sick?

Loni had asked the marmosa trees to fill the pit with their sap. Now she stood before a baby Bonta tree saying, "Thank you, but we only need marmosa sap." Leaves started to fall from the little tree and it started drooping. Loni touched her ring saying, "Beauty, please to thank this tree." Instantly flowers of every color appeared on the tree. The Bonta smiled and held its sap.

The pit was almost full. The streams of orange sap were slowing down, as the rosy fingers of the sun began to streak across the horizon. GreeHee stood on the edge of the pit, fists clenched, scales rigid, face strained.

Loni said, "I'm ready when you are."

Okay Loni, I sure hope this works," said GreeHee as he stepped into the pit, grimacing at the sticky stuff. The dragon rolled over several times, smoke rising from his nose as he attempted to coat it with the sticky sap.

"It looks like you have a good coating," said Loni as she flitted about, checking the dragon. "Okay GreeHee, I'll become a moonbeam and sit in your ear so I can see what is happening without getting hurt."

"How long can you stay in that form?" he asked surprised by the golden ball of light in front of him.

"Ten to fifteen elides." Loni bounced into GreeHee's ear.

With a deep sigh, the dragon flew into the dawning sky.

GreeHee saw the band of terrotacs not far behind him. He dropped quickly throwing the big black one out of reach, but the terrible purple terro moved in. Now GreeHee flew high and turned southeast, hoping to outmaneuver them. But they closed in. The smaller two flew low, while the big purple and black one moved in from behind.

The smallest Terro flew in below GreeHee, just out of reach of his fire breath. The stench of rotten breath hit GreeHee like a putrefied wall. Laughter rumbled as the big black Terro swooped in biting his left thigh. Loni shouted cuing GreeHee and he turned, burning more than the Terros speckled belly. He burnt his face. The Terro screamed and pulled back, but not before he tore away some of GreeHee's hide.

One of the younger Terros flew up, attacking GreeHee's vulnerable belly, while the powerful purple Terro moved to GreeHee's right side. GreeHee tumbled in the air, shooting fire at the purple one and smacking the young one in the face with his tail. But before GreeHee could move out of range the young one bit down on his tail, pulling him down.

GreeHee did everything he could to fire on the Terro including singe his own tail. The Terro held fast. Then within eight leets of the ground he let go. Holding his stomach and hollering in pain, the young Terro hit the ground. GreeHee took off close to the ground, maneuvering between the trees. Darts of pain shot through his body as the branches tore into his bleeding thigh. The youngest Terro and the terrifying purple one hovered above him. The others had disappeared. Was the marmosa working? GreeHee came to the end of the trees. "Loni we've run out of cover!"

"GreeHee look up!" Loni screamed.

The two Terros descended upon him. He turned straight up facing his attackers. Breathing fire for all he was worth, GreeHee burnt their bellies, tails, and necks.

GreeHee headed into the sky. The purple Terro lurched forward extended his neck and sunk his teeth into GreeHee's right foot. Screaming with pain, GreeHee turned firing upon him. The powerful Terro would not let go. Instead he whipped his tail into GreeHee's face, almost knocking Loni out of his ear.

Regaining his senses, the dragon heard Loni scream, "GreeHee, on your left!" The young Terro moved in on his left, mouth wide-open, ready to bite into his already wounded left thigh. The purple Terro pulled GreeHee downward. Gathering every bit of power and strength, the dragon whipped his tail to the right, knocking the purple one in the head. He loosened his grip on GreeHee's foot. Recalling how his father had disarmed many a terrotac, the dragon aimed his most powerful fire in a direct stream at the young one's left eye. The Terro shrieked, let go and gave up the chase.

Then the purple Terro began moaning. Holding his stomach, he let go of GreeHee's foot and flew after the others.

GreeHee sighed with relief, gritted his teeth against the agonizing pain, and flew high trying to spot a place where he could wash off the sap and clean his wounds.

About ten yonts later, they came to a wide clear lavender river.

"What luck!" cried Loni once more in her full form. "This is the great Brentippees River. It borders the land of Narsor, king of the giants. They've been friends to fairies for over six hundred linglorns. We'll definitely be welcome here!"

Despite his pain and tiredness, the only thing he could think of was washing the sticky sap off his body. "Loni, jump!" he shouted. "I'm diving in."

Loni landed on the warm dry grass. But as soon as GreeHee hit the water, she was soaked. "Whoa!" she exclaimed, flapping her iridescent wings and shaking out her long blonde hair. Loni found a drier spot on the bank and sat down.

GreeHee made quite a spectacle in the lavender water. Floating on his wide green back he washed his face, stomach, arms, legs, and tail. Then he turned over and began using his tail to wash his back. Each time he started to scrub he lost his balance and rolled face down into the water. Over and over again GreeHee tried to keep his balance only to end up dunking himself again. Loni began to laugh.

GreeHee's frustration turned to anger he blew fire. Only each time the fire started, he lost his balance and rolled into the water, leaving little clouds of smoke. GreeHee stopped to catch his breath. He poked his head out of the smoke clouds and looked at the lavender river mottled with orange sap. He noticed Loni laughing and realized how ridiculous the whole situation must appear. GreeHee started laughing too.

Once the fairy and dragon regained their composure, Loni said, "Let me help you scrub off the last bits of sap."

"Oh now you want to help me. Now that you have laughed yourself silly at my expense." Eyebrow raised, he cocked his head sideways. "You know it feels good to laugh."

Loni helped GreeHee. Then they looked at the wounds.

"Most of the cuts are already healing," GreeHee said looking at his arms and stomach.

"These are the worst," said Loni pointing to his tail and right foot.

"And this one here. It really hurts." GreeHee pointed to his left thigh.

Her eyes widened and she shook her head, "Oh, that looks really badly. It must have reopened in the water. You need a salve to heal that gash. Let me see what plants are around here." Loni began to search the riverbank.

Spotting prickly comfrey, she asked, "Please, would you help my friend?"

"Take a piece of my footing," replied the comfrey.

"Thank you," Loni taking part of its fleshy root.

GreeHee watched the fairy, wondering at her wisdom. He was too tired to fight his feelings, so he relaxed and let Loni take care of him.

"Can you squeeze this?" asked Loni. "It will help you heal faster."

GreeHee did so without saying a word.

Loni rubbed the salve into GreeHee's wounds. When she finished GreeHee mumbled, "Thanks Loni, I think what I need now is a good nap."

They both fell asleep in the warm sunshine on the broad banks of the beautiful Brentippees.

As he slept, GreeHee tossed and turned. Every step of the battle replayed in his dreams. He saw Loni laughing by the river and a voice kept echoing, "She saved your life…she saved your life." GreeHee turned away from the voice only to see his terrible father holding twenty fairies, and eating them one by one.

GreeHee screamed and woke. Loni was in a deep sleep. How unsuspecting she was, so trusting and kind. She really seemed to care about him too. Oh what to do! Could he really kill her and her family? Oh why was he born a dragon? He was nothing like his father. Why couldn't he be a fairy or a giant or anything else? GreeHee started to cry. Then he heaved a deep sigh. Determined that he would forget it all, he fell back asleep.

Loni slept in a deep trance. Fairy children sang an ancient song.

> A dragon mean, with teeth and fire
> A fairy queen took straight to die
> But unicorn so young and kind,
> Did hear the scream; arrived in time.
> A dagger thrust, his horn did take
> In two the dragon's heart did break
> The blood that spilled was only mean
> In time the rest grew great and clean
> In waking time, this pregnant one
> Would have a runtling dragon-son
> Who in his turn, would have to pay
> In blood or kindness for her way.

Round and round the song ran in her head. She kept seeing the image of the unicorn thrusting its horn into the heart of the enormous beast.

Slowly the scene changed. Loni found herself in the comfortable familiar surroundings of her father's private chambers. There amidst emerald satin and white wooly carpets, the rose-colored light glowed through the quartz walls, illuminating her father's face etched with sorrow. He held her mother, who cried in his arms. Eulool stood before them, issuing words of comfort. "Loni is all right so far. We must keep a positive embrace around her. She is much closer to home now."

Then Eulool looked straight at Loni saying, "The time approaches quickly! Remember the star! Events are happening fast, child. If you don't get home soon you may be lost. Hurry, wake up now, and wake the dragon!"

Startled Loni woke up. She shook herself, flapping her wings briskly. The star of knowing gleamed in her enchantment band. She turned to wake GreeHee. He mumbled in his sleep, little wisps of smoke escaping from his nose.

"GreeHee! GreeHee!"

But GreeHee didn't budge.

Loni hopped onto GreeHee's shoulder and started to shout into his ear. GreeHee turned over in his sleep, knocking Loni to the ground, nearly crushing her. "Oh good grief, my wing is stuck."

GreeHee began mumbling in his sleep, "Why me? Why me? I don't want to do it. Oh, why me?" He seemed very sad.

"Oh Beauty, how shall I get out of this mess before GreeHee rolls over onto me?" asked the fairy trying to pull her wing out from under the dragon. A sharp shell sparkled on the ground beside her. Picking it up, she pressed it into GreeHee's skin right above her wing. As he moved away from the pinching sensation Loni pulled herself free.

"Whew, that was close!" exclaimed Loni.

She flew above the sleeping dragon and landed near his ear. In her loudest voice she hollered, "GreeHee, wake up!"

His eyes opened wide. "Under attack? Are we under attack?" He jumped up and would have tossed Loni to the ground, had she not hung on tenaciously.

"No, everything is okay. But we must leave now. I can explain as we fly."

Pulling himself together, GreeHee said, "Wait a moment, Loni, I've got to get a drink first, then we'll go."

As the water hit his stomach, he realized how empty it was. "I need to get something to eat. We haven't eaten for more than twenty-four senes."

"GreeHee, I feel we should get closer to Narsor's castle. Perhaps we could eat there. Besides I don't see a whole lot to pick from here."

GreeHee looked around. The bank was barren. The area showed no signs of life for many yonts. "Okay, let's go," he said. "We'll stop if we see a good spot. Otherwise we'll see what the king has to offer. Though I'm not sure I'll be welcome there."

Loni hopped onto his back and off they flew.

"GreeHee, you're not like other dragons. I think King Narsor will like you as much as I do." Then, she asked, "GreeHee is something bothering you? Is there a problem I might help you with? I know I'm only a little fairy and certainly not wise like Eulool our wizard. But if you talk about it maybe we could figure it out together."

No one had ever offered to help him before. No one had ever asked what was bothering him. His father only called him names, gave him orders, and was actually so ashamed of him that he seldom ever shared anything with GreeHee, least of all affection. But Tereem was still his father. He wanted to scream thinking about how different he was from other dragons. Who ever heard of a dragon that couldn't even eat a fairy? Oh, what could he do? If he were home, he'd crawl into his cave and go to sleep.

"Please GreeHee, talk with me. Sometimes when we talk about things, they don't seem as overpowering as when we keep them inside."

"Oh Loni, you're too kind. You don't know me. I'm not what you think!"

"No, no one is ever what anyone else thinks they are. But actions speak louder than words," replied the fairy waving her arms. "When we first met you didn't harm me, another dragon might have killed me. You fought those Terrotacs, bravely defending both of us. You're a good, courageous dragon and I'm proud to be your friend."

That did it. GreeHee landed. He wanted to look Loni in the eye and hear her say that again. "Loni, look me square in the eye and say that again," commanded the dragon as he held the tiny fairy before him.

Loni stammered, "Which part? You mean about what you are?"

"Yes! Tell me what you see."

"Well, you are a gentle, thoughtful courageous dragon, and I am proud to be your friend!"

Putting the fairy down, GreeHee sat pensively for a long time.

"Loni, I like you. Despite how a dragon should feel, I like you. But I'm torn inside. I came here to prove myself and so far the only thing I've proven is that my father is right -- I haven't the heart to be a great dragon. I'm only a sniveling runt of a dragon. Perhaps that's all I will ever be."

Loni raised her right hand pointing at GreeHee, "But you have too much courage to believe those words! Think how well you fought those Terrotacs. It took courage." Loni paced and waved her right index finger to emphasize each point. "You were outnumbered, but you didn't give up. You flew for senes bleeding and didn't complain or cry once. You have the qualities of a great dragon!"

"Yes, but not the fierceness!" blurted GreeHee before thinking.

"Look, perhaps the problem you face is not a lack of fierceness but one of identity. Stop comparing yourself to other dragons. Look at yourself and see who you are."

He wanted to roar, "I'm GreeHee the Fierce, son of Tereem the Terrible!" But it was so absurd that he broke into a pathetic laugh saying, "I wanted my father to be proud of me; but I haven't the heart to be what he is. Oh, if only I were born a fairy or a giant or anything except a dragon."

GreeHee sighed. "Loni, I'm a simple-natured dragon with no fierceness. I wish I knew how to make my father happy and still be the simple dragon I am."

Loni's enchantment band began to hum. The fairy moved her hand toward him saying, "GreeHee if you want to know how, the star of knowing will tell you. Take it!"

GreeHee's eyes widened with amazement. In Loni's hand danced a five-pointed blue star. It danced into his hand growing larger, humming and twinkling. Then it began to sing:

> The dragon comes with greedy hands
> To fix red death upon the land.
> But when a dragon's heart be pure,
> Then one alone can close the score.
> Now if you question how to be,
> Just be yourself alone, GreeHee.
> Think not on other's names or words
> Yours is a gift, dragons unheard.
> While through his life your father greeds
> Upon a time, you'll set him free
> And then he shall as all Tamoor
> Be proud of you, so search no more!
> Now as you go along life's way,
> Take heed of these few words I say:
> To your heart be true! This is your test,
> Each time you do, you are your best,
> Then you will earn the highest score,
> Freedom, Wisdom, and Power forever more."

The star faded. Stunned, GreeHee didn't move. He stood with his right hand outstretched where the star had been.

Loni exclaimed, "Look, at your palm!" They both gazed at the spot. There sat the blue star, smack dab in the center, as if it had always been there.

"Wow!" GreeHee said, rubbing it with his left thumb. "To your heart be true," he whispered as a smile burst across his face. "Now that's what I like to do best of all! Oh that's so much easier!" Loni smiled too. "Hop on Loni, let's go to Narsor's castle and have dinner. Dragoonas! Do I have a lot to think about!"

Except for his swollen, throbbing thigh and foot, GreeHee never felt better in his life. The huge burden of being a dragon had been lifted from him.

They flew silently into the forming darkness. By the time the three silver moons of Tamoor had risen, GreeHee began to wonder if they would ever get to Narsor's castle. "Loni, I'm so tired and hungry, are you sure this is the right direction?"

"Yes, GreeHee, yes! See, my enchantment band is glowing white," she extended her hand for GreeHee to see. "That means we're almost there."

Tiny lights appeared on the horizon. As they drew closer the enormous roads and buildings clearly revealed a community of giants. GreeHee flew lower trying to make things out in the agricultural and forested terrain below.

Only six yonts from the castle, a rock hit GreeHee in the head knocking him out. He spun hurtling toward the ground. Loni hung on tightly screaming; "GreeHee, wake up! Wake up! Wake up! Please wake up!"

Chapter 3

LAND OF THE GIANTS

GreeHee did not crash to the ground. Instead, as fortune would have it, he fell into the tops of some bonta trees. The thick fur-like leaves held him as comfortably as any bed. Loni landed near him. She returned to her full form. Hopping over to his ear, she shouted, "GreeHee, wake up! Please wake up!"

Loni stared, her wings twitching. The dragon did not move. No wisps of smoke came from his nose. What to do? Looking to her enchantment band for comfort, the fairy's mouth fell open. Beauty glowed strangely, first red than blue. It couldn't seem to make up its mind! Friend or foe? Oh, if only GreeHee would wake up.

Clash! Crash! Zing! Sounds of metal shattered the silence. Her enchantment band was going wild. Afraid, yet curious, she wanted to fly down to see what was happening. But what if GreeHee woke while she was gone? Torn between fear of the unknown and knowing, Loni decided GreeHee would be all right for a few moments while she quietly explored below.

As she reached the lower limbs of the furry bonta tree, Loni could make out voices.

"You thought you had us, did you? Size is no match for Tana's power"

"I spit on your power!"

Loni got closer. Two carrons stood beneath the tree in which she hid. Carrons, large bird-like beasts, had yellow eyes and long strong yellow beaks. These carrons wore black armor.

But what were they doing in the land of Narsor? And why did they knock GreeHee out of the sky?

Their captive, a handsome dark haired, giant, stood defiant, his hands tied behind his massive back. He too wore armor. His sword, as tall as the Carrons, rested against the tree beside them, its hilt glittering below Loni.

What to do? If GreeHee remained unconscious, the giant is my only hope. Loni secretly hopped across the trees, landing behind the giant. While the three continued to throw insults at each other, The fairy formed into a moonbeam. Then she floated under the giant's helmet to his ear. Whispering ever so softly, Loni said, "Friend, take no notice of me, but listen." The giant's shoulder jerked but he said nothing. "I am a fairy and shall free you by burning through your ropes, so do not worry if your wrists get hot. When I am through, continue to stand still and I will distract the carrons so you can overpower them. If you understand, scrape the ground."

The giant responded. Loni hovered by his hands in her full form. She held her enchantment band to the ropes whispering, "Beauty please no sound do make, but singe these ropes that they may break." With a tiny spark the ropes burnt through. The giant grasped them in his hands.

By now the carrons were speaking to each other, taunting the giant. "Virgil, I'll wager one flask of the finest brimwinery that this yellow-livered half-bred beast of a giant can't go three elides in the arena with a boron."

"Eh, I don't know," replied Virgil, "as slow as he is I think--"

Branches snapped behind him. As the two carrons turned, the giant seized his sword. In a mighty blow he killed Virgil. Terrified the other carron ran through the trees. The giant, right on his tail, grabbed him by the neck with his powerful fist, nearly strangling him. "Where is your power of Tana now, you filthy excuse for a bird? Perhaps if we can wash and pluck you clean enough our dogs might eat you!"

With his free hand, the giant pulled a dark green sack out of a pouch on his belt. It was made of tortorsall, an impenetrable mail-like material produced by the gigantic tortoises of Narsor. Then the giant stuffed the carron into the sack and tied it shut.

Loni flew back to the treetop to check on GreeHee. But he was not there. Where is he? Loni flew in and out of the trees searching for the dragon, perhaps he awoke and went on to the castle.

Loni flew to the ground. The giant called out softly, "Fairy! Fairy! Where are you? Please come out…"

"I'm here."

The giant pivoted. "Oh! How can I ever thank you? You saved my life!"

"Well," said Loni, "perhaps you can help me. I'm Loni of Ooden and I came to Narsor with a friend. But he has disappeared. We were flying over these trees when he was hit in the head. I don't know where he is. I hope he went to the castle. He knew that's where we were headed. Can you help me find him?"

The giant leaned forward, head tilted sideways, one eyebrow raised, he asked; "What kind of friend is he?"

"A dragon."

"Oh, no!" cried the giant raising his hands to his head. "I shot your friend! I thought he was a friend of the Carrons. Dragons are normally enemies. We must hasten to the castle. Your friend's life is in great danger."

The giant threw the sack over one shoulder and Loni rode on the other.

"What is your name, giant?"

"I am Potemkin, Captain Superior in the Guard of his King Narsor," the giant said as he started jogging toward the enormous stone castle.

At each checkpoint, the giant asked about the dragon. But no one had seen him. Loni figured GreeHee must have used more discretion in getting to Narsor's castle.

As they crossed the enormous drawbridge to the towering fortress, Loni looked to Beauty for help. "Please, Beauty, look and see, where is my friend GreeHee?" But Beauty just shone white. Exhausted, hungry, and very sad but having no other ideas, she recalled the words of Eulool: "All things are in perfect order even though you do not understand them at this moment. Trust in this. It is so." These words always helped her through tough situations. So she took a deep breath and let go of her fears, switching her attention to the giant.

"Commander, the king is in session in the central greeting hall. He has been asking for you," said a heavy built, red bearded guard as he saluted Potemkin.

Potemkin, his voice flat, empty of hope asked, "Have you seen a dragon?"

"No sir. What would a dragon be doing here?" asked the guard raising his thick bushy eyebrows,

"It's a long story," Potemkin said, shaking his black wavy head. Then handing the sack to the guard he continued, "Here's a Carron I captured in the forest, have one of the guards to take him to the dungeon."

"Yes, Sir," the guard snapped his heels together with a salute.

Loni and Potemkin went down a long hallway made of huge granite stones and lit by enormous torches every ten leets. The hall must have been twenty-four leets high and Loni felt tiny seated on the shoulder of the giant.

At the meeting hall Loni hopped to the cold gray rough-hewn floor. Two guards, dressed in armor with green armbands, equally tall, came to attention saluting Potemkin. As he returned their salute, the guards opened the immense, ornately carved, wood doors and Loni's eyes met those of the king. They were kind, green eyes shaded by bushy gray eyebrows. His hair was the color of salt and red pepper. Shorter than Potemkin, he stood about fourteen and a half leets high. Narsor was striking with his billowing white silk sleeves sharply contrasting the mottled-green tortorsall breast cover and the dark forest-green suede pants. His black leather boots came to his knees, which were almost as high as Loni's waist.

He stopped in mid sentence and looking at Potemkin asked, "Commander, who is the little fairy with you?"

Before Potemkin could answer, a young fairy dressed in beautiful blue-green armor said, "Your Highness, this is my sister, Loni, the youngest princess of Oberlon!"

Loni flew to hug her brother. "Yorkin! I'm so happy to see you! I have so much to tell you --"

Yorkin whispered: "Hush, Loni." He deliberately turned them both to face the king.

Clearing his throat, the king shifted his gentle eyes from Yorkin to Potemkin saying, "Commander, I am certain you have much to report but considering the appearance of Princess Loni, we will take a one-sene break and then continue our discussion of new strategies."

The group broke up and the king came down from the platform to personally greet Loni. "Are you hungry child?" he asked in a fatherly manner.

Loni bowed deeply to the king. "Yes, your Highness."

Turning to a young giant who was walking past, the king said, "You, Shermoit, go to the kitchen and tell Bertrand the King requires an immediate spread of food in the meeting hall."

"Yes, my king!" said Shermoit, bowing and scurrying toward the kitchen.

"Well, Potemkin, tell me how you found Loni."

By the time the meal was complete, Loni had told the whole story of how she met GreeHee and their journey to Narsor. She sighed, frowning, so Yorkin put his arm around her.

"My dear child," said the king, his green eyes soft with kindness, " we will do what we can to find your dragon but it is unlikely he will turn up here. My own wisdom tells me he either left when he became conscious or one of our enemies has carried him off. Either way, we will be hard pressed, in the midst of this war, to find him again."

Loni could not hold back her tears.

"I assure you, we will do our best, but in the meantime we need to get word to your family that you are safe. Your brother, Yorkin, will be responsible for you while you are here and--"

"Pardon me, Sire," Yorkin said, "but I would like to take my sister home. I know you don't have giants to spare, but would it not benefit all of Narsor and Oberlon if both Potemkin and I took Loni home? Then we could also scout the area for other actions of the enemy."

Stroking his beard and searching Potemkin's face for reactions, the king said, "What do you think of this, Commander?"

"King Narsor, the idea has strong points. I feel obligated to take care of Loni since she saved my life and I shot her dragon. I also agree with Yorkin. Together we could scout the perimeters of our kingdom and Oberlon. The strength of the giant and the magic of a fairy make a powerful match against the stealth of Tana."

"All right then," the king said his face strong with conviction, "in the morning we will go over the locations of all outlying guards. I will send enough men with you to relieve those in the outposts. We will use your journey to change the guards and to gather intelligence on the state of affairs at the edge of the kingdom. I will also give you extra giants for protection and a female to look after Loni. We'll work out the logistics in the morning. By the following sunrise you will leave for Oberlon. This will give Loni a little time to rest before continuing her journey. Are we all agreed?"

"Yes!" came the hearty response from Potemkin and Yorkin.

"Thank you, your Kingship," said Loni, still thinking of GreeHee and wondering why Beauty was silent.

As the giants assembled once more, Loni left the hall with Yorkin. She asked, "So what's going on, Yorkin? When did this war start and how long do you think it will last? And Mom and Dad, are they in danger?"

"Whoa Loni, slow down. Let me tell you what has happened since you disappeared." With his arm around her shoulder, Yorkin began, "Two beedites ago, we received word that the power of Tana was on the move again for the first time since the Primengeer. Eulool had predicted it, but no one wanted to believe it. Even father was hoping Eulool was wrong."

Yorkin stopped at a huge door flanked by two beautiful copper lanterns. Tortoises decorated the shades lighting the hall with dancing shadows. The solid oak door towered eighteen leets high, it would take the strength of a giant to open. But inset at the bottom center of this oak masterpiece was a much smaller door. This petite version, the giants lovingly called the 'Child Way.' Yorkin opened it for Loni. "This is your room while we are here."

The enormous room felt warm and welcoming despite its size. Numerous lanterns and beautiful tapestries hung on the stone walls. Opposite the bed blazed a colossal fireplace decorated with unicorns. The air wafted with fragrant scents of piney rosemary and sweet lavender and a peaceful feeling pervaded despite the war outside the castle wall.

A lovely young chambermaid, about twelve leets tall waited for Loni. She wore a white blouse embroidered with Narsor's shield on the sleeves and a common black skirt under a simple green apron with the words: "Narsor's Dynasty of Peace" embroidered in white across the top.

As the fairies entered, the young giantess bowed saying, "I am Sarolla, here to serve you, Princess. I have warmed your bed, but it is enormous. I could get a cradle out of storage for you if you prefer."

Loni's eyes twinkled with laughter as she looked at the gigantic bed covered in gold and white brocade and six pillows, each of them large enough to be a bed for her. "No, it will be fine, Sarolla. There's no need to change anything. I can float onto it and make myself comfortable. Though, I doubt anyone will be able to tell I slept here in the morning."

"Is there anything else I can do for you, Princess, before I leave?" asked the gentle chambermaid.

"No Sarolla, thank you. You have made me very comfortable. Everything looks wonderful." Loni smiled. Sarolla bowed and left.

Loni and Yorkin sat on the king-sized cushions in front of the warm fireplace. Yorkin loosened the leather straps of his breastplate, rolled back the teal blue silk sleeves of his shirt and shook out his wavy blonde hair as he continued. "At the end of the Primengeer, the power of Tana was broken. She was forced out of lower Tamoor to the City of Teeth in the North. According to Eulool and fragments of prophecies told for nearly six hundred soars, Tana's power relied on a star and that star was broken in the Primengueer. I asked Eulool what the prophecy meant about a star but he never answered me. I don't think anyone really knows what it means. However, I feel it's the key to Tana and to winning this war." Yorkin drew a deep breath, then continued, "In the meantime, Tana moves. Eulool says the star must have been reconstructed in order for Tana's power to be on the move again."

"But what does that mean, Yorkin?" Loni asked, "If you're saying Eulool doesn't know, then who does?"

"Yes, that is a problem. When Father asked Eulool to look further into it with all his magic, Eulool came back to say it would take five to solve the mystery of the star and break Tana's power now."

"But when Father asked what Eulool meant by five. Eulool could only answer, 'I see five moving figures but I cannot make them out. Two are small, one large and long, one large and tall and one enormous compared to the rest, but they are in shadow and I cannot see them clearly.' Eulool was distraught for beedites looking into his gazing ball. But despite his efforts he could not tell Father anything more."

"So that means until these five appear, there will be war?" asked Loni.

Yorkin nodded his aquamarine eyes shining in the firelight. "I believe that is what it means. And as we wait, Tana gains more strength each beedite. All we can do is defend our homelands and hope that these five soon appear."

Chapter 4

MYSTERIES OF THE PRIMENGEER

Loni woke filled with questions. How did they win the Primengeer? Where was GreeHee? Will I see him again? Can Eulool answer these questions? What do Potemkin and King Narsor think about Tana's power?

The lanterns glowed and the flames danced in the fireplace, making the huge room warm and comfortable. Loni sat up, the chambermaid said: "Princess Fairy, I have brought you water and a yellow gown my mother saved from my first yule blessing. I think it will fit you."

"How thoughtful, Sarolla!" Loni said, touching the long silk dress.

"As soon as you're ready I'll take you to the dining hall, your brother is waiting for you."

"Wonderful! I'll be ready in a tithe."

Sarolla led Loni down a wide staircase. Loni didn't recall climbing stairs the night before. Before she could question the young giantess, Sarolla said, "I don't think you could have found the hall on your own, I'm certain you came upstairs a different way last night."

Loni tried to visualize the hallway that Yorkin had used. "Is there a passage without stairs?"

"Yes, princess," said the gentle maid. "It was designed so horses might move the royal ones out quickly in case of war."

Loni's mind returned once more to the power of Tana and the present war. "Sarolla, do you know anything about how the Primengeer was won, so many soars ago?"

Chuckling, the chambermaid said, "Me? Only what my grandfather told me and what I overheard during the schooling of Prince Destoor."

"Please tell me what you know."

Sarolla spoke slowly, her dark brown eyes searching the floor, "Well, Grandfather said we must always be on the alert for the power of Tana. He said it was not dead, only sleeping. He said the time would come when it would rise again and it would take a new kind of power to win the war this time."

"Sarolla, what did he mean by a new kind of power?"

"I asked that question myself. But grandfather did not know the answer."

As they reached the dining hall, Loni stopped and touched the chambermaid's hand asking, "Before we go into the hall, please Sarolla, tell me what else you heard about the Primengeer."

The young giantess knelt beside the fairy, her dark brown hair peeking out from under the black kerchief, "Once while I served Prince Destoor I overheard his history instructor say that the Primengeer was the result of a merging of three beings who wanted control of Tamoor. When they merged, they took the power of a star. I didn't really understand this. Then he continued saying, once the star was broken the power was gone. But, I remember getting a chill over my whole body when he added, 'If they discover how energy can be used to mend the star, then Tana could rise again." Sarolla fell silent and stared off past Loni.

"So that's what happened. That's why we're at war now," whispered Loni.

Sarolla stood up and Loni thanked her for the information.

The cavernous hall bustled with sounds, deep voices, tinkling silverware, and clanking armor. Swords as tall as Loni hung by their sides and they wore bows and quivers filled with arrows slung across their backs. Sprinkled amidst the mottled green armor, a few giantesses wearing simple green skirts carried overflowing trays of food. Long oaken tables filled the hall rubbed to the rich color of cherry-wood. They ran horizontally along the center aisle. Tapestries of dyed wools and furs that told the story of the three dynasties of giants covered the walls to the right and left of the entry.

The warm doughy scent of bread and the sweet smell of sugar aroused her taste buds. The tables, with their enormous bowls of fruits and yogurts, buns and biscuits, looked inviting. It was a feast fit for the giants who occupied this land. As she scanned the room and its enticing assortment of foods, she saw Yorkin and Potemkin at the last table on the right.

"Welcome, sister!" Yorkin said getting up to embrace Loni. Potemkin bowed to the tiny princess and they all sat down to breakfast.

"I have so many questions," said Loni addressing them both. "I want to know more about the Primengeer and how it was won." She looked Potemkin straight in the eye.

"You are filled with surprises, Princess Loni!" stated the giant as he eyed her closely. "First you show up with a dragon and now you are going to solve the mystery of Tana. You go straight to the core of the beast don't you? For such a tiny Fairy princess you have quite a mind."

"Thank you, Potemkin. My father was always impressed with my ideas and my inquisitive mind. It is why he feared I would stray beyond the safe boundaries he set for me. And I guess he was right. After all, that's how I got here. But please, will you tell me of the Primengeer and how we won. We must win this war and I want to help!"

"Okay, little one, I will do my best to tell you what I know of the Primengeer, but I have an appointment with the king in a little while and you would be better served if you went to the king's library. You will find more answers there."

Loni said, "What a great idea! I will do it right after breakfast. Will you come with me, Yorkin?"

"I cannot Loni, I must attend a meeting for scouts in a little while."

"Oo-kay," Loni said feigning a pout. Then turning again to Potemkin she said, "Please share what you know with us, Potemkin."

Loni waited while Potemkin buttered a huge roll. She noticed how beautiful his enormous hands were. He was a handsome giant, clean-shaven with dark brown eyes hidden beneath, thick lashes and combed eyebrows. He leaned back in his chair speaking between bites, "Well I don't know very much about how we won the Primengeer because it has been kept secret for more than six hundred soars. What I do know is that the three beings who took the power of the star and merged to destroy Tamoor were, Maduk a troll; Beastera a powerful female dragon, and Felleen a female bird-beast liken to a carron, but who was the last of her breed.

It is said when they bled their magic, they became one and the star brought them the power to rule. When they entered the land of Narsor, which at that time was called the land of Nadeckador, Nadeckador's wizard Draydel faced them. He then disappeared into thin air right in front of the eyes of both armies. It is said that a cry of despair rang from the giants of Nadeckador and the power of the three that is Tana strengthened and moved forward onto our soil.

Despite, the destruction that took place for the next two leedites, a strange and unusual thing happened, which ended the war and silenced Tana till this beedite.

It is said that a star appeared in the sky and it's blue light flowed over both armies. The voice of Draydel could be heard in a song. But the words have never been repeated and no one knows what they were. Once he finished, the light cleared and the armies of Tana literally flew backwards past the boundaries of Nadeckador.

Later that evening, the body of Draydel was found in his chamber dressed in a robe painted with the Wizards' Web. Around him glowed the colors of the mystic mountains.

As for Tana, no one can explain how she came to power again." The giant washed the words down with juice while the fairies watched.

Potemkin rose. "I will see you at dinner," he said to them. Then in mid stride, he turned to the fairy princess and said, "Loni, I will want to hear everything you find out about Tana and the Primengeer!" It sounded more like a command then a request. Loni nodded as he left the room.

Like everything else in the castle, the library was enormous. The books were much too big for the tiny fairy to lift from the shelves, so Loni looked for someone to help her. Strangely the place was silent. The dusty shelves filled the walls. They began about three leets from the floor extending to a height of eighteen leets. A huge fireplace burned brightly on one wall between the bookshelves. In the center of the room, sprawled three gigantic tables. Books both open and closed lay scattered on them. In the center of each table, sat a lantern but none were lit. The sunlight streamed in through three colossal windows on the wall opposite the door.

Loni floated along the bookshelves, searching for references to the Primengeer or Tana. Deeply entranced in her thoughts she nearly hit the ceiling when a voice bellowed: "Can I help you find your answers plain, but what of war, and a friend who's slain?"

Loni turned, "Oh, eh what, yes, please."

Loni floated down to the floor and stared at the librarian, who looked odd and small for a giant, maybe eight leets tall. She had gnome-like features, somewhat becoming but strange. Instead of the common skirt and blouse worn by giantesses, this creature was dressed in a one-piece thing. All emerald green and split for legs, like the pants that giants wore but baggier. Loni realized she was staring at the librarian. "Oh forgive me, I didn't mean to be rude." Loni said.

"Never a Be-gee have you seen, not in real life or in a dream?" the librarian sang out, as if about to do a song-and-dance routine. "Well that's me, as you can see. A Be-gee me! Oh yes, faerie. The gnome part makes my brain real bright, smart and thinking beedite and night. It also makes me see things far, into the future or on a star. The giant in me is strong and true, so I can get some books for you!" With this the Be-gee gracefully swung onto the ladder that rolled across the shelves. Loni stared with her mouth wide open while the Be-gee swept through the shelves taking three large volumes and quickly placing them on the table in front of her. "It's here you see the things you want, the Primengeer and Tana's haunt." The Be-gee opened the first big green book and turned to a page titled "The Primengeer."

"Wait, how did you know what I was looking for? And can you please speak without all that rhyming

"A Be-gee rhymed since time began, it's how we resonate with the land. It's in our hearts and in our minds and we simply cannot stop the rhyme! As for your wants, it's plain to see, questions are all over thee."

Loni didn't feel comfortable with the rhyming language, so she decided to read the books and only ask questions when necessary. But she did wonder what the Be-gee's name might be.

"My name is Teese, it means I is, but you can simply call me Liz!"

"Liz?" Loni asked.

"Liz is easy and it's short, the best name to use in court."

"Oh, I get it." Said Loni. "Easy to say, easy to remember and that makes it easy when you're announced to the king."

"You are bright as bright can be, I like you, Princess Loni. You have a riddle and a dragon too. You're most unique, heroic you. You want to know of Draydel's death? The answer is at Wizards' Web. I also see inside your eyes, you want to know who are the five. But you must learn this on your own, I'm told by the part that's gnome. It says you'll know six beedites hence, the five as one on peace intent. And GreeHee too, the dragon true, is deep in sleep, he questions you."

"How do you know about GreeHee? Can you see him on me? Can you tell me where he is? Is he all right?"

The Be-gee's odd nose moved up and down as she nodded flashing a wide smile, "Oh yes, oh yes, it's all so clear but I cannot tell you where."

Before Loni could ask another question, the door opened and another customer entered the library seeking help from Liz.

Loni was left to ponder the words of the strange Be-gee. The answer was at Wizard's Web? Good grief, Wizard's Web was so far away-- across the Azura Kah and deep in the Mystic Mountains. She had never heard of anyone but the unicorns who could travel the Mystic Mountains and find their way. And then to Wizard's Web, no one ever even spoke of it. Eulool must know more about this. "I must talk to him!" Loni muttered out loud.

No one heard her. The Be-gee rhymed with a giant at the far end of the room.

And what of GreeHee? What did she mean by 'he was in a deep sleep and questions me'? Yikes, of all the core eggs in Tandem, this was a puzzle.

Loni began scanning the pages for information that she had not heard about the Primengeer.

The books contained references to this battle and that battle and who won and how many giants died. Nothing surfaced about the end of the war except the same things that Potemkin had said. The information on Tana was also missing. It said nothing about the forming of the star or what star it was or what it looked like The only mention of Tana stated she was three, again naming the three-- Maduk, Beastera, and Felleen. No mention existed, of how they bled together, as Potemkin had said.

At the moment Loni noticed her hunger, Liz rang a bell announcing, "Oh my, oh my the dinner bell, the library closes now, that's swell!"

Chuckling, Loni said politely, "Thank you, Liz," as she left the room.

In the dining hall, Loni spotted Potemkin and Yorkin. She joined them and asked Potemkin, "What do you think of Liz, the Be-gee? Does she have some magic powers?"

"Oh, I should have warned you about Liz!" he said smiling. "But she only works there once in a moontide, so I wouldn't have known you would meet her. How very interesting?" Potemkin tapped his right hand on his cheek pondering, "What did she say to you? She is very psychic but also speaks in rhyme, so you're not always sure what she's saying."

"I know," said Loni. "She said that GreeHee was in a deep sleep, that he was questioning me, and that she could not tell me where he was."

"Really!" said the giant, eyes widened and eyebrows raised.

"And," continued the fairy, "she said that the answer to how Draydel won the war is at Wizard's Web."

Yorkin asked, "Wizard's Web? No one goes to Wizard's Web! You have to go across the Azura Kah and then through the mystic mountains to get there and only unicorns can travel that land, and even they never speak of Wizard's Web. You know, Loni, I've never even heard Eulool talk about it."

Potemkin looked at the two fairies. "I can't help you with this at all. Giants only cross the Azura Kah after they die. No giant has so much as stepped a foot in that river. So I'm not going there. Did she say anything about the star?"

"No we never got to that. Someone came in. Besides, with all that rhyming Liz is not the easiest person to talk to."

"Well, little princess, try to give it a rest. All things work out in their own time and this war will be no different. Certainly the great ones will not put the weight of this puzzle on your tiny shoulders. We giants carried it before, we will do it again."

Loni's melodic voice turned cold, her face serious, "But they said it must be done differently this time, remember? Maybe that's why we're here."

"When did they say that?" asked the Commander.

"Oh," Loni's voice softened, "I forgot to tell you I also asked the chambermaid if she knew anything about the war." Loni cowered a little. "She said her grandfather told her Tana's power was sleeping, and Tana might rise again. And if that happened, the war must be won in a different way."

Potemkin nodded, "Well that makes sense if you look at the facts. King Narsor doesn't have a wizard like Draydel. He was the last of the giants' wizards. So there is no one like Draydel to end this war. It will have to be done differently."

Yorkin nodded. "And then there is the question of the five. That's certainly different. Who are the five? Did Liz say anything about them, Loni?"

"Oh, yes. I forgot to tell you. She said that in six beedites we would know who they are and that they would work to bring peace. She also said something about me learning this on my own whatever that means?" Loni shrugged.

Potemkin said, "Well, that is very good news. It's the best news I've heard all beedite. Loni, cheer up, you have told us that the war will not last much longer than six beedites. If the five will bring peace and they get together in six beedites, I would imagine it won't take them too very long until they break the spell and remove Tana's power."

Loni began to smile and so did Yorkin.

Potemkin said "Later you must share these details with the king, I feel it will give him hope. I know it gives me hope!" And he began to eat with gusto.

King Narsor listened with fervor to everything the little fairy princess said. He approved of her work and commended her, "Princess Loni, your family will be very proud of you when they learn how hard you're working to solve the puzzle of Tana's power. You are a gemstone in the line of Oberlon!"

Loni blushed. But as the king smiled, the questions she had been planning to ask him tumbled out. "King Narsor is there any other bit of information you may know that could help us unravel this puzzle? Are there any records of Draydel's private writings?"

The king's mouth dropped for an instant, then he said, "You are truly amazing. Why didn't I think of that? There could be an ancient book of wizardry in Draydel's rooms in the old castle of Nadeckador, which lies to the West of here." He turned to Potemkin and continued, "I will leave it up to you, Commander. If you feel it is not too far out of your way, go to the old castle. If not, I will--"

"Please Potemkin," Loni said, "can we go? I feel certain this is important to the destiny of Tamoor." Then she turned sheepishly to the King. "Sorry I interrupted you, your Highness."

"That's all right, my dear," The king said, patting her on the head, and then turning to the Commander, he asked, "What do you say, Potemkin?"

"We will go there, my king. It's not too far out of our way and we'll send a messenger to you stating what we find."

"Excellent!" The king said his eyes sparkled with delight. He rubbed his big, ruddy, jeweled, hands together saying, "I expect great things from the three of you. I feel the fate of Tamoor may be somehow aligned with your journey." He pondered for a moment his silver head resting in his hand, his square fingers running through his close-clipped beard. Then, he snapped back into his regal stature and stood to leave, saying, "I will break bread with you at morning tide. Good night."

Potemkin bade good night to Loni and Yorkin saying, "I will send someone to wake you before dawn. Till then, may you rest well."

Yorkin walked Loni to her bedchamber, and they did travel through a wide passage without stairs. The stone floor was carved with deep horizontal lines. It must have been for more traction for the horses - all very interesting.

Then her mind switched to GreeHee. "What do you think Liz meant when she said GreeHee is in a deep sleep? Do you think he is dead?" Loni asked Yorkin, eyes wide, a furrow on her brow.

"No, Loni. I'm certain if he were dead, she would have said that. Maybe someone is taking care of him and they gave him some sleeping medicine. Let's think positive. As much as you care about him, I feel certain you will see him again. Take heart, little sister, dream wonderful dreams." He opened the 'Child Way' door and hugged her good night.

Chapter 5

CAMP OF THE CARRONS

"**I**s he awake yet?" came the deep demanding voice of Carron General Maltor, a very tall, slim, blue Carron, as he pulled back the flap of the tent and entered with his prominent entourage, handsome, golden-feather, Captain Bartet and gray-beaked Admiral Jarteen. The three birds stood perfectly erect, each fitted in their intricate breastplates of black cloisonné. The armor told the story of their war experiences. It included the deaths of creatures less fortunate and also the many medals they had been awarded by the power of Tana. The colors ranged from vivid violets to deep merlots, swirling with flourishes for which the Carron bird artists were known.

Doctor Paychente slowly turned to survey the intruders. "No, not yet," he said staring at the trio. "General, you needn't bother to ask again, as I have told you for the last three beedites, I will send one of the guards to alert you as soon as our hero awakes. So please, leave me to my work."

"Listen Paychente," the General hollered, "I will come and go as I please. I need this dragon at the front and it's your job to get him there as soon as possible, so see that you do! I am impatient! Have you forgotten we are at war?"

Paychente slowly turned away, drawing out each word as he spoke, "Yes, General, I know we're at war. I will send word as soon as the dragon awakens."

The General and his officers started to leave when GreeHee moaned, "GrreeHee...yes...GreeHee." Wisps of smoke rose from his nostrils.

Doctor Paychente rushed to GreeHee's side, massaging his cheek and coaxing him to speak. "Tell us, dragon, who is this greedy? What are you saying? What is your name?"

General Maltor and Officers Bartet and Jarteen moved closer. Standing next to GreeHee's ear, Maltor bellowed, "Speak to us dragon! What is your name?"

The question shot through GreeHee like lightening striking him, "GreeHee..." he whispered.

The doctor demanded, "Please, General, you must be more gentle in your approach. We don't know how sick this dragon is."

Paychente asked in a kind, caring, voice, "Is your name Greedy, dragon?"

Oh how soft. That is nice. Who was speaking? GreeHee forced his eyelids open. Big, brown, eyes stared back, and the dragon whispered "GreeHee, yes." Wisps of smoke curled from his breath.

"Greedy! Yes that is truly the name for a dragon!" exclaimed the general strutting about the tent. "He is obviously a mighty dragon for one so young. Look at those scars!" the general continued his chest swelling, pointing at GreeHee. "Look at this leg, burnt and deeply gashed, it shows courage and honor! Get him well, doctor! That is an order! I need this dragon and I hold you responsible if he is not on the front lines soon!"

The doctor stammered, "But General, I can't guarantee that--"

"You heard the General, Doctor." Jarteen said pointing at Paychente. "Do it! We don't want to hear whimpering excuses." Then the threesome left the tent.

As GreeHee lay semi-conscious, he continued to see the image of Doctor Paychente's big brown eyes, more like a field doe than a Carron. How odd? And, what a nice, soothing voice he has.

GreeHee heard Paychente moving around. There was the sound of drops falling into a bucket and the sweet fragrant scent of lavender. He felt a warm damp clothe on his forehead. "Come now young dragon, let's wake up," the doctor said gently. "Greedy, wake up."

GreeHee's body relaxed and Paychente started humming an old Carron lullaby. GreeHee's mind filled with song, eyes unfocused, and glazed, he spoke in short, faltering, sentences. "Loni that feels so nice. Do you really like me?"

"Greedy, I'm your doctor. Can you hear me?" Paychente inquired gently.

"Loni... friend...friend...I..." Then GreeHee tumbled back into the well of his subconscious.

The doctor took a small jar from one of the many pockets in his coat. He snapped off the top and held it under the dragon's nostrils saying, "Inhale. Breathe this, Greedy, it will make you feel stronger."

In a tithe, GreeHee opened his emerald eyes. He stared at the short, white-jacketed, yellow-beaked carron, "Uh! Who are you? Where am I?" He tried to get up but fell right back.

Keeping his hand steady on GreeHee's forehead, the doctor said, "calm down, Greedy. I'm Doctor Paychente. You've been injured and I'm here to help you."

"Doctor? A doctor?" questioned GreeHee, glazed eyes opening even wider.

"Yes, Greedy, I'm a doctor. You were hurt in battle and a squad brought you here. Do you remember what happened?"

"I don't know," GreeHee hesitated, rubbing the side of his head. "I can't seem to remember anything."

Paychente removed the compress saying, "Well, don't worry about that now. I am certain it will all come back to you in a short time. First we must get you something to eat. You have been here for three beedites and I have been watching you lose weight even as you slept."

GreeHee said nothing. He searched his mind for answers. Who am I? What battlefield? How did I get here? His mind swirled as he watched the strange doctor writing something. The doctor left the tent and GreeHee watched his silhouette and listened.

"Corporal Gento, immediately give this to Chef Baskoote," Paychente said to the thin carron at the right of the entrance. "You will wait for him to give you a roast, two pots of potatoes and vegetables and a pot of tortoise soup. Enlist whatever help you need and bring the food here double-time!" The silhouette disappeared and Paychente turned to the other guard, his silhouette appeared bent, old and overweight. Paychente handed him a note and said, "Corporal Potsote, deliver this message to the General. You must put it in his hand, so find him wherever he may be in camp."

GreeHee watched Paychente re-enter the tent. He placed the compress back on GreeHee's forehead. With a deep sigh, GreeHee said, "Doctor how did I get here?"

"A squad of Carrons brought you from a battle in Narsor's forest. They found you unconscious lying in a tree. Can you remember that at all?"

GreeHee slowly closed his eyes and frowned saying, "No. I don't remember the battle. I remember flying and being hit in the head, then nothing."

"While you were unconscious, you said certain things. Perhaps these can jog your memory. You mentioned the name, Loni. Do you remember, Loni?"

"Loni?" GreeHee, eyes still closed, rolled the name around in his brain. "Loni. I don't get a picture of anyone… But the name feels good. Isn't that odd? The name feels good?"

"Well, this is because you associate some pleasure with this individual or the name. Or whatever Loni is, suggests pleasure to you," the doctor explained. "Eventually you will remember everything. Don't try too hard, relax and let things come to you. Whatever pops into your head will help us discover the thread of who you are. You also said your name was Greedy. Is that correct?"

"Greedy? That feels kind of right. It sounds pretty good. Greedy? Well I can't say for sure but I will answer to it. Okay?" GreeHee asked opening his eyes and looking directly at the doctor.

"Yes, that will be fine. Let me know when you discover what is wrong with the name, or if you suddenly realize what your name is."

Corporal Gento walked in with two other Carrons carrying food. GreeHee turned as the warm, meaty aromas filled the tent. "Oh, now I know I'm hungry. That smells so good!"

"Place it here in front of him," Said the doctor pointing to the long table. The three carrons gingerly stepped forward putting the food down. GreeHee tried to sit up, Paychente attempted to support him and stumbling said, "Gento, help me with my patient."

Gento, backed up and stammered. "Uh, you're friendly aren't you dragon?"

GreeHee said, "I won't hurt you, Carron."

"No he won't hurt you, Gento, just help me!" the doctor commanded. He pulled Gento into position next to him, so that they could support GreeHee's right shoulder as he moved into a seated position to eat.

Gento moaned, "Ugh, you're really heavy."

"You should see my father!" blurted GreeHee.

Paychente said, "Your father? Tell us what you remember about your father. What's his name?"

"He's the most terrible dragon in all of Tamoor. He's at least four times my size. But then I'm only thirteen soars you know." Seeing the doctor's eyes widen, GreeHee added, "Didn't you know that?"

"Well Greedy, I haven't worked with many dragons before, but considering your size, I assumed you were young. I just didn't think you were _that_ young! Do you remember your father's name?"

"Yes! Tereem! Do you know my father?" GreeHee said smiling, showing his enormous teeth.

Paychente's eyebrows rose as he stared at GreeHee's teeth. "Yes, I have heard of him. Haven't you heard of him, Gento?"

Corporal Gento crept closer to the door of the tent, his eyes fixed on GreeHee's teeth as he replied, "Yes, Doctor Paychente, I have. Isn't he the dragon who ravaged a whole village in the valley of Borterleen last soar?"

Before Paychente could answer, a voice bellowed through the flap of the tent. "So you finally got up eh, Dragon Greedy!" General Maltor strutted in, Bartet and Jarteen directly behind him. "I am General Maltor, your Chief Commander. I want to know everything that happened to you. How you got those scars." He pointed to the many scars that covered GreeHee's body. "And how many giants you killed. You may have a medal coming for doing battle beyond the call of duty. Who enlisted you? We have no records of a dragon your age in the service of Tana, but then of course, dragons are known to be independent and we welcome your desire to destroy our enemies!" The general chuckled, patting GreeHee on the shoulder. GreeHee watched tongue-tied as Maltor continued.

"We want to know everything about you! My aide Captain Bartet will write the historic record of your honor and courage. So speak, Dragon Greedy. What a fine name for a dragon that is!" The general made himself comfortable on a rough wooden chair by the table.

"I," GreeHee began, his upper lip twitching, the way it did when his father asked questions. GreeHee looked to the doctor for help.

Paychente stepped between the dragon and Maltor, saying, "General Maltor, please, let Greedy eat a little food before asking him so many questions. The dragon hasn't eaten for more than three beedites! He's been in battle and injured severely and needs a little sustenance before you can expect him to remember all the details you want."

The general smiled tapping his left wingtips on the table. "All right then, we'll eat along side our big hero and we can make some small talk until the meal is over. Corporal Gento, go to the kitchen, and tell the Chef I will have my meal now."

"Yes, sir!" replied Gento.

As the Corporal began to leave the tent, the general added, "Make sure you bring enough cups and flasks of my private brimwinery for all of us. Do you understand?"

"Yes, sir!" snapped a reply from Gento as he scurried out of the tent.

"Well, my fine Greedy, I am anxious to hear about your courageous battles, but since our good doctor insists," he said, scowling at the doctor, "we will keep things light while you eat." Pointing to the pots of food in front of GreeHee, he added, "Please, go ahead and start without us. We all had lunch and are not as hungry as you. Besides, I want to hear how much you like our chef's food."

GreeHee began to eat, eyeing the General. What had he gotten himself into? He was pleased that he remembered his father Tereem. But as he continued to think about his father, sadness crept over him, his shoulders drooped. Then he recalled the words, 'sniveling runt.' Yes that is what my father called me. GreeHee felt the need to prove himself.

"Greedy, where is your home?" asked the General.

"I'm not sure, sir. I do remember that my father is Tereem the Terrible. Does that help?"

"Beloved Margots! You mean you are Tereem's son? But he never spoke of you? How old are you dragon-son?" asked Maltor.

"Thirteen, sir," answered the dragon, shrinking back.

"Why, you _must_ be Tereem's son. He is the most terrible dragon in all Tamoor as far as I'm concerned. And here you are not even out of school, taking in the war and killing giants and who knows what else. Your father will be very proud of you when he hears the news. I am certain there is going to be a medal in this for you. Why, I have a mind to present you to Tana myself for your aggressive heroism. I only wish I had a son like you! You make a Carron proud!" The general's chest swelled, as he said these words. GreeHee started to smile, but it was only a reaction, his heart still felt heavy.

Wasn't this what he had always dreamed of happening? The moment he had waited for since he began his lessons in the dragon art. But what was this other feeling inside him, like some traitor under his skin? Some part of him felt he didn't deserve this honor. It must be all those fears he harbored as a dragonling, thinking he would never amount to a fearsome dragon, no less a heroic one. Yes, that's what all these feelings must be.

Corporal Gento entered with the brimwinery, and behind him Carrons followed with food. "Come in. good man, Gento," the General said. "Serve up the winery, so we can toast to this adolescent dragon, covered with scars of honor, and the lineage of greatness."

The cups were made from the white belly of tortoise shells dyed blood red. Carved on them in Carron scroll were the words: 'Mightier than mountains.'

The general stood up, raised his cup and the other Carrons followed. "In appreciation of Greedy, mighty young dragon with a heart for blood! May he explore greatness in the service of Tana!"

In unison they said, "To Tana, may she reign over all Tamoor and kindle us with her power!"

GreeHee raised his cup, feeling proud to be a dragon, but something was wrong, he felt a chill run down his spine at the mention of Tana. He noticed Paychente standing in the background watching. How odd, the doctor did not drink or join in Tana's praises.

The tent glowed orange from the setting sun, as the group drank and ate heartily, and a feeling of comradeship settled over the Carrons. GreeHee listened to them, his ego swelling as they likened him to the heroic dragons they'd known. He listened to stories of his father and the incredible number of creatures he killed. How Tereem instilled fear in all who knew him, even when they fought on the same side. But despite all this patronage, GreeHee felt a knot in his stomach when he tried to recall the battles of his own scars.

By the time the dragon finished his entire meal, the Carrons, with the exception of Doctor Paychente, were so drunk that the General said, slurring his words, "We will declassify you in the morning, Greedy. Get a good night's sleep and be ready after breakfast."

Then, turning to the other officers he said, "Let's go, we've had a fine feast, and can thank Tana for enlisting a brave young dragon. One dragon is equal to a hundred Carrons!" They ambled out of the tent and GreeHee heaved a deep sigh.

"So how are you feeling, Greedy?" asked the doctor.

"I feel full and tired. I'm worried about my inability to remember the battles with the giants. I can't seem to recall them at all."

Paychente touched GreeHee's shoulder saying, "That's all right. You made a breakthrough by remembering your father and it certainly has paved the way for friendship with General Maltor. Now that's something to be thankful for. He was ready to give you a medal tonight! What an impression you have made!"

"But I didn't say anything, and what if I never remember the battles? What if--"

"Hush my little Greedy," the doctor said in a kind voice. "Be grateful for this moment. Tomorrow will take care of itself."

As the doctor began clearing away the dinner mess, he asked, "Do you feel well enough to lie down on your own or should I call Gento in to help you?"

"Let me try. I've been so long in this position that I'm not certain if I can move, and if I can, I would really like to take a little walk outside this tent, you know what I mean, Doctor?" He said, pointing to his bulging stomach.

"Oh yes, how unaware of me!"

GreeHee tried to stand. He shook out his front arms one at a time, exercising them. In a few moments he stood upright, stretching his legs.

The doctor watched and waited. Finally he said, "You seem to be doing all right. How do you feel?"

"Aside from my head and the pain in my thigh, I feel pretty good. I'd like to get some fresh air. Can I leave now?" He started to pace a little, kicking up dust with his tail.

"Okay, let me check the guards and decide which direction will be best." Then, looking GreeHee straight in the eye, he said, "You understand I must go with you. You are in my charge until you are fully recovered. Understood?"

"Yes."

A few tithes later they walked out of camp, noticed only by the few guards on duty. Each silently saluted the doctor and backed away from the dragon.

When they reached ten leets beyond the perimeter of the camp, GreeHee found a spot to relieve himself.

He returned to where the doctor waited. Flickering stars filled the clear night sky.

"Tell me, Greedy, when you look at the stars, do any memories surface for you?" asked Paychente who now sat upon a large boulder.

"I feel a sense of freedom, but I don't remember anything," he replied staring at the magnificent indigo sky. "Wait a minute! I remember a star was very important. Yes, but which star and why is it important?"

They sat for a while in silence, then GreeHee exclaimed, "I think the star was blue! Is there a blue star in the heavens?" Together they looked. Several stars looked blue. GreeHee murmured, "They seem so small. I think it's supposed to be big. Oh, well."

A few moments later, GreeHee said, "You know, Doctor, I don't feel like killing anyone. Is that normal for a dragon?"

"That's a very interesting comment, Greedy. As I observed you, I saw no signs of aggressive behavior. It is rather odd for a dragon to be so congenial. Can you recall anything of your childhood? What kind of games you played? What your father taught you? Anything about the battles surfacing?"

"Not really. I get a picture of a jeweled mirror. I see myself with a scowl. But it all feels like a game. I don't feel angry, simply sad." GreeHee searched the Carron's face for answers.

Dr. Paychente scratched his chest as he spoke, "Greedy, I think I could be of greater service to you if I told you a story. It's the story of a very unique Carron. He was born with large eyes that reflected his large heart. Carrons usually have small close-set eyes, but this little baby bird was different. He didn't like to bite baby beasts. He didn't dream of winning wars, medals, and fame. He wasn't interested in proving himself on the battlefield. His parents were dismayed by his nonchalance, when it came to the usual Carron games. He was more interested in saving the lives of the unfortunate creatures his companions terrorized with their beaks, swords, and arrows. It seemed there was no place for this Carron in the world of Carrons. He didn't fit in, and no matter how his parents tried to teach him, it was to no avail.

When he went to fencing classes, he stopped before striking and took the blow instead. When he went to stalking classes, he trapped his prey but never teased them or poked them with his beak. In every class his response was so unlike the rest of his peers, that finally as he reached twelve soars, his parents were asked to remove him from school because he was unfit to continue. They were ashamed of him. The town, his parents, and even his brothers wanted nothing to do with him. So he was asked to leave the community of Carrons forever." While the doctor had been speaking he stared at the stars. Now he turned and looked at GreeHee. "Tell me Greedy, what are you feeling as I tell you this story?"

GreeHee had been staring at the ground, his eyes filled with water, trying to contain his feelings. He didn't want to talk about them. He didn't feel they would make any dragon proud. He felt confused. After a moment he looked up at the doctor and said, "I feel sorry for the little Carron." Then staring more intently at the doctor, he said, "It was you, wasn't it? You're the unusual big-eyed Carron, aren't you?"

"Yes, it is I."

"But you're a doctor! You're accepted by your people, aren't you?"

The doctor nodded. "In some ways, yes. But it took soars of loneliness to find my path. I spent far too many soars in anguish and tears. I was alone, and all I did was hate myself and throw insults at the ancients for letting me be born like this."

"Then one night, I helped a little peto bird recover the use of his wing and he could not thank me enough. He said to me, and I remember his exact words, Paychente said staring at GreeHee. "In all my life, no one has been so caring, helpful or kind to me. You have given me a new life with your medicine and a new heart with your love." It was a profound moment for me. I realized I felt happy and proud. I was important. I had a purpose." The doctor hesitated as he wiped the tears from his soft, brown eyes.

GreeHee had never seen a grown-up cry. He felt puzzled and wanted to cry too. He wanted to hug the Carron, but he held himself back.

The doctor continued." I'm sure I felt happy before, but I never realized it until that moment. Then, I discovered my being different could serve a purpose. I could be happy just by being who I am. I realized that being me, this simple non-Carron-like bird, allowed me to do something better than any other Carron. I could heal others and thus share my love, be happy, and make others happy."

He stopped for a second and stared at GreeHee. Then he continued, "Now I know, being different is a gift. Different is wonderful when you understand how to use the gift."

The doctor fell silent. GreeHee said nothing. "Well, let's get back. Think about what I said and perhaps you will find some gemstone you can use."

Chapter 6

NARSOR'S DREAM

Even before dawn, Loni awoke. She had been flopping like a fish out of water for the last few senes. Her wings now twitched out of control, as though they wanted to fly off without her. She had dreamt of being in Draydel's rooms and finding an important book. "Oh, I can't wait to get to Nadeckador's castle!" she said as she flew from the bed.

Sarolla asked, "Princess, is there something I can get for you?"

Startled Loni jumped nearly hitting the ceiling. "Oh, I didn't realize you were here!"

"Sorry," Sarolla said, covering her mouth with her fleshy right hand, her brown eyes twinkling with laughter.

"I feel this need to get going. My mind is riveted on all the things I am going to do. Is anyone else up yet?"

"Yes Loni, I overheard your brother, Yorkin, laughing in the hall when I came up the stairs."

Loni quickly got ready.

Sarolla looked down shyly, "Princess Loni, I know you're going on a long journey in a little while and the King has asked me to go with you, if you would like my company. May I accompany you? I have never been outside of the castle and I would love to see more of the kingdom. I can be very useful to you too, I can mend clothes and make food and make medicines and." A heavy knock resounded on the door.

"Time to rise," came a deep voice. The footsteps continued down the hall.

"Oh Sarolla, I would love to have you come with us." She hopped up and gave the surprised giantess a hug.

"Thank you, my lady! Thank you!" The young giantess bowed. "I have already put together some things for the journey. As soon as you release me, I will gather everything we will need to be comfortable."

"I'm ready now! I can't wait to get on the road."

"Shall we go?" said Sarolla, opening the big door and waiting for Loni to lead the way into the hall.

In the dining room, Potemkin and Yorkin were already eating. Loni could hear Potemkin say, "To make the journey as swift as possible, the King has given us horses. They are rigging them up, even as we speak." Then turning to Loni, Potemkin said, "Good morning, Princess, are you ready for a long ride?"

"I'm not only ready, I am so excited!" said Loni beaming. "I can't wait to get to Nadeckador's castle. Do you think we will get there by nightfall, Potemkin?"

"It is possible if we ride hard and if there is no interference of any kind," answered the giant while spreading jam on a large steamy biscuit.

"What do you mean by interference?" asked Loni.

"Well, Princess, we are at war and it is hard to say what we may encounter on the road to Nadeckador's castle. I really don't expect anything but there is always the possibility." Potemkin looked at both Yorkin and Loni. "Do both of you know how to ride?"

Yorkin nodded. "But we have only ridden the tiny ponies. So it will be an adventure riding a giant horse."

"Well, the King himself has chosen a special mare for you. I am told she is very well mannered and highly trained. I think she was one of the Queen's horses. She will respond to all the same commands you use with ponies. Indeed, she will enjoy having you aboard instead of one of my men. Even with both of you riding together, the horse will be carrying less than one-quarter of the weight she is used to. So she should be very happy." Potemkin smiled, his deep dimples showing.

Loni looked past him, Potemkin stood up and turned around. The king stood behind him. "Oh, Sire, I did not realize you were there. Please forgive me." The giant bowed to the king.

"That is fine, Potemkin, I had only hoped you had eyes in the back of your head. I would feel much better if I thought you could see behind as well as in front in these wartimes," the king said with a grin.

Then to Loni, he continued, "I have found something that should be of interest to you. Last night before retiring, I had a strong urge to look for the original floor plans for this castle. I knew that our architect Tarktor had studied Nadeckador's castle before designing this one. Here is what I found." He pushed aside some of the food and laid the architectural plans on the table. "These are the sketches that Tarktor drew of Nadeckador's castle. Here in the North Tower are Draydel's rooms." He pointed to a suite of rooms at the upper right part of the drawing. The castle faced south and the North Tower was in the Northeastern corner.

These would be the rooms of a wizard. Loni considered the variety of fireplaces, much like Eulool's that Draydel certainly used for more than cooking or heating. Then the special windows set in the ceiling of two of the rooms. Tarktor had drawn a picture near the first of these sky-windows. Loni immediately pointed to it, saying, "This looks like the scopetron that Eulool uses to look at the stars." Then looking up at the king and smiling, Loni added, "Eulool used to let me look through it. It was lots of fun."

"Yes, my dear child, I believe it is a scopetron." And then winking at Loni, the King added, "And it is lots of fun to look through, I have one of my own!"

Loni smiled back at Narsor. "This is wonderful, your highness! It will make it much easier for us to find whatever Draydel may have left us."

Looking more closely at the plans, the king pointed to a wall that was noted by Tarktor. "Here Potemkin, Tarktor's note indicates he felt there was something else hidden in this area, perhaps a trap door or a secret room. The wizard Draydel was very powerful and kept his secrets hidden in puzzling places." Narsor pointed to the space. "But Tarktor never found anything to substantiate his idea."

"I see, Sire," Potemkin said, "It looks like there should be a room between these two walls." The giant studied the plans. "We will meticulously examine this area when we get there. These plans will be a great help to us. Thank you!"

King Narsor had also placed a map showing the area of Nadeckador's castle on the table. "Oh, the Crystal River!" exclaimed Loni, pointing to the map. "I know where this castle is, we used to weave stories about it when we traveled in spring to the river. It sits on the hilltop far across the river. Remember, Yorkin? Oh, we will soon be home!" And she added with tears in her eyes, "I didn't realize how much I missed home until now."

Yorkin held his sister while the king and Potemkin looked on.

In the front courtyard of the castle stood fifteen giants and Sarolla. Eighteen horses stood saddled and ready to ride, as well as, three packhorses buried under the famous tortorsall blankets and sacks.

Potemkin pointed to a blue roan saying, "Yorkin, you and Loni will be riding that mare."

"Oh!" Loni. gasped, "She is beautiful."

Loni flew to the mare. She had black feet, mane, tail and ears. The rest of her was a mix of gray, white, and brown spots. Her face was a deep charcoal gray with little white spots and a beautiful long white strip that stretched down her nose to her black nostrils. The stripe widened between her big blue-black eyes and looked like a tall star.

"What is her name?" Loni asked the red-haired giant holding her reins.

"She is called Starina Ronella. But we call her Starry for short."

Loni patted the beautiful horse.

"I will protect you little one as though you were my own foal," came the sweet whisper of the mare.

Loni's eyes widened and she asked the giant, "Can Starry speak?"

"Well…" he said stroking Starry's cheek, "I wouldn't want to say that in public, but I have certainly heard her speak. I could tell you tales but there is no time for that now. Let me help you up, princess." The giant held out his arms and lifted Loni onto the horse.

Loni petted Starry's neck, "I think I heard her speak."

"Of course you did, Loni! I not only speak, I am really smart too. I know the trails throughout the forests of Narsor and will take very good care of you,." Starry said, giving a little whinny and flagging her upper lip to emphasize her words.

"I must be the luckiest fairy in all Tamoor to get such a wonderful companion for my ride home. Thanks for being here for me, Starry!" exclaimed Loni.

"Who are you talking to?" asked Yorkin, finally taking the reins from the giant and getting ready to mount the horse. The giant formed a foothold for the fairy to step into and Yorkin began to mount the mare.

"I was speaking to Starry, our horse! We are in for a real treat, Yorkin, our horse is going to protect us," Loni said, extending her small hand to Yorkin as he climbed up.

"Okay, Loni, if you say so. I know you are my most sensitive sister and you probably do hear the horse." Then turning to the giant, he asked, "Do the horses of giants speak?"

"Well, Prince Yorkin, some do and some don't and most giants never hear them. But there are plenty of tales of horse voices offering wisdom in times of war and peace. You have one of the Queen's best mounts. This mare was bred specifically for Queen Beetrea. Starry was her most beloved mare. You will be very safe on this horse. She was trained to know all of Narsor and I personally have heard her speak. She is a very brave, wise horse and I think that is why the king himself insisted that you have her. I wish you well on your journey." Then he turned to the horse, "Starry, I hope to see you again soon. Be safe. Travel under the guidance of Percheera, the horse star. May she protect and keep all of you!" The giant turned back to the mare, patting her neck and rubbing her muzzle. Then, with his head down as if he had lost a dear friend, he walked off, waving to the fairies.

"What a strange giant." Yorkin said.

"I think he didn't want you to see how much he will miss Starry. I think he loves her," said Loni.

Yorkin reined in the horse and turned her to ride alongside Potemkin.

The king approached and said: "You will be safe on this mare. She was my wife's best horse. Queen Beetrea used to tell me how she spoke with her, and how Starry guided her to some very special places in the kingdom. Since you are both small and precious to me, I wanted you to have her. I know if my queen were still alive, she would have chosen this mare for you." The king took a deep breath and looked down for a moment swallowing hard. Then clearing his throat, he said, "Princess Loni, I had a dream last night. I saw the powerful wizard Draydel, and my wife stood beside him. First Beetrea spoke to me and said she would be with you to protect you, so you should call on her if you need the care of a mother and her wisdom. Then she stepped back and Draydel introduced himself to me. He wanted me to assure you that this journey will be blessed." Looking directly at Loni, the king continued, "Draydel said you will find what he hid for you so many centuries ago. Then he showed me something that is very important for you to remember. He pulled out a piece of paper and there was a symbol on it. It looked like this." King Narsor handed the little fairy a piece of parchment with two triangles on it. The triangles had sides of equal length and one faced up while its base touched the base of the second one, which faced down. Together they made a kind of diamond with two lines in the middle.

Loni took the paper and said, "Sire, did he say anything else about this?"

"Only that when the time came, you Loni, would know what to do." Then he turned to Yorkin and Potemkin. "Loni is an important key to this puzzle. I know this from the dream. Draydel also said something that you both need to know." The king hesitated. He straightened, his eyebrows knitted close together. He placed a hand on Potemkin's hand and the other on Yorkin's, and in a deep, serious voice commanded. "You two are guardians of Tamoor and must work in tandem. You share the power of two moons." All three stared at the king. Yorkin broke the silence.

"Sire, what does the power of two moons mean?"

"Yorkin, I don't pretend to know. I only know that this dream was very real and the power that Draydel had is somehow connected to you and Potemkin through two moons. It is all a riddle to me. I am certain though that it is important, and that both of you will need to remember what Draydel said."

Yorkin and Potemkin stared blankly at each other. Potemkin turned to the king and said, "My king, we will remember all that you have said. I will hold it in my heart and we will protect Princess Loni as well. Are there any other instructions you wish to give us before we leave?"

"That is all," said the king with sadness in his eyes. "I only wish that I could go with you. I shall in spirit and I shall keep all of you safely in my thoughts." With this the king stepped back and raised his right hand in the flat-palmed salutation of giants. Potemkin, Yorkin, and Loni raised their right hands with their fingers together, pointing at the sky and their palms facing the king.

Potemkin turned his horse, an enormous dark brown steed, away from the castle. Yorkin followed and Loni waved to the king saying, "Thank you for everything, King Narsor. We will honor you in our journey!"

"Good speed, may the ancients protect you!" replied the King.

Potemkin led the horses single file through the courtyard away from the castle. Loni and Yorkin rode behind him. Sarolla was behind them, and the rest of the group followed.

"Good speed!" "Safe passage!" "Ancients protect you!" "Ancients guide you!" Came the many exclamations from the crowd gathered to see them off.

In a few tithes, they were at the gate. Loni turned and noticed the king still stood in the same spot. He looked very handsome in his dark green cloak embroidered with gold symbols of longevity and prosperity. His gold crown shone brilliantly in the orange glow of the sun as he waved goodbye to the troop. Would she ever see him again?

Chapter 7

THE CITY OF TEETH

The icy wind cut like a razor across Colonel Bravort's face as he flew into the city of Teeth. The younger of the two carrons with him began to complain.

"Colonel, how much further is it? The weather has dropped and my beak feels like frostbite is setting in," whined Corporal Rant, shivering and wishing he had not been so anxious to meet Tana.

"Keep your attention on your assignment, Rant, and forget your beak! Promotions are for brave soldiers not whiners!"

"Is that the entrance, Colonel? There at five shadows?" questioned Sergeant Petri, pointing at a dark cavernous opening in the mountains to the southeast.

"Yes! I believe it is," responded Bravort. "Let's fly a little lower and hold out the flag of Tana, so they know who we are."

Sergeant Petri pulled a flag out of his pack and held it with his right wing tips. The red-on-red background gave the appearance of droplets of blood. Across the top were three pale yellow moons set in an arc above a gold graphic that radiated out to them. The moon in the center was a full one. The other two were crescents. The moon on the left was a last quarter moon and the one on the right, a first quarter. The graphic was made up of a gold circle in which two half circles stood back to back, vertically. Below all of this was an inscription in indigo. Written in an ancient Tamooran language, which perhaps only Tana understood.

With the flag held in front of him, Petri led the trio. They flew to sixty leets above the ground and began following a rocky path between sheer cliffs to the mountain entrance.

Mountain spires filled the steel-gray land. It felt cold and looked colder. There were no signs of plant or animal life.

"Sir, the place feels deserted," Rant said.

"That's exactly what Tana wants you to think!" stated Bravort. "It's a perfect tool of war to mislead the enemy into feeling safe. But I assure you, you are being watched every tithe! Nothing goes unnoticed in the city of Teeth. Tana sees all. Remember, this is a land of incredible magic. So don't be misled by appearances."

They landed in front of the ominous charcoal entrance. Carved into the psilomene mountain, it stood eighty leets high. The smooth stone appeared seamless, giving no hint of a door. But without question, this was the entrance to Tana's citadel.

Before the Colonel could catch his breath to speak, a rumbling began and boulders crashed behind them. With a flash of swords the trio turned but no one was there.

Then Bravort began the proclamation that he had been practicing in his mind since he left the General's camp. "In all the lands no greater stands, then Tana. We hail you and commend you. We bow and will defend you. In blood and all that's gory, we'll follow you to glory! As soon as we win this war, Tana shall rule all Tamoor! Hail Tana!"

The trio raised their heads and wings in the Carron solemn salute, right wing over the heart and the left wing tip raised in a fist.

In moments the fortress wall of stone dissolved and they entered a courtyard of magnificent light. Enormous oak trees, blankets of emerald meadows and the hypnotic fragrance of wildflowers filled the air. The path before them was a mosaic of red and gold woven with the symbol of the flag. As they stepped forth, the wall behind them became solid once more.

The Carron warriors marched single file. Colonel Bravort led the way, his chest puffed out and a stern Petri followed, holding the flag high. At the rear Rant kept moving his head from side to side, staring at everything they passed, his mouth hung open in awe.

Directly ahead the walkway widened into a circle in the center of which there stood an enormous fountain with a fascinating statue. The statue depicted a troll, dragon, and bird beast merging into a huge column of red light. Around the circumference of the fountain smaller statues depicted the many creatures of Tamoor bowing to this central image. In front of the statue stood a figure cloaked in a deep purple cape, which from a distance appeared to be black. The being stood perfectly still, his arms in the traditional Tana welcome, right arm extended with fist facing downward. Only his intense, black eyes moved.

Colonel Bravort stopped ten leets in front of the figure and extended his right wing forward with wingfist clenched downward saying, "I am Colonel Bravort of the Carron Command Forces stationed on the Narsor front. I have news for Tana from General Maltor."

"Welcome!" came the raspy reply. "Follow me."

A chill ran through Bravort. The being he now followed seemed emotionless and appeared to have no blood in its body. It walked with a machinelike cadence, had no facial movement when it spoke, and even with Bravort's incredible sense of hearing, he could hear no sounds of breathing coming from the cloaked figure. Bravort's mind raced searching for any bit of knowledge he might have about such a being, but nothing surfaced. Was it only an apparition used by Tana and not a living creature at all?

They were leaving the manicured courtyard and entering a cavernous hall. Skins from many different animals covered the floor. Directly in front of them was a dais and there sat a figure, which was certainly Tana. It had the hideous face of a troll with the beak of a Carron. Its body looked like that of a dragon, including its hind feet and tail. It had the wings of a carron and the hands of a troll. Tana was almost too much for anyone to take in at once, a mesmerizing combination of three creatures fit into the size of a small dragon.

"Your most High, I have brought the messengers," announced the lifeless cloaked being as it bowed before Tana.

The threesome stood at attention right wing fists extended downward.

A guttural voice chilled the air with its seductive nature. "Aha, what information have you brought to me, Carron Colonel Bravort?"

Bravort jumped. Then he bowed, "Your Highest and Ruler of all Tamoor, I have news from General Maltor concerning the actions at the front."

The scintillating icy voice with a demanding arrogant tone said, "Yes, I know, Bravort! But what are they?"

"The General gave me specific instructions that I am to tell you three very important pieces of information. First, we are fighting the war exactly as you have commanded. Secondly, we have killed over one hundred giants and injured at least as many. We have taken no prisoners. We have lost about two hundred and fifty creatures in death or disability. Only seventeen of our creatures have been captured and no one above the rank of corporal. And thirdly, we have enlisted the aid of a dragon named Greedy who has fought valiantly. He is the only son of Tereem, the great dragon."

Tana emitted a hissing sound and smoke came from her nostrils. "What is this? What is this? A dragon named Greedy? We have not seen this on our globes. How is this possible?" Tana seemingly talked to herself and not to Bravort at all.

Then she looked straight at the colonel and demanded in a tone that could cause a lesser Carron to retreat. "How old is this dragon you have enlisted?"

Employing discipline, Bravort answered, "I am not certain, Your Highest, I believe the General said he is thirteen soars."

Tana stopped moving and stared straight through the Colonel. She didn't seem to notice Petrie doing his best to stand still holding her flag, or Rant's squirming. Transfixed, as though conversing with someone in another dimension, after a moment of total silence she looked at Bravort once more.

"What thirteen soars? Where did you enlist him?" Tana paced, placing her troll hands on her hideous blue face, which was now clouded with smoke.

"I am told he was found on the battlefield wounded and unconscious, Your Highest," replied Bravort, concentrating to keep his voice level. He had thought she would be pleased, even happy.

"Colonel Bravort, I want you to take a message to General Maltor. Tell him I want you to bring this dragon Greedy back to me within the next twenty-eight senes, do you understand?"

"Yes, Your Highest. As you wish, it will be done."

The hissing icy voice of Tana demanded, "You will leave in the next sene! You can eat and then leave immediately! I expect you to deliver the dragon to me within twenty-eight senes! Do you understand, Colonel?"

"Yes, Your Highest." Answered the Colonel, keeping his terror and curiosity under his armor. He had no idea how they could achieve such a feat, why Tana wanted the dragon, or how they would leave in a sene when they had only now arrived after one continuous sixteen-sene journey. But soldiers do not question their commanders, and certainly don't question the power or magic of Tana.

"As for the rest of the news your General has sent, I have heard it and I have seen it. I would not say we are winning, but we are holding ground. I will be sending in a Special Forces unit of trolls very shortly and then we shall see how Narsor likes that. You can tell your Commander, General Maltor, within five beedites the Trolls Special Forces Unit will arrive. They will announce themselves to the General only, and they will not interface with your military. But I am giving your General direct instructions to do whatever the Troll Commander demands. He is to have overriding privilege in this war. Whatever he needs or wants will be given. Make sure you are totally clear on this and that you pass this on to General Maltor. I have an edict you will carry to the General that states what I have told you. However, if any but your hands or the General's touch it, it will disappear, so remember what I have said. This is very important." Tana's eyes turned red, fire shot from her lips as she stared into the Colonel saying, "What is your prime objective upon return to General Maltor's camp?"

Bravort almost let his terror slip. Trying to keep from stammering, he replied, "Bring the dragon Greedy back to you within twenty-eight senes and give the edict to General Maltor."

"Hissssss...yes! See that you do exactly that Bravort. When you return with the dragon you may receive a reward for your courageous efforts." Tana finished her sentence with a burst of fire that sent the Carrons scurrying back a few paces.

Tana turned to the cloaked figure to her left at the end of the dais and said, "Take care of their needs and see that they leave here within one sene."

Then Tana flew down from the dais and Colonel Bravort bowed, hoping she would not notice how badly he shook. Rant fainted.

"Take this," said Tana, glaring down at Bravort and handing him a rolled parchment with a red wax seal. "Be very careful where it is placed. Remember if anyone beside you or General Maltor touches it, it will disappear immediately. I will be watching you on your journey, Bravort, so travel in haste and pride me. Your reward awaits your return." Her huge orange eyes drilled the message into his brain. Bravort would not forget this.

Colonel Bravort placed the parchment in his pack and then bowed to Tana. When he looked back up, Tana had disappeared.

The cloaked figure stood waiting while Colonel Bravort attended to Rant.

Shaking the young white Carron fiercely, Bravort commanded, "Rant get to your feet. We have no time to waste here."

"Oh, I thought I would be burnt to death. I felt like a bird on the Barbie, Colonel. I thought it was all over, I--"

"Enough Rant. Close your beak and get your talons in order. We leave here in less than a sene and I would like to at least get something to eat if I can't have a decent night's sleep."

Bravort's mind raced at the thought of traveling all that distance back to camp and then immediately back again. How was this mission to be accomplished? Oh, the dragon...of course, that's how! A smile crept over Bravort's face, his feet felt light as he realized he would fly back atop a mighty dragon. Oh, yes! That's how. Of course Tana already realized this and was simply testing my allegiance.

Once they had completed their meal, they stuffed their packs with extra rations and were escorted back to the entrance. Nothing had changed. The light was still the same, temperature, and flowers, all exactly as they had been one sene hence. Now they would leave the citadel. But how would they have enough stamina to keep going? How much stronger he felt after eating! The fears were gone and he felt good. Only the dread of the journey made him weary. "Colonel Bravort," came the chilling voice of the cloaked figure as they reached the huge stone door. "I am to give this to you." It handed Bravort a small round bottle. The Colonel looked at it curiously and then at the figure, "When you feel too tired to continue, place one drop on your tongue and give a drop to each of your soldiers, it will revive you and fill you with the strength to continue. Tana guards you. Her power is the greatest in all Tamoor and you are now under her protection."

Chapter 8

A VISIT FROM THE QUEEN

The crack of thunder suddenly brought Loni back from her thoughts.

"That sounded awfully close!" exclaimed Yorkin.

Before Loni could answer, lightening struck a huge tree in front of Potemkin's horse. The horse reared as a thick, thirty-leet branch fell across the narrow path.

"This storm will get worse before it gets better," Potemkin said turning his horse to face the group. "We need to find some shelter quickly. Does anyone know a place close by where we can get in out of the rain?"

The small group stared at each other hoping someone might speak.

"There's a cave not far from here," came the sweet voice of Starina; but only Loni could hear her.

"Starina knows a cave nearby. She can take us there!" Loni shouted over the now pouring rain.

Bushy eyebrows raised, Potemkin pointed to Yorkin, saying, "Please lead the way."

"Give her free rein, Yorkin, and Starina will take us there," Loni whispered in Yorkin's ear.

Starina began a fast walk up the path and then said, "Oh, there it is," and then turned east into the dark forest.

"How far is the cave?" Potemkin shouted.

"About two yonts," replied the horse.

"Almighty ancients, I heard the horse!" exclaimed Potemkin. The entire group burst into laughter.

"So what did she say, Commander?" asked Yorkin, chuckling under his teal green hood.

"About two yonts, is that right Starina?" Potemkin asked.

Starina whinnied. The forest darkened the further they traveled. Towering oaks and evergreen trees became so thick that the rain stopped altogether.

"Starina, how can you tell direction in this darkness?" questioned Loni.

"By the smell in the air and the ground cover on the trail. Look down and you will see the ground gets deeper in moss as we approach. Do you hear the sound of rushing water ahead? It means we are almost there."

"Yes, yes I do," Loni said.

Yorkin asked, "Loni will you share your conversation with the rest of us?"

"Oh, yes. Starina said that the water up ahead indicates we are getting close to the cave."

"Well, that is really something. I didn't hear any of that, yet I heard the mare speak clearly a moment ago!" said the Commander.

"I can direct my thoughts to only one person in much the same way you whisper," replied Starina.

"Well, that is marvelous! You truly are the queen's horse!"

The path widened into a scrubby field and pounding droplets of rain mixed with the crashing of the rushing creek. Starina stopped. "The creek is usually not this strong. I'm not certain how safe it will be to cross under these conditions," said the mare loud enough for all to hear.

Potemkin rode up and studied the situation.

"There's the cave, Commander," Starina said, pointing with her nose.

Potemkin, Yorkin, Loni, and Sarolla looked across the creek to a spot set high in the eastern hill, the cave obscured by rain and trees.

"If you say so, Starina. I can't see it clearly," stated Potemkin. Looking up and down the stream the Commander added, "I don't see any place that looks better. I think we had better try crossing here. We will do this with the strongest men downstream as the fairies and Sarolla cross. How does that sound to you, Starina?"

" I think that is about the safest idea, I only hope we can get a sure footing and hold our ground in this creek."

Potemkin signaled for the men to move into position on the furious creek. "Tyron, you are my strongest. I want you to go first and test the current. Take your time."

Tyron carefully coaxed his mount into the perilous waters. The horse slipped but then caught a foothold. He positioned himself in the center of the creek and the other soldiers followed. Then Potemkin signaled for Yorkin, Loni, and Sarolla to cross.

"Please, sir, I am terrified of the creek, can I wait here until the storm is over?" begged Sarolla who was now as gray as the sky.

"No, Sarolla. Let your horse do the work and hang on. Cover your eyes if you must, but go!" commanded Potemkin.

Sarolla covered her eyes and began chanting the ancient sound of Tamoor.

"Oool..aaamm Oool...aaamm Oool…aaamm." The rest of the giants began to chant with her and the rain seemed to let up and the horses calmed.

Once all the soldiers had crossed, Potemkin entered the water. As he reached the middle of the creek, lightening struck a boulder upstream, the rock split. Instantly it crashed toward Potemkin. Sarolla screamed. Loni pointed her ring toward Potemkin shouting: "Beauty please, a circle of light; protect my friend with all that's white!"

Suddenly an intense white light encircled Potemkin and his horse. The rocks bounced off and continued downstream.

The troop cheered, shouting 'Potemkin' and 'Loni'.

When Potemkin reached Loni, he said, "What just happened?"

"I asked for help and Beauty did a little something to protect you."

"I am once more grateful to you little one. I hope I can repay you in some way." Smiled, Potemkin squeezed Loni's tiny hand.

"Potemkin, you are repaying me by taking me home and helping save all of Tamoor from Tana."

The Commander's smile faded, "Let us hope that the ancients will guide us to save all of Tamoor. All right, Starina, lead us to the cave before we drown in our saddles."

Starina climbed the rocky slope, maneuvering between the low myrtle bushes and thick bonta trees.

"I see it. I see it!" exclaimed Sarolla.

"Yes, there it is and it looks like a nice large cave, big enough for the horses," Exclaimed Potemkin. Then in a quieter voice he added, "But of course, Starina would only find us a cave such as this one!"

Finally inside the giants built a fire and unpacked dry clothes.

Hands on his hips, surveying the space, Potemkin announced, "We may as well plan to settle here for the night. There's no reason to take any more chances this beedite. Let us thank the Ancients, Starina, and Loni for our safe journey." Potemkin bowed his head and every giant followed in suit. They sang out in unison: "Oool...aaamm, oool...aaamm, oool…aaamm."

Potemkin looked up, a twinkle in his eyes, smiling broadly, he clapped his hands sharply saying: "Okay everyone, let's get to work setting up camp." Turning toward a wiry little giant the Commander added, "Pazard ready the evening rations, this weather makes a warrior hungry!"

"Yes, sir, Commander. It will be my pleasure," replied Pazard.

Pazard, a jovial giant, enjoyed telling jokes, laughed easily, and loved creating beautiful food. He had a penchant for light fluffy crème puffs and delicately spiced cream sauces.

Removing his hood, Yorkin asked, "Loni, I'm going to help Potemkin, can you take care of Starina?"

"Oh yes, it will be fun. I bet Starina has some great stories to tell me and maybe she can show me more of this cave," Loni responded taking the reins from Yorkin who had dismounted.

"Okay, but don't go too far. I have no idea how big this cave is or who else might be here."

"Don't worry, big brother, Starina and I will take care of ourselves. And I'm sure you'll feel better knowing I'm with the Queen's horse and not a troll."

Yorkin smiled and patted her leg.

Loni and Starina walked deeper into the cave. GreeHee came to mind. What had happened to him? It seemed like a lifetime since the moonrise when he had disappeared. Loni looked to Beauty for some guidance, but Beauty showed no signs of concern. So Loni turned her attention to the beautiful mare.

"Starina, this cave is enchanting. Does it have a tale to tell?"

"Now that you mention it, it does. The first time I came to this cave I was with Queen Beetrea. There was a side to the Queen that few people knew, but I had the pleasure to watch and know intimately." The horse sighed with satisfaction. "She was schooled in the magical arts."

"Oh my!" exclaimed Loni. "No wonder she could hear you."

"Well actually, it was the Queen's magic that made my speech plain And it was the Queen who taught me to throw my thoughts in a controlled fashion, so only one person might hear me."

"How incredible! I feel the Queen is nearby when you speak. Oh my, I can see her presence to the right of your muzzle! She is very beautiful."

"Right again, Princess Loni. Queen Beetrea is standing here with us." Replied the blue roan mare.

Queen Beetrea's hazel eyes sparkled under delicate eyebrows, her long auburn hair flowed in waves to her waist and long narrow fingers touched the mare's neck. The Queen's oval face was beautiful, skin glowing, chiseled nose and full, perfectly formed lips; no wonder King Narsor had fallen in love with her

"Starina, can you ask the Queen questions for me?" Loni asked.

"Actually, you can ask her yourself. She can hear you as clearly as I can."

By now out of earshot from the rest of the troop, they had reached a place where the cave widened considerably. Droplets fell from the stalactites hundreds of leets above into a small pool in the center. Because the space was so dark, Queen Beetrea appeared almost real.

Loni dismounted and bowed before the apparition. Beetrea smiled touching Loni's head with her jeweled right hand.

"Your highness, may I ask you some questions about the prophecy and how Draydel won the First Primengeer?"

"Yes, my child, but I may not be able to answer all your questions," came the soft voice of the Queen.

"Who are the five that are mentioned in the prophecy?"

"This you will know in less than one leedite. The ancients would not want this revealed before then because it could endanger the mission of the five."

"Oh! How did Draydel win the Primengeer?"

"This is a question for Draydel and not for me. However, I will give you a clue. It was through the magic of merging centered power. Once merged it was then directed to expand and cleanse all negativity in its path."

Looking directly into Loni's eyes, the Queen added, "You have this power, but are not conscious of how to use it. I am here to teach you something about power that will be very important to you in your journey."

"Oh, Queen Beetrea, I am ready to learn. Please teach me."

The Queen turned, her golden dress flowing across the rough stone as she floated to the cool dark pool. Starina quietly watched. The sounds from the rest of the cave disappeared and only the trickle of water filled the air.

Loni followed Beetrea to the pool. The Queen pointed for Loni to look into the small circle of dark water. As she stared, a drop fell from the ceiling of the cave. It filled the pool with sky blue, the color rippled outward, permeating the pool with light.

"Loni, look into this pond and see your power," the Queen said, still pointing and patiently waiting for Loni's awareness to take hold.

Mesmerized, as if she had fallen into a deep well, deeper into a trance where time and breath had stopped, she heard the roar of a windstorm. The wind began to push her gently, then with force and then ruthlessly. She didn't move. She felt her essence drawn down into the Tamooran soil, deep into her center. The Life mother whispered, "I will ground you, Loni, guardian of Tamoor." A surge of strength rose through her. Then a bolt of lightening shot from the sky, striking through her into the Tamooran mother. It filled Loni with energy and she felt the strength of all nature coursing through her tiny form. The wind filled with apparitions. It changed from Carron to dragon to toothless troll. Each charged toward her. But none could touch her. They bounced off as if she were a mirror. Finally the air settled. The wind whispered and caressed her. The sky cleared and the Tamooran mother spoke. "Well done, daughter of Tamoor, guardian of Ancient Power."

A shiver ran through her body as an ice-cold droplet of water splashed onto the back of her neck. "Oh, what was that? Did the great Tamooran mother speak to me?"

A silky smile crossed the Queen's red lips, "Yes, she did. Remember this experience. You will need to be conscious of this power in the near future."

"But what about me? Guardian? What does that mean, Queen Beetrea? Am I not simply a fairy?"

"My dear child, we are all much more than we appear. And you, Loni, are quite special. In time you will know more. It is your journey to discover. But remember when the time comes, the Great Tamooran Mother and Father Lightening will be there for you. Simply trust them and know they will help you center your power."

The queen disappeared. Loni turned to Starina hoping to hear her opinion of what had happened. But the mare was fast asleep, standing exactly where Loni had left her.

Back at the camp, Loni found Yorkin and Potemkin sitting by a huge fire, eating and deep in conversation.

"So you think the Carrons will join with the trolls to initiate further attacks on Narsor?" asked Yorkin.

"Definitely," replied the Commander. "I guarantee that, unless we put an end to this war quickly, the trolls will enter and then the wildebeests, hyhenats, and sawtooths. Tana has power over any being whose hearts are filled with greed, ego, and self-righteousness."

Yorkin gripped the cup tightly, his handsome face strained with fear, "But that leaves only fairies, giants, and the ethereal ones like the unicorns, pegasi, and centaurs to fight for the good of Tamoor. Oh, and there are the Tamooran soil folk at the very south tip; they are certainly egoless. But none of these beings really know much about war, except for we giants and fairies. It doesn't look like very good odds to me!"

Loni touched his shoulder and giggled.

"Why you little brat!" he rushed at her. Loni flew to the top of the cave. Yorkin followed in hot pursuit. "I will get you little sister and when I do --"

"You'll do what Yorkin?" snickered Loni.

"I'll tickle you, that's what I'll do."

Still looking behind her at Yorkin, she hit the top of the cave. "Ow!"

"Gotcha!" Yorkin said, grabbing her wing and pulling her down to the ground. "Oh, you're no fun." The tone of his voice changed to a caring one. "Are you all right?"

"Yes. Sorry, well kind of, sorry." She looked at him with a mischievous twinkle in her eyes. Then they burst into laughter.

"You are not! You're just a little fairy trouble, that's what you are," Yorkin said, tugging on her hair and then hugging her. Then standing up hands on his hips, wagging his right index finger, he demanded, "So how long were you standing there, Princess Loni?"

Dusting herself off, Loni answered, "Long enough to hear about the woeful fight between wickedness and integrity." Then looking at both Potemkin and Yorkin, Loni added: " But I'm certain we will win despite the difference in numbers."

"Well, Princess Loni, may we all have your great heart," said Potemkin. "Please sit down and I will have the chef bring you dinner. Pazard! Bring Loni some food."

The cook nodded.

In a serious voice Loni began, "The Queen's presence travels with us. She was schooled in magic and I feel she will be a great help to us in this journey. We will win this war with magic. It was the way of Draydel and it will be our way as well." Loni was not sure what she was saying but felt very good when she had finished.

"Yes, it will definitely take magic. But none of us are schooled in it!" exclaimed Yorkin thumping his fingers nervously. "I guess I should have stuck with those classes Eulool started to teach me when I was a child."

"Yorkin, did Eulool teach you how to stay centered in your power?" asked Loni.

"Good grief, Loni," Yorkin said, eyes wide. "He repeated those words all the time. I never really understood them. When I worked with his changelings, he would say, 'Stay centered or they will take your power.' I guess I stayed centered because they never got away with anything. Yet, I never really understood what I was doing. Why do you ask that?"

"I had a chat with Queen Beetrea and --"

Potemkin asked, he and Yorkin leaning toward her. "You did what?"

"I saw the Queen, she appeared to me and we had a short conversation."

"And, what did she say?" asked Yorkin touching Loni's shoulder, while Potemkin leaned even closer.

"She said, oh how did she put it?" Loni put her finger to her lips and closed her eyes. The others said nothing, waiting for her to speak. "I asked her how the first war was won and she said it was through the magic of merging centered power. And then she added something about directing it to expand and it would cleanse everything negative in its path." Loni opened her eyes and stared directly at Potemkin and Yorkin.

"My most magical dish," exclaimed Pazard, presenting a plate of creamy pasta to Loni.

The trio jumped. Potemkin knocked into Pazard's arm. The two giants fell into each other with the plate of pasta all over their faces.

Sitting up and licking the cream from his face, Potemkin said, "That is really good, Pazard, but I prefer to eat it on a plate."

"Me too!" added Pazard.

They laughed.

Sarolla came to help the Commander stand up. Pazard picked up the plate and taking a dishcloth from his apron, began cleaning up the mess. Then he stood up and said, "I will offer my largest crème puff to anyone who can correctly answer my favorite riddle?"

"Is it a really large crème puff?" asked Tyron, the enormous curly red-headed giant, now towering over the wiry little chef."

"Yes! Easily twice the size of all the rest!" said Pazard, still cleaning pasta from his clothes.

Potemkin said still shaking the cream sauce off of his tunic, "All right, you might as well tell the riddle, we know you will anyway. So please, Pazard, before Princess Loni starves."

"Okay, what do you get when a troll marries a carron?"

"A feathered roll?" asked Tyron proudly tapping his thick hands on his enormous chest.

"No. A carol too ugly to sing," said Pazard.

Loni laughed. Yorkin sighed. Sarolla frowned. And Tyron stood there puzzled, scratching his head.

"Oh good earth, I think you had better stick to your cooking, Pazard, and save the comedy for the jesters," said Potemkin with a dry laugh.

Sarolla took the dishcloth from Pazard, saying, "Here, let me do that for you, Pazard, then you can get more food for the Princess."

"Good thinking, Miss, I'll get on that right away."

Tyron said following the chef, "Pazard, wait, don't I get that big crème puff? I'm the only one who gave you an answer."

"No. You will have to try another of my riddles first…" Pazard said as they strode off together, the wiry little chef and the enormous rotund soldier.

Potemkin signaled for Loni and Yorkin to follow him to a more comfortable spot. "Now what were you saying about centered power merging, Loni?"

"I'm not certain of its meaning," replied Loni, "but I have some thoughts about it." Loni straighten, her left eyebrow angled, and continued, "I think the Queen was referring to Draydel centering his power and merging it with the power of a blue star and perhaps some other power. I feel he had to keep all of this centered and then somehow use magic to direct it to clear Tamoor of evil. That power forced all negativity backwards. And I think we will have to do something similar in our time to win the war. But instead of one mighty wizard, it will take the merging power of five this time. Does that sound like it makes sense to both of you?" Loni said looking from Potemkin to Yorkin.

Potemkin nodded, lips pursed, deep in thought.

Pazard gently whispered, "Princess!" as he touched Loni on the shoulder and carefully handed her another plate of food.

"Oh, thank you, Pazard. It looks delicious." Loni inhaled the pungent scent of the warm cream sauce. Pazard made a show of tiptoeing away with his finger over his lips. The trio chuckled at him.

Then Yorkin said, "Loni, that explains how the armies disappeared from Narsor's land. But the real question now is who are the five and how do they merge their power to win the war?"

"I don't know, but the more I think about it, the more I feel we may be three of the five."

Potemkin stood up, overshadowing the two fairies and with a sweep of his great right arm said: "May the ancients bless us if this is so. But I must say no to this quest. I cannot cross the Azura Kah while I live and I don't know what good I could be to anyone dead."

Loni stood up, firmly stating, "Potemkin, you must trust the Ancients to guide and protect us. If we are to cross the Azura Kah, I am certain they will find a way for you to do so. Don't you agree Yorkin?"

Yorkin sat back, his eyebrows raised, "Yes, but why us? Eulool said he saw five; two small, one large and long, one large and tall and one enormous compared to the rest. I guess we could be the two small and Potemkin could be the large, tall one, but who are the others? And why, with all the wisdom of the Ancients, would they choose us?"

Loni reminded him with a question, "Yorkin, remember what King Narsor told you and Potemkin before we left the castle?"

"That Yorkin and I have the power of two moons," answered Potemkin before Yorkin could reply.

"Oh yes, that strange statement," Yorkin said turmoil pouring from his voice. "I really don't understand it and no matter how I try, I cannot fathom what it means in any practical way!"

"I'll drink to that," added Potemkin. "I have pondered that statement for senes, and I too cannot understand what it means or how I could possibly carry this power."

"Well I am certain in time we will all understand," said Loni.

"I certainly hope so," Potemkin added throwing his hands in the air.

Sarolla, stepped in. "Though I am certain I have no right to be listening to your conversation, I could not help but hear you, and I immediately remembered an ancient phrase my grandfather made me learn as a child. May I share it with you? I think it would help."

Potemkin raised his cup and shook his head. "Please Sarolla, perhaps your grandfather had a better understanding of the Ancients then we do."

"The phrase he taught was: 'In all the times of fair and woe, you can be sure the Ancients know, their wisdom great, yet ours is slow, so trust and trust, give them your hand and then in time, you'll understand.'"

Chapter 9

PAYCHENTE HELPS

Captain Bartet had the job of interrogating GreeHee. He stood alone in the tent with the dragon, quietly pleading. "Please, Dragon Greedy, you must give us the details. The general will wait no longer. He becomes angrier each beedite you are silent." Then in a near whisper, the Captain continued, "I have written a complete story of your heroism; all you have to do is sign it and it will make the General happy. You will get a medal of honor and everyone will be happy. Would you like me to read it to you?"

GreeHee's eyes widened and he stared bewildered by the Captain's dishonesty. "You made up a story Captain?"

"Yes Greedy, it is perfect and will make everyone happy. Let me read it to you. Surely a dragon like you will enjoy this slight deception. I give you every honor."

Smoke rings curled from GreeHee's nostrils, his tail tapping against the sides of the tent, "Bartet, leave the story here. I will think about what you have said. I only wish I could remember the details myself." The Captain's beak turned white, he backed away, leaving the story on the table in front of the dragon.

As the doctor entered the tent, he said in a gentle voice, "Greedy, is there something you want me to read to you?"

"Doctor, I am not sure what I should do. I still don't recall all the details and now Captain Bartet is pressing me to sign this story." He pushed the papers toward Paychente.

The doctor picked up the papers with his left wingtip and signaled to the dragon for silence. He carefully crept to the tent opening and looked through the slit in the flap. Then he stepped back to GreeHee and whispered, "Greedy, it is time to give you a little advice and to help you make some important decisions."

"I need all the help I can get, Doctor. I'm all ears," replied the dragon.

Paychente pulled up a stool and sat close to the dragon. "Let me take a quick look at this." Moving his feathered fingers across the pages, the doctor completed the story. Then looking at the dragon, he continued, "Well, Greedy, as I see it you have a few choices, but before I speak about any of them, let me ask you a simple question." Paychente hesitated for a moment then moving very close to GreeHee whispered, "How do you feel about going into battle?"

"I," stammered the dragon, "I don't want to kill anyone."

Drawing in a deep breath and smiling the doctor continued, "As I suspected. Then there are several options you have. Do you feel strong enough to fly?"

"I'm not sure. Could we go out tonight and see?"

"Yes. We will. But first let us take a look at your options. One, you could sign this tale of heroism and make Maltor happy. This would bring great relief to the entire camp, making you a hero. Then as soon as I say you are fit, you will be directed to the front lines to go back to war."

"I really don't like that option, although the hero part is nice," he said with a frown.

"Well, you could still have the first part and then we could devise something about your health which could prevent you from going to the front lines again. How does that sound?"

"Now, that might be okay but I'm not sure I want to sign anything that is a lie. I don't feel right about it."

"Yes…" said the doctor tapping his left wingtip on his knee. "Now, that's the dragon I've come to know." The doctor patted GreeHee on the shoulder. "I think your best plan would be to leave camp tonight."

"Do you think I'm strong enough?"

"Well, my friend Greedy, I suspected it might come to this and so I made a special medicine to increase your stamina. I believe there is enough here to help you fly beyond harm's way. Would this be your choice?" asked Paychente gently touching GreeHee's chin.

"Yes! I really want to leave here and go home. I want to unravel what has happened. I feel so harassed." Then quickly looking directly at the doctor, GreeHee added, "Oh, not by you, but by everyone else. I hope I can fly!"

"Well, Greedy, in a few senes we will find out. In the meantime, I will prepare this medicine I have been storing. You should rest, this could be a very long journey for you and you will need all your strength."

The doctor stood and went to his worktable at the far end of the tent. There he took out some bottles and began mixing the medicine. As he worked he hummed. The little tune comforted GreeHee and he fell asleep.

Several senes later, Paychente said, "Greedy, wake up."

GreeHee woke with a puff of smoke. The doctor jumped.

"Oh sorry, I'm not used to anyone waking me. It's the way dragons wake when disturbed. Luckily, I noticed you before the fire stage!" He chuckled as he stood up.

The doctor shook his head while waving the smoke aside. "The Ancients are with us, Greedy," he whispered peering through the flap of the tent. "They have filled the night sky with clouds so there is very little light. It's perfect for your get-away."

Quietly, doctor and dragon moved through the camp. They headed for the west gate, the same one they used every night. A hundred leets beyond the gate, the doctor steered them north around the camp and then further to the east.

Finally far to the east of camp, the doctor said, "Greedy, here you can test your strength."

With a massive stretch of his wings, the dragon leapt into the darkness. "I can do it, Doctor. I feel tired but I also feel great. I love flying. I didn't realize how much I missed it!"

"Shsh..sh" Paychente said, "I hope no one heard you!"

"No, I don't think so," whispered GreeHee. "I could see only a couple of carrons moving about and they were on the south side of camp."

"Good," said Paychente. "If you are to leave tonight, you should fly due east until you are clear of the land of Narsor. Travel to Oberlon and then head north to go home. Once you begin to fly west, you will have to be very watchful. Armies of carrons, trolls, and others may be marching from the north. I know Maltor sent a small squad to the north three beedites ago. I don't know what they were sent for, but they could be bringing more soldiers back. You will be safest east of here."

"Yes, I see." He nodded. "I have never been to Oberlon but since it is a fairy kingdom, I don't think I need to worry about anything there."

"No, I have already thought this through for you, Greedy. Oberlon has lots of resources. You should find food easily and I don't think most fairies would go anywhere near a dragon. If you were to fly south you would have to cross all of Narsor and that could be deadly. If you flew due west or north, you would fly over numerous troops of Carron soldiers and this could be deadly for both of us. East is the only direction which offers safety. There are no other Carron camps to the east and there is not much giant activity there either that I have heard about, so it should be safest. I know it means a very long journey home but it is the safest."

"But what about you, Doctor? What will happen to you when the General finds out I have disappeared?"

"Not to worry, my fiery friend, I will tell the General that when we came for relief, you took off and I waited for you to return exactly as I have done every night. When you didn't return quickly, I feared something might have happened to you and I went looking for you. Then I will tell him the next thing I remember was being knocked unconscious. By the time I became conscious again, you were gone. That will be my story. So in case you get caught, you will know what I told the General. Now, dear Greedy, here is the medicine I made for you. It is best if you take all of it now. Here, swallow it completely." He handed the young dragon a small brown bottle.

The dragon drank all of it. "Yuk, that is disgusting," he said, slapping his tongue in and out of his enormous mouth. "You could have warned me!"

"No," chuckled the doctor, "If I had, you would have hesitated or refused." Paychente broke into a hearty laugh as he watched GreeHee gagging and acting as though he would die from the taste.

Then in a more serious voice he continued, "Greedy, that medicine will take effect in about four senes and I figure you probably have the strength to fly for that long before you will need help. Once it takes effect, you should be able to go eight or ten senes without getting too tired. So you need to keep going as long as it has effect. By that time you should be in Oberlon and out of harm's way."

"Thank you so much for all your help." GreeHee frowned, his emerald eyes watered. He wished Paychente would go with him. Then he added sheepishly, "Would you like to go with me? You could ride on my back?"

Patting him lovingly on the shoulder, the doctor said gently, "No Greedy, my place is here with my species. But thank you for inviting me." Then in a stronger voice, Paychente added, "You need to get started. So go, fly east. Remember don't head north until you reach Oberlon."

"Okay, but how will I know when I get to Oberlon?"

"Oh, that's right, "said Paychente, slapping his forehead with his left wingtip. "You've never been there. It's easy. Look for the Crystal River. Once you cross it, you'll be in Oberlon. Take care and may your journey be blessed." The doctor patted the dragon's shoulder.

"I'm so grateful to you, Doctor. Thanks for taking care of me. I hope you will be safe." GreeHee flew into the air and vanished into the cloudy night.

Chapter 10

A QUESTION OF DEATH

Just before dawn, Paychente prepared himself to meet the General. He rolled in the dirt and bruised his head and neck against a rock. Then, he flew into camp to tell General Maltor that the dragon had disappeared.

As Paychente reached for the flap of the General's tent, the General was coming out. He knocked into the doctor. "What the bomb gardeners are you doing here, Paychente! I was on my way to see you and get the dragon." The general pushed away the two corporals who had immediately started to rescue him.

"General Maltor, I have come to inform you that the dragon is missing," said Paychente standing up and dusting the dirt off his coat and feathers.

"What! What are you saying, Paychente? How could the dragon be missing?" bellowed the General.

"Sir, I took him for relief last night and he didn't return as quickly as he has every night, I immediately went looking for him. Instead of finding him, I was knocked unconscious and when I awoke he was nowhere to be found. I came here immediately to tell you sir," the doctor said with a salute.

"What are you saying, bird! Are you telling me you lost the dragon?"

"Not exactly, general." Paychente squirmed.

"This calls for a full investigation. This problem is bigger than you could even imagine, Doctor Paychente, and you may have to explain this to Tana!" Paychente did not move a feather. Why was the general turning red with anger over the dragon? "Captain Bartet!" Bartet stood right behind him, covering his ears.

"Oh, there you are, Bartet, get a search party together and take Doctor Paychente with you. He will show you where he last saw the dragon. As my most trusted tracker and personal aid, I want you to check the ground and see if the giants had anything to do with this, or if the dragon had ideas of his own. In the meantime, I must meet with Bravort. Go now," the General commanded Bartet who stood staring at him. "What in Tamoor are you waiting for, bird? Go!" Bartet jumped into action.

Paychente showed Bartet where the accident happened. Bartet, was a very quiet soldier, he went about his work efficiently while Paychente watched. What should I do now? Should I knock this kind bird out and fly off? Is this my only chance to save my feathers? Certainly a visit to Tana can't be good.

Before Paychente could decide, Sergeant Petrie landed in front of him. "Doctor, you must come with me immediately there has been an accident and the General sent me to get you."

Bartet looked up from his magnifying glass. "Go, I don't need you. I only needed to know where the incident took place."

Paychente flew back to camp with Sergeant Petrie. "What happened Petrie? Is the General all right?"

"Sir, it is not the General, it's the Admiral. He was struck by lightening."

"Struck by lightening? That's impossible, the sun is shining."

"Sir, I saw it with my own eyes. It happened when the General handed him a parchment."

Paychente shook his head. What in the world is this about?

Entering the General's tent, Paychente immediately assessed the situation by examining Jarteen.

"Well, Paychente, what do you make of this?" inquired the General.

"Sir, I am afraid there is no sign of life. The Admiral is dead. May I inquire as to the circumstance of this sudden death? Sergeant Petrie mentioned lightening and this wingtip is seriously burnt."

Maltor ignored the question, "Are you saying there is nothing you can do to revive my Admiral?"

"Sir, he is dead." Repeated the doctor. The General's body sagged and he fell back into his chair.

"Okay, Paychente, remove his body to your medical facility." Then turning to the Colonel, Maltor continued: "Bravort, rest up, you must leave right after mid-moontime. Now leave me alone all of you!"

Paychente began a systematic examination of Admiral Jarteen's body. He should do an autopsy but something kept stopping him. Each time he looked at the Admiral, he felt he might wake up. But clearly the Admiral had no heartbeat. Even after several senes the body did not become hard, rigormortis was not setting in. This made no sense whatsoever. What had happened to the Admiral? Lightening could cause the burn on Jarteen's right wingtip. It could even cause death, but where did it come from?

Paychente sat in his chair pondering the situation. Exhausted, the doctor fell asleep.

Around three in the afternoon, the Doctor awoke. He walked over to Jarteen's body expecting it to be cold and blue but it was still warm and filled with color. In fact it looked and felt exactly as when he first saw it early that morning.

"Corporal Gento, go to General Maltor and ask him to come here. I need to consult with him about Admiral Jarteen's death."

"Yes, sir!" said the lanky athletic Carron.

"What is it now, Doctor?" growled the General entering the infirmary.

"Sir, the death of Admiral Jarteen is very puzzling and I need more information as to the circumstances of his demise. Actually, I am not sure he is dead but I am convinced he is not alive!"

"Paychente, what gibberish is this? Not dead but definitely not alive? What are you saying?"

"Sir, look for yourself." The doctor pointed to the Admiral's body.

"Oh, unseen Tamoor!" exclaimed the General. "Jarteen looks as though he is asleep." Then touching the Admiral, Maltor jumped back. "He is still warm! How can this be?"

"Well, General, that is exactly my question. How did the Admiral die? Based on what I am seeing, it appears to be some kind of magic?"

"Doctor I am not at liberty to give you all the details of his death but I will say this, it is the work of Tana!"

"Tana? But Tana is on <u>our</u> side. Why would she hurt Admiral Jarteen?"

"It was all a misunderstanding but now I know what I must do," the General said in a whisper, staring at the floor. He turned to the Doctor. "Paychente, pack your things, you will be leaving with Bravort at mid-moonrise. Get some sleep. You have a very long journey ahead of you. That is all." Maltor turned to leave the tent, then turned again saying, "Oh, also leave one of your corporals in care of my Admiral's body. Blanket him as if he were asleep, and give your bird orders to watch him and report to me immediately if there is any change in his condition."

Chapter 11

NADECKADOR'S CASTLE

GreeHee thought of the doctor as he flew, hoping he would be safe. At the very darkest time before dawn, a wave of weariness overtook him and it took sheer determination to keep flying.

Then, a few elides later, a surge of energy raced through his body. "It must be the medicine!" GreeHee mused, "The doctor was right." So he continued flying well past dawn.

By late afternoon the sky was still cloudy and the light drizzle of the last two senes turned to rain. Shivering, stomach growling, though GreeHee could make out a river in the distance, he must rest for a while. He needed to dry off and get something to eat. As he scanned the countryside, the forests thinned to rocky meadows. "I will be much safer where I can see what is around me. The forest may harbor creatures that want to kill me. I'll stop on a hill in the clearing."

Flying over the open ground, he noticed roads clearly in use and others in disrepair. Following an overgrown road would be safer. On a hill a few yonts further stood massive broken walls and some large stone buildings partially intact. It looked like it had been a small town centuries ago. At the very peak of the hill, the tower of an ancient castle poked into the sky from walls completely overgrown with vegetation. The perfect place for a dragon to eat and rest.

As he reached the hill, he realized the Crystal River was no more than eight senes away. "Maybe I should keep going like Doctor Paychente advised." But then, "Kaaah-choo!" His whole body shook. "Aaah, ka-choo! Instead of smoke, his nose was dripping a greenish liquid. "Oh, my nose is leaking! I need to get warm."

GreeHee landed in the overgrown courtyard at the top of the hill. He ripped aside some vines and pushed open what had once been a pair of enormous doors. "Truly a giant's castle. Perfect for a young dragon like me!"

GreeHee entered what had once been the great hall. At one end stood the remnants of an enormous fireplace. It was intact except for the vermin and dried leaves from the deciduous trees that towered seventy leets high and stood about ten leets in front of it. "Perfect!" GreeHee began heaving. A few puffs of smoke spiraled out but no flames. A chill ran through him. "Kah-choo!" The sound echoed through the cold stone walls. Pieces of stone crashed to the floor. Should he try again?

Shivering, he must try again. A little spark. Then a flame. And finally, a fire! Yes, a beautiful enormous, fire! He felt better the more he blew fire through his nostrils. It cleared the sneezy feeling. In a few tithes, the dead wood began to burn and GreeHee kicked everything loose into the fireplace, clearing the area around it. The fire burst into high gear. GreeHee stood close to the flames. "Oh, this feels so good, I'll curl up on these leafy vines and rest for a while." GreeHee fell into a deep sleep.

A voice screamed, "Help! Help! Someone please help me? Please!"

A surge of fear coursed through his body. What was happening? He couldn't see anything. Everything was black. Then a wave of heat burst through him. He was asleep, deep in some dark dream. He could hear and feel sensations but could see nothing. Then a sudden heavy thud and all was silent and peaceful. "What was this? What was happening? Where am I?

GreeHee found himself staring into the ancient gold eyes of a magnificent unicorn. A soft, masculine voice spoke in his head: "It saddens me that I had to kill your mother to protect a fairy queen, but you, little one will live. You will be called GreeHee and in your life you will repay this debt to the fairy kingdom. You shall have all that your mother lacked: a heart filled with love, a desire for peace and a mind that shall reason. In your thirteenth soar your heart will lead you to a new world of harmony with all life. The Ancients shall bless you with all you need to accomplish your task and one of my own will help you find your way. After your long journey you will find joy.

"Sleep peacefully. When you wake, you will remember." A burst of emerald light flowed over the young dragon and he fell back into a calm healing sleep.

The sky, still drizzling and misty, now turned from orange to violet as the sun dipped below the horizon. Loni shouted, pointing at a hill in the distance, "I see it! Look! There's the tower! That has to be Nadeckador's castle."

"I believe you are correct, Princess." Said Potemkin, coaxing his horse into a trot.

"We will rest before dark!" resounded through the tiny troop. They spoke of dinner, warmth and a weary journey that would soon be over.

When Potemkin reached the crest of a small hill and could see the castle more clearly he reined his horse in and stopped. He held up his hand for the rest of the troop to be still and silent.

Leaning forward on his horse, hand holding the rain from his eyes, he squinted, "Smoke? Can you see it, Yorkin? I can certainly smell it!"

"I see it all too clearly," said Yorkin reining Starina closer to Potemkin.

"This may portend danger! Who could be there? It is awfully far for the Carrons, and the trolls could also have taken a more direct route," said Potemkin as he rubbed his chin with his right hand. "Well, it could be some old giant who has made a home in the ruins. Let's hope so."

At the bottom of the hill, Potemkin addressed the small troop. "Yorkin and Tyron, choose two scouts each and then meet me over there for your orders." He pointed to his right. "Everyone else dismount and keep silent."

Once the six scouts were gathered, Potemkin said, "Soldiers, we are depending on you to scout the area. Tyron, take your giants and check the east side. Yorkin, you will scout the west. I expect you to meet around the back of the castle walls. Then using discretion, go inside. See who is camping there. Take no action. Return here and report what you find to me. Do you understand?" Both fairy and giant nodded. "It is certain that if the enemy is here, they will have scouts of their own and only the Ancients can protect us if that is the case. We are no match for an army. Okay, Soldiers, go and be careful we will wait here for you."

"Yes sir, Commander," Yorkin said, saluting the Captain. Tyron and the rest of the scouts did the same.

They disappeared into the rapidly approaching darkness.

"Potemkin," said Loni as he returned to the group. "I don't believe we are in any danger."

"Why is that?"

"Beauty has not shown red and even when I ask now," she said holding her enchantment band up for him to see, "She continues to shine white."

"So, that means we are safe?"

"Yes. Beauty has always warned me when I am in danger."

"Well, let us hope she is right." Then looking up at the sky and pulling his cloak closer around his strong muscular body the giant continued, "It is truly a gift of the ancients that this nasty misty weather has held and that we have arrived at dusk. If our enemies are present, the weather may be the cover that has saved us from sight. At any rate, we will soon know." He sat down on a large flat rock and added, "We might as well get comfortable while we wait."

Loni sat patiently, watching the sky turn to deep indigo. What was taking so long? "Beauty are you sure everything is all right?" The enchantment band blinked a bright white.

As the three-silvered moons of Tamoor rose, Loni heard sounds. Potemkin whispered, "Keep silent." Then scurried toward the castle.

Loni strained to hear her brother's voice but sounds were muffled by the wind and rain. In a tithe, Potemkin, Yorkin, and Tyron stood in front of her.

"Sir, what can I do for you?" asked the little fairy standing up and shaking water from her dark green cloak.

"Princess Loni, it seems your Beauty may be right," Potemkin said pacing. "There are no signs of danger around the castle, but inside it there is a dragon!" He stopped in front of her.

"Oh! Oh! Is it GreeHee? Could it be GreeHee?" Loni said, turning to Yorkin and Tyron.

"I don't know. It is possible," said Yorkin. "All I know is, he is asleep and does not look full-grown to me. Did he have any distinguishing features that you remember?"

"Uh, his belly was yellow. Oh, in the battle with the Terrotacs, he suffered a deep wound to his left thigh and it must have a long scar."

"Great Moons of Tamoor!" came Tyron's deep rumbling voice. "This may be your dragon. I did see the scar on his left thigh, but I really couldn't see his belly the way he was curled up."

Loni bounced up and down. "I can't wait!"

Walking back to camp, Potemkin said, "When we get to the castle, Yorkin, you will take Loni in and see if she can identify the dragon before we all enter and hopefully before he wakes."

Yorkin nodded.

Then turning to Loni, Potemkin added, "Princess, I must warn you not to become too excited, this may not be your dragon. Lots of dragons have scars and if this is not GreeHee, you may be in danger, and so may we all. But if it is a small dragon, we have a good chance of killing him especially if he is still asleep when we get there. So Tyron and I will go inside the castle with both of you and you will let us know if this is GreeHee or not. Do you understand, little Princess?"

"Yes, sir," said Loni, looking down and then with her big eyes back up at him said smiling, "I have a really good feeling about this, Potemkin!"

Smiling back, Potemkin said, "May you be right, little one. Now let's hurry and hope we get there before the dragon wakes."

With the rest of the troop situated outside the courtyard walls under the umbrella of some enormous marmosa trees, Potemkin, Loni, Yorkin, and

Tyron entered the castle grounds. Aside from the patter of rain on the stones and the scent of smoke in the air, it felt deserted. As they approached the colossal carved doors of the castle, Potemkin put his hand on Loni's shoulder and said, "Loni, Tyron and I will get in position first and then you can enter." Loni attempted to speak but Potemkin put up his hand and continued, "We cannot know how this dragon will react even if it is GreeHee and my job is to protect you, so we will do this my way. If this is not your dragon or if he does not recognize you, we may have to wound him or even kill him. We will be ready to act." Loni's eyebrows touched and her smile faded. She wanted to protest but something told her to keep silent, so she did.

Potemkin turned to Yorkin, "As soon as I give you the signal, you and Loni can enter. Do you understand?"

"Yes, Sir," the handsome fairy whispered, readying his bow.

Then Potemkin and Tyron, with arrows drawn, stealthily entered the castle. They seemed to disappear as the vines camouflaged them completely.

Potemkin waved to Yorkin. The fairies entered the castle.

Loni's smile became a grin the closer she got to the dragon. "It's him, Yorkin! It's him. It's GreeHee!" she whispered beaming.

"Okay, Loni," said Yorkin, taking her hand. "I want you to do this a certain way. I will stand behind you and you can call to him. But in case he gets angry I will take over." Yorkin put his hand gently over Loni's mouth as she tried to protest. "Little sister, we're at war and I'm going to protect you, so don't even try to make me change my mind!" Then changing his tone, Yorkin added, "Are you ready?"

Loni nodded and flew a few leets in front of the dragon's face.

"GreeHee! GreeHee! Wake up, it's me, Loni!" the princess called out in a soft friendly loving voice.

"Wha..who is that? Loni? Loni? I know Loni," the dragon said from a deep sleep. As he spoke a little fire escaped from his nostrils. Loni and Yorkin dodged it easily but Tyron, terrified of the beast, nervously released his bow and an arrow flew through the air barely missing GreeHee's right eye. It lodged in one of the spikes that rose out of the top of his nose.

"Ooww!" screamed the dragon, involuntarily breathing fire.

"GreeHee, GreeHee, let me help you!" cried Loni. But Yorkin pulled her away from the dragon who was now standing, fire shooting in large flames from his nostrils. He looked to his right, but could not see Tyron who was now covered in vines hiding from everyone.

"Who did that?" cried GreeHee.

"GreeHee, it was a mistake, I am sure Tyron is sorry. GreeHee, let me help you," Loni pleaded, breaking away from Yorkin's grip. She flew to the dragon.

"Loni? I remember Loni. Oh my Ancients, Loni!" His wrinkled scowl disappeared and GreeHee smiled.

"I missed you, GreeHee. I tried to find you, but you were gone," Loni said as she landed close to the spot where the arrow had struck. "Here, let me help you get this nasty arrow out of your spine." Loni began to pull on the arrow but could not tug it out.

"Wait, Loni, let me do that," Potemkin said as he stepped out of the vines.

"Who are you?" asked GreeHee, taking a step back.

"I am Potemkin," said the Commander as he approached the dragon.

"GreeHee, Potemkin is my friend, "Loni said, "He has tried to help me find you. Please let him help. He can get this out."

"Wait, Potemkin," Tyron called, "I am the one responsible for this terrible mistake. Please, Mister Dragon, accept my apologies," said Tyron now fully visible and bowing to GreeHee. "Please let me be the one to take it out for you."

"Whoa, wait an elide, how many of you are there?" questioned the dragon backing up a bit.

"GreeHee," Loni blurted, "we have a whole troop of giants with us and this is my brother Yorkin." She pointed to Yorkin, who bowed to the dragon.

"Nice to meet you, I am sure," said GreeHee.

Potemkin ordered, "Tyron, I will take care of GreeHee. I need you to get Pazard and ask him to bring bandages and ointment immediately!"

"Yes sir, Commander!" said Tyron racing out of the castle.

"GreeHee, if you will put your head down here so I can reach the arrow, I will get it out as painlessly as I can," said Potemkin.

"Uh, okay. Since Loni says you won't hurt me, I guess it's okay."

GreeHee did as he was told and the Commander cut the point of the arrow off and then pulled the rest out clean. Blood started to spurt and Potemkin held it as tight as he could.

"Does it hurt a lot, GreeHee?" asked Loni.

"No, actually I don't have a lot of feeling in my spines, so it's okay. It will probably stop bleeding on its own in a few elides."

"Well I will put some pressure on it," Potemkin said, "and that will help. Pazard will have some ointment that will stop the bleeding very quickly."

"Thanks. So what are you doing here, Loni?" the dragon asked.

"The giants are taking me home and I wanted to stop here at Nadeckador's Castle to investigate the wizard's tower room. I think it may contain some information that will help us win the war. You know we are at war, don't you? And where have you been all this time?"

"Yes, I know we are at war. That's how I became separated from you. The

Carrons took me to their camp. But that's a long story --"

"Here's the ointment sir," shouted Pazard, running toward the Commander and then stopping dead in his tracks when he realized Potemkin was standing on top of a dragon's head. Potemkin stood pressing with one hand on a big bloody dragon spine while he extended his other hand for the ointment.

Seeing the look on Pazard's face, Potemkin chuckled, "No need to be afraid, Pazard. GreeHee is a good friend of Princess Loni. He will not harm you."

Pazard's whole arm shook as he handed the ointment to Potemkin.

"As a matter of fact, Pazard, I am willing to bet if you made one of your delicious meals for GreeHee, he would even love you!" Potemkin said, winking at GreeHee and Loni.

"Whoa! I would be happy to accommodate you Mister GreeHee, but I doubt I have enough food to satisfy a dragon," Pazard said, bowing and backing away at the same time.

"Well, maybe you could make him one of your fine crème puffs. I wager he's never had a crème puff, have you, GreeHee?" the Commander asked.

"No I haven't. I have only read about them in books. I think I might like to try one or two. Actually as soon as you put that ointment on, I will need to get something to eat. Can I safely go outside without being shot at?"

"Yes, as soon as I explain who you are to the troop, you will be more than safe. We will guard you!" Potemkin said as he stepped away. The wound had stopped bleeding.

"Uh, sir," Pazard hesitated, "I think everyone already knows about Dragon GreeHee. Tyron started confessing how he accidentally wounded the dragon as soon as he came to get me. I am certain everyone knows."

"Okay then," said GreeHee. "I will be back once I've had my fill."

Yorkin, Potemkin, Loni, and Pazard stepped out of the way as the dragon flew straight through an opening in the roof.

"Princess Loni, I declare to the Ancients you are indeed our lucky charm. In my wildest dreams, I could not have imagined a dragon so gentle and well mannered. And I will also admit that 'Beauty' was right!" Potemkin grinned and lifted her off her feet with a hug. "Thank you for being with us on this journey!"

Loni blushed.

Chapter 12

PROPHECY AND THE UNICORN

By the time dinner was over, the entire troop had been introduced to GreeHee and Loni had filled him in on the details he could not remember about their travels. "So that is why I didn't feel I had killed any giants." Looking at the big sweet eyes of the tiny fairy, her animated little hands, her soft laugh like a breeze in summer, GreeHee's heart swelled, his muscles relaxed and the corners of his mouth turned up naturally. "Ah," he breathed a sigh.

Loni told him about Queen Beetrea's visit and he remembered. "Loni, something happened when I fell asleep here. I met a unicorn!"

"What?" Yorkin couldn't help saying as he looked up.

"Aaagh," Potemkin nearly choked, spitting sassafras juice everywhere, "Did I hear you say, you met a unicorn, GreeHee?"

"Well, yes I did. He was in my dream. But he was very, very real!"

Loni asked, "Did he come to tell you something? You know these old ruins contain Draydel's magic. There is no telling what we might learn asleep or awake here."

"The unicorn was very old. He had a long beard and golden eyes. He told me he was sorry that he had to kill my mother, but that I would live." GreeHee stopped, trying to hold back a tear.

"Here now," said Potemkin patting GreeHee's shoulder. " My mother died giving birth to me and I often thought while a giantling that I had killed her. It hurts not to have her and it's even more painful to think you might have been the cause of her death. I know how it feels. If it's any consolation to you, I have learned through war that the Ancients have a much bigger picture. They have a greater plan and we are all playing a perfect part in it. Knowing that has given me some peace." The giant squeezed GreeHee' shoulder and GreeHee let the tear fall.

He sighed a deep breath and said, "I have never spoken about my mother before. My father seldom spoke of her and I only know I miss having a mother. She has always been a nice dream to me. Someone who might be there if you needed comfort."

"Oh, dear GreeHee," said Loni as she flew to touch his cheek, "we're here to comfort you. That's what friends do for friends, you know. And we are your friends. Aren't we Yorkin? Potemkin?" she said looking to her brother and the Commander.

"Yes," they said in unison.

GreeHee took in a deep breath, "I am just learning about friends. Until I met you, Loni, I had no idea what it felt like, and then there was Doctor Paychente. He was so nice to me. I hope he is all right. He is nothing like the other Carrons."

Potemkin stiffened, backed up, "Now that I would have to see to believe. I have seen far too many Carrons to believe there might be one who is good!"

"But you have never seen a dragon like GreeHee either, have you Potemkin?" asked Loni, her big eyes drilling him.

"Princess, you certainly can cut to the quick. I have to admit that is true, but GreeHee is only thirteen and--"

"Commander," she began frowning, "you know the Ancients have much to teach us and I feel we need to learn that a gentle spirit can take any form."

"Hmm. I will think about it, Loni." Potemkin scratched his chin thoughtfully. "In the meantime, let's hear the rest of GreeHee's encounter with the unicorn."

Yorkin said, "Yes, do tell us more about the unicorn."

"Oh yes, the unicorn, he apologized for killing my mother and I remember a warm feeling came over me when he said it. I felt his compassion. Then he said I would repay the debt to the fairy kingdom--"

"Wait, what debt to the fairy kingdom?" interrupted Yorkin. "What did the unicorn mean by that?"

"Oh, before I met the unicorn there was something going on. Someone was screaming. I think my mother was about to kill someone. But the unicorn killed my mother instead. Based on what the unicorn said, my mother must have been in the process of killing a fairy queen. Yes, I remember feeling a sense of heat. My mother must have been getting ready to blow fire."

"Wait a minute, GreeHee, where were you?" asked Loni.

"In his mother's womb," answered Potemkin. "Don't you see -- the unicorn told him, he would live but his mother would die?"

"Oh, now I understand," said Yorkin beginning to pace. "It is what we in Oberlon call 'The Wisdom of the Unicorn'. If a unicorn should pierce anyone with its horn, the evil will die but any good therein shall live and thrive. You remember, don't you, Loni?" Yorkin stopped and pointed at her.

"Yes, of course." Loni sighed. "We were taught that in a nursery rhyme: 'Wisdom of the unicorn, should it pierce one with its horn, evil dies and good is born, t'is the wisdom of the unicorn.' Yes I remember! Why do you think it refers to it as wisdom? I have never understood that?"

"Eulool answered that question for me once," replied Yorkin. "He said it is because wisdom is the power to cut through illusion. With wisdom you can distinguish good from evil in all things and that is exactly what the piercing of the horn does."

"Amazing things you learn from fairies!" exclaimed Potemkin slapping his knee. "But can we hear the rest of GreeHee's dream now before I fall asleep wondering. I am so tired, I don't know how much longer I can stay awake."

"Well, he said I would repay the debt to the fairy kingdom some beedite and that I would have everything my mother lacked. Let's see." The dragon stopped. He scratched his head. "A heart filled with love, a desire for peace, and a mind that shall reason, yes that is what he said!" GreeHee exclaimed, sitting taller, eyes flashing, chest puffed.

"My Ancients, but that is what I wish for my giantlings and companions!" Potemkin's eyebrows raised, expressive hands extended. "What a blessing and totally unknown to dragons before you, GreeHee!"

"Was that all he said?" asked Loni poking the dragon gently.

"No, he added some really scary, strange stuff after that." GreeHee stopped, screwed his face, tapped his nose and burst out, "Oh Blessed Dragon Eyes! It was about this soar of my life!" All eyes were glued to the dragon. "He said in my thirteenth soar my heart would lead me to a new world of harmony and that the Ancients would bless me with everything I need to complete my task. Then he added that one of his own would help me find my way. And something about after a long journey I would find joy? I really don't know what that is? What is joy?"

"Oh, GreeHee!" Loni said, "joy is when you laugh and there is nothing else in your head, no worries, no sadness, no painful thoughts or regrets, only laughter. That's joy! You remember when you were in the Brentippees River and you started laughing at yourself?"

A big smiled crossed GreeHee's long green face. "Yeah! That was funny. I didn't notice all the pain. I felt happy."

"Can I interrupt?" asked Potemkin running his right hand through his wavy black hair. Everyone looked at the Commander. "What did the unicorn mean when he said the Ancients would bless you with everything you need to complete your task? What do you think they meant by your task?"

"I don't have any idea. What do you think, Potemkin?" asked the dragon.

"Well, we haven't told you all about the prophecy and the war with Tana; but I am inclined to believe that you are part of it." Then turning to Yorkin and Loni he added, "Don't you think GreeHee must be the enormous one?"

"Oh my! Oh my!" exclaimed Loni flittering in the air. "Oh my! It is all falling together now! I am starting to see the picture."

"What picture? What prophecy?" GreeHee whined, pulled back, little bits of smoke spiraling in the air. I'm going home tomorrow – And I don't like being called the enormous one either." Whack, tail flicked high then snapped to the floor.

Potemkin jumped up, pointed at GreeHee, "Well, how would you like to be a giant who has to cross the Azura Kah and die before finishing the journey?"

GreeHee moved closer, tapped his upper lip, eyebrows touched," The Azura Kah, that is not even in the direction of home. I need to go to sleep and talk to that unicorn. I thought my journey almost over when I got here."

"Whoa, hold your ponies!" said Yorkin standing, hands on his hips. "No one is sure that any of us are the five. We could be jumping to conclusions, so let's cool it and get some sleep. In the morning we can tell GreeHee the whole prophecy and--"

"And we can search Draydel's tower!" Loni flew around the trio. "Then maybe we will know better who's who and what to do." Loni landed, yellow silk dress glowing in the diminishing firelight, she pointed to Yorkin, "But remember, Draydel told King Narsor that you and Potemkin hold the power of two moons. So there is little doubt you're both part of the powerful magic it will take to win this war."

Yorkin's mouth contorted, brow furrowed, "Well maybe Draydel was mistaken. I don't feel powerful."

"Excuse me, Yorkin. Your first idea of getting some sleep and starting fresh in the morning is best right now," Potemkin yawned, stood up, bowed to the dragon and added, "I'm glad you're with us, GreeHee." Turning to the fairies, he said, "I wish you a restful sleep. May the Ancients protect us all!"

Chapter 13

POTEMKIN'S ENCOUNTER

Before going to bed, Potemkin checked on security measures for the camp. Past the courtyard to a ridge high atop the crumbling stone ruins of the ancient castle walls, he met Tyron on first night watch.

"Tyron, how do you feel after such a long ordeal this beedite?"

"Very well, Commander," the robust warrior saluted. "A surprising turn of events this night -- I am relieved the dragon is a friend. I felt terrible when I let that arrow fly. Sir, it was an awful mistake."

"Tyron, we all make mistakes. No need to berate yourself over it. The Ancients are certainly guarding our journey. What a beautiful moonrise this has turned out to be." The sparkle of stars and the light of the three-slivered moons filled the clear night sky.

"Yes, sir. It is perfect weather. It would be hard for any enemy to get past a watchman under these conditions."

"Very well then, I'll go to bed now and rest soundly knowing you're here."

Snores and sounds of shallow breathing filled the Great Hall. Moonlight shimmered casting soft shadows in the hushed glow of the tired fire as Potemkin snuggled into his bed sack and fell asleep.

"Potemkin, you will die, if you continue this journey! I can save you and give you immortality. Come to me -- to your real home in the Northland." Potemkin struggled to make out the source of the voice. A whirlwind roared around him. A rush of air pushed him forward.

"Do you want to die, soldier?" said the neutral voice.

Potemkin swallowed hard, "No."

"Then say you serve Tana and I will protect you from the prophecies!"

"Tana? I have no allegiance to Tana. I serve my King!"

"Your king is a powerless old man. His wife had the power and she is dead! The Carron army has overtaken Narsor. You will become my slave," the voice laughed. The tone changed, seductive, "I can save you -- come to me now."

"Show yourself! I do not talk with the wind and will not make commitments to a voice without a face," demanded Potemkin.

"Aaah, I thought I would spare you but so be it!" Tana taunted. A lovely woman appeared, gleaming in an exquisite pale blue satin gown, the bodice covered in pink pearls, long lace sleeves extended to delicate wrists and slender jeweled fingers, her skin smooth ivory, red hair swirling in curls around her bare shoulders, soft green eyes shaded by long lashes. "I didn't want to tempt you with my beauty, but since you demanded it, here I am."

"Holy Stars," Potemkin sighed in a near whisper, his heart pounding, "you are more beautiful than any giantess I have ever imagined."

"You see, I am not at all what you have been told." Tana said sweetness dripping in each syllable. "I am the giantess you seek and I find you very strong and handsome, Potemkin." Tana touched his cheek, desire shot through his body. "We are meant to be together. Do not go to the Azura Kah." She pouted tempting him, caressing his neck, igniting his passion. She unbuttoned his shirt, stroking his furry chest, exciting him. Potemkin's breath increased. She pressed against his chest, staring up at him, lips parted. Potemkin embraced her, inhaling her fragrance, roses, sweet, intoxicating. He pulled her closer, his hand captured silky ringlets, heart pressed to her voluptuous breast. "You are everything I desire," he whispered looking into her eyes. As his lips thirst to moisten hers, lightening flashed.

"Don't!" Queen Beetrea commanded, appearing in front of Potemkin. Her eyes flashed like daggers, her brilliant purple wand held high swept in an arc, "Get out! You have no power here!"

In a tithe, Tana's beautiful face transformed into the hideous troll, scowling, orange eyes intense, feathered blood red body, gangly troll hands clutching, dragon tail whipping. Potemkin shrank in horror. "Ha Ha Ha, you are fools. Beetrea, I murdered you and you're still not settled in your grave. Isn't that too bad," Tana taunted, her huge head shook, nasty mal-formed troll finger wagging, blue lips curled, "Ha Ha Ha I don't need Potemkin or anyone else to win this war. But it's such fun toying with your handsome giant!"

"Out and don't return!" commanded the Queen, hazel eyes riveted, right arm outstretched, wand pointed.

Tana's laugh faded and the warm emerald light emanating from Beetrea grew stronger.

"Potemkin, look at me," the Queen said touching his shoulder.

"My Queen. I am so ashamed. I cannot bear to look you in the eye."

The Queen's delicate fingers lifted Potemkin's chin, "You need not be ashamed. Your will is strong. Your weakness is your fear."

"But my Queen, I don't want to die."

"Potemkin, you will only die when it is time, not one elide before."

Brow furrowed, Potemkin frowned, "but how can I cross the Azura Kah and live?"

"I cannot explain that now. But I will tell you this -- you will live! You will live and have many giantlings in your lifetime. I know this to be true."

"I shall keep these words in my heart throughout this journey and look to you for comfort."

The Queen's eyes held his, her white silken gown glowed under the purple velvet overdress, gold cords dropped from her tiny waist, her jeweled crown shimmered in the fading light, "Do so, I will journey with you. All of Tamoor shall be grateful for your service. I leave you now. Rest your heart -- give Tana no room to find fear!" The Queen vanished and Potemkin woke.

His skin crawled, "Ugh, yilk!" He spit, thinking how he almost kissed Tana. How close he had come to a dishonorable death!

Chapter 14

DRAYDEL'S MAGIC

Even before the sun had reached the horizon, Loni was up looking for Potemkin. GreeHee still slept, as did Yorkin. Actually in the Great Hall the only one up and about was Pazard, busy starting a fire and mixing batter for muffins and breads.

"Have you seen the Commander?" Loni asked.

"No Princess," replied the chef, "maybe you should look outside."

"Yes, I will do that, Pazard. Thanks!" The fairy floated through the great hall and into the courtyard. She could hear Potemkin's voice coming from the direction of the horses.

"Well Starina, your Queen is really something," he said to the mare when Loni touched his shoulder laughing.

"And what are you laughing about, Princess Loni?"

"You, Potemkin. You look very funny sitting on that upturned bucket talking to a horse!"

"Well, I will have you know this is not just a horse. Starina has told me more interesting stories than I have heard from any of my soldiers," Potemkin said smiling.

"Yes, I am sure that is true but you still look ridiculous sitting there like a school child under a horse's nose!"

"Starina, what do you think of that?" Potemkin said, rubbing the mare's muzzle. "And you thought Loni was so sensitive! There you have it," He pointed to the laughing fairy.

"There's no accounting for humor, Commander," said Starina. "Funny bones are a very personal matter and I never try to second guess them."

"A wise horse you are indeed!" Then turning to Loni, Potemkin added, "So, I suspect you could not contain your excitement any longer and you want me to give you permission to enter the tower?"

"Yes, that is exactly why I am here," Loni said, swallowing her laughter.

"Unfortunately, I cannot let you go on your own. So we will need to wake Yorkin. We should also consider if GreeHee would be of any assistance.

What do you think, you know him better than anyone else?"

"I really don't see what help GreeHee may be in this matter. And I'm not sure he will fit through the stairwell to the tower."

Potemkin stood up and patted Starina's neck. "I will talk with you later, Starry. Thanks for all the comfort. You are a wonderful friend."

"Anytime Commander, I'm here for you!"

"See you later Starina," called Loni over her shoulder, still snickering.

Loni and Potemkin headed back into the great hall. Potemkin went to his supplies to get the floor plans of the castle, while Loni flew across the room, planning to pounce on Yorkin.

"You lazy little fairy!" she said as she landed squarely on his stomach.

"Oh, yeah!" came Yorkin's voice landing behind her, pinching her wings.

"Oowh!" Loni screamed, "You big bully! I was supposed to scare you!"

"It's about time I got one in on you, Loni," Yorkin said. "You need to learn to watch your back, you little fairy brat." He laughed as he tugged at her wings and hugged her. "So what's the status on our mission to the tower? Have you been waiting long?" Yorkin teased.

"Forever, you sleepy head," Loni smiled. "Actually we're ready to go."

"Okay then," Yorkin said.

With drawings in hand, the threesome headed for the tower.

"Wait an elide, Commander!" shouted Pazard, white apron flapping, holding up three sacks, "Take some food with you. Who knows how long you will be gone." Pazard ran to Potemkin, handed him the bags of fresh muffins, yogurt and juice.

"Thank you, Pazard, if we don't make it back until the moon rise, we should have enough food." The Commander chuckled.

Potemkin, Yorkin, and Loni walked and ate.

The stairwell was easy to find but climbing it was another matter entirely. Stones, debris and vermin, filled the winding broken stairs. Vines strangled the walls shooting here and there across the steps.

"It looks like we'll need more giant power to get through these vines." Potemkin said, shaking his head as he surveyed the staircase.

Loni said, "Potemkin, Yorkin and I could fly through all of this and get up to the top easily. Perhaps there is a better way for you to get there too?"

"What do you mean?" asked Yorkin.

"Well, I was thinking that GreeHee could fly Potemkin to the top of the tower and if we're already up there we could open a window to let him in. What do you think of that, Potemkin?" asked the fairy princess.

Potemkin, scratched his head, pushed out his lower lip, "Hmm, that sounds like it could work. Do you think GreeHee will cooperate without you being there Loni?"

"I think so. Just tell him that I need him to do this for me. I feel he will be very helpful. In the meantime Yorkin and I will keep going."

"Okay," said the Commander, "but Yorkin is in charge and I expect you to do whatever he says. That's an order Loni."

"Yes, sir, Potemkin!" Loni saluted, pouted, then grinned.

"Excellent, sir!" said Yorkin.

Loni and Yorkin made it to the top of the tower stairs in less than twenty elides. But they could go no further. The chamber was locked behind an enormous wooden door.

"Holy Ancients, why didn't we think of this?" Loni said. "Without Potemkin, how are we supposed to open this door?"

Yorkin and Loni sat down to consider the situation.

"I got it!" shouted Yorkin, jumping up. "We'll moonbeam it. Look at that lock," he said pointing to the gigantic keyhole. "You and I can get through that in a tithe, like we used to get into Eulool's forbidden rooms, remember?"

"Great idea!" Loni said forming herself into a moonbeam.

In a tithe they were both inside Draydel's chambers.

The rooms were bright and spacious. The first one had huge windows at either end, polished blue marble floors and bookcases along the entry door wall that ran from floor to ceiling. To the left of the entry, the room extended about thrity leets and to the right about fifteen. Directly across from the door was a stone corridor leading to the rest of Draydel's chambers. On the right side of the opposite wall stood a slate fireplace with a solid oak mantel and a map of Tamoor. On the left side of the room Draydel had a dark blue circular couch arranged around a scopetron that was aimed at a skylight in the ceiling. At the far end of the room beyond the scopetron was one of the wizard's worktables laden with a variety of beakers and measuring tools. Above the table hung numerous star maps.

"Look, Yorkin doesn't this scopetron look a lot like Eulool's?" Loni touched the stargazing apparatus.

"It certainly does." Yorkin looked through the lens piece at the sky.

"Look at the variety of books!" Yorkin said, "What odd sizes?"

"And over there," Loni said, pointing to still more shelves that lined the wall to the left of the doorway. "They are very odd."

The rooms continued through the wide stone corridor. It was empty except for a magnificent mirror that leaned against the left wall. The mirror, fifteen leets high and about eight leets wide, set in a silver frame that was intricately carved with magical symbols. "Isn't this mirror exquisite, Yorkin?"

"It is beautiful," Yorkin ran his hand along the frame.

The corridor opened into two more rooms. The one on the right was a bedroom. Inside a big wooden bed ran along the right wall. A window identical to those in the entry poured light onto the meticulously carved wooden desk below it. The room overflowed with books. They filled the shelves around the big slate fireplace on the left wall and sat in stacks on the floor, around the desk and on the bed. Candles perched on wrought-iron pedestals by the bed, in gold and silver candleholders on the desk, on the window ledge, and on the heavy dark wood mantel above the fireplace. Delicate embroidered tapestries of stars and constellations hung over the bed. Though the room was giant size, it felt cozy embellished with Draydel's personal things.

In the room at the end of the corridor stood the wizard's kitchen work area. It had a raised river-rock fire stove and a large rectangular walnut table with six odd size chairs. Various hanging baskets filled with herbs and roots, and shelves stuffed with neatly labeled jars of all sizes, lined the immense gray and charcoal stone walls. A window in the ceiling filled the room with a glorious column of light.

"Loni, isn't it unbelievable, that after six hundred soars these rooms are still intact? Except for the tiniest amount of dust, it looks like Draydel could have been here last night."

"Right you are," came a voice out of nowhere.

The fairies jumped. Yorkin drew his sword, shielding Loni with his body as they crept into the corridor.

"Who is that? Is someone here?" Yorkin asked, his sword extended in front of him.

"I am the keeper of the wizard's chambers and I have been waiting for Princess Loni. Come here and look in the mirror."

A brilliant light flashed across the room leading them to the magnificent mirror that rested in the corridor. As they peered into it, only their faces reflected back. Then an unseen hand erased their faces, and a knurled old oak tree filled the silver frame.

"Are you a tree?" asked Loni.

"Not exactly though that is how I appear. I was once a lovely young giantess who worked for Draydel. When the Primengeer began, he asked me if I would be willing to serve my country at whatever cost. I asked if it would hurt and he said no. I asked if I could become more powerful and learn more of the wizards' ways if I did what he asked and he said yes. I have been promised that when my service is over I will be returned to a giant form. I am to be born to an important giant and will be raised as the first in a new line of wizards."

"Wonderful!" exclaimed Loni. "I'm sure Narsor will be glad to have a line of wizards again."

"So what do you have to do to be born again and why did he make you a tree?" Yorkin questioned, his blonde eyebrows touching, fine nose wrinkled.

"I'm here to guide Loni to the information that Draydel left for her. I have been here protecting it for more than a linglorn." The animated tree said.

"Why didn't you give it to Tarktor when he came?" Loni asked.

"Because he was not the right one. Draydel left this information for Princess Loni, the youngest fairy princess of Oberlon in the six hundredth soar after the Primengeer. That would be you, Princess. Only you can release me from this form."

"How can I do that?"

"By finding the book."

"But why are you a tree instead of a giant?" asked Yorkin again, placing his sword back into the scabbard.

"Because a tree can never get senile, it only gets wiser with age," answered the leafy old oak in the mirror. "And as a tree, I do not have the fears or passions of a giant, so I could never betray my mission. It was the safest and easiest form Draydel could find for me."

"Well, do you have a name?" asked Loni.

"You can call me Lovely."

"Okay Lovely, what is our next step?" questioned Yorkin.

"You will have to go through the door behind this mirror."

"I don't see any cracks or cuts in the stone that imply an opening," Loni said, floating about the wall. "But wasn't this the area that Tarktor questioned, Yorkin?"

Yorkin surveyed the wall and rooms. "Yes, it was. Actually, when you look at the rooms on each side of this wall, it does seem like there must be something more between them."

"Excuse me," said Lovely, "if you will move this mirror to the opposite wall, the glass will light the wall and then I can show you what to do next"

Yorkin examined the framed glass. "Okay, but I'm certain we couldn't move this mirror, even if our lives depended on it. This mirror is huge."

"Yorkin, let's try anyway, maybe Draydel magically made it appear heavy."

Yorkin groaned, "Ugh. Loni this mirror is not going anywhere if you and I are the only ones moving it."

"Is there a magical word we should use when we lift, Lovely?" asked Loni.

"Sorry, but Draydel left me no instructions for moving the mirror."

"Hmm, what about Potemkin?" Loni asked Yorkin.

"Yeah! Let's see if GreeHee and Potemkin are outside."

Loni and Yorkin went to the window and peered outside. The window ledge was as high as Loni, so both fairies floated up to it and looked out.

' I don't see them, Loni." Said Yorkin. "Let's open the window and call to them."

The fairies pushed against the window, first with hands, then shoulders, then on their backs using their feet, but they could not get it to budge.

"Oil, try some oil," said Lovely, tree limb pointing to an oil-can on the floor in the corner behind the door.

"Great idea!" said Yorkin, flying to the can. Straining to lift it, he sighed, hand on his brow, "Whew, these giants have some mighty heavy stuff."

"Wait Yorkin, let's take some oil out of the can and pour it onto the window clasp. There must be a little cup or saucer around here somewhere we can use." Loni scanned the room. "There," she swooped across the room to a little chest." Perfect!" She held it up.

Once filled, Yorkin carried the saucer to the window and poured the oil over the clasp. "Okay, say a little prayer and let's give it a push."

Loni and Yorkin pushed and pushed at the clasp. Suddenly it gave way and they both fell out of the window.

"Draydel, where are they?" screamed Lovely.

"Not a problem, Lovely. We have wings remember?" Yorkin said, laughing and pulling Loni back onto the window ledge.

"I still don't see GreeHee, or Potemkin," Loni stated, grimacing, arms folded across her chest.

"Maybe they're around the other side of the tower. Let's try the other window." Yorkin said.

Before they moved GreeHee shouted, "Any fairies up here?"

The fairies looked out the window again and saw nothing.

"Halloo up here you little twinkle toes!" hollered the dragon, giggling.

GreeHee flew above the tower with Potemkin on his back.

"I have a giant delivery," the dragon said, peering in the window.

"Thanks for the lift enormous one!" said Potemkin as he jumped onto the window ledge. "I sure am glad you're enormous, I could never feel safe flying on anything smaller."

"Glad to be of service, Commander," said GreeHee bowing his head.

"Good morning, you big loveable dragon." Loni placed a little kiss on GreeHee's right cheek. "I'm so happy you're back in my life."

"Me too, you know what I mean," said GreeHee blushing. Then he added, "Potemkin, how long do you think you will be? Should I wait on the roof?"

"Give us about a sene and then come by and check on us. If we are any sooner, Loni will fly down and find you. Thanks again, GreeHee." Potemkin waved as the dragon flew away.

"Potemkin, we need your help to move this mirror." Yorkin said pointing to the mirror. "There's a trap door behind it with information from Draydel."

"But it doesn't look like there's a trap door here?" said Potemkin, feeling the wall behind the mirror. "How do you know this?"

"Because I told them, Commander." Lovely said.

Potemkin stood perfectly still, mouth dropped open, eyes widened, "Is that, the mirror speaking?" The fairies smiled and nodded. He turned to the mirror. "Are you speaking to me?"

"Yes Potemkin, I have already explained everything to Loni and Yorkin. Trust me on this, there is a trap door behind this mirror, move me to the opposite wall and I will show it to you," Lovely insisted.

"Her name is Lovely, Commander," Loni said as Potemkin readied himself to move the mirror.

"You know for a mighty wizard, Draydel could have put this mirror on wheels," Potemkin said as he strained. "My Ancients, I think it weighs as much as GreeHee!" The fairies laughed. "Yorkin, Loni, perhaps if you helped push, we could move it." They all pushed, but the mirror wouldn't budge.

"I'm afraid it's not going anywhere with only the three of us," said Potemkin. "We may need Tyron and two other giants to move this. I guess we'll have to call GreeHee back." Potemkin started toward the window.

"Wait an elide, Commander, maybe Lovely knows something we have missed. Any suggestions Lovely?" Yorkin asked the tree.

"Don't you know any magic? Surely one of you has been schooled?"

"Not that again!" sighed Yorkin. "No, none of us has been schooled, but I'll put that down as number one on my list of things to do when – and if – I ever get home again."

"All right then, it's settled. I'll call GreeHee." Potemkin said.

"Wait Potemkin, I have an idea." Loni pointed Beauty toward the mirror. "Beauty please be sweet, give this mirror four swift feet."

In a tithe the mirror sprouted feet and moved to the opposite wall.

"Incredible Stars, your Beauty is most amazing!" Potemkin grinned.

"Well, it's about time we started using magic instead of the brawn we don't have, little sister." Yorkin said, chuckling.

"You know, Yorkin, I was only taught to use Beauty in emergencies. I don't think of her when it comes to moving furniture," Loni said, hands on her hips. Then her mouth dropped open and she pointed, " Look there's the trap door!"

"Unbelievable! That simply could not have been there a moment ago! Okay, now how do we open it, Lovely?" asked Potemkin with a wry smile.

"And to think I felt strange talking to a horse? Now look at me, I'm talking to a tree in a mirror!"

"Well," Lovely replied, "I'm really a giant disguised as a tree, but that's no matter. Let's get on with this project so I can get on with my next life."

Potemkin, blinked, slapped his forehead and stared at the mirror.

Lovely pointed a limb at Loni, "Princess, there are two stones on the left side of the door about three leets above the floor. They should be a perfect reach for you since Draydel designed it on your behalf."

"Let me see." Loni placed her left hand along the smooth rocks to the left of the doorway. She pushed and pulled but nothing moved. "Wait." She stepped back and surveyed the wall. It was a smooth mix of uneven charcoal and gray stones, each fitted perfectly to the next, with no consistent pattern. "Look these two stones are similar to the picture Draydel gave to King Narsor. The only difference is there's a stone between them" Loni pointed to the rectangular stone that separated the two triangular ones. "I think this stone has to come out or go in." She pressed on the rectangular stone. Immediately it sank into the wall and disappeared. The other two stones came together forming a diamond -- exactly like the picture in Draydel's drawing!

"Perfect!" Loni exclaimed backing away.

The door slid back into the wall. The light from the mirror illuminated a little room. Loni began to enter. "Stop!" Lovely shouted.

Loni froze.

"Not before you do one more thing. Draydel set a booby trap in case someone was to move the mirror and find the door. Only I would know the booby trap and I was forbidden to tell anyone but you, Loni."

"Okay, what should I do next, Lovely?"

"Behind this mirror there is a tiny gold envelope, remove it first."

Loni looked behind the mirror and found the envelope. She held it up, and asked, "Now what should I do?"

"Stand before the portal and open the envelope, inside it you will find some gold dust, throw it into the chamber."

The gold dust flashed like a thousand candles lighting the room and Loni could see everything inside. "Is it okay to go in now, Lovely?"

"Yes."

"Wow, that was amazing," said Yorkin. "Too bad you had to use all that dust, it could have come in handy later."

The little room had lots of small books and a desk with little inkwells and nice pens. A small glass of water sat on the desk.

"Lovely this is really eerie, everything in here is my size? I don't understand, wasn't Draydel a giant like you?"

"Actually that is one of the keys to the mystery of Draydel. He was not a giant; he was a great, great, great, great Granduncle to both you and Yorkin. That is why you both carry the magic and the power to win this war."

"Blessed Ancients, no wonder you two have been called in!" exclaimed Potemkin. "Blood carries the ancestral powers. And you both have Draydel's blood."

Loni sat in the petite chair at the wee desk, overwhelmed. "My dear Granduncle gave his life to save Tamoor and now we are here to finish the work. I hope we can do it, Yorkin," she said, starting to cry.

"Now, now little sister. If our Granduncle knew we would be born and that we would be the ones chosen, he must have also known we could do it. Aren't you always telling me to trust the Ancients? Now it's my turn to remind you," Yorkin said, squeezing Loni's shoulders. "Loni are we supposed to find something important in this room? Let's start looking before this gold dust wears off."

"Loni will <u>know</u> it as soon as she sees it," stated Lovely.

"Okay, let's look." Loni stood and scanned the room. One corner seemed shinier than the rest. To the left of the little desk were three small shelves. "Yorkin, look at how bright the middle shelf appears. I think there must be something important there."

Loni stood in front of the shelf. Red bookends kept the row of tiny books in place. "Something about these bookends..." She placed one on the desk and picked up the other one. "Look, these bookends are like the two triangles in the drawing. I wonder what will happen if we put them together like that?"

Loni put the bookends together so their flat bottoms touched, forming the shape of a diamond. They began to glow.

"Step back, Loni," Yorkin said, pulling Loni away from the desk. "They look like they're going to explode or something."

Smoke escaped from the stones and a sizzling sound, like cold water on a hot grill. The bookends changed color from red to indigo.

"Look," Loni said, "They're merging together and forming a five-pointed star!" The transformation stopped. On the table lay a small blue book with a star on the cover.

"Potemkin, did you see that?" cried Loni.

"I never moved my eyes from the moment you picked up the first one. I saw it all and can't believe what I saw." The Commander shook his head, his eyes glued to the book.

"Yorkin, I <u>know</u> that star, I have seen it somewhere before. I'm sure it will come to me." Loni stared at the book in her hands.

Yorkin begged, "Loni, aren't you going to open the book? I'm dying of curiosity to see what's inside?"

The tower started to rumble. The floor began shake.

"Well maybe we'll look at that book later," Yorkin said grabbing Loni. "I think we better get out of here now!"

"Wait, Yorkin!" Loni said, pulling free of his grip. "There is one thing I have to do before we go." Loni picked up the little glass of water that had been sitting on the desk for the last six hundred soars. She drank it saying, "I love you Uncle. Thank you for taking care of us. May we honor you in this journey."

"Let's get out of here," Potemkin said, pulling the fairies through the doorway, "this tower is not going to last much longer."

But Loni's sight turned to Lovely. "Blessed Fairy Mothers, look at Lovely!" she said, racing to the side of an old woman lying on the floor beside the mirror. Potemkin and Yorkin did as well.

To Loni the ancient giantess whispered, "Thank you for freeing me." Then moving her moist brown eyes to Potemkin, she added, "I will see you again, father." Her eyes closed and she died.

"Where did she come from and what did she mean by that?" asked Potemkin, hands on his face, shaking his head, his eyes enormous.

The tower trembled. Books fell from shelves and the floor rolled like the Azura Kah in a violent storm.

"We'll explain later, Potemkin!" Yorkin shouted, pulling Loni into the air and out of the way of a crashing stone.

Potemkin didn't move. He stared at Lovely oblivious to the danger.

"Potemkin!" Yorkin shouted again, pulling on Potemkin's sleeve. "We have to get out of here now, the tower is collapsing."

"Yes..." Potemkin whispered, still not moving.

The tower shook and the floor cracked through the center of the corridor. Yorkin tugged Potemkin's arm. "Potemkin, look -- there's your ride!" Yorkin shouted once more, pointing to the window where GreeHee waited.

GreeHee bellowed, "Hurry the stones are crumbling. They're crashing everywhere out here! Hurry!"

The Commander heard the dragon, "Yes, let's go!" Yorkin still on his arm, Potemkin leapt through the window onto the dragon.

"Okay then, that's one way to mount a dragon!" chuckled Yorkin.

"It's about time," Loni said.

GreeHee flew up and away from the tower. As they looked back, the walls shattered like glass, stones crashed like acorns in a storm, and the roof crumbled like an overbaked cookie.

"I knew it. I knew it," shouted Loni. "Draydel held that tower together with magic all these soars. That's why it was the only one left. Now that we have his book, the magic is gone."

As GreeHee, Loni, Yorkin and Potemkin landed at the bottom of the hill, the troop cheered.

"Good work, Tyron!" said Potemkin bounding off GreeHee's back. "Is everyone safe and accounted for?"

"Yes sir, Commander!" replied Tyron," Everyone is safe."

"And you, Starina," Potemkin said, "have done an excellent job teaching the horses not to fear the dragon. Bravo! And Dracor?" The Commander searched for the soldier who would report back to King Narsor.

"I am here, Commander," said a young ruddy giant on a gray horse. "Do you wish to add something to the report?"

"Yes, a short note. The King needs to know about Draydel." Dracor handed Potemkin pen, ink, and parchment. While writing the message, he looked up at Dracor and said, "You take this directly to King Narsor. Do not allow anyone to read it and that includes you. Give me the sealing wax."

"Yes, sir!" Dracor said, heating a bit of red wax in the small torch he carried for this purpose. Then he dripped the wax onto the parchment.

Potemkin pressed it with the ring on his right hand, sealing the note with the Crest of Falcongard. Under it he signed his name: Potemkin Falcongard, Commander in the Royal Army of Narsor. "Now take this and one soldier and go as quickly and as safely as possible. We'll follow as soon as Loni is safe in Oberlon."

"Yes sir, Commander!" Dracor saluted and placed the parchment in his breast pocket. "Bearsord, come with me." The two young soldiers rode west.

Potemkin mounted his horse, "Yorkin, ride with us. Loni, would you prefer to ride Starry or fly with GreeHee?"

"Sir, I'll go with GreeHee."

"Okay." The Commander rode up to the dragon, his horse snorting loudly. Pulling the flag of Oberlon from his saddlebag, he handed it to Loni. "I want you to hold this high when we enter Oberlon so there will be no question about GreeHee's allegiance."

"Yeah, no more rocks to the head!" GreeHee smiled.

"You are really on top of it, Commander," Yorkin smiled, saluting.

Potemkin chuckled, "That's why I'm the Commander."

Chapter 15

PAYCHENTE'S STRUGGLE

The drizzle had turned to rain and the temperature continued to drop as they traveled north. Paychente was cold. What was he doing on this journey to the City of Teeth. Neither warrior nor messenger, he should be back at camp keeping abreast of Admiral Jarteen's condition.

"Colonel Bravort, please tell me again why I am part of this squad to relay information to Tana," said the doctor as they rested a moment under a high rocky ledge in the barren foothills of the Wolfking Mountains.

"Doctor Paychente," frowned the Colonel shaking his head, "for the fourth time, General Maltor ordered you to come with us and stand before Tana because you were the last Carron to see the dragon."

"I simply cannot figure out what good I am to my species, to the war, or to Tana by making this miserable journey," Paychente said shivering under the armor they had suited him in and his thin white coat that he had insisted on wearing despite the weather or war. "I'm a doctor and should be caring for the sick not trekking across Tamoor to visit the Queen! What in the Carron Stars am I doing here? And what in Tamoor does it matter who last saw the dragon? What does Tana care about an adolescent dragon?" He wanted to fly away from this insanity. He was tempted to leave his command in the Carron army. He felt General Maltor had sent him on this mission as a scapegoat for losing the dragon. He felt deep in his feathers that if he made it all the way to the City of Teeth, this mission might be his last.

"I wish I could tell you more but General Maltor has instructed me to give you only a few details about this mission," Bravort said as Petrie peered out from under his hooded coat.

"And you Petrie, have you also been instructed to remain silent?" questioned the doctor.

"Sir, I follow Colonel Bravort's orders. I am sorry, sir," Petrie replied.

"Colonel, what exactly does Tana want with an adolescent dragon?" Paychente pleaded. "Please answer this one question and I will be satisfied."

"Doctor Paychente, you are exasperating me!" Bravort replied in a controlled voice. "I have no idea whatsoever what Tana could want with the dragon. All I know is that when we mentioned the dragon and his age, Tana became extremely volatile. I do not want to be the bird that tells her we don't have him. And what's more I do not want to be late for our appointment with her. So let's forego the rest of your questions and hit the sky!" Bravort demanded, standing up.

"Colonel please, wait, I cannot fly another leet. I'm not an athletic warrior, like you and Petrie. I'm tired and shivering, and can't continue at this pace. Please, I need to rest. Can't we stay here until the rain let's up?" begged Paychente, not wishing to move until he decided on a plan of action. He must get away from Bravort and Petrie. If Bravort were afraid of what Tana would do to him when he showed up without the dragon, what would Tana do to the bird that let the dragon disappear? Paychente needed a solution; one that would keep him alive, even if it meant he would become a fugitive from his species. How heavy my heart feels, he thought. Ahh, that is the answer.

"Doctor we cannot stay here any longer, we must leave <u>now</u>!" Bravort shouted, his wings raised.

"Oh!" cried the doctor. "My heart! Oh the pain, it's my heart!" Paychente clutched his chest.

Bravort grabbed Paychente, who doubled over with pain. Petrie got behind the doctor and pulled up his head.

"What's the problem, Doctor?" demanded the Colonel.

"Colonel Bravort," rasped Paychente, "I have had a heart condition for several soars and the pain…oh the pain." Paychente writhed as he had seen so many Carrons do in his sick bay over the soars. "I think I'm having a heart attack! Oh, Holy Mother of Carrons, I need my medicine, please give me my medicine."

"Where is it, Doctor? Where is the medicine?" urged Bravort.

"Uh, my left breast pocket, a bottle - small pink pills. I need four of them. Please hurry!" The doctor rolled his eyes and collapsed while the frantic Colonel Bravort searched the coat for the medicine.

"Here it is!" shouted Bravort while Petrie continued to hold the doctor.

"Great!" shouted Petrie, "but how can you give it to him? He's unconscious?"

"Pray to the Ancients, Petrie! I'm going to force them down his throat." Bravort pulled open Paychente's beak and tossed the pills to the back.

"Doctor Paychente! Can you hear me? Please answer me. Doctor, can you hear me? You have the pills, you should get better now!" shouted Bravort.

Petrie held the doctor while Bravort pulled Paychente's bedroll out of his pack and fastened it around him. They warmed him up and made him comfortable. Paychente did not move.

"Is he dead, sir?" asked Petrie.

"No, Sergeant." Bravort kept checking Paychente for a heartbeat.

"Sir, I'm frightened. What if the doctor dies? What will we do?" said Petrie his left wingtip in his beak.

"I will have to decide that when, and if it happens," Bravort stood up and paced in front of Paychente, "What is worse Sergeant Petrie is, if he lives but stays unconscious. There is the real problem." Bravort continued pacing. "Petrie, one of us may have to go to Tana while the other stays behind with the Doctor. Do you think you could handle looking after him, if it comes to this?" asked Bravort.

"I don't know sir? I have never done anything like this before. I've never been around anyone who is ill," whined Petrie. "But sir, I' will certainly do my best. I'm sure I can guard the Doctor and keep him comfortable until you return."

"You know, Petrie, I never imagined I would have thoughts like I'm having now. This has become the hardest assignment of my military career. Returning to the City of Teeth without the dragon will make Tana angry and bringing the doctor was a kind of peace offering. But now for me to arrive alone without dragon or doctor, I may be headed for certain death. I feel like leaving my military post now. I have very bad feelings about this."

Paychente shifted and sighed. Yes, I was right, they needed a scapegoat. He wanted to speak but the pills had taken effect and he could not move his beak or his limbs.

The sky cracked with thunder.

"You miserable birds! I'm waiting for you and the dragon, but you have let the dragon escape!" Tana's words flew like knives through a bolt of lightening that landed less than five leets from Bravort's feet.

Jumping back and immediately saluting the darkness, Bravort addressed the Queen's voice, "Your Highest Tana, I brought Doctor Paychente to explain the dragon's disappearance." The Colonel pointed to Paychente, who didn't move despite the thunder and lightening that roared around him.

"Your Doctor Paychente will tell me nothing. I know he is not devoted to my cause. He is useless to me. Time is essential to this war and since your army has lost the dragon, it will be your responsibility to find him!" shouted Tana, as she appeared before Bravort in her hideous form, orange troll eyes glaring. "Colonel Bravort, I will now give you your orders and be assured that I know your every thought. If you decide to leave this mission undone, I will destroy you. Do you hear me?"

"Yes, your Most High Tana. Yes!" Bravort bowed, pale beak shaking.

"Listen to me closely Bravort and you too Petrie!" Tana said, turning to Petrie who sat crouching behind the Doctor."

"Yy, yer, yes your Highest." Said Petrie, stuttering and trembling as he tried to stand and bow at the same time.

"Go back to General Maltor and tell him <u>this</u>," Tana threw a fireball from her right hand at Colonel Bravort." Bravort jumped back. When it landed on the wet stone, it became a piece of parchment. Bravort stared at it, not daring to move. Petrie also stood frozen in place.

"Pick it up, you stupid bird! Pick it up now!" Tana bellowed.

Bravort jumped and picked up the paper.

"You will tell Maltor that I expect you to lead a squad of Carrons to capture the dragon. He will be on his way to Oberlon with a troop of sixteen giants and two fairies. You must ambush them before they get to the castle of the fairy kingdom. Kill all the giants and bring the dragon and fairies back to me. These are your orders and the parchment will confirm them. You will also tell Maltor that if he does not want to spend a linglorn alive in a dead body like his friend Jarteen, he will make sure to give you his best men."

"Yes, Tana." Bravort bowed and placed the parchment inside his armor.

"I will await your victory, Bravort. When you arrive with the dragon and fairies, you will receive a medal and be promoted to Admiral."

"Your Highness Tana, what should we do with Doctor Paychente?" the Colonel asked, "He has had a heart attack and--"

"Do nothing with or for him!" shrieked Tana with another flash of lightning. "Leave him to die. He is nearly dead now and I will send a wind so cold that he will not be able to survive. He is not worth your worst efforts <u>or</u> mine. Now go! There is no time to spare. I am watching you, lest you forget it, here is a little reminder for both of you!" Tana hissed, fireballs shot from each of her hands and struck Bravort and Petrie, knocking them down. When the two stood back up, Tana was gone.

"Petrie!" Bravort pointed, "The seal of Tana is on your forehead."

"Sir," hesitated Petrie, "it is likewise on yours."

Both birds felt their foreheads. Bravort shook himself and then looked at Doctor Paychente, who had not moved a feather since before the appearance of Tana. "Is the Doctor still breathing, Petrie?" asked the Colonel.

Leaning over Paychente, the Sergeant listened for his breath and tried to feel his heartbeat. "Barely, Colonel. Just barely," said Petrie in a sad voice.

"All right then, let's move the Doctor closer to the wall and make sure he is comfortable before we leave him. I will not have the death of this Carron on my heart."

Petrie grabbed Paychente's shoulders and cradled his head while Bravort held the Doctor's covered talons. Carefully the two Carrons moved Paychente close to the wall of the ledge. They tucked his pack under his head and made sure his bed sack was wrapped tightly around him. Colonel Bravort stood erect over the Doctor and raised his left wing in the Carron salute. Petrie followed.

"May the Ancient Carron Warriors protect you, Doctor, or lead you home to your place of honor or disgrace." Bravort saluted Paychente as though he were already dead.

Paychente heard them fly away. He would not be able to move for over two senes unless he could get two pills from his pocket into his mouth.

The wind howled as though it were a giant wolfing coming for him. The temperature dropped, and even though he was securely wrapped in his bedroll, he felt it bite at him through his face feathers. He struggled to touch his right pocket but when a gust of wind blew in, he knew chancing freezing would be worse, so he decided to snuggle as deeply into his bedroll as possible. He pushed his beak under the down blanket and prayed for protection as he fell asleep.

A few senes later, the Doctor woke to a loud, wheezy, purring. He felt warm. Where was he? What had happened to him? A big hot, furry blanket leaned against his right side. The space was dark. He tried to focus. Wait, my eyes need to adjust. Then he realized he was in a cave and that furry blanket was alive. Afraid to move, Paychente listened. It sounded like a cat, a huge cat, probably a sawtooth. Holy Mother of Carrons, what to do now? Four times his size, sawtooths could pick him apart in a tithe. Could he sneak out without being noticed?

Once again he lay perfectly still and listened. The breathing, purring, and wheezing were not synchronized. Two cats! Paychente's beak shook. He started to panic. No way could he outrun or outfight two sawtooths. No pill was going to save him now. He had to get away before they woke.

Whoosh, a burst of frozen air brushed his beak. The cat next to him curled tighter pulling him closer. What luck, my beak faces the entrance. Though the cat held his talons, the bedroll had a little wiggle room. So very carefully, very gently, very, very slowly he began to free himself from the bedroll and crept along the wall to the opening of the cave. The purring continued. Thank the ancients, Paychente thought as he listened and slid his feathery body along the wall. Bones and other crunchy things covered the cave floor, so he gingerly placed each talon hold. Gently, gently. Any sound would cost him his life." One talon at a time he moved toward the cold opening. Each time he touched something that made noise, he tried to smother the sound with his feathery body.

Finally he reached the cave entrance, he could still hear the sawtooths purring. He looked outside at the tiny cracked ledge. As he slipped into the freezing wind, a rock dislodged and crashed down the mountainside. Paychente froze. The cats growled.

"Bounder, get up, the bird is trying to escape!"

The doctor saw their big yellow eyes and sharp incisors flash. They vaulted toward him.

Paychente threw himself into the air and flew straight up as fast as could. Looking back, he saw two enormous sawtooths clambering up to the top of the mountain, growling and cursing each other for their loss.

Chapter 16

CROSSING THE CRYSTAL RIVER

The was sun setting when the small troop of giants reached the Crystal River. "We have had quite a beedite and I'm not certain we will find a good crossing place before dark, so we'll camp here for the night and ford the river at dawn," The Commander stated.

"Yes, that sounds like a good idea," said Tyron, dismounting.

"Potemkin!" Loni shouted from where she sat on GreeHee hovering over the troop. "I have a bad feeling about that. Please could we cross now? GreeHee and I can find a good spot easily from the air."

"It would be safer in the morning, Loni. Why do you want to chance crossing when there is so little light left and everyone is tired?"

Loni and GreeHee landed. "Sir, Beauty keeps flashing little bits of red when you say stay and that means there is some danger on this side of the river. It's not here yet, but there is no doubt some menace is headed our way." Loni stretched out her right hand for Potemkin to see. A short sequence of red flashed from the ring.

"Well," said Potemkin, "considering how Beauty has saved my life before I suppose it is best we cross now." The Commander scratched his strong chin, sighed, and rubbed his tired eyes. The troop had been talking about dinner for the last two senes.

"Okay, Starina," Potemkin called out as he reined his horse to Starry's side, "do you know this river?"

"I have only crossed it once, Commander, and that was much further south. It is very wide but easy enough to swim across for a horse. Here it seems to run a little faster. Perhaps the dragon can see if it is narrower anywhere nearby?"

Potemkin said, "GreeHee, I will go with you and we'll take a look. Loni, come with us, perhaps Beauty will have something to say." In the air, Potemkin said, "GreeHee, let's go further north and see if the river narrows."

The river glistened like a silver ribbon in the twilight. "There!" exclaimed Potemkin. "Where it turns to the east, it seems to narrow by about three hundred leets. Loni, what does Beauty think of that?"

"She's not flashing any warning signals, so it should be fine."

"All right then, we're agreed. Let's go get the troop," Potemkin said.

The dreary troop rode to the bend in the river and Potemkin sent Yorkin and Starina to test the water. Even though it was deep, Starina crossed. "Not a problem, Commander!" hollered Yorkin from the Oberlon side.

GreeHee and Loni hovered above the river watching each giant cross. By the time Potemkin entered the river, the three moons of Tamoor had broken through the clouds and looked like silvery sprites dancing on its surface.

Everyone cheered as the Commander climbed onto the Oberlon side.

Loni landed and rolled in the deep grass. "What are you doing?" asked GreeHee. "Is that a fairy ritual or something?"

"No, you silly dragon. I was rubbing against the Tamooran mother to thank her for Oberlon. I'm so glad to be home. I will see my Mother and Father tomorrow. I'm so happy!"

Yorkin joined them. "Loni why don't you open that book while we're waiting for dinner?"

"Yes Loni! I would like to hear more before I leave for home in the morning," added GreeHee.

Loni jumped up, her big eyes flashed, "GreeHee, you can't leave for home now. You're part of this team. You're part of the mix that will save Tamoor! Besides, don't you think you would be happier with your friends rather than alone in your father's cave?" Loni made direct eye contact.

GreeHee threw down his hands, "Well, I don't know. I don't see how I can be of service to Tamoor. I'm only a young dragon. I would need to know why I'm part of this mission. Does anyone know what the mission is really?" GreeHee shrugged, and looked at the fairies.

"Perhaps the book will explain it to us." Yorkin asked.

Loni held up the indigo book. "Let's go sit next to the fire and see if the book can tell us what to do next."

The trio sat down and Potemkin joined them with several heaping plates of food. Sarolla arrived with an enormous bucket of delicious smelling meat. "Here, GreeHee," Sarolla said, placing it in front of the dragon. "Pazard made this just for you. He said he hopes you like it. And to tell you that everyone in the troop is grateful that you are here with us," Sarolla added with a bow.

GreeHee's, mouth fell open, big emerald eyes widened. "Thank you," he said, inhaling the delectable aroma, "My mouth is watering!"

Potemkin lifted his flagon and pointed to the rest of the troop who had gathered round the blazing fire, holding their cups in the air. "Three cheers for GreeHee, a noble dragon and true friend to giants and fairies!"

"Hip, hip, hooray! Hip, hip, hooray! Hip, hip, hooray!"

"Oh, thank you, you are all too kind. Thank you!" GreeHee bowed, he swallowed hard and blinked back a tear.

"GreeHee," Pazard stepped forward saying, "we wanted you to know we really appreciated the way you took care of our Commander this beedite."

GreeHee, smiled, wiped back a tear and bowed, "I really appreciate how you have all welcomed me into your lives. Thank you so much. I feel like I have a family!"

"Well, we hope that we can always honor that bond," said the Commander. Then he signaled for the troop to disperse so GreeHee could eat and they could talk in private.

"See, GreeHee," said Loni, "you belong with us. We are your family now."

GreeHee took a deep breath and smiled, "I must admit I have never felt so loved. He started eating, licking his fingers, he added, "and this food is delicious!"

As the foursome completed their meal, Yorkin said, "Loni, please open the book, and tell us what secrets Draydel left for us?"

Loni put down her cup and wiped the last bits of moisture from her lips. She moved closer to the fire, so the firelight poured onto the indigo book. Potemkin and Yorkin sat on either side of her peering at the tiny tome.

As Loni opened the book, a small white envelope fell from its pages.

"Whoa!" shouted Yorkin, catching it before it fell into the fire. "Here, Loni." He handed the envelope to his sister.

Taking the envelope and staring at the pages of the book, Loni said in a daze, "I don't <u>see</u> anything in the book. What about you? Yorkin? Potemkin? Do you see anything?"

GreeHee leaned over the threesome. Eyes wide, he scratched his head saying, "I don't see anything either? That is too strange?"

"Loni, open the envelope. Perhaps it has a clue," Potemkin said.

"Hmm, yes perhaps the envelope." Loni closed the book and held the envelope up for everyone to see. Blue ink began writing a word across the outside. "G..r..e..e..H..e..e GreeHee!" shouted Loni.

"Holy Mother of Tamoor, out of thin air your name has appeared on this envelope!" whispered Potemkin, swallowing hard.

"Here, GreeHee," said Loni, handing the envelope to him, "do you want to read it?"

"Oh no, Loni, why don't you read it? I don't want to touch it," said the dragon, his voice filled with trepidation.

Loni opened the envelope while Yorkin, Potemkin, and GreeHee stood, their gazes glued to her movements.

> "Dear Young Dragon GreeHee,
> It is time for your heart to lead.
> Your destiny calls and you
> must go beyond Oberlon to
> complete what you were born to do.
> Look at your right hand and remember!"

GreeHee placed his big green and purple right hand in the firelight for all to see.

"There it is!" pointed Loni. "I <u>knew</u> I had seen that star before. It's the Star of Knowing! GreeHee, you remember don't you?"

The star lit up and filled the firelight with its blue presence. It began to dance and sing:

> "Trust your heart that is your test,
> For when you do, you are your best!"

"Oh my silver moons, I do remember!" said the dragon, standing.

But before he could continue the shimmer of blue light changed to an emerald green and before the foursome stood a brilliant white unicorn.

It spoke in a rhythmic voice: "In another beedite we shall meet and, then as one we shall defeat, the Queen of three with the power of five, it is our time to come alive." The unicorn faded into five points, each a different color -- white, yellow, blue, green and red. Then the five points merged into a star that sparkled golden, danced, and dissipated into the fire.

Yorkin was the first to speak. "GreeHee, you asked and Draydel answered. It seems we are all in this together."

"I am amazed! I don't know what to think but my heart says I'm home with the three of you." He looked at each of his companions. "You are my friends and I guess if you're going into danger, I should be there with you. But where are we going?"

Loni looked at GreeHee, her big soft eyes twinkling, "Wherever Draydel leads us, GreeHee. Only he knows."

"Loni, look!" Yorkin shouted, pointing to the book in her lap.

"Oh!" said Loni.

Draydel appeared in the book seated at the desk in his secret room. He wore a long white silk robe embroidered with gold symbols, his pale face wrinkled, aquamarine eyes twinkled, thin lips smiled and honey blonde hair and beard shimmered in the firelight. In his right hand he held the Star and said: "You will journey far and I will journey with you. You're not alone. Keep your hearts pure. Fear is the only enemy that can lead you astray. Know your heart, follow it, and know there are many who watch you. Be careful and leave camp early." Draydel disappeared.

"Well, I understand exactly what he meant by fear," Potemkin whispered, staring into the fire.

"Commander, is there something you haven't told us?" asked Yorkin.

Potemkin slapped his knees, drew a deep breath and in a serious tone said, "Yes, my friends. I had a visit from Tana last night."

"Tana!" All three said in unison.

"Yes, Tana. She appeared to me as the most beautiful giantess and tempted me. She appealed to my pride and pushed me, using my fear of crossing the Azura Kah. I almost fell for her."

"What happened?" asked GreeHee, leaning over Loni to get a closer look at the Commander.

Potemkin answered, "Queen Beetrea rescued me. We are truly protected. I felt ashamed and then Tana appeared in her real form. She is most hideous! I am so glad Queen Beetrea protected me from that monster. I would like to wield my sword and cut her throat!" Potemkin stood, slashing his sword through the air. The threesome backed away.

Loni smiled, "Well, that's really good news, don't you think?"

"Uh, yeah," said Yorkin, staring at Potemkin.

"Yeah. But why is it good news?" asked GreeHee tapping his cheek.

"Now, we all know that Tana is hideous looking and so she can't use that illusion on us anymore. And we also know that Queen Beetrea is guarding us! That is excellent news. That's the way I see it. Doesn't everyone agree?"

"Well, when you put it that way. I see what you mean," said GreeHee.

"Me too," said Yorkin, grinning. "There is one more thing you missed."

"What?"

"If Tana appeared to Potemkin, there can be no doubt that he is part of the five." Then to the Commander, Yorkin continued, "Potemkin, did you learn anything more about the Azura Kah?"

Potemkin beamed, his dark eyes danced in the firelight, "Ah, yes, that is the best part! Queen Beetrea implied I would cross the Azura Kah without dying!"

Chapter 17

A PLAN TO ATTACK

Colonel Bravort was deep in thought as the sun set and his platoon flew over the ruins of an old castle. He could not believe how quickly everything had happened. Now under his command, flew the finest Carrons in Tana's army. General Maltor had been like a child when he showed up with Petrie. The mark of Tana on their foreheads sent chills down the spines of everyone, even the fierce Maltor. No Carron in the army could look at Bravort or Petrie without staring at their foreheads. Then whatever Bravort told them, they did without question. Now with a platoon of seventy-five Carrons, Colonel Bravort would attack the tiny troop of giants. Bravort's only concern was the dragon. He still didn't understand what Greedy the dragon was doing with the giants or if his strategy to take the dragon would work.

"Colonel," the voice of Captain Bartet interrupted, "there are visible tracks around the castle below. Sir, do you want to see them?"

"Yes," the Colonel stated. Turning to Sergeant Petrie, Bravort added, "Petrie, instruct the platoon to land inside the courtyard below and ready the evening meal. The Crystal River is only a few senes from here and with the developing darkness our timing should be perfect. Tana indeed is guiding us," he said, his handsome golden face, brightening with a smile.

"Yes sir!" replied Petrie. He turned and shouted to the platoon, "Birds, land in the courtyard below and get ready for dinner and further assignment!"

"Oh, and Petrie," the Colonel added, "follow us down the hill. I want to speak with you when Bartet and I have finished."

Captain Bartet held the title of best tracker in the Carron Army. He wasted no time examining the ground around the castle while Colonel Bravort and Sergeant Petrie watched.

"What do you make of these tracks Bartet?" asked Bravort.

"Sir they're not very old. They were made about five or six senes ago."

"How many horses?" asked the Colonel.

"It seems there are twenty-one. But from the looks of it, two went back to the west while the rest headed east." Bartet pointed as he spoke.

"And can you tell if there is a dragon with them?"

"Sir, it seems there is definitely some enormous beast with them, one that flies." Bartet pointed to several footprints that spanned seven leets and had claw spreads of five leets. "Considering the marks left by Greedy in our base camp, these appear to be identical in size and weight." The Captain added, kneeling over one of the prints.

"Any other comments, Captain?" asked the Colonel.

"Well sir, they left here at a walk and I will have to follow the tracks for a while to see if they began to trot or gallop. If they continued to walk all the way, it is possible that they have not reached the river yet."

"Ah, very interesting," replied Bravort, twirling a leather fob in his right finger feathers. This new habit began after he left Tana on that freezing rainy night. He had placed his right wing fingers inside his pack to check on the safety of the parchment and found this leather fob - blood red with the symbol of Tana stamped on it. It gave him comfort whenever he touched it, so he often held it tightly and twirled it between his finger feathers.

"Well then, Bartet, eat quickly and scout the area ahead. Take another bird with you. I want to know if these giants are strolling to the river or racing. Then I will know exactly what strategy to take. So get moving, bird. I expect a report in two senes."

"Yes sir, Colonel!" shouted Bartet as he flew toward the courtyard .

"Petrie, come with me."

Sergeant Petrie followed the Colonel to the courtyard. They filled a plate each and then flew to a large boulder on the edge of the hill where they could watch the sun set and converse in private. The evening glowed orange and violet across the scrubby grasslands below, in the distance to the northeast, the glistening white of the Crystal River was fading fast.

"Sergeant, I have not mentioned to anyone what I have been experiencing since the night we left Paychente. But since you also wear the mark, I wondered if you have had any strange occurrences with Tana?"

"Sir, I have not discussed my experiences with anyone either. I'm not even sure if they are real or if I'm starting to lose my mind, but I..." Petrie stared at the ground.

"Petrie speak, I'm certain you're not losing your mind. Tana is speaking in your head, isn't she?" stated the Colonel, gripping Petri's right wing.

Petrie snapped an icy look at Bravort. "Yes! You know? You too?"

"Yes Petrie, we are in this together. Tana said she would be watching us. She is doing much more than that. I can feel her presence and if I start to say something she does not want me to say, I feel a pain in my head." Then holding up his red leather fob, the Colonel continued, "This is the only thing that gives me comfort. I feel as though caressed or soothed by Tana when I hold this leather. We're under her spell for life or death."

"Yes sir, I know. My will is no match for the magic of Tana. I feel angry and yet sometimes, I feel grateful. I know Tana will use her power to keep us safe. We are vehicles for her magic." Petrie sighed.

Bravort nodded. "Tana's magic will easily destroy these giants. As for the dragon, I am still uncertain exactly how it will be done. But I feel even as I say it, Tana has yet another card she will pull from the deck. This time when we return to the City of Teeth, we shall have a hero's welcome and receive the promotions we deserve."

"Sir, if you don't mind me asking, how are we going to take the dragon? I know we have seventy-five mighty Carron warriors, but do you really think we can take a dragon?"

Bravort jumped up, streams of hatred flew from his eyes. Petrie trembled and shrank back. "Petrie!" Tana's voice shot through Bravort. "I'll take the dragon! You and Bravort follow my orders. My magic will take the dragon!"

Bravort slumped forward, shook himself, and sat down. He held his throbbing head between his feathered hands and added in his own placid voice, "Sorry about that, Petrie, it's not a good idea to doubt Tana. She has control over this situation and us. She needs us to kill the giants and get close enough for her to take the dragon."

"Well," Petrie said, still shaking, "I will do whatever you ask, Colonel."

"Okay then," Bravort said standing and rubbing his forehead. "Let's get the platoon back into the sky and head for the river. Tana gives me the impression that we must catch them before they touch the soil of Oberlon. It will make our task easier."

The two birds flew back to the courtyard.

Colonel Bravort noted the location of the Crystal River in his mind. "Don't worry, I will make sure you get to the River," came the eerie but soothing voice of Tana. Bravort relaxed a little. He was tired but somehow he kept going. He had not slept since the night in the Wolfking Mountains. He could not recall how long it had been. "You don't need sleep, Bravort. I have others sleeping for you and their energy is fed to you by my magic."

So that is why I can keep going, thought Bravort.

"Yes," came the reassuring voice in his head.

"Colonel?" Bartet asked. "It seems the giants alternated their pace. I'm only guessing, but I believe based on the tracks I followed that they have already reached the river."

"Well, I'm not surprised. If it was my army I would have pushed my soldiers," Bravort said as the two flew side by side. "The real question is will they cross the river in darkness? Or wait until dawn?"

"I cannot say, Sir. If it were my decision, I would wait till dawn to assure safe crossing. But, then, we Carrons don't have these problems"

"Yes Bartet, we are lucky to be Carrons! Take your scout and let me know as soon as you discover where the giants have camped for the night. I will fly the platoon close to the ground to make sure we are not seen. I am depending on you to show us where their encampment is and the most secluded route to get there. Go!"

"Yes sir!" Bartet shot out ahead of the platoon with Milkoor, a rookie scout nervously flapping to keep up with him.

A sene and a half later, Bartet returned, "Colonel, the giants were getting ready for bed when we saw them. They have made camp in a meadow right across the river. The location is a few yonts upstream. The curve in the river can give us plenty of cover, if you choose to cross in the South."

"Splendid news! Was the dragon with them?" asked the Colonel.

"Yes sir, he is definitely there. From what we could tell he seemed to be very comfortable with the giants."

"Did they have any scouts or lookouts in the southern area?"

"No, sir! From the looks of it, the dragon was at the south end. We couldn't see the horses, so I suspect they must be at the north. There were three lookouts along the river as best as we could make out. But no one actually south of the camp."

"Okay, then we will set up camp south of the bend in the river, inside the forest. It will give us time to rest for a few senes before we attack." Then Bravort turned and looked directly into Bartet's eyes. The Colonel made a hissing sound, an evil ugliness streamed from his eyes. Bartet's eyes widened in terror, he backed away. Then with a sardonic smile, Bravort added in Tana's guttural voice, "We will kill them before dawn while they are in their deepest sleep."

Chapter 18

SURPRISE WARNING

GreeHee nestled into a deep patch of Oberlon grass. He lay at the south end of camp facing north so he could see the river on his left and the forest on his right. Straight ahead of him, Loni and Yorkin slept and the rest of the troop rested beyond them. At the far north of camp, the horses stood silently sleeping. Everything felt peaceful.

GreeHee took a deep breath, sighed, and released the tensions of the beedite. Something moved in the trees to his right. GreeHee raised his head and studied the area. Giant guards watched the river. No one had noticed. GreeHee decided to rest his head but keep his right eye open and watch. For a few tithes nothing moved. Then a rustling sounded in the trees closer to him. He looked to his right. He saw a flash of white and thought he heard his name.

"Greedy!"

GreeHee quietly walked to the trees.

"Greedy!" once more came the voice.

Not wanting to wake the rest of the troop, GreeHee looked into the forest and whispered, "Who is there?"

"It is I, Doctor Paychente."

"Doctor Paychente? Come out here so I can see you."

Paychente stepped out of the trees. "Greedy, I have come to warn you."

"Oh, Doctor Paychente, I'm so glad to see you! I remember everything about my life now and I have so much to tell you," GreeHee began and then he stepped back, "Warn me? You came all this way to Oberlon to warn me? What is happening?"

"Greedy, you're in terrible danger! Tana has sent an army of Carrons to capture you. I am really surprised that I found you before they got here."

"Oh, we will have to tell Commander Potemkin about this," said the dragon, brow furrowed and hands on his head. "Oh, by the way Doctor, I found out my name is GreeHee, not Greedy."

"How very interesting. That is a most unusual name. But before we start chatting, we need to inform your Commander. I will wait here. No reason to get myself killed by these giants."

"Don't be silly Doctor, these are my friends."

Before the dragon could turn around, Loni appeared. "GreeHee I heard you...uh who is this?"

"Loni, this is Doctor Paychente, he has important news for us."

"You took care of GreeHee, didn't you? He told me all about you --"

"Loni, please," the Doctor said, "we can chat later. This is a matter of great urgency. Could you get your Commander so GreeHee and I don't have to walk through camp and wake everyone."

"Yes, I'll go and get Yorkin too." Loni flew back to camp.

"Doctor, you look terrible. Have you eaten? What has happened to you? Did General Maltor harm you after I left?"

"No GreeHee, not exactly. It's a long story but I am too tired to tell it right now." The doctor sighed.

"Come with me," said the dragon, leading Paychente to the fire ring at the edge of camp where the foursome had spent the evening. "Here we can sit down and I will get a fire going in a tithe so you can warm up."

"Wait, no! Please, GreeHee!" Paychente said jumping up, his wingtips outstretched. "Better not to draw any more attention to ourselves than we already have. The Carron army could be watching us right now."

"Oh, I see what you mean. Well, here comes Commander Potemkin."

Potemkin approached sword drawn, held close to his side, his eyebrows knitted together, ready to strike. Loni and Yorkin followed behind him.

Paychente stood up and spread his wings, saying, "Commander, I'm not armed. I'm a friend of GreeHee's. I am Doctor Paychente formerly of The Carron Army, not because I believe in what Tana is doing, but because I am a Carron. Tana and my birds have betrayed me. Through some miracle I have survived and felt it necessary to find GreeHee and warn him about Tana's plans. You're in grave danger."

Potemkin glared down at the Carron. "How do we know we can trust you to tell the truth? What is in it for you?"

"Friendship sir, simply friendship." Paychente touched GreeHee's shoulder with his right wingtip.

"That is very touching, Paychente but rather hard for me to swallow." To GreeHee he added with disdain. "Do you believe this Carron, GreeHee?"

"Yes, Potemkin, I do. He saved my life and risked his own to help me leave the Carron camp. He's a good bird and a real friend."

"Please Potemkin, can we listen to what he has to say?" Loni asked. "I feel he's telling the truth."

"And you, Yorkin, what do you think?" asked the Commander.

The Prince stared at the Carron, his green nightshirt blowing and blonde hair swirling in the night breeze, "Sir I agree. Why would a Carron take a chance coming into this camp? We could kill him in an instant. I think we should listen to him and see what he has to say. If he is leading us into a trap, we will know it."

"All right, Doctor Paychente, give us the news you carry." Potemkin crossed his massive arms, still holding his sword.

"Sir, Tana has sent an army of Carrons to kill all of you and capture GreeHee and the fairies. I heard her say this while I lay nearly dead in the Wolfking Mountains. She knows where you are and that is how I knew where where to look for you. I have seen the platoon led by Colonel Bravort. He has close to a hundred warriors and I'm certain they're not far. They may be as close as a sene away. You need to have a plan of action. Tana's magic is great. I don't know how you can defeat them."

Potemkin's fingers tapped his upper lip, his dark brown eyes stared at the Doctor, "Where are they coming from, Paychente?"

"Sir, they're following your trail from the west."

"Commander, look!" shrieked Loni, pointing her enchantment band to the west. It flashed almost continuous sequences of red.

"Does this mean Beauty agrees with this Carron?" Potemkin asked.

"Beauty is definitely saying there is danger coming from the West and it is getting very close! Once the sequence is constant the danger is present."

"Ancient Mother of Tamoor, we must act quickly. There's no time to lose. GreeHee since you, Loni, and Yorkin are so important to Tana, you must fly them to their father's castle. No Carron in Tamoor will be able to catch you before you're safely under the protection of King Allielt. I will stay here and fight the Carrons. I will hold them back so you will be safe."

"No Potemkin, I cannot do that," said the green and purple dragon, crossing his arms and tapping his right foot. "I can kill more Carrons in a tithe then all your men put together. I should stay and protect you."

"I'm not leaving your side either, I must fight with you," said Yorkin.

Potemkin stood, hands on hips, "I really appreciate your loyalty but I promised King Narsor you would get home safely and we're much too small a troop to expect to win. So this is an order, Yorkin, take Loni and Starina and ride as fast as you can to your father's castle. Starry will carry you quickly and safely. Not as fast as GreeHee but," continued the Commander looking directly at the dragon, "GreeHee is right, if we plan our strategy properly, together we could win this battle. Are you with me?"

"Yes, Potemkin, I'm with you."

"I, too, pledge my honor to follow your command and care for any wounded," said the Carron doctor, in his torn white coat, raising his right wing tip attempting the flat-palmed Giant salute.

Potemkin smiled. "Okay Doctor, I pray the Ancients have sent you for good and not evil. I welcome any help I can get now." Then turning to Yorkin he said, "Yorkin, go! Right now, take Loni and Starry and go!"

Yorkin jumped, saluting, "Yes sir!" He pulled Loni's hand and said, "Loni, let's get our things and go home. Potemkin, we'll send re-enforcements from Oberlon."

Loni cried as Yorkin pulled her away, "GreeHee, Potemkin, Ancients keep you!"

Clouds covered Tamoor's three moons as Yorkin and Loni galloped into the pitch-black Oberlon Forest.

Chapter 19

THE GOLDEN WATERS

Starry galloped for nearly forty-five elides and then began to slow. "Is anything wrong Starry?" asked Yorkin.

"No Yorkin, I just need to trot for a while. Even the horses of giants can gallop for only so long. How are you and Loni doing?"

"I have to admit I'd love to get down and walk around for a few minutes. One begins to cramp after a while sitting in such a tense position," Yorkin said. "What about you, Loni?"

"I'd love to stop for a minute and stretch. Could we do that, Yorkin? Do you think we're safe?"

"I don't see why not. There haven't been any signs of danger and we're over twenty yonts from camp by now. Wouldn't you agree, Starry?"

Starry slowed into a walk. Tiny columns of moonlight filtered through the leaves of the dense trees illuminating bits of ground on the dark path. "I figure we have traveled about twenty-three yonts. That is usually the distance I can go at a gallop before feeling the need to slow down. I think we're safe enough if you would like to stop for a moment. But I really would prefer to wait until there's enough light so we can see clearly.."

"I suppose that would be much wiser but let's compromise by stopping as soon as we come to a small opening in the trees. Is that okay with you, Loni?" asked Yorkin.

"Yes, that will be fine. I can't wait to get home. I want to hug Mother and Father and fall into the soft downy silk of my little bed. Oh, how I long for my little bed!"

Yorkin said, "I have so many questions to ask Eulool. I wonder if he has been watching us? I hope he helps Potemkin and GreeHee. By the way, Loni, what does Beauty have to say?"

Loni loosened the grip of her right hand and looked at her enchantment band. It gleamed white. Then she pointed it to her right. It still gleamed white. To her left the same and then she pointed Beauty back toward the giant's camp. Beauty flashed red in short sporadic bursts. "Beauty indicates that the danger is behind us. From the way the red flashed, she's saying no one follows."

"Well, that's good to hear. Look, Starry," Yorkin said, pointing to an opening ahead lit with a shaft of moonlight. "There's a perfect spot to stop!"

"As you wish, Prince Yorkin. The grass looks terrific to me. Do you expect we'll come to any water soon? I'd like to get a drink."

"Yes, in another sene or so we'll come to the 'Moat of Golden Waters' and we can all drink and get giddy with the excitement of being home at last."

"Oh, the Moat of Golden Waters! It always marks home for me. It should be close to dawn when we reach it. I love dawn when everything is golden and feels brand new!" said Loni as Yorkin helped her dismount. Starry began to eat and Yorkin stretched. Loni rolled in the thick grass. As soon as she lay flat on her back, she fell asleep.

Loni felt the warm embrace of her father. His soft voice soothed her senses. "My darling child, you must keep traveling! Mount the horse and don't stop until you cross the golden waters. We'll be waiting for you there." Loni felt as though her father had tugged her to her feet. Opening her eyes she saw Yorkin.

"Come on little sister, I could hear father too. We must go now. Even if we only trot, we must go now."

The two fairies flew onto Starina Ronella and continued their journey.

"Father said he would be waiting for us at the golden waters. I'm so excited, Yorkin. Listen! The trees are speaking Oberlean!"

"Wellenright Princessest ed Princt! Gloreeonum! Gloreeonum! Loveth thee-en!" came the melodic voice of the trees.

"Yes! I hear them!" Yorkin exclaimed. Then he sang out, "Gloreonum duo! Loveth thee-en altooth! Ne-en loveth thee-en altooth!"

"It is such a beautiful language, Yorkin," said Starry. "Gloreeonum! Gloreeonum!" she sang prancing and trotting in a high step through the Oberlon Forest of talking trees.

As the sky grew brighter, the trees sang louder. Cardinals, robins, and blue jays joined in, and Yorkin and Loni began to sing an old Oberlean song.

"Loveth thee-en altooth Oberlean, altooth Oberlean,
I-el loveth thee-en. Mathet Tamooran,
I-el loveth thee-en, I-el loveth thee-en
Mathet Tamooran, Mathet Tamooran!
In-ith altooth cavornan, alith creaatin eth
Gloreeonum, Ah Gloreeonum

Altooth Gloreeonum, Altooth Gloreeonum!
I-el loveth thee-en Oh, Oberlean,
Altooth Oberlean Forest-thee-en ed all creaatin,
Altooth Gloreeonum! Ah Gloreeonum!
Altooth Gloreeonum! Gloreeonum!
Glo-oo-ree-onum!"

A sharp crack of thunder reverberated. A tremor of terrifying proportions shook the ground beneath the trio, forcing Starry to stand perfectly still with all four hoofs outstretched to keep her footing.

As the mare gathered her courage to walk again, a howling wind swept through the forest like an icy knife.

"There's something behind us!" Loni screamed.

Starry pivoted. Lightening lit the sky. Trembling, Starina stood still. Loni and Yorkin did not move. Some unknown force held them entranced.

They had been traveling uphill for yonts. Now facing the direction of the sound, they could see across the expansive forest all the way to the Crystal River. They watched, lightening struck again in the middle of the river. Blackness formed, like a cloud of evil, in the sky above it. The trio, immobilized like statues, watched with horror as lightening struck again and Tana appeared. She was enormous!

"Holy Mother of Tamoor, we must run now!" Yorkin said in a trancelike whisper as he stared at the monstrous figure.

Then lightening shot from Tana's eyes. The trio stood transfixed with terror as Tana's voice pierced the confidence of their souls. "You will never be safe from me, Princess Loni and Prince Yorkin! Sing as you will, Oberlon cannot protect you from my power. Ha Ha Ha!" The hideous laugh echoed through the forest.

Yorkin yelled, "Stop looking!" He covered Loni's eyes and turned Starry back around, headed toward home. "Starry, gallop! Go as fast as you can! Potemkin and GreeHee are probably dead. We must get home. We must not let Tana steal our power to live! Hurry!"

Starry flew into a gallop at Yorkin's command. Tana's laugh continued. It iced the forest and chilled their hearts.

"Are you all right, little sister?" asked Yorkin.

"I, I never realized how powerful she could be," Loni said, trembling.

"Loni, remember Draydel. Think of him instead. He defeated Tana and he believes we will do the same."

"Prince Yorkin may I speak?" questioned Starry in a voice focused through a rhythmic gallop.

"Please Starina," said Yorkin.

"Queen Beetrea taught me long ago a simple law of power. It states that what you focus on you shall have. So if you focus on Tana's words, you forfeit your power to her. Instead, if we focus on Draydel, as you have suggested Yorkin, we will absorb Draydel's power into our own."

"Oh Starry, you and Yorkin are great gifts to me. You're both so incredible!" Loni said with renewed optimism.

"Thank you, Loni. I'm glad to be of service to you and Yorkin."

"Look! Look!" Yorkin pointed. "There's the Moat of Golden Waters!"

"Home! Oh, we're almost home. Can you see Father, Yorkin?"

"No, not yet, but I'm sure he'll be there to greet us."

"I will get you there in no time," said Starry.

Loni heaved a deep sigh of relief and held Yorkin tighter. "Home at last. Home at last!" she whispered, closing her eyes.

As they approached the Moat, Yorkin shouted, "Look at the ground! Loni are you awake?"

"Uhh, what did you say?" Loni asked, opening her eyes. "I wanted to nap until I could fly into Father's arms."

"Loni, look at the ground!" Yorkin repeated.

"What has happened? It looks trampled and bare? What has happened, Yorkin?" Loni asked shaking her head, eyes wide with panic.

"I don't know? But it looks like the work of trolls. I'm not sure we will find father at the moat."

"It smells like trolls!" added Starina, her nose twitching.

"Let's not panic, Loni," Yorkin said, squeezing Loni's hand, "remember Eulool protects the castle, so perhaps we'll find Father waiting. I shouldn't have said we wouldn't find him. I jumped to a conclusion. Are you okay?"

"Yes, kind of, I'm going to call on Queen Beetrea to protect us like she told me to. I'm also going to imagine Father waiting. We'll be there soon enough."

The Moat cut a channel seventy-seven leets wide in a complete circle three yonts from the walls of Castle Farion's courtyard. "Oh look, see it's going to be fine!" Yorkin shouted, shaking Loni so she would open her eyes.

"Oh, the heart of Oberlon! It's still green and beautiful. The trolls must not have made it across!" said Loni. "Do you see Father?"

"Not yet, but I bet he'll be here soon."

Starry said, "I'm going to dive in and get a drink! Are you both ready?"

"Yes!" they grinned.

The sun had not crested the horizon yet but the sky had turned a beautiful orange and the waters looked like melted amber. Starina Ronella jumped into the moat and the fairies slid off her back into the golden wet embrace of ancient fairy energies.

"All pain and sadness washed away, in Oberlon I love to stay!" Yorkin sang out.

Loni laughed and flitted her wings as she glided on top of the water.

As they reached the Castle side of the Moat, a voice called, "Children! My wonderful children!" King Allielt trotted down the tiny road on Alabastar, a magnificent white ponykin stallion with a thick long mane and tail. The king's purple velvet cloak edged in gold brocade, covered a white tunic embroidered with golden symbols of fairy lore: the staff of Wizen, intricate leaf patterns, rainbows, ancient Oberlean words, and colorful graphics of the gentle creatures of Oberlon. On his chest, he wore the Crest of Fairies -- a large pendant of gold embellished with amethysts and emeralds, the precious stones of his kingdom.

Other voices greeted them. "Loni! Yorkin!" came the voices of brothers and sisters, and the multitude of fairies that came to see the tired pair.

The King reached the river's edge and dismounted. "Loni your mother and I have dreamed of this moment." Allielt extended his arms.

"Father! We have so much to tell you!" cried Loni as she flew into his embrace, splashing water from her wings.

"Oh, my child." He brushed the liquid from his whiskers. "I am so happy to see you! We have been worried about both of you. These are very dangerous times."

"Where is Mother?" asked Loni.

"Your mother is making sure everything is perfect for your welcome home!" Then he added in a whisper, "Honestly I think she didn't want everyone to see her cry when she greets you." The king winked at Loni and they hugged.

"Father!" Yorkin exclaimed, as he bowed to the King.

"Yorkin, I am very proud of you!" King Allielt extending his jeweled right hand to his son and pulled Yorkin to his chest in a hug. "I have heard good things about your journey. I'm proud of your bravery and the way you have protected your sister." Then looking directly at Starry who stood close behind Yorkin, the King added, "Now aren't you the famous Starina Ronella?"

"Yes, sir, I am Starina." said Starry, bowing to the King.

King Allielt hugged the mare's neck, "Thank you for taking such good care of my children."

"It has been a great honor, your Highest," replied the mare.

With a big smile, the King said, "Let's go home and celebrate." Loni rode with her father while Yorkin rode Starry. The rest of the fairies followed on ponykins or in carts as well as on dragonflies and birds. Like a parade, they entered the delightful castle courtyard of the tiny fairy kingdom.

Loni sighed. The Courtyard of Castle Farion was an enchanted paradise. The road leading to the castle was made of smooth river rock in soft pastel hues. Fragrant flowers of every kind blossomed along the sides, bursting in rainbows of color, interspersed with majestic Cedars, Eucala and Magnolia trees. Beyond the road paths led to small round stone houses trimmed in lavender, pale green and pink. A bubbling creek ran through the courtyard and colorful stone bridges topped with lavender wood crossed it in many places. Gentle waterfalls tumbled over crystal rocks in the distance. Colorful buntings, warblers and tanagers sang and the flowers' hypnotic fragrance evoked enchanted dreams and intoxicating romance.

As Alabastar crested the final hill of the courtyard road, Castle Farion came clearly into sight. "Oh Father, how I love our home!" said Loni with a deep sigh. "It's the most beautiful castle in all Tamoor!"

"I agree, Loni," said the King.

The Castle Farion was built of lavender, violet, pink, and green crystal stones. The windows were designed in pairs; each pair having a unique shape from round or octagonal to diamond or hexagon. All shimmered in rose or lavender glazes, trimmed at the bottom with golden flowerboxes dripping with fuchsia bougainvilleas and yellow honeysuckle. The subtle hints of color shimmered from the pearlescent wood that wrapped each window. The castle sparkled with rainbows in the early morning light, its walls gleamed as the pearl and gold embellishments threw back the orange glow of dawn.

"Oh Father, you remembered!" exclaimed Loni noticing the castle doors.

"Yes, Loni. You always loved how the doors opened when a royal procession came to visit, so I made sure they would be ready to open for you."

Loni loved to see the magnificent doors of the castle swing open in celebration of a formal affair. They formed an arch ten leets high and were one of the most treasured possessions of Castle Farion. Made from Golden Pearlwood Trees that grew in only one place in the Mystic Mountains. The wood was whitish gold with a pearlescent sheen that changed color all beedite long, the same way that unicorns changed color.

Over six linglorns ago, long before the Primengeer, Wizen, then Master Unicorn commissioned this door as a present for King Farion's new castle. It was blessed and bestowed with magical powers for protection and success. The magic instilled feelings of love and security in any who came in contact with it. Loni had always felt the magic of these doors. Even before she could walk, she loved to look at the doors and touch them.

As they approached the castle, the doors slowly opened. In the entry stood Queen Marleenah wearing a resplendent gown. The bodice had a scooped neckline with sleeves puffed at the top and fitted in the forearm. Six tiny lavender star-shaped buttons lined each sleeve from cuff to elbow. The top was made of emerald green velvet, gathered tightly and embroidered with tiny lavender stars. The velvet dipped below her waist into a sweeping full skirt of iridescent lavender silk embroidered with mint green fairies and shooting stars. The Queen's long red hair flowed gracefully over her shoulders. She smiled, green eyes sparkling from tears.

"Mother!" Loni exclaimed, flying to her. "How I missed you!"

Queen Marleenah could not hold back her tears as she hugged Loni. "I missed you too." Then looking up and extending the slim long fingers of her right hand, she added, "And you too, Yorkin." The King joined them in a family embrace and together they went into the castle followed by the multitude of fairies in the courtyard.

Inside, the castle was aglow with crystal candelabras in the shapes of unicorns and doves. Beautiful silk banners in bright teal, purple, rose, and emerald, flowed down the walls filling the spaces between high arched white-shuttered openings under the eaves. The room glittered with crystal. Cherry-wood tables stretched the length of the hall, adorned with beaded runners of peach and turquoise velvet laden with porcelain and gold bowls of whipped cream, yogurt, berries, nuts, granolas and delectable berry and chocolate sauces; fairy-wing crystal pitchers held colorful juices, and tall, brilliant crystal vases reached high, with spiking flower arrangements of white orchids and star lilies. The combination of crystal, golden flatware, and sharp white porcelain threw rainbows dancing across the room and onto fairy faces creating a magical atmosphere.

"Father," said Yorkin as they began to eat. "Where is Eulool?"

Loni listened, watching her father's expressions as she ate.

"He is in his tower, I believe. He said he had some very important work to accomplish before…" The King hesitated. He moved closer to Yorkin and continued in a whisper, "…Before you and Loni leave on the rest of your journey. But let's not talk of this now." Winking at Loni and Yorkin, he added, "Your mother does not know all the details and I want her to enjoy you while she can."

"Okay, Father. I have so many questions, do you think Eulool will see me when we're finish eating?"

"Considering how tired you and your sister look, I think it might be better if you both get some rest and ask Eulool all your questions this evening."

"Yes, I know you are right. It will be wonderful to sleep in my own bed for a change," he added, "Father, before Loni and I got to the Moat of Golden

Waters, we crossed an area of ground that had been destroyed by trolls. Are you aware that they were that close to the castle?"

"Son, please keep your voice down," King Allielt whispered. "We are aware and there is much that needs to be addressed in this matter. But now is not the time." The King touched his son's shoulder and grasped Loni's tiny hand. He smiled, "I am proud of both of you. You are destined to save Tamoor."

Chapter 20

AMBUSH

As soon as Loni and Yorkin had left, Potemkin instructed GreeHee and Paychente to create a decoy of a sleeping dragon. "Use whatever you must but try to make it look as large as you are and we'll pray the clouds will create enough shadow to make the illusion work."

Paychente scanned the area and pointed, "Look at that boulder over there, GreeHee. I think we could move that and add some dirt around it to make it look like you." The odd pair set to work.

Meanwhile Potemkin began the job of waking the troop. "Sarolla," he said, gently touching her exposed arm. "Sarolla, get up quietly and help me wake everyone."

"Huh, is it morning already, Commander?" She asked, stretching and rubbing her eyes.

"No, but I want you to get up quietly and arrange your bed sack so it appears you're still in it. Then without making a sound, crawl to the next giant and have them do the same. When everyone is finished we will meet in the forest for further orders. Do you understand?"

"Uh, I think so. Are we in danger?" Asked the giantess, eyes widened.

"Yes. But, we must not panic. Do as I say and we will be fine."

Sarolla crawled out of her bed and stuffed it with everything she had.

Within twenty elides, the giants, along with GreeHee and Paychente had completed their tasks.

"Well done, Giants of Narsor!" Potemkin whispered. "Look at our camp. It looks peaceful and we still have several senes before dawn."

GreeHee, Pazard, and Paychente sat high above the group, about twenty leets away in the top of an enormous Marmosa tree waiting to hear Potemkin's plan. "My fellow warriors, we have information from a Carron friend of --"

Before he could continue the troop began to whisper, "A Carron? A

Carron, where is this Carron?"

"Quiet, please and listen!" demanded the Commander.

"Hush!" added Tyron. "The Commander knows what he is doing."

"Giants listen to me," stated Potemkin firmly. "I have verified the information and it is reliable. It may well save all our lives."

Once again whispers ran through the small troop.

"Listen to me and pay attention. I do not want to hear another whisper of any kind. We have to be ready for an attack and though it may appear we are ready, there is still more we must do."

"Attack by whom?" asked a young slim dark-haired giant standing ten leets from the Commander.

"By a Carron army guided by Tana!" Potemkin replied.

"Oh no!" resounded the troop, heads shaking. Potemkin raised his hand and they fell silent.

"They are very close and there are many of them. We are a tiny fraction compared to their army, so we must be shrewder and braver. We have a chance with the element of surprise. That is why we have laid this trap."

Giants smiled at one another, sighs rolled through the group.

"Each of you will take a position here in the trees facing the camp. The south end will be under GreeHee the dragon's watch. Tana wants the dragon and the fairies."

"What? Why does she want the dragon and the fairies?" asked a tall mustached giant to the rotund blonde giant next to him.

"Where is Princess Loni?" asked Sarolla, her eyes wild, searching the troop.

"Both Loni and Yorkin are safely on their way to their father's castle. We needn't worry about them. We are here to fight and destroy as many of these Carrons as we can. With GreeHee's help we have a good chance of winning this battle. I want every single Carron destroyed. There must be no one left to send a message to Tana. Are you with me?"

"Yes!" came the voices of the giants in unison.

Potemkin raised his hands to silence them. "Okay, Tyron will show you your stations. No one is to shoot an arrow or spring a rock or make themselves known in any way before I give the order."

Then pointing to GreeHee, Paychente, and Pazard in the tree behind the little troop, Potemkin continued. "GreeHee and his friend, Doctor Paychente, as well as Pazard will keep watch for the enemy. From their post with the spyglass they can see up and down the river. No Carron will cross it unnoticed. In the meantime, each of you must know your stations. Then everyone is to help the Rocker brigade collect ammunition. Once this is complete, you will return to your stations and wait until I give the command to fight. Does everyone understand my orders?"

Everyone nodded.

"Are there any questions?" Potemkin asked.

"Sir, will GreeHee also engage the enemy?" asked the big blonde giant.

"Yes, he is our secret weapon and will be following my plan of attack. Now, follow Tyron to your stations and help the Rocker Brigade collect ammunition."

As the troop followed Tyron along the edge of the forest to the north end of camp, Potemkin signaled to GreeHee.

GreeHee landed in a clearing a few leets from Potemkin. "What now, Commander?" asked the dragon.

"Fly me to the lookout. Then I will explain my plan for you, Pazard, and Paychente."

In a tithe, they landed in the treetop.

"Pazard, how are you getting along with Doctor Paychente?"

Pazard grinned and slapped Paychente on the back, "Sir for a Carron, he has a decent sense of humor. I told him my Carron-troll joke and he laughed!"

Paychente smiled and Potemkin chuckled, saying, "You must be a unique Carron if you can bear to listen to Pazard's riddles, and even a little warped if you laugh at them!"

"Sir, it is quite a delightful change of pace to be around someone with a sense of humor even if it is poking fun at my species."

"Well then, I welcome you, Paychente. You are definitely unlike any Carron I have ever met. I suppose that is why you feel such a kinship for GreeHee?"

"Yes sir, Commander. GreeHee is much like me. We have traveled a similar path."

"Hmm, I see." Potemkin held his chin in his hand. Then he placed his hand on the hilt of his sword and began, "Let's get to the business at hand. Pazard do you see any activity through the glass?"

Pazard, who had been watching during the conversation, handed Potemkin the spyglass and said, "Here sir, look for yourself. I am having a hard time seeing anything at all. Only when the clouds move aside for a moment can I see the river clearly."

Potemkin took the glass and looked. "I see what you mean," he sighed. The glass was dark except now and again a sparkle of water shot back, exposing the silent moonlit river. "But we can see intermittently and I don't think a whole platoon could pass without notice."

"I hope you're right, sir," Pazard said. Then he quickly reiterated, "I mean

I am sure you are right, sir!"

"Ha. I am quite certain the Queen of Giants will not let us miss these creatures of ill will," Potemkin added.

Paychente held out his right feather fingers for the glass, "Sir, I probably have the best eyes for this. Do let me keep watch."

"Paychente, I pray you are for real. It does us little good to be prepared if you mislead us in this matter."

GreeHee scanned the river. "Potemkin, I can vouch for Paychente and besides, I don't need a spyglass to see. My eyes are designed for night vision. I can see clearly down to the river and have not seen anything pass yet."

"Okay then, I'm counting on the three of you to inform me as soon as you see the Carrons. Now let's get down to what we will do once they come into view. GreeHee, I'm going to fly with you so you will have eyes in back of your head and a sword to protect your back. Our job will be to attack them as soon as they try to capture what they think is you. I suspect this will be the first part of their attack. It would be mine. I expect them to use a net, so it should be very easy to spot them as they approach. Once the net is dropped we will fire upon them. My biggest question is will they charge across the river or pour in from the south through the forest. Hm?" Potemkin tapped his upper lip and then turned to Paychente. "Tell me, Carron Doctor, what do you think this Carron Commander will do? You must have some experience with their practices."

"Sir, I don't know for sure what Bravort will do. He seems very conservative to me, so I guess he would choose the greatest cover he could get and that would be to cross the river where they will not be seen and then make a surprise attack from the closest proximity."

"Then that means they will cross downstream and come up along the edge of the forest."

Doctor Paychente added, "that is my estimate. While traveling with Colonel Bravort, he always exhibited pragmatism. He is very calculating, a good soldier. He would never jump into a situation and endanger his birds."

"He sounds like an accomplished Colonel. Whether he comes across the river or along the edge of the forest, we will be ready for him. Once they are in view, I want you and Pazard to continue to monitor their approach while GreeHee and I ready the troop for them. Understood?"

"Yes, sir!" doctor and chef said in unison.

GreeHee pointed south "Sir! I see movement downstream!"

Potemkin grabbed the spyglass from Paychente. "Holy Mother of Tamoor! How many are there?"

"Sir, I have counted sixty thus far," GreeHee said.

"You have incredible eyesight, GreeHee! I can barely make out the movement. There is no way I could actually count the number of Carrons! And you, Paychente," Potemkin said putting down the glass, "you <u>are</u> a friend to GreeHee! You are vindicated in my mind and I value your friendship." Potemkin slapped Paychente on the shoulder.

"Whoa, thank you, Commander," said Paychente, as he fell sideways.

"Oh, so sorry," said Potemkin, his eyebrows raised, grabbing the bird. "I forgot you're not a warrior but a doctor." He helped Paychente back onto his talons. "Doctor, you not only pegged this Carron Colonel correctly but it is definitely a large platoon. We will be ready for them. GreeHee take me down so I can speak with Tyron."

"Paychente, you and Pazard watch as best as you can. We will return." GreeHee flew Potemkin to the camp below.

Potemkin said to Tyron, "They're coming from the south and they'll be traveling along the edge of these woods. There are more than sixty of them, so we need to reinforce the south end and not worry about the north."

"How long before they get to us, Commander?" asked the huge red-haired giant.

"Not sure, Tyron." Potemkin said, shaking his head. "The Carron marching distance may be a sene or less - certainly not more. Has the troop created a strong supply of rock munitions for the brigade?"

"Yes sir, Commander, come and see for yourself." Tyron began walking and pointed to the thick piles of rocks along the tree edge.

Every giant was schooled in the art of rock firing, but in this troop of Giants, Narsor had insisted that Potemkin take five experts. The Rocker Brigade, Potemkin called them. Potemkin himself had numerous medals for his rock-firing expertise, but his great love had always been wielding the sword. Potemkin Falcongard came from a long line of Sword Masters. At the tender age of three, Potemkin began his instruction with the sword. He had won twelve championships in the last seventeen soars.

"Everything is in order, Tyron. Our warriors have done an excellent job."

"And me too, Commander! I helped too," Sarolla said.

"Ah, Sarolla! I have a job for you. The Carrons are on their way and I want you to stay with the horses back in the forest. Build a camouflage around yourself with bushes and wait until we come to get you or when everything is still. If we are defeated, you must ride to King Allielt's castle and tell him what has happened here. Do you understand?"

"But, but," whimpered Sarolla, "I don't know where the King's castle is?"

"Now, Sarolla," Potemkin said, lifting her round chin with his huge right hand. "Just ride east. Eventually you will either see it or come to a road with a sign or someone will find you. Yorkin will be riding back this way with an army of fairies. I am certain you will be safe. Okay?"

"Yes sir, I will do my best."

"Good, you will make your king proud." Potemkin continued walking with Tyron down the firing line. All right, Tyron, I will go back to the lookout with GreeHee. Tell all our warriors that they are not to take any action until they see GreeHee spew fire on the Carrons. That will be their signal to fire."

"Yes sir, Commander. Ancients bless us all!" Tyron bowed and clasped his enormous hands over Potemkin's right hand.

Potemkin pulled him into an embrace, saying, "You are my dear friend, may we enjoy many seasons yet to come." Then Potemkin jumped onto GreeHee's back and they flew to the treetop lookout.

"All is ready below. Now it will be up to me and GreeHee to set fire to these evil beasts of Tana!"

The wiry Pazard nodded, pressing his thumbs into the air.

The Commander added, "Present company aside, we're only here to destroy those who wish to destroy the freedom-abiding creatures of Tamoor."

"Understood," said Paychente.

"Have you noticed anything new?" asked Potemkin.

Paychente said, "Sir, I thought I saw movement in the trees about three yonts from here. It may be scouts. They don't seem to have enough action to be the whole platoon."

GreeHee pointed. "There, in the trees you can see a flash of gold from time to time. It looks like two Carron scouts to me."

Taking the spyglass, Potemkin focused on the area. "Yes. Okay, we will have to take them out before they get close to our camp. It must be done without a lot of noise. I will do it with Tyron's help and yours, GreeHee. Let's get Tyron."

They flew silently above the lowest trees toward the Carron Scouts.

"Stop here, GreeHee," Potemkin whispered. "This tree is an easy climber. Tyron and myself will get down and be ready for them. Wait for us here."

"Don't you want my help, Commander?" questioned the dragon.

"You are helping, GreeHee, just wait. This will be easy work for the two of us."

"Okay," GreeHee sighed.

In a few tithes, Potemkin and Tyron were on the ground hidden behind two trees on either side of a narrow path -- the most likely spot the Carrons would take. "Crunch, shwish, crunch, crunch," came the sounds as the Carron scouts approached. Potemkin smiled at Tyron. They stood with swords drawn and raised.

"Milkoor, quiet, we don't know how acute the dragon's hearing may be."

"Yes, Captain Bartet, I will move more slowly and quietly."

"We're almost there and no signs of life yet. Tana has made this easy."

Whoosh! Down came Tyron's sword clear across Bartet's neck.

"Ahhgh!" screeched Milkoor. Whoosh! Potemkin's sword slashed across the Carron's back, as he froze for an instant behind his fallen Captain.

"Okay," whispered Potemkin to Tyron, "let's hide them deeper in the forest. Then cover the tracks and get back to GreeHee."

"I heard a screech? Do you think the other Carrons heard it?" asked GreeHee when Potemkin jumped onto his back.

"Hard to say, my friend, but it does not matter. They will figure out what happened soon enough. Let us hope it doesn't ruin our little surprise."

GreeHee dropped Tyron off at the front and flew back to the lookout.

"Did you hear a screech while we were gone?" Potemkin asked Pazard and Paychente as they landed.

Pazard, scratching his thinning hair, said, "Yes we heard something. Not sure what it was. It was distant. Could have been an owl or some other creature or…" he paused and stared at Potemkin's wide grin, "murder of a Carron scout?"

Potemkin said, "The scouts are gone. That's two out of sixty or seventy. Let's pray the rest will be as easy. It won't be long."

"Potemkin, I can feel them!" said GreeHee, eyes wide with surprise, "I can't see them yet but I can feel a tremor in the tree. It's coming from the ground. The tree is telling me they are coming. Do you feel it?"

"Why yes, I feel it too!" said Paychente. "I have never felt anything like this? Are these trees filled with magic or…?"

"I don't know but considering we're in Oberlon, anything is possible. Fairies are known for their enchantment of nature," said the Commander. Pazard had his eyes closed and was swaying back and forth with a smile on his face. "Pazard, what are you doing?"

Pazard continued content, swaying, eyes closed.

Potemkin shook the skinny giant, "Pazard! What are you doing?"

"Uh? Oh? Commander Potemkin? Oh yes, I was …" The chef looked about, his eyes widened, mouth dropped open, "I don't know? I started to dream and it was lovely. I don't know what happened."

"They're coming, Potemkin, I can see them now!" GreeHee yelled.

Pazard jumped up, grabbed for the spyglass but Potemkin took it from his hand. "Yes, I see them," Potemkin said handing the glass back to Pazard.

"Okay, this is it. GreeHee and I will go below. You two stay here and watch. If we win, we will all leave together. If not, you two should remain hidden until the Carron army has gone. Then, Doctor, it will be your job to check the wounded and see how many you can save. Pazard, you will find Sarolla. She will be waiting with the horses inland. Once she is safely with you, you will come back and help Paychente. Do you understand my orders?"

"Yes, Sir!" both doctor and chef said in unison.

Then Potemkin hugged them simultaneously, saying, "May the Ancients protect us all!"

GreeHee and Potemkin flew slowly across the thick treetops toward the Carron soldiers. They waited atop the bonta tree where GreeHee had first seen Paychente. Each moment GreeHee could feel the Carron Platoon move closer. Each moment still closer they came. GreeHee and Potemkin waited. GreeHee began to tremble.

"Are you afraid GreeHee?" Potemkin whispered.

"No Potemkin, what you feel is the dragon fire building in anticipation of a fight!"

"Oh! I will tell you when, okay?"

"Yes, Commander, at your word I will strike."

The Carrons formed a line of battle below them. Even in the darkness their armor threw back little glimmers of light from the moons of Tamoor. They had not noticed any of the nine giants standing nearby, whose armor of dark green tortorsall made them undetectable amidst the trees.

Carron whispers rose in the night air. GreeHee and Potemkin listened.

"What a stroke of genius, Tana has created for us. The dragon continues to sleep while we are only forty leets from him," a Carron soldier whispered. GreeHee smiled.

"Net carriers line up," another whispered.

Fifteen Carron soldiers lined up, holding an enormous mail net.

"On my command of 'Fly,' you will fly forward swiftly and cover the dragon," said a commanding Carron. He motioned for the other soldiers to move up along the forest edge and get ready to kill the rest of the giant troop. They moved along the perimeter of the forest not more than ten leets in front of Potemkin's force.

"These giants are so sure of themselves that they have left no one on watch?" said one of the carron soldiers.

"No, can't you see they have three lookouts and they are all asleep. It must be the magic of Tana," said another soldier.

"You fools, it is probably the work of our scouts," Said yet a third.

"Quiet, all of you fools!" said the leader. "In another tithe I will give my command and you will foul everything up with your jabbering!"

Silence. The Carron leader watched his birds signal they were ready. Then in a strong voice, he said, "Fly!"

In one great swoop the Carron soldiers threw the net over what appeared to be the dragon. At the same time the rest of the Carron platoon charged, swords drawn, onto the piles of bedrolls.

Potemkin said, "Now, GreeHee!" The dragon swooped across forty leets, spewing fire. Five Carrons were caught in the flames. The Carrons charged at the dragon. GreeHee fired upon them and took another two out of the air.

"Drive them closer to the rest of the camp, GreeHee!" said Potemkin.

Three Carrons managed to get behind the dragon as he pushed the others forward with his fire.

Potemkin stood on GreeHee's back brandishing his sword at them. Leaning to his right, the Commander cut off one's head. A Carron had landed on top of GreeHee and sliced into Potemkin's left arm. Potemkin swung his sword across the Carron's neck and killed him.

On the ground the Carrons had discovered the folly of their attack too late. Giants threw rocks at them, killing several at a time. Arrows flew from both sides. The Carrons were exposed while the darkness made the giants nearly invisible.

GreeHee continued to fire upon the Carrons on the ground. The camp was ablaze. Carrons everywhere screamed a-flame. Many lay dead, burning on the ground.

A bolt of lightening struck over the river. The sky itself opened. Without thought or perhaps by magic, the Carrons and giants turned and for an instant the fighting stopped. Even GreeHee spun to look.

In the middle of the river Colonel Bravort stood on the water, transformed into the hideous form of Tana. She shrieked. Lightening struck from her hands but could not reach the camp of the giants. It could not cross the river. Her hideous blue troll face and sunken orange eyes turned red, she hissed and shrieked, "Retreat before you all die, you miserable Carrons! You have made me a fool and you will pay for your folly!" Then she glared at Potemkin and GreeHee. "You think you have won, don't you? But this is only the first battle and I will have both of you before this war is over! Heed my warning and surrender now and you will save your fairy friends from harm. Surrender!" She shrieked, lightening bolts striking from her eyes. "You will soon know pain as never before. All that you know will be destroyed. And dragon, if you think you can play with fire, wait until you feel mine!" Then with a ground shuddering crack of thunder and a huge strike of lightening, she disappeared. In the river floated the body of the Carron Colonel charred beyond recognition except for the brand on his forehead.

The Carrons flew across the river, screaming in all directions.

GreeHee and Potemkin landed. The troop ran to greet them.

"Save what you can and..." Potemkin fell unconsciousness.

Tyron caught the Commander. "GreeHee, get the doctor."

The dragon flew to get Doctor Paychente.

"Let me see him," said Paychente flying to where Tyron stood holding Potemkin. "If any others are wounded, please bring them to me." Said the doctor as he tore the clothing away from the Commander's left shoulder.

"Will he be okay, doctor?" asked GreeHee.

"His heart is still strong. He has lost a lot of blood and will need to rest for a while. I don't think riding a horse will do him much good either," said the Doctor looking up at Tyron.

"Doctor what if we strapped the Commander to my back?" asked GreeHee. "Would that help?"

"It would be better than putting him on a horse," said Paychente, "Could you do that Tyron?"

"I'm sure if GreeHee is willing we could work something out."

Two other giants were brought to the doctor with minor wounds.

Before ninety elides had passed, Tyron and Pazard had created a harness for GreeHee to safely transport the Commander. They made it out of the net the Carrons had brought to capture GreeHee.

"There GreeHee, it should be snug but comfortable. How do you feel?" asked Pazard.

"I think it's fine," said the dragon.

"Does anyone have the flag of Oberlon with them?" asked Tyron, taking command of the troop.

Pazard said, "I think Princess Loni had it in her pack."

"Okay then, GreeHee, you will have to carry the flag of Narsor instead and you will lead the way to King Allielt's castle." Tyron wound the flag into the harness so it stuck upward above the lowest spike on GreeHee's neck. "Doctor Paychente, can you ride a horse?"

"I can fly, Tyron, I don't have to ride a horse," answered the doctor.

"Sir, we will be riding hard and I think you may find it difficult to keep up and since we have an extra horse--"

"It's okay, Tyron, the Doctor can fly on my back when he gets tired and that way he can look after the Commander too," said GreeHee.

The exhausted little troop of giants entered the forest of Oberlon.

Chapter 21

CASTLE FARION

GreeHee could not consider how tired he felt, getting Potemkin to safety was his first concern. Doctor Paychente stayed close, riding and flying, checking on Potemkin and bolstering GreeHee's spirits. GreeHee looked at the Doctor in his torn bloodstained coat, his face drawn, eyes sunken, still smiling and humming. He is a true friend. Too tired to speak, GreeHee flew as fast as he could toward the rising sun and Castle Farion.

"Any sign of the Castle yet, GreeHee?" Asked Paychente. "We should be coming upon it soon."

"Look, Doctor," the dragon pointed, "There is water, could be a moat."

"Yes! I bet that's the Moat of Golden Waters. We're almost to Farion!"

"I can't think of better news," sighed the dragon.

After a few elides, GreeHee shouted, "Yes, there is the Castle!"

Paychente grinned, pointing, "There's the King and I think, his wizard!"

In a tithe, they landed, the King smiled, waving to them. Before he could speak, Eulool stepped forward, white beard blowing and blue robes dancing in the breeze, "Welcome, GreeHee, and you must be Doctor Paychente! This is King Allielt, father of Loni and Yorkin."

GreeHee and Paychente bowed.

"We're honored Your Highest," Paychente beamed, in his ragged coat.

GreeHee said. "Yes, I am honored too, King Allielt and…" GreeHee paused, eyebrows raised, looking at Eulool.

"I am Eulool, fairy wizard and counsel to the King."

"Please, Your Highest," said the Carron, face strained, pointing to Potemkin, "We have a sick giant here. Could we move him to a bed?"

"Yes, yes of course. This must Potemkin, he is too large for us to move. Are there any other giants with you?"

"Yes sire, there are more. They should be here shortly."

"I see one now," said Eulool.

Dismounting and bowing at the same time, Tyron stood before the King and Euloоl. "Your Highest, I am Tyron Darborday, second in command under Commander Potemkin in King Narsor's Army."

"You are welcome here Tyron." Allielt pointed to Potemkin who lay motionless tied to GreeHee's back, "Please take care of your Commander. We have been expecting you and have some comfortable rooms prepared."

"Yes sire," Tyron said, rushing to remove the mail net that held Potemkin in place. While Euloоl and Allielt watched, Paychente and Tyron managed to move the Commander gently to the ground. Potemkin started to mutter as Tyron leaned the Commander against his right shoulder. Before Tyron could begin walking Potemkin into the Castle --

"Wait let me help you!" shouted Pazard as he jumped from his trotting horse forcing the King and Euloоl to move aside quickly. "Oh pardon me. Pardon me!" said Pazard, trying to bow to the King and place his left shoulder under Potemkin's right arm at the same time.

The King pointed to the entrance of the castle. "Take him inside. The fairy there will guide you to a room. As for the rest of your troop we will find them some accommodations in the visiting quarters at the west wing of the castle. We actually have some beds large enough for giants there."

"Allielt, I will go with them and see what can be done for the Commander." said Euloоl, bowing out.

"Yes. I will join you as soon as the rest of the troop and GreeHee is situated," replied the King waving his hand.

Allielt turned to the dragon. "I have heard wonderful things about you, young GreeHee. Thank you for taking care of my children." GreeHee began to speak but the King raised his right hand. "We will talk later. I know you are tired and should rest. Go with them," he said, pointing to the giants who were now riding around the west end of the castle. "I will send fairies out with food for all of you." GreeHee bowed. The King turned and went into the castle.

Four senes later, Potemkin regained consciousness. Loni and Yorkin were waiting by his bedside playing, "Double Die," which consisted of five dice. The object of the game was to be the first to score two hundred twenty-two points. Points accumulated each time the sum of one's dice throw resulted in double-digit numbers. However, any time someone rolled three or more matching dice, such as three threes or four fours, etc., they would shout, "Double die!" Then the sum of the identical dice would be subtracted from the other player's total, this made the game difficult and required intense concentration, so they didn't hear Potemkin's first words, and the Commander sat up staring at the two fairies for a few tithes before either noticed him.

Loni jumped up, shouting, "I won! I won!"

"Finally!" said Potemkin. The fairies jumped.

"How long have you been awake? We've been sitting here for thirty elides hoping you were okay." Yorkin said.

"Uh huh. I can see that," said the Commander laughing.

"Are you all right?" Loni asked.

"I feel pretty good except for my shoulder and stomach. Is there any chance I could get something to eat?"

Yorkin charged to the door, "I'll get you some food right away."

"And I will get my father. He told us he wanted to see you as soon as you woke up," said Loni.

"Wonderful to see you awake Commander!" said GreeHee peering in the window. "I have been out here waiting to hear your voice again."

"Why you wonderful dragon!" Potemkin grinned at the big smiling face, peering in the little rose-colored fairy window opposite the foot of his bed.

In a few elides, the King, Eulool, Loni, and Yorkin, had crowded into Potemkin's room, while GreeHee continued to watch from the window. The King spoke first.

"Now that we are all here. It is of the utmost urgency that you four understand the importance of what Eulool is about to reveal. Because..." he hesitated, staring for a second at each face, "you are the hope of Tamoor."

"I have been watching your travels since Loni first met GreeHee," Eulool began, his voice serious, his hands animated, fingers combing through his beard, "The ancient riddle was written with you in mind. There is only one piece missing to this puzzle, but he is on his way to the castle and should be here in the morning."

"Who is it, Eulool? Asked Loni, "Who is the missing piece?"

"It is Boldor, the greatest grandson of Wizen," replied the Wizard.

"You mean the Unicorn?" asked Yorkin.

"Exactly," replied Eulool.

"Yes," Potemkin leaned forward, "we thought it must be a unicorn. But Eulool, why are we the five. Actually, I know why Loni and Yorkin and GreeHee fit the riddle. But why me?"

The wizard sat erect in his sky blue robes, deep indigo eyes staring somewhere above Potemkin's head, strong nose and chin prominent, hand rested on the Staff of Wizen, he looked at Potemkin and patted his hand, "Yes, you Potemkin, that is a good question. Loni and Yorkin carry the blood of Draydel so they are the two small ones. GreeHee is the son of Reatora, the dragon who attempted to kill Deandrea, Queen of the Fairies, over six hundred soars ago. So he is here to repay the debt by protecting fairies from Tana's darkness. Boldor carries the blood of Wizen, so he must be part of the purity of light to torch the darkness of Tana. But what exactly do you, Commander Potemkin, have to do with this riddle? Are you an ordinary giant thrown into the mix by accident?" The wizard leaned back, ran his hand through his silky white beard, raised his eyebrows and waited.

Potemkin stammered, "Uh, I don't know…"

"No, you are no accident! There are no accidents in the universe. You, sir, are the carrier of blood that descended from Draydel's assistant, Laramadeera. Or as you know her, Lovely."

Yorkin leaned forward, "But, Eulool, Lovely died. We saw her. How could Potemkin be her descendant and besides, she said he would be her father in this life? I don't understand?"

"Child, blood is in a continued lineage. Even as he will be her father in this life, he has already been her father in that one," said the wizard wagging his long bony finger.

Potemkin straightened, rubbed his chin and shook his head, "Blessed Ancients, are you saying we're born again in lineage and so we are in essence our ancestors? That is very confusing and I don't know that I can believe such."

"Believe it or not, matters not. It is so. We simply continue to turn the wheel of time and reenter until we decide to move to a level beyond this one. It is the way of learning, mastering, and change," stated Eulool.

"What about me?" asked GreeHee, eyes wide, at the window, "My mother died when I was born but she died six hundred soars ago and I'm only thirteen. Even the longest recorded dragon birth doesn't come close? Do you have an explanation for me?" the dragon asked confused beyond measure.

Eulool stood, walked to the window, "The reason it took so long for your birth was because the negative dragon patterns had to be balanced inside you first. You could not be born until all was in harmony. And naturally the timing was exact. It is how all life works. Your father still recognized you, did he not?'

"Yes. He never mentioned how long it had been till I was born."

"No but did you not hear him say, your mother's name was Reatora?"

GreeHee nodded.

"Your father also called you a runt of a dragon because you didn't have the fierce temperament that he demanded, didn't he?" continued Eulool.

"Yes, he said that all the time."

"Well, that is the sign of who you are. There can be no question that you are the enormous one. There is no other dragon that is of right mind and conscious soul. You reveal yourself by your kind heart and unfierce ways.

Your mother was Reatora!"

"Yes that is what my father said." GreeHee shrank back, shoulders sagged, head slumped, to hear these details spoken so clearly for all to see.

"Then you indeed are the longest birth of dragon in the history of Tamoor. And you, my dear GreeHee," the wizard softened, "are one of the five. You should be proud because you will become the most famous dragon of all time. You are already famous in the rhymes of fairy children. They just don't know whom they are singing about yet. Why, even I didn't know until recently when you appeared," the wizard reached through the window and patted GreeHee's cheek.

Yorkin jumped up, face tense, arms extended. "But please, Eulool, will you tell us what we are to do?"

"And what does crossing the Azura Kah have to do with any of this?" Potemkin asked.

"Potemkin, you will have to wait a little longer before I can tell you that. Tomorrow, when Boldor arrives, I will give you the keys to the rest of the riddle. Till then, I will leave you with this," the wizard drew a deep breath, "the danger has only begun. You must link your hearts and your minds. You must quickly learn to rely on each other for strength. None of you must allow another to fear. If you do, you will give Tana what she needs to destroy Tamoor."

"Please, Eulool, are we safe here?" asked Loni.

"Yes, my little princess. Tana scared you with lies. She is very good at that and will continue to try. But you are safe here. Tana can say what she will but she cannot enter Oberlon or Castle Farion. As long as the star of five remains intact, she has no power in Oberlon. And all of you shall be safe here. As for Boldor, you needn't worry about him, he has Wizen's blood and will strengthen each of you." As Eulool began to leave the room, he added, "We'll talk more tomorrow. In the meantime, Potemkin, your job is to get well. You have a long journey ahead and will need your strength."

Chapter 22

EULOOL SPEAKS

Sunlight streamed in the window as Loni awoke. She slowly became conscious of her surroundings. Home! In her own bed covered in pink silk. It felt so nice. Leisurely Loni stretched. Oh! Boldor the unicorn might already be here! She jumped out of bed and flew around the room dressing.

In the great hall of Castle Farion, food had already been served.

"Father, has Boldor...?" shouted Loni as she scrambled into the hall. Boldor stood facing the King at the High table. "Oh! How do you do, Boldor? I am Loni." She came to a sudden stop as gracefully as she could while his large soft dark blue eyes held her gaze.

"How do you do?" said Boldor, bowing to the young princess. His coat flashed a variety of pastel colors. The unicorn stood about five leets to the shoulder; his neck and head towering over the King and Eulool. Boldor's horn twisted like an old vine to a fine point at the tip. It was golden white. Encircling his neck a flat forest-green velvet band about one pinch wide hung down against the center of his chest where it ended in a small pouch branded with the crest of the Crystal Forest. Boldor used his telekinetic abilities to give Loni a hug.

"Oh!" said Loni. "That is so nice, Boldor." She walked up to him and hugged his neck.

"Thank you too, Loni," replied Boldor flashing a bright pink.

"Ah, have you been here long?" Loni said backing up a little. " I hope I haven't missed anything. Have I?" She looked first at Boldor and then at her father and Eulool.

"No my dear, come and sit here between your mother and me." King Allielt said, making room for his baby girl. "Boldor has been telling us about his journey here. I think you will find it interesting."

"What about Yorkin, Potemkin, and GreeHee?" she asked.

"I expect they're in the courtyard setting up a meeting place that will be comfortable for everyone," said the king.

"We are ready your Highest." Potemkin said as he entered the Great Hall. "Oh, Loni! Good, you're up. We're ready for the meeting."

Loni flew down to Potemkin and carefully touched his bandaged arm. "How are you feeling?"

"Fine! I'm healing quickly with Eulool's magic and Paychente's care. See how well I can move it now." He swung his left arm into the air.

The King, Eulool, and Boldor joined them. Queen Marleenah brought a bowl of berries and cream to Loni saying, "Dearest, here, eat while you talk. I picked your favorite plum berries this morning."

"Oh, Mother!" Loni said, giving her a hug. "Thank you."

Potemkin led the odd group into the sunlit courtyard. Loni held the bowl and nibbled as they walked.

"Your castle is enchanting," said Boldor. "I'm glad to have this opportunity to visit but sorry it is under these perilous circumstances."

The King nodded, his eyes cast toward the ground.

"GreeHee, how are you?" asked Loni.

"Fine Loni, you little sleepy head," replied the dragon with a smile.

Arranged in a circle stood King Allielt's favorite outdoor throne, four chairs with bright-colored cushions, and deep comfortable moss for GreeHee and Boldor. In the center stood a simple round wooden table.

The King and Eulool sat and everyone else took a seat.

Eulool looked left to right to assure the fairy watchers were positioned and no one else was in earshot. Then he began in a low voice, "It's time to reveal to you all that I know about the journey you must now make. It is a dangerous one but hopefully I will prepare you well to conquer Tana."

"Are you coming with us, Eulool?" asked Loni.

"No, I cannot. I must stay here to protect Oberlon. Without my magic, Castle Farion would have already been destroyed."

Yorkin said, "Are you referring to the trolls?"

"Yes, and to other efforts made by Tana to ruin Oberlon," Eulool frowned, his deep eyes shadowed by thick white eyebrows.

Yorkin asked, "Can you tell us more about the trolls? Where are they? What are they up to now?"

"They're headed west. I believe they have already arrived at the camp of Carron General Maltor. They are being used by Tana to destroy Narsor."

Potemkin jumped, "Eulool, I need to go to Narsor to protect my king."

"No!" Said Eulool, motioning for Potemkin to sit down. "You are one of the five and it will take all five of you to destroy Tana. Never let another doubt about this enter your mind. Those doubts are fears, which will be used against you by Tana. You're safe here while I'm with you, but heed my words; once you leave Oberlon, you must remain strong and not let any thoughts of Narsor's possible defeat, or any question of your own loyalty, enter your mind. It could be your downfall and that would give Tana reign over all Tamoor. Do you understand, Potemkin?"

"I will do my best," said Potemkin, Eulool's resolute eyes in his glaze.

"No sir, you will do it! As I say, you will do it!" Eulool stood, waved his glowing pearlescent staff, eyebrows set together, left hand pointed at the five. In a softer voice, he continued, "Before I go any further, I will give you the gifts I made for you. After considering each of your strengths and weaknesses, I created certain magical potions to compensate for your vulnerabilities."

From under his robes of purple and gold, the wizard removed five tiny bottles, each containing a liquid of a different color. He placed them on the table and chose the green one first. Turning to Potemkin, he held it up, saying, "This is optimism and I made it for you, Potemkin, because you're a realist. Even as being such is one of your strengths, it is also your most significant weakness. Anytime you begin to doubt yourself or the success of your mission, place a drop of this on your forehead or hold it close to your heart and you will regain an optimistic viewpoint."

Potemkin took the bottle staring at it curiously. He placed it inside a pocket above his heart. "Thank you, Eulool. I will treasure your wisdom and use this when I need it."

Then Eulool picked up the bottle of blue liquid, "Yorkin, because you have a quick, curious mind, sometimes it rushes forward before wisdom takes hold. I give you Clarity. A drop of this liquid placed on the tongue will clear the mind of desire to act before assessing all the details."

"Thank you," Yorkin took the bottle.

Eulool handed to GreeHee the bottle of gold liquid, "GreeHee, you have a great heart but do not know how to love yourself. It is only now that you are beginning to discover love and friendship. When you feel unworthy to be a part of this quest, unworthy of love or friendship, place a drop of this liquid on your heart. It has the power to open your heart to loving yourself. You're our hero because out of this entire group, it takes more courage for you to step forward than for any other."

"I don't know what to say?" the dragon said, his big green eyes watering.

Eulool pressed GreeHee's hand closed over the bottle and added, "You need say nothing, GreeHee. Be yourself and you will succeed."

Then turning to Loni, Eulool took the tiny bottle of pink liquid, saying, "Loni, you are the heart of this journey. Your innocence, optimism, and love are key to opening the doors in Wizard's Web, but because you have no understanding of evil, when it approaches you are terrified. This liquid will waken the heart and give you the realization that love is power beyond evil. Take it and place a drop on your left hand when Beauty warns you of danger, and evil will shrivel powerless before you."

Solemnly, Loni took the pink bottle.

"Then finally, Boldor. You have wisdom and courage but live in a world, which to the rest of us is illusion. Because of this, illusions in our world may seem real to you." Then handing a bottle of crystal clear liquid to the unicorn, Eulool continued, "This liquid placed on the base of your horn will give you sight to see through illusions, so you will not waste precious time fighting an unreal battle."

"Thank you, Eulool!" said the unicorn as his telekinetic power placed the bottle into his velvet pouch.

Arms extended, staff raised, Eulool addressed the group, "Even as you each have a personal potion, it will be the love you have for each other that reminds you to use them. You must be a team. Together you will defeat Tana, not one of you can do it alone and no others in all Tamoor could come close. The fate of Tamoor rests on the success of your journey.

"All right now, let's examine what this journey is really about and how you are to accomplish it." Eulool pulled out a map from under his robe. The group moved in closer as he placed it on the table.

"Here is Castle Farion in Oberlon." He pointed to a mark on the map. "To our east are the Crystal Mountains and in the midst of these mountains is the Pool of Reckoning, the entrance to the Crystal Forest where Boldor lives. This is where you will go first. Boldor knows how to take you from there to the Mystic Mountains and Wizard's Web. At Wizard's Web you must pass through the Doorway of Time and the Hall of Mirrors to get to the Seat of Stars. It is in the Seat of Stars that you will fulfill your destiny."

"Master Eulool," said Potemkin, "what exactly must we do to fulfill our destiny in the Seat of Stars?"

Eulool drew in a deep breath, his fingers running through his beard, "Well, for me to explain that I will have to give you some information about Tana and how she attained her power. Unfortunately no one has all the details about this, so I can only give you the clues I've found and my hypothesis."

Eulool sat back in his chair and everyone did the same.

"Tana is a combination of three creatures: Maduk a troll, Beastera a dragon, and Felleen a Carron-like creature. Each of these beings had one desire -- to control all of Tamoor. Each had the goal to destroy anyone that got in the way. But each also brought something different to the mix. Maduk brought brute strength, a barbaric talent for crushing his enemies, and an affinity with marshes and sordid places. Beastera brought fire, incredible eyesight, a dynastic lifespan, and staying power. Felleen brought the ability to kill with speed and agility. Together these qualities are formidable. But how did they combine into one onerous creature? This is where my hypothesis begins." He took a deep breath, searched the faces of the group, "I believe the magic came from Felleen. But first let me give you the foundation to my reasoning. It has been told throughout the legends of wizardry that in the early beedites of the planet, there was an indomitable wizard. His name was Oraculus Potenteerum and it is said he had the power to create stars!"

"Ahh, so that is where the power originates!" said King Allielt, finger to his lip, his blue eyes flashed, gold hair glowing under his emerald crown.

"Yes your majesty, that is what I believe." His long beard dancing in the breeze, "And I will now reveal how I feel it fell into Felleen's wingtips. But before I start again could we get some water. I'm sure I'm not the only thirsty one in this group."

Loni flew to the castle.

"So Eulool if I understand correctly," began Potemkin, "you're saying the magic of wizard Oraculus somehow ended up in Felleen's possession, and this magic gave her the power to create a star from the three creatures vying for control of Tamoor?"

"Basically, that is correct," answered Eulool reaching for the goblet Loni held for him. She had returned with several fairies carrying trays of goblets and two crystal pitchers, one of sweet berry nectar and one of water.

"Did I miss anything?" asked Loni.

"No, Loni," said Eulool holding his goblet up, "Thank you!"

They all raised their cups in gratitude. Loni sat down and Eulool continued, "Okay, legend has it that Master Wizard Oraculus Potenteerum discovered the magic to create stars and of course, we must suppose that he also had the power to destroy them, because once we learn how to create we also learn how to destroy." The wizard held up his hand, index finger extended.

"And then that would mean that Draydel knew this magic, because it was Draydel that destroyed Tana's power in the Primengeer!" exclaimed Loni.

"Astute observation, Loni, but perhaps not totally correct," said Eulool. "We do not know exactly how Draydel stopped Tana but we do know that he did not totally destroy her power. Therefore, he either did not know how or perhaps he did not have all the power necessary to completely destroy her. But he certainly knew more than we know."

"Tell him about the book, Loni. Tell Eulool about the book!" said GreeHee his eyes big, tail whipping.

"What book?" asked Eulool and King Allielt at once.

"Oh Father! Eulool, I didn't have a chance to tell you but when we went to Nadeckador's Castle we found Draydel's secret room and this little book that he left for me." Loni pulled it from a pocket in her overdress. "Here it is!" She handed it to Eulool. "But it looks empty until we need it, I guess, or we ask a question or something."

Yorkin stood up, his eyes wide, arms animated, navy velvet cape floating, "Yes in camp before we knew about the Carron attack, we sat at the fire to look at the book and GreeHee asked a question. An envelope fell out of the book and suddenly GreeHee's name appeared on it and a letter from Draydel told GreeHee he was part of the five. Then when we looked back at the book Draydel appeared holding the Star of Knowing."

"Yeah! The Star of Knowing! GreeHee show Eulool the star," Loni said tapping the dragon's arm.

The King and Eulool had flipped through the blank pages of the little indigo book and now stared at GreeHee.

"Uh, here it is," said the dragon stretching to display the purple and green palm of his enormous right hand for the King and wizard to see.

"Ahh!" said Eulool, his eyes wide, fingers touching the blue star, "You, my dear dragon, are wearing a mark of power. This is one reason why Tana desperately wanted to capture you!"

"Huh? I don't understand?" said the dragon.

"Star power is what this is all about, my dear GreeHee, and it seems you already have the mark of a Star!"

"But, but…"stammered Loni. "Didn't you give GreeHee the Star of Knowing, Eulool? I remember you came into my dream and gave it to me and told me to give it to GreeHee when he asked. Wasn't that you?"

"No, it was not I!" said the wizard, eyebrows raised.

"T'was I!" came a voice from the indigo book that Eulool held. Within a tithe the phantom form of Draydel materialized before them, only a pinch taller than Eulool, wearing a soft white cotton robe with a wide yoke neckline embroidered with stars, his long dark blonde hair flowed into his honey-colored beard, gentle rounded eyebrows shaded his light blue eyes, his left hand held an emerald wand.

"Draydel!" exclaimed Loni.

"Draydel," echoed a whisper throughout the group.

"Yes Loni, it was I who sent the Star of Knowing to GreeHee." He turned to GreeHee, "The star is part of the power. You are a key and will discover all at Wizard's Web. I will be with you throughout your journey."

"Draydel, is my theory about Tana correct?" asked Eulool.

"Yes! Felleen found the ancient manuscript that had been hidden for hundreds of linglorns, in the City of Teeth. You see the city of Teeth some seven thousand linglorns ago was a flourishing metropolis created by Oraculus. He hid the manuscript because his ego would not allow him to destroy it. Felleen found it and used it to merge the three into Tana. Now Tana is not only the power of three as you described, but the power of nine, because the creation of the star brings the number to the third power. That is why it will take five to defeat her."

Eyebrows knitted, Loni tapped the side of her face, "But Draydel if she has the manuscript, couldn't she recreate herself all over again?"

"Yes, but by the time you have taken the action to disperse the power of Tana, it will take her many more linglorns before she can build up enough strength to use that magic again."

Potemkin stood up, eyes riveted, "So that means we must also find the manuscript and destroy it before that happens?"

"Yes, but that is for another time. Right now your mission is to destroy Tana before she conquers all of Tamoor. Narsor is not safe and you five must travel fast and light as soon as dawn breaks in the morrow, or all may be lost. The trolls are taking their toll on the army of giants and Narsor cannot hold out for more than three or four beedites." The apparition began to fade. "I must go now. Stay together and do all with cooperation and love and you will succeed."

Silence fell over the group as they stared at the spot where Draydel had stood. Eulool, the first to speak, handed the indigo book back to Loni, "This is your link to Draydel and as we have all witnessed, he will come to your aid through it. So guard it carefully and use it wisely."

Nodding Loni putting the book back into her pocket.

"Do you have any questions?" asked Eulool standing.

Potemkin said, "I am certain we will be filled with questions in no time but, as for myself, I cannot think of one right now."

All agreed.

Eulool, hand shading his eyes, looked skyward, "The sun has passed its zenith. Let us enjoy a noontide meal. Once we have had our fill, there may be more I should address."

"Yes, let us partake of food!" added King Allielt smiling. Queen Marleenah waved to him from the corner of the castle. He waved back and added to Loni and Yorkin. "It seems your mother has been waiting for us to come to dinner." Then turning to GreeHee, Potemkin, and Boldor he extended his right hand, saying, "Come my friends, let us eat."

Chapter 23

NEW ORDERS

"**W**e were ambushed! Even with Tana's help we lost the battle," Petrie told Maltor, burnt feathers over much of his body. "Many were killed. I don't know the numbers, sir." He continued, eyes fixed on the General, Tana's brand in sharp contrast to his white forehead feathers.

The General turned from his gaze, "You say Tana appeared and was only capable of talk? Incredulous! Are you certain of this, Petrie? Perhaps the burns on your body confused your sight? Huh? Perhaps that's it?"

"No sir, General Maltor. I saw it plain as the beak on my face. Tana appeared but her lightening bolts could not reach across the Crystal River."

"Well, I have a mind to go after that dragon myself. How dare he eat our food, live under our care, and then take up with the enemy. He is sicker than I could have imagined. And to think I almost awarded him the 'The Iron Talon'! And what of that gibberish, saying he is the son of Tereem? What did Tana say about that? Petrie, what did Tana say about that Greedy dragon?"

"Sir, she told us nothing about him. Absolutely nothing! Tana said she wanted him captured and taken to her unharmed. She said that we were to kill all the giants and then bring the two fairies and the dragon to her." Petrie placed his right hand inside his breast pocket and touched the leather fob that had belonged to Bravort. Even though he had been in terrible pain, he had waited till the giants left and then he pulled Bravort's dead body to shore. Petrie found the fob tightly clutched in Bravort's right feather fingers. He took it from the dead Colonel for comfort.

"Listen to me, Sergeant Petrie, there is more to this little dragon than meets the eye." The General feathered his chin with his right wingtip. "Gento get Sergeant Faltaz. I need to see him immediately."

The Corporal saluted and left.

"Tell me, Petrie, what else do you recall of the battle? Reports indicate that we're missing sixty-three soldiers. Are they all dead?"

"Sir, as I said earlier, the dragon killed many Carrons setting them aflame. The giants killed many more with rocks and arrows. And after seeing Tana's wrath and her inability to save us, as well as the death of Colonel Bravort, many soldiers deserted, incensed or insane. They are probably wandering in the barren northlands of Narsor," Petrie said, eyes drawn, frowning. "Sir what would you have us do? We expected a quick victory but nothing we expected happened." Petrie whined.

"General Maltor, you summoned me?" interrupted Sergeant Faltaz, a very neat, armor polished, blue-feathered Carron.

"Yes Faltaz, as chief historian, I need some facts from you. The battle that took place a few beedites ago at the Crystal River seems to have a few quirks that I cannot piece together. Are you familiar with the battle?"

"Well, sir, I have been gathering details about it from every Carron who has returned, so I guess I know a bit about it."

"Okay, did everyone tell you that Tana appeared over the Crystal River?" asked the General, sitting behind his desk.

"Yes sir, I heard that from everyone. They described her and every one said that Tana shot lightening bolts towards the Giants but that none of these met their mark."

"Faltaz, first, you are hereby ordered to leave that information out of any account you write concerning this battle. Secondly, I want to know what facts you have that can explain why that happened. And the third matter of business is the dragon. I want you to tell me why Tana wants the dragon and why he is to be delivered unharmed." The General signaled for Faltaz to sit in the chair to Petrie's left.

"Sir, I do not have answers to these questions, only suppositions. From all I've read and heard, legend claims that Oberlon is surrounded by enchantment and protected by a powerful wizard. If this is true, then perhaps the wizard's power prevented Tana from striking the giants."

"Okay, that sounds reasonable, but if that is true how did an army of trolls get through Oberlon? Tell me that!" The General pounded his desk.

"Sir, I don't know. I have not interviewed the trolls so I cannot say what may have transpired on their journey through Oberlon."

"Tell me, Sergeant, what you think?" demanded the General.

"Sir, I'm not paid to think beyond the facts. I'm an historian and that means I put the facts together. I don't make them up." Faltaz said, words pouring from his orange beak.

"Well, toll the bell in tandem, son, but I don't give a boron beast's butt what your job description calls for; I want to know what you think! Facts or no facts, what is your opinion in this matter!" Maltor stood up, eyes bulging, he poked the historian's chest.

Faltaz backed up, beak gaped, "Okay, sir, but please note that this is off the record. I believe the trolls did not try to attack or kill anyone in Oberlon and so they were allowed to pass through the country without harm. Tana, on the other wing, intended to attack creatures in Oberlon. The protective magic intercepted her attack and prevented her from hurting anyone there."

The general sat down, drew a long breath, "I see your point and it is plausible. But let's take a hypothetical situation. What if the trolls had begun their march through Oberlon and then while in Oberlon decided to attack someone, would the magic stop them?" asked Maltor squinting.

"Sir, again, I have little to go on here but, based on the actions of our own birds, I believe once on Oberlon soil, an army could attack and sustain a victory. After all, our birds did attack the giants, it was Tana who could not."

"I see, so it is magic against magic," the General mumbled. "The magic may only work in defense of magic and has little to do with ordinary soldiers." Maltor scanned the historian's face. "And the dragon? What in Tamoor does he have to do with anything? Why does Tana want him? He has been a weed in my seed since he first appeared. What can you tell me about him?"

"Sir, information on this particular dragon is simply non-existent. We saw him and he seemed ordinary. He did not display the natural tendencies of a dragon but he was sick and this may have mitigated his nature. Personally, I cannot see any reason why Tana should want this little dragon Greedy."

"You know what, Faltaz, that is not my question. I personally don't care what you personally saw!" said the General wing-fist pounding. "I want to know what legend or history has to say about a young dragon. Is there some tidbit you can throw me that can help unravel this enigma, Sergeant?"

"Well, sir, nothing comes to mind about a young dragon. I do not believe we have anything in Carron history books about a young dragon; only stories of battles against or with dragons." Sergeant Faltaz wrinkled his brow and continued, "I think you're asking me for some prophecy concerning a dragon but Carron history precludes prophecy sir. I cannot recall any instance of it in our books."

The General began to speak and then pursed his beak. He stared at his desk and then again at Faltaz. For a moment his gaze landed on Petrie hunched in the chair. Finally he said, "All right, get out of here." Faltaz got up to leave and the General added, "If you hear anything at all that might give me insight into this dragon, you will inform me immediately!"

"Yes sir, General!" Sergeant Faltaz saluted and left the tent.

The General turned to Petrie, "You look like you know something, Petrie. What are you hiding?"

"Me, sir? Nothing. Nothing at all."

"Then why are you hunched over like that? What is wrong with you?"

"I...I think Tana has the answers."

"Of course Tana has the answers, you fool. But she isn't sharing is she?" said the General, mimicking Petrie's high-pitched voice. "I need the answers. I need to know what to do next. I have no word from Tana and the trolls are running the war on Narsor. My army needs direction and as their commander, this hideous battle in Oberlon has cursed us with defeat. My birds need a direction that will assure victory and if Tana needs this dragon, I must find a way to get it for her." The general paced.

A hiss came from Petrie. Maltor pivoted. Petrie's eyes glazed with anger. He stood up and said, "I will tell you what to do, you miserable Maltor. I have an assignment for you, if you have the courage to take it." The voice of Tana clearly emerged through Petrie. His eyes began to swirl. "I need that dragon and those fairies. They are on the way to the Pool of Reckoning in the Crystal Mountains. Take your entire army and capture them. I will send a dispatch of ogres to back up the trolls. I will send you a secret weapon. Maltor are you ready to give your life for Tana?" Tana's eyes swirled gold and orange, round and round, holding Maltor's gaze.

"I...I...I will." Maltor stammered, his eyes locked with Tana's.

"Then I will give you a gift for your allegiance!" she said -- a bolt of lightening flashed from Petrie's right feather fingers opening them to reveal the red leather fob. Immediately it flew from Petrie's wingtip, suspended in the air before Maltor. As his feather fingers closed around it, the sizzling sound of burning feather ensued, yet Maltor did not move, even as smoke rose from his right wingtip.

Tana's guttural voice continued, "You will have your friend back too. You will need him. You will leave by dawn for the Crystal Mountains. You will not fly over Oberlon. You will not rest. You will go directly to the Pool of Reckoning and wait on the Eastern side until the fairies, dragon, giant, and unicorn appear. You will capture or kill the fairies. And you will capture the dragon, render him harmless but do not damage his right hand in any way. Do it right this time!" The voice hissed again and Petrie collapsed.

"Aaagh!" shouted Maltor holding his right wingtip in the air and opening it. The leather fob fell to the ground. Petrie opened his eyes and leapt for it. Maltor grabbed Petrie's wing with his talon. "What is this? Have you been hiding something from me? Something you received from Tana that she has now given to me? And you want it back?" The General pulled Petrie to his talons. "Speak, you treacherous Carron!"

"Sir, I wasn't hiding anything," stammered Petrie. "That fob was mine from Tana, it gave me comfort. I dropped it and wanted to pick it up."

"You lying fool! Tana gave that to me! Don't you remember?" questioned the General.

"No sir. I must have missed something. The last thing I remember was Sergeant Faltaz leaving the tent."

Maltor let go of Petrie. Tana's instructions were for him alone. "Then you missed Tana! She was here and gave us new orders." The general picked up the blood red fob. He held it affectionately in his right wing tip. He noticed the scar. Once the leather touched it the pain was gone. Tana had left her mark but honored him with discretion. Probably because I am a general, he smiled. Turning again to Petrie he said, "Get to work right now, ready the army to fly at dawn. We have much to do and I will see to it that all is done properly. Go now Petrie!"

Before Petrie could salute, Corporal Gento rushed into the tent shouting, "General, Admiral Jarteen is awake!"

Chapter 24

THE CRYSTAL MOUNTAINS

At dawn, GreeHee, Boldor, and Potemkin stood waiting for Loni and Yorkin. "Do you think Eulool had some other magic to give them, Potemkin?" asked GreeHee, scratching his chin.

"No. He wanted to show them something in the gazing ball and since none of us have fairy blood, we wouldn't be able to see it."

"Oh, so what does fairy blood have to do with seeing in the ball?" GreeHee questioned.

Boldor answered, "It has a bond with the crystal and allows fairies to see and feel things across time and space."

"We're ready!" Loni said as she flew to the threesome.

"What did you see, Loni?" asked GreeHee.

"I think Yorkin should tell you that, perhaps we can talk while we fly?"

"Yes, we need to get going if we are to reach the Pool of Reckoning before moonrise," said Boldor.

"Don't you want me to come with you? I can fly and I can be of help if someone gets sick?" asked Paychente.

Yorkin patted his wing, "Yes, you would, but Boldor says it's dangerous enough for the four of us and anyone else will make it more dangerous."

"Loni and Yorkin can fly with me." Boldor said, "Then Potemkin can have GreeHee all to himself and be comfortable."

"Goodbye children!" Queen Marleenah gave Yorkin and Loni one last hug. King Allielt stood watching, biting his upper lip, and forcing a smile.

"I will miss you, Father," Loni said as she gave her father one last hug.

Yorkin mounted the unicorn. "Father, I will take good care of Loni and we will return soon."

"I am certain you will, Yorkin," said the King, touching his shoulder and then lifting Loni onto Boldor's back. We will keep good thoughts around all of you. Good speed!"

Eulool smiled weakly in the entrance of the castle, his long white beard flowing, Staff of Wizen glowed, and he waved. In the courtyard fairies and giants shouted 'goodbyes' and 'good speeds.'

Once in the air above Castle Farion, Boldor began, "Before we get to the Crystal Mountains I must warn you about their energy and how they affect those who are not pure in all things."

"What do you mean by pure in all things?" questioned Potemkin.

"Hmm, let me explain." The unicorn hesitated then continued, "I think I need to explain what they are first and then my meaning will become clear. The Crystal Mountains are amplifiers and generators. Whenever a being travels through them, whatever is in their thoughts will expand. Then the mountains will generate an image to fulfill the thought. Can you see the impact this can have on a creature whose mind is not pure?"

"Are you saying that whatever is in the mind of a creature will be created into something physical?" said Potemkin eyebrows angled, head cocked.

"Yes! That is one reason we are flying. Even if we had the time to stroll to the Pool of Reckoning, it could be deadly walking through the Crystal Mountains. By flying over them, your thoughts are still amplified, but instead of thoughts being created externally, they will turn inward and grow internally. Does everyone understand?"

"I think so," said Yorkin. "So if we have a fear about something, it will grow inside our minds? Is that correct?"

"Precisely!" said the unicorn. "That is why no one has ever reached the Pool of Reckoning without invitation. However what I have told you is a secret and known only to unicorns because it is our home and our magic."

"You mean even Eulool does not know this?" asked Loni.

"No, he does not. That is why I have waited until now to tell you. I cannot divulge this information to anyone because it is in the pact of unicorns. Before I came to Oberlon, I met with the Unicorn Counsel of Elders. We had a heated discussion. Many said this information would not be safe with the four of you and could cause an end to unicorns in Tamoor. But due to the war with Tana and the nature of the cure being the prophecy which includes all of us, the Elders finally reached an agreement."

"But we can keep a secret!" said Loni.

"Ah, but it is not so simple, my dear friends. Once the information is placed in an 'un'pure mind, it can be retrieved by magic, and that is the concern of the Elders. So I am going to ask each of you to agree to the terms stated by the Counsel of Unicorn Elders. If any of you lack the heart to agree, I will not give protection to you in the Mountains and that means you might as well turn back."

Potemkin extended his arms, "Please tell us what the agreement is, I am certain there is none among us who would not agree."

"The agreement is that upon return from Wizard's Web, you will pass through the Mirror of Memories. It will erase this knowledge and all your memories of the Crystal Mountains."

All four agreed.

Potemkin asked, "But can we not remember a little bit of this journey? Are we to forget it all?"

"I know your ego wishes to retain some control in this matter, Potemkin, but to do so would be to endanger the lives of all unicorns. However, I can give you this. You can visit in your dreams, but upon waking you will simply feel the peace and joy of being in the Crystal Forest, but not recall any details. Are you agreed?"

"Yes. For Tamoor, my King, Oberlon, and the Kingdom of Unicorns, I will release my control of my memory."

"Then we are agreed," said Boldor, coat flashing joy, pink and lavender.

"Look at the colors of those mountains!" exclaimed GreeHee.

The foothills of the Crystal Mountains stretched before them, filling the horizon with breath-taking rainbows. Some looked like enormous berry ices, others more like ice crystals or glass. Many peaks were so clear, you could not tell where one mountain ended and another began. Glowing in morning light orange, rose, and lavender, they enchanted one to dream.

"Home!" Boldor sighed, "I think it is the most beautiful place in Tamoor." Then added, "Now it would be best to focus on something, someone, or someplace you love. Fill yourselves with love and it will amplify, thus protecting you as we enter the Crystal Mountains. So to help each other we should talk only of the treasures in our hearts, we must not discuss the journey, only cherished thoughts that are easy to focus on."

Boldor continued, "Potemkin, tell us about the loves of your life."

"Ho hmm, hmm." He cleared his throat. "Well, I really haven't had any loves to speak of yet, so--"

"Of course you have, your mother, your first toy, your sword, your medals…you see what I mean," said Boldor.

"Well, I must admit I have never looked at love quite that way before. And I've never discussed these things with anyone. It is going to be a little hard for me, could someone else go first? I'm feeling uneasy with this assignment."

"Oh, maybe I can help you," said Loni. "What if we choose something and each of us talks about it. For example, I love the color green. I love the trees and how they dance with their green fingers waving like a waterfall of emeralds in the sun, glittering and shiny and lovely," Loni smiled at the Commander, "Potemkin, what's your favorite color?"

"I love blue," the Commander blurted. "The sky when it is clear either during sun time or sunset. My father gave me a dark blue velvet cape when I went to my first fencing competition and I loved that cape. I felt like a king in it. Ever since then, I have loved the deep rich color of blue."

Boldor said, "You are doing it, Potemkin! That was perfect. Don't you feel wonderful?"

"Why yes, it feels very nice. Indeed it feels nice." The Commander beamed. "What about you GreeHee, what is your favorite color?"

"Gosh, that is a hard one." GreeHee said his tail twitching, "I think I like a lot of colors. Looking at these mountains, I don't see a color I don't like. They're all beautiful."

Yorkin asked, "But if you had to live in a place where you could only have one color and the rest of your world would be black and white, what color would you choose?'

"I guess it would be lavender. It is soft and doesn't intrude into your mind. It's gentle and quiet but definitely there. It makes me feel like taking a nap sometimes and reading at others. Yes, lavender would be the color."

"GreeHee you are sooo amazing!" Loni exclaimed. "Lavender is a great choice. It's the first step to purple, the color of kings."

Boldor smiled and winked, "More importantly, purple is the color of wisdom and lavender is the first step to wisdom."

Loni added with a chuckle, "GreeHee, you have chosen the color that will help you follow your heart! How very you!"

"I did? Well that's amazing!" replied the dragon, his eyes wide, grinning. Then he asked, "What about you, Yorkin? Do you have a favorite color?"

"I like green and blue mixed together. I guess it's called turquoise. It's the color of the Azura Kah. I have watched the mists rise off the Kah like the ghosts of ancestors leaving behind the glorious turquoise waters. Sometimes a huge golden-orange fish will leap from the Kah, taunting me with his playful spirit, his brilliant scales sparkling against the blue-green waters. Yes, I would have to say turquoise. It makes me feel at peace. It soothes my mind and relaxes my soul." Yorkin sighed deeply.

"Wait an elide, Yorkin, when have you been to the Azura Kah?" asked Loni, her eyes wide..

"Oh, Loni, you remember when I took lessons from Eulool, don't you?"

"Yeah, but--"

"Well, I loved peering into his gazing ball and I always ended up on the north shore of the Azura Kah at dawn. It was fun!" Yorkin smiled.

"Oh, by the way, are you ever going to tell us what Eulool showed you in the gazing ball before we left?" asked GreeHee.

Boldor said. "I think we had better save that until we get to the Crystal Forest. Then if it brings up any fears, it will be okay. Okay?"

Yorkin nodded, "Yes, that is the best idea. Would it be all right if we take a break for a few elides to stretch?"

"Yes, but remember to stay focused on beautiful things. Keep your hearts open and we will be fine."

They headed for the beautiful meadow that ran along the south ridge of the mountains, high above the Upper Crystal River. The fivesome landed on a ledge bursting with blue and violet flowers, close to a pristine waterfall that danced gracefully in the sunlight on the crystalline wall, into a shimmering pool and then spilled over the ledge plunging a hundred leets into the river below. "Breathtaking!" Potemkin inhaled the intoxicating air.

"There's no grass here? Why is that, Boldor?" asked Loni.

"No, the Crystal Mountains really are made of crystal so grasses don't grow here. But by some amazing act of Creator, we have these incredible flowers. Look closely at them and you will see what I mean."

GreeHee drank from the pool, while watching Loni examine the flowers. "Why they are moving!" exclaimed Loni.

Potemkin scratched his chin, "Are they another life form? A creature that can move about?"

Eyes twinkling, Boldor shook his silky mane, "Well, yes and no. Actually they are another life form, as are all the plants and rocks but because we have no soil in the Crystal Mountains, the flowers weave their roots together to sustain themselves. Their intertwined roots keep them on the mountain but not in one place. If you come to this very spot next soar, it's possible the whole meadow will have moved over there." The unicorn pointed with his soft pink muzzle to the next ledge.

"Amazing!" exclaimed Potemkin, sitting on an enormous crystal outcropping and beginning to eat lunch. "Does anyone else want to eat?"

After a short while everyone with the exception of Boldor napped in the warm sun. Boldor watched the clouds move across the sky. "What is that?" He said. "GreeHee, wake up!"

"Uh, what is it Boldor?"

"There in the Southern skies can you tell what that dark moving cloud is? It looks like enormous birds or something?"

"It's Carrons! A whole army of Carrons!" exclaimed the dragon.

"Are you certain?"

"Yes, there is no doubt! I can see them clearly. They are armed, wearing armor and appear to be moving in the same direction we're going!"

"You are gathering fear, GreeHee," Boldor said in a low voice. "Think of something beautiful right now. Think of lavender!"

"Uh, shouldn't we discuss this first?"

"No! Do what I say. You need to be calm and thinking loving thoughts. Hatred will destroy you and all of us. Tana will win if you do. Take three deep breaths and clear your mind of everything and fill it with lavender. I see lavender seeping into your mind." Said the unicorn, taking a deep breath with the dragon. "That bottle of Self Love, anoint yourself with it."

GreeHee did as Boldor dictated. He sat down and concentrated on lavender. He anointed himself and began to relax.

"Good," said the unicorn. "Now I'm going to need your help. When I wake Potemkin, say nothing of what we have seen. I have a plan trust me on this. Can you do that?"

"I will remain silent. I will keep thinking about lavender. I think this magic potion is helping. I feel light and loving."

"Excellent." To Potemkin he said, "Commander, time for us to continue our journey." Using telekinesis, Boldor shook Potemkin at the shoulder.

"Oh, yes. I am ready." Potemkin, blinked, stood, stretching, "Oh, would you look at those little fairies. I hope some beedite I have children who are as wonderful as these two."

"I think you will, Potemkin," said Boldor. Then added, "Commander, it is time to anoint yourself with the Optimism oil that Eulool made for you."

"But I feel fine, Boldor. I don't need it right now."

"Please trust me on this. I'm extremely intuitive and you will need it soon, so put it on now."

"Okay, if you think it is best." The giant scratched his thick neck and reached inside his pocket for the oil.

"Yorkin, Loni, time to get going," said Boldor, throwing his thoughts at the two fairies, who rose suddenly.

"Yorkin, it would be good if you anointed yourself with your oil. Do you have it handy?" said the unicorn.

"Why, I don't feel like rushing into anything?"

"No, but that is why you should put it on now before you do."

"You're certainly cryptic, Boldor. Is there something you're going to tell us?" asked Potemkin, seeing GreeHee sitting peacefully by himself.

"Yes I have something to tell everyone. But I want to preface what I am going to say with a picture of what can happen when evil thoughts enter the Crystal Mountains."

"But I thought we were all doing fine." Loni said arms extended, shaking her blonde head, "Aren't we doing what you asked Boldor?"

"Yes, you have each been following my instructions exceptionally well.

So do not personalize what I will now tell you. Evil thoughts amplify evil and in flight it will turn inward, while on the ground in these mountains it will generate into reality. Is everyone following me?"

They all nodded.

"So if hypothetically, we were to encounter evil in these mountains, what would be the best thing for us to do?" asked the unicorn.

The Commander said, "Well, if what you say is correct, the best strategy would be to wait until the evil inside the creatures generated by the mountains manifested and destroyed them. Is that correct?"

"Exactly! It is a very simple process here in the Crystal Mountains. The magic of unicorns is the ultimate magic because we never have to lift a sword to protect ourselves. Our magic allows evil to devour itself. Do you now understand the depth of this magic?"

"Amazing!" said Yorkin. "Why don't the unicorns place it everywhere in Tamoor, then there could never be evil again!"

"Yes, that would be wonderful. Couldn't you share that magic with Father?" asked Loni.

"No, used throughout Tamoor, too many would die," said Potemkin.

"It is the magic of the pure of heart, Loni, and though most fairies are close to this, certainly more so than giants," Boldor said, while Potemkin grinned, "There are still many who have not reached this level. Tamoor is home to many levels of consciousness and it would be unfair to take that freedom of choice away. Each creature will eventually master it's mind, body, and emotions."

"That is so understanding, Boldor," smiled GreeHee, nodding.

"Yes, it makes perfect sense," said Potemkin, tapping his big knee, "But there is another reason you have told us this, isn't there Boldor?"

"Yes. Now that you understand the ramifications of the Crystal Mountains I will tell you what GreeHee and I discovered. To the south of here a Carron army appeared to be flying towards the Pool of Reckoning. It seems Tana knows where we are headed and intends to ambush us."

Loni jumped, eyes widening, "Oh! But --"

"But we will let them get there first and we will watch from a safe distance as evil devours itself! Now I believe each of you can fully understand why the Counsel of Elders have kept this secret and why you must as well."

"So we're safe. I thought so," Potemkin grinned, juggling three red and gold crystal stones.

Loni, Yorkin, and GreeHee laughed. Potemkin joined them. Their laughter amplified throughout the meadow and Boldor shook out his mane, letting out a long deep breath.

Chapter 25

EVIL

Boldor and GreeHee flew along the inside of the Crystal River gorge. The warm afternoon shot brilliant rainbows across the chasm. Florid meadows painted the variegated quartz ledges with jewel tones and flowering vines in palettes of fuchsia and gold dripped over the pastel walls. Interspersed throughout the multi-colored crystal chambers, waterfalls trickled like delicate bridal veils revealing myriad rainbow hues from the striated rock beneath, while other waterfalls plunged in fury like avalanches sharp white against the delicate crystalline tints. Water melodies echoed throughout the rainbow gorge, splashing, trickling, plummeting, and flowers waltzed in the gentle breezes.

At the base of gorge, the Crystal River cascaded over vibrant rocks, splashing against stained-glass walls; and here and there beneath powerful waterfalls, it formed deep whirlpools foaming into rainbows mists.

After a while the sun began to dim and the sky turned a soft orange. Clouds muted the horizon line softening the purple mountains into gentle shades of lavender and pale blue. The river narrowed the further they went, till it became a trickling stream, bubbling over the crystal rocks of violet and green.

"How much further is it, Boldor?" asked Potemkin "I'm starting to get anxious. I think the magic oil is wearing off. I don't feel like everything is going to be all right any more."

Boldor studied Potemkin. His face creased, lips frowned, right hand gripped the head of his sword, his left clenched in a fist. "We're almost there Potemkin but you need to think of beautiful things. You need to concentrate on love. Can you do that?" Boldor asked.

"I don't know. The only thing I can think of is that I must kill the Carrons. I keep seeing blood. My head is starting to swim."

"Okay, we'd better land now," Boldor insisted. GreeHee followed.

"Put the oil on again, Potemkin," said Boldor, "before you burst."

"I really don't feel like it and I don't know if I can. I'm getting very angry and I want to…" Potemkin swung his sword in the air flashing it at some unseen assailant. "I will kill you Carron!"

"I can help you, Potemkin!" shouted Yorkin, pulling an arrow from his quill and firing at the air.

"Boldor, what should we do?" cried Loni. GreeHee stared, eyes wide, eyebrows high, mouth gaping, as Potemkin and Yorkin fought the invisible Carron army.

"I'm not sure, Loni. Potemkin and Yorkin are carrying their own remedies but we can't reason with them now. If we don't do something quickly, they may turn on each other and that could be fatal for both of them." The unicorn's forehead furrowed with thought. "Loni ask GreeHee to try knocking Potemkin into the water and then perhaps he can pin the giant down and keep him still until we can get the oil. In the meantime, I'll snatch Yorkin's quill."

"Loni flew to GreeHee and asked for his help. The dragon positioned himself behind the now raging giant. With a whisk of his tail he knocked Potemkin into the creek, throwing him totally off guard. Then GreeHee flew over the Commander and pinned him down. Potemkin screamed. GreeHee began blowing smoke at his face.

"Let me go, you overgrown bag of smoke! Let me go! I'll kill you when I get up. Make no mistake about it, you're one dead dragon!" But try as he might, Potemkin could not free himself from GreeHee's grip.

"I will save you, Potemkin!" shouted Yorkin attempting to pull an arrow from his quill. "What's going on? Where are my arrows?" He jerked around, trying to see the enemy.

"Yorkin! Yorkin, use your oil!" shouted Loni, floating above him.

"What oil? Who are you?" squinted the fairy Prince.

"Yorkin, I'm your sister Loni! Yorkin you must remember!" Yorkin pulled out his sword and began to charge toward his sister. "Surrender? I will not surrender, I'll kill you Carron!"

"Yorkin!" shouted Boldor. Boldor charged. He caught the fairy's arm with his horn and the sword fell. Loni grabbed Yorkin's wings and struggled to stay behind him as he twisted around to catch hold of her. Loni shouted, "Beauty please, make Yorkin see, I'm Loni, it is me!"

A flash of white light and clouds dropped from Yorkin's eyes. "Yorkin, the oil!" Loni said. "Use the oil Eulool gave you. Use it now!"

"Uh, the oil? The oil?" Yorkin blinked, staring.

Loni took it from his pocket. "Take a drop on your tongue and you will see clearly." He did so without a struggle.

"Can anyone help me over here before Potemkin hurts himself?" cried GreeHee still standing over the struggling giant.

Boldor had been standing on Yorkin's sword waiting for him to come to his senses. Now he went to GreeHee's aid. Using his telekinetic abilities he raised the oil out of Potemkin's pocket, opened the jar, and carefully dropped it onto the cursing giant's forehead.

"You disgusting dragon, I'll kill you as soon as I get free!" Potemkin shouted, arms flailing.

"Give him a few more moments, GreeHee, and he should come to his senses," said Boldor as Loni caught the bottle of oil and recapped it.

In a few tithes they were sitting by the stream. "Now I understand what you meant Boldor." Potemkin frowned, kicking a small rock. "All I could see was blood and I could easily have killed everyone I love. I am sorry."

Boldor telekinetically squeezed Potemkin's shoulders, "Well, we're almost to the Pool of Reckoning and we might as well wait a bit. I'm not sure I want to see the blood and destruction that is taking place there now. What happened here, to us is minor compared to a whole Carron army."

Yorkin stood, pointed to the mountains, "I think these mountains are better than any army could ever be. I wish we could lure Tana here. That would take care of everything wouldn't it Boldor?"

"Interesting thought, Yorkin," Boldor's brow furrowed, upper lip pulled in, "I am not totally sure of that. She is much more intelligent than anyone realizes. But she is filled with anger. At any rate she has probably figured out our secret by now since she follows the Carrons with her inner sight!"

"Why does Tana want Tamoor?" asked Loni. "Why is she so angry?"

"Yes, why does she want to hurt everyone?" added GreeHee.

"Why is she so evil?" asked Yorkin.

"All very good questions," said Boldor. "But before you can know that you must answer another question. Is evil genetic or a learned attitude?"

"I don't know?" said Loni.

"I think it's due to a life of difficulties – a loveless life," said Yorkin.

"No, I disagree." Potemkin said shaking his dark wavy head. "Evil simply is! There has always been evil in Tamoor and so perhaps it is genetic. After all," he turned to GreeHee, "present company aside, dragons have always been evil. It is inherent in their genetic makeup. Almost all Carrons I have known, with the exception of Doctor Paychente, are evil. So it must be in their genetic makeup. I think some species are simply the embodiment of evil. And Tana is a combination of three very evil species."

"And you, GreeHee? What do you think?" asked the unicorn.

"This is a very complex question for me. I have never thought of my mother or father as evil. I always wanted to please my father and make him proud of me. I guess to do that I would have had to do some evil things, but I simply didn't have the heart to do them." GreeHee hesitated, his hand held motionless in front of him. Then he continued, "When I stayed with the Carrons, I didn't think of them as evil. I simply didn't want to go to war for them and start killing anyone. They took care of me. Doctor Paychente told me how he grew up an outcast of his species because he, like me, did not have the heart to kill anyone. So because my father and most Carrons want to kill, you think that makes them evil? I guess what I am asking is, what is evil?" GreeHee turned his gaze to Boldor.

"Exactly!" the unicorn exclaimed, throwing his mane. "First we must define evil, then we can decide how it fits and how to handle it. Does everyone agree that evil is the opposite of good?"

Everyone nodded.

"Then perhaps we should first define good," said Boldor.

"That's easy," said Loni. "Good is when we are filled with love and we do things to keep everyone happy."

"Yes, that sounds like good to me," said Yorkin, rubbing his slim chin.

"So then, good is a feeling of love paired with an act of love, is that what you mean?" asked the unicorn.

"Feeling and action resulting in a happy response. Yes, I agree with that," said Potemkin.

"But we missed something, it begins with thought then feeling then action. Doesn't everyone agree?" said Yorkin.

"Yes," they responded.

Boldor paced, brow furrowed, "All right then, if good is the thoughts, words, and actions designed to bring happiness, then evil, it's opposite, would be the thoughts, words, and actions designed to bring sadness or pain. Does everyone agree with that?"

They agreed.

"So that proves that it must be the result of a loveless life or why else would anyone want to inflict pain on another?" said Yorkin.

Boldor nodded, "I believe you're both right. Evil can be a learned attitude as a result of a loveless life. The individual never experiencing love may only know how to give back what it has received – pain. On the other side, there are species that for generation after generation have only experienced a loveless life and therefore may appear to be, or may actually become genetically evil."

"But if those statements are true how can we explain GreeHee or Doctor Paychente?" asked Loni.

"An excellent question," said Boldor. Then he turned to Potemkin and added, "Based on our knowledge that dragons and Carrons have always been evil, and that GreeHee and Doctor Paychente are the only two exceptions in thousands of linglorns, then we cannot say they are genetic throwbacks and we cannot say they have a learned attitude either, so that puts us back at square one. How does one become evil?" The unicorn hesitated, his companions stared blankly at him.

"The answer to this question is hidden in the very beginning of Tamoor. When Tamoor was first created, there was only sun time. There were no moons, no stars, no darkness, and no death. There was no pain, no sorrow, no needs. Each creature that graced the planet was a unique creation of Creator. Each had no flaws and no desires. Each felt the continual love of Creator. So there was bliss throughout Tamoor.

"This went on for linglorns until a time when Creator's heart grew even larger and It decided to give the ability to create to Its creations. So Creator considered how It could give all of Its creatures this new freedom to be Creators, knowing in Its great wisdom that the ability to create also held the ability to destroy. So Creator decided that the best way to do this would be to create a reflection of the universe It had created. This would be a safety net for all the beings Creator loved. Here they could create and also destroy, thus developing greater love and compassion for all creation, without ever hurting themselves.

"In this reflective Tamoor, all life would be a dream of creation and only appear real to those who centered their consciousness there. So this is where we live in the 'Reflected Universe of Tamoor.' Here we think we can die, we think there is evil, we think there is some final act but in reality, we're only living in a reflection. At the very same time we're still living with all the comfort and love of Creator while we may choose to believe we have separated from It or even been abandoned by It. Thus we, as the juvenile creators have created evil, death, and pain. So now do you understand what evil is?"

"Not really," said Loni.

"Does that mean evil is an illusion?" asked the dragon.

"Yes and no," answered the unicorn.

"Huh?" said Yorkin, blinking at Boldor.

"Yes, evil is an illusion but in this reflective world we believe it is real and therefore it has the full effect of being real, just as death has the full effect of being real and so on with all creation."

"So, you are saying Tana is only as real as we believe she is?" asked Potemkin his bushy eyebrows squeezed together with intensity.

"Yes! But you must understand that to undo the evil you must undo the belief that has been ingrained in your lineage for linglorns."

"I don't think that is possible," said Potemkin, sitting back again, crossing his huge arms against his armored chest.

"So does that mean that Tana is not really evil?" asked Yorkin, forehead furrowed, elbows on knees, hands at his temples.

"Yes! Exactly! <u>Now</u> you're getting it!"

"But she looks hideous and she murders innocents." Potemkin stood, face contorted, hands in the air, "I cannot believe she is anything but evil. If she were not evil, why would we bother to be on this journey and why would we be at war at all."

"Because she does not know she is not evil," said the unicorn gently.

"Are you saying it's our job to make Tana understand this?" asked Loni.

"Yes and no. It is our job to offer the truth but we must remain indifferent to her choice. We must join with one vision and see Tana exactly as Creator sees her – with love!"

"I can't do that!" Potemkin, shook his head, folded his arms against his armor and sat down.

"That is one incredible challenge," said Yorkin tapping his nose.

"I am not certain I can do it either, Boldor," said Loni.

"I can do it!" shouted GreeHee. "I can do it!"

Fairies and giant looked at him mouths gapping.

"Yes, GreeHee," said Boldor. "That is why you are the star of this journey. You are the only one in Tamoor who can look upon Tana with compassion. She is composed of a part of you!"

Chapter 26

THE POOL OF RECKONING

As the group flew into the highest elevations of the Crystal Mountains, the setting sun embraced the bluffs in red and orange casting long shadows like traveling giants over the ridges and ledges of the crystalline walls. The last vestiges of the Crystal River sparkled and disappeared into the rocks and the fivesome crossed over a translucent pass of striated smoky quartz entering the sanctuary surrounding the pool of reckoning.

GreeHee, flying ahead of Boldor pointed, "Wow, look at those peaks!" to four colossal mountaintops glowing in waves of pale-blue, indigo, and violet, cornered to the four directions.

"Those are the four protectors of the Pool of Reckoning. They appear to be mountain peaks but they're really ancient guardians," stated the unicorn.

"Do you mean they could come to life?" asked Potemkin.

"Oh yes, if someone threatened the Guardian at the Pool and attempted to enter the Crystal Forest. Yes, then they would come alive."

"Look at the Pool of Reckoning," said Loni, pointing to the keyhole shaped pool in the center of the valley below. It shimmered like an amethyst embraced by a wall of vibrating emerald crystals. "It looks like a doorway to another world."

"Oh, my ancients!" Potemkin pointed, "There is blood everywhere!"

Bodies of Carrons were strewn across the rocks like bloody feathered mats. The sharp light of sunset pierced the crystal peaks with the glare of blood-spattered iron. "This is too hideous to look upon," said GreeHee. "It makes the attack at the Crystal River look like child's-play."

"It looks as though the insides of the bodies have been removed and the outsides are cut and scattered," said Yorkin, shaking his head, hand covering his gaping mouth.

"Slow down, GreeHee," Boldor said. "Let's be sure no one is still alive." The unicorn took the lead and GreeHee searched with his keen sight.

"There! By that big purple boulder. I see movement!" said the dragon.

"Yes I see it too!" exclaimed Yorkin.

"Oh no, turn back or land now!" screamed Loni.

"What?" asked Boldor craning his neck to see Loni.

"It's...it's getting bigger," said Potemkin. The black mass moved.

"Land now or turn back! It's coming! It's evil and it's coming!" Loni shrieked, staring at her enchantment band.

GreeHee began, "What should we do, Boldor? What..." A dark cloud rose from the boulder into the sky in front of them.

"You will fall to your knees before me! That's what you should do, dragon!" Tana demanded, her troll face dripping with blood.

"Aaagh!" shouted Potemkin, flashing his sword in the air.

"Love!" commanded the calm voice of the unicorn and a wave of white light embraced the small party.

"Oh," said Potemkin, putting down his sword.

"You see what I have in my hand, you stupid scourges!" shouted Tana holding out her hand.

"They look like us?" said Yorkin in a weak voice.

"They are you! And I'm going to eat each one of you. Devour you whole." She placed what appeared to be Yorkin in her mouth. She began to chew and blood spilled from her lips.

Yorkin stared, mouth open, his body quaked but he said nothing.

"I can't watch," Loni covered her eyes.

"Put your oil on now, Loni," whispered Yorkin.

"Love!" repeated the unicorn keeping the white light around the group.

"NO!" shouted Potemkin as Tana picked him out of her hand, laughing. She held him by one foot, dangling him in the air. "Big strong giant, you're but a morsel to me." Tana placed him between her teeth, concentrating on Potemkin. He screamed as she crushed him.

"Potemkin, it's only a ploy to get you angry," whispered GreeHee. "Feel the energy Boldor has around us. It's real."

"Ah. You are right GreeHee," Potemkin said, breathing deeply.

"Aaargh!" Tana shouted. Her eyes turned blood red and she closed her right hand with Boldor, GreeHee, and Loni screaming inside it. "I will crush you!" Tana said, tightening a fist over them. "Like this!" The sound of screams and breaking bones filled the air. Then silence as blood oozed through her fingers.

"Your blood will run in the valleys with all of your kind! Why even now, giant," Tana said, drilling Potemkin with her scarlet eyes, "Your king suffers a great blow and shall soon lose his kingdom to me!" Her chilling laughter echoed through the mountains. She faded before them. As the cloud dissipated, a body fell to the ground.

"General Maltor," said GreeHee. The group stared at him. "He was the Commander of the Carron Army."

Potemkin surveyed the carnage, "It looks like the whole army has been destroyed. There are hundreds of bodies." Potemkin's face tightened, frowning, he asked, "What did Tana mean, Boldor? Is my king in danger? Will Narsor be lost to Tana?"

"Potemkin, please don't let Tana's lies draw you in. She paints vivid pictures but they're only pictures. If we believe her pictures we will not complete our mission and then the pictures will become reality. Let's finish this beedite in peace." They landed near the pool and Boldor turned to the group. "You fulfilled my expectations. This encounter with Tana has served to make you stronger. We will win this battle if you can continue to trust your own hearts."

"Welcome!" a voice echoed like the wind in a canyon. The being sparkled like a million droplets of water. "I am the Guardian of the Pool of Reckoning. This is the entrance to the Crystal Forest and each of you may pass."

"Thank you," the weary group replied almost in unison.

"Please know that in this pool you will see whatever you desire. So make you minds clear and focus on your happiest moments or, if you dare, your deepest question. It is up to you. The experience can be filled with delight or steeped in torment. For here you will reckon with parts of yourself you may not understand."

"Guardian, could we have a moment to consider what you have said?" asked Yorkin, arms extended.

"By all means. Boldor can help you make wise choices," the Guardian said. Then he disappeared.

"Let's sit for a moment. Take a deep breath and rebalance," said Boldor.

They sat atop the glowing emerald crystals edging the pool. GreeHee faced them with Boldor to his right.

"Is this pool really water?" asked Loni, looking into it.

"No," replied Boldor.

"No?" asked Potemkin.

"No, it appears to be water and contains all the energies that water represents but it is vibrating energy."

"You're tired aren't you Boldor?" asked Yorkin.

"Yes."

"Do you think it would be best to wait until we have rested before entering the pool?" asked the Commander.

"No. We'll be nourished and energized once we enter the Forest. I don't have the strength to wait here till dawn," Boldor replied.

"I don't want to sleep here with so much death nearby," said Loni looking toward the war zone beyond.

"Yes, you're right. But I'm afraid to enter the pool," Potemkin said.

"Me too," said GreeHee.

"Why are you afraid, GreeHee?" asked Loni.

"I don't have a lot of happy memories and I don't think I want to see who I really am. I don't know but that's what I think."

Loni touched his shoulder, "We're all here with you. Don't worry, think of love like we did in the air in front of Tana. That felt good didn't it?"

"Yes, but I think something else will come up that I don't want to see."

"Okay," Boldor said taking charge of the situation, "Now fears are rising in each of you and if we sit here much longer none of you will enter the pool. I'll surround you once more with the light and you will feel love." The unicorn closed his eyes for a moment. "We will enter together. Gather round and face the pool. On the count of three, everyone will jump in."

The Guardian appeared above the group. "I will count for you, Boldor," said the echoing sparkling entity. "One, two, three!"

Together they plunged into the pool.

"You disgust me! You disgrace your ancestors," roared Tereem.

"But father, I will make you proud," replied GreeHee.

"Never. You're no son of mine. I should have killed you when you were born. An old dragon warned me that a birth so long in coming was a bad omen, but I called her a fool. I could not believe a son of mine and Reatora could be anything less then the most terrible of dragons. But look at you, consorting with fairies and unicorns. You've made me the laughing stock of Tamoor!" Tereem turned his back to the young dragon and then disappeared.

Reatora appeared, huge purple dragon, fire flashing, tail whipping, eyes brimming with tears, "If I had killed that unicorn none of this would be happening, so in some ways, son, I blame myself! I failed you. I'm sorry."

"Mother! Oh Mother, how I have longed to see you," said GreeHee.

"Son, the best you could do is to go home and hide. Do not go any further. You're disgracing your father, all your ancestors, and me. Go home and stay there. If you cannot be the proud dragon you were born to be, you should hide yourself, so you do not dishonor us any further."

"But, Mother, I must be true to my heart, mustn't I?"

"What heart? You don't <u>need</u> a heart. You're a dragon! Your fire is your heart and it's meant to destroy. Dragons are not bound by morals. We take whatever we want. We're the most powerful species in all Tamoor. GreeHee, the destiny of all dragons lies in your future. There are very few young dragons and if you become this pansy 'heart-following' creature, you deny the power of dragons. It will be the beginning of the end for our kind. Please son, go home and reconsider who you are." Reatora faded but her pleading golden eyes and outstretched purple-green hands would never leave GreeHee's mind.

"Your world is changing, my little one, and you are on the verge of discovering who you are!" said Draydel appearing through the mists of dancing colors.

Loni asked, "Draydel will we complete this journey? How can we touch Tana's heart? Is she as cold and untouchable as she appears? I'm afraid of her when I see her. She is truly hideous. I --"

"Now, now child, you have many questions and some cannot be answered at this time. Let me see," said the wizard, running his hand through his dark gold beard. "what can I tell you? Tana's heart, hmm, that is a most interesting question? Love can pierce any veil, yet time is part of the formula necessary to do so and I do not believe you have enough time to accomplish this. Her heart is cold beyond your imagination but I will not say it is impossible. As for your fear of her, this is unnecessary. Her size and her looks shake you, but she is no match for your love. Stay centered in your power and Tana cannot touch you. You're safe."

"What about the mission, Draydel? Will we win this war?"

Draydel's white robes reflected the colors around him, his golden hair and beard danced, his pale blue eyes held Loni's. "That is yet to be determined. I will say it looks good but time is running out. Narsor is about to fall to the trolls and even Oberlon will be threatened if you do not move quickly. I don't want to worry you, Loni, yet you must keep your hearts together to win this war. I'm with you as are all your ancestors."

Draydel faded and Loni blinked, fingers to her lips.

"How can we use Tana's pictures against her?" asked Yorkin.

"You're a fast study, Prince Yorkin, your father will be proud!" said Eulool, dark eyes flashing, blue velvet robes dancing in the swirling vortex. "You can send the pictures back to Tana by making your mind a mirror and holding it up to her."

"But what if I want to send her a picture? Can I do this?" asked Yorkin.

Eulool's eyes twinkled, finger wagged, "Yes you can, but you must be completely focused on the image and know it is real to the depths of your being. It's a dangerous act of magic for the neophyte because without practice you can fall into the picture and lose yourself."

"But I can do this, correct?"

"Yes, but as I said you must be careful."

Yorkin, eyebrows knitted, extended his hand, "Can you tell me what picture could destroy Tana?"

"That is a very complicated question and I'm not positive that I can answer it so take what I say with a grain of salt. Since Tana is composed of troll, dragon, and bird-beast, her greatest fear is the loss of control. Projecting a picture of no strength, no fire, and no ability to fly would be debilitating to her. How you would do this will be your own creation based on your knowledge, not mine. Be careful, fairy prince, this is a very dangerous choice." Eulool, finger wagging, disappeared into the ethers.

"How can I be wise?" questioned Potemkin.

"By asking before acting," Queen Beatrea said, her beautiful oval face gleaming, long auburn hair flowing.

"But how can I do this when there is no time to ask before acting?"

"Ah, but there is always time. You have allowed the concept of time to cloud your power. Time is within your control. You must know this. Without understanding this fact you cannot acquire the wisdom you seek and death may become part of this journey."

Potemkin scratched his strong chin, eyebrows angled, "My Queen, can you give me some other clue in this matter of time? I have been taught to react to danger with immediate action. It's the way of the warrior. How can I change this?"

"I will give you this secret and you must apply it. I cannot do it for you and I cannot give you a token to carry or a magic potion like Eulool has given to you. The secret is this. There is no time! It is an illusion. You can expand or collapse it to suit your needs. Use this information wisely. I will help you in any way I can. Be blessed, Potemkin." In a shimmer of rainbow colors the queen disappeared.

Boldor, question free and filled with love, simply passed through the Pool of Reckoning, yet the five arrived in the Crystal Forest at exactly the same moment.

Chapter 27

BOLDOR

Tinkling, clinking, dinging, crunching, sounded, but the light was so bright Boldor alone could see.

After a few elides Loni's eyes adjusted. "Wow, that was amazing. I spoke with Draydel and… oh, look at this place…" Loni's mouth fell open. A vast vibrant forest of immeasurable crystal trees shimmered in multicolored crystalline leaves, tinkling like goblets in the sweet fragrant breeze. Trees, etched and knurled of citrine, ametrine, striated pink and green tourmaline, stretched high into a canopy of rainbow gemstone leaves -- brilliant emerald, deep purple amethyst, indigo sapphires, rich rubies, spectacular golden topaz and dazzling diamonds. Light poured through from an unseen sky, sending rainbow sprites dancing. Gemstone leaves blanketed the smoky quartz ground, crunching and crackling underfoot. Beautiful crystal boulders jutted out of the rocks lining a path to a clearing in the distance. Despite the crystalline nature stones, they felt soft, embracing, soothing, and delightful.

"I can't see a thing," said Potemkin.

"Give your eyes a moment to adapt," Boldor said.

"Holy Mother of Tamoor is this the Crystal Forest?" Potemkin asked.

"Yes, and in a little while you'll be able to see more than the rainbows and the crystal trees." Boldor said his voice increasing in strength with each word. "Once your eyes become accustomed, you'll see my family of unicorns. They're everywhere here and they're waiting to meet each of you."

"Oh, this is amazing!" said Yorkin. "I had no idea that the Crystal Forest was really made of crystal."

"Yes, so it appears, but in reality it is made of light, lots of swirling rainbows of light. Exactly as we unicorns are made of light."

"It's more beautiful than I could have imagined," GreeHee said, making music by running his hand through the leaves of a citrine tree.

"Oh, a baby unicorn!" Loni jumped, a tiny unicorn nuzzled her wing.

In a tithe, baby unicorns surrounded the five, silky rainbow tails and manes, tiny pastel candy-cane horns, and brilliant jewel toned hooves flashed as they giggled, reared and pranced. The little ones were curious about the enormous purple and green dragon. They hopped on top of GreeHee, tickling him with their muzzles, horns, and tiny hooves. The dragon started laughing and ended up on the ground with little unicorns on top of his huge belly.

"I feel so energized here," said Potemkin to Boldor, chuckling, watching the baby unicorns frolic on the dragon. He swung his left arm around, "My arm feels like new!"

"The Crystal Forest can heal anything as long as you still have the energy and desire to make it so. This is a center for healing used by spiritual beings. You four are the only ones we've ever allowed here in physical bodies."

"Really?" Yorkin pivoted, eyes wide.

"Really. You can come in one of your light bodies, as in the dream state, but to physically be here is an honor of distinction."

After a round of playful interfacing, Boldor led the five to a serene meadow at the edge of the forest. Vibrant emerald green with intermittent patches of rainbow colored flowers, it rolled down to a deep aquamarine pool that thrashed under the thunderous cascades of a gigantic waterfall. The sounds of crashing water clamored for attention and a fine mist sprayed the five as Boldor led them across a rocky path to a rose quartz cave hidden behind the falls.

"This is where you will rest until dawn breaks in Tamoor. Then we will journey to the Mystic Mountains and Wizard's Web. You will be healed of any ailment and rejuvenated in this environment. Oh, and as you may have already noticed, you will not get hungry here and there is no need to eat."

"Why is that?" asked GreeHee.

"Because you are vibrating at a level higher than the physical. There is no need for food here. Breathe deeply and the air will nourish you." Then he asked, "Are you comfortable?"

They all answered yes.

Snuggling into the soft moss-like rock, the melody of the falls lulled them to sleep.

"Time to go," said Boldor, eyes bright and coat flashing like the sun.

"I would love to stay here for the rest of my life," said GreeHee, stretching. "It feels like we left Tamoor lifetimes ago."

"Yes, I feel that way too," said Loni.

"The Crystal Forest has that effect because there is total peace here."

"Why does the sun shine all the time here?" asked Yorkin.

"Because the vibrations here are too high for darkness. If you take another look, you will realize there are no shadows either. No shadows, no darkness, no pain, and no negativity of any kind. But enough about the Crystal Forest, we need to get to the Mystic Mountains, time is passing in Tamoor and it's now past dawn."

The unicorn led the group deep into the cave, the sounds of water disappeared and they entered a dark passageway. "Take a moment for your eyes to adjust." Said Boldor. "It is not really as dark as you think."

In a few elides, the group continued through the colorless cavern.

"What is this place, Boldor?" asked GreeHee. "It seems big and small all at the same time. I can't quite put my tongue on what I mean."

"Yes, I understand. This is the Tunnel of Passage. It adjusts to the size and needs of those who enter it. It has no real size. It is a vibrating space that lets you move through to any place in the worlds you wish to go. You need only direct the energy. That is why I am leading because I know how to direct the energy to the Mystic Mountains, an error in judgment could leave us at the bottom of the Azura Kah. So trust me and we'll be fine."

Potemkin swallowed hard and started whispering, his eyes closed and hands on GreeHee's tail, "I trust Boldor, I trust Boldor, I trust Boldor."

Except for the Commander's whispers, the company walked in silence. Finally, the five reached an opening of blinding light. The sweet scent of jasmine and amber filled their nostrils.

"This is wonderful!" said Yorkin inhaling deeply.

Potemkin knelt and kissed the warm ground. "Ancients, bless Tamoor!" Then he kissed Boldor's horn, "Thank you, Boldor! I'm still alive and I've crossed the Azura Kah!"

Everyone smiled.

"Okay, let's mount up," said Boldor drawing a long breath. "Loni and Yorkin ride with me. Potemkin, you fly with GreeHee." Leaping into the bright blue sky, he added, "Follow me, GreeHee."

Cool invigorating scents of orange blossom and peppermint wafted on air currents, clouds floated lazily in the bright sunshine and the majestic Mystic Mountains clustered in chains below, between them foothills ranged with colorful trees of all sizes stretching to touch the blue, violet, green and coral meadows of the gentle rolling valley floor. At the very center flowed the swirling, dreamy Mystic River ebbing over colorful smooth psilomene rocks and quartz outcroppings.

Potemkin pointed to the massive river placidly lapping against the northwest side of the Mystic chain, "The Azura Kah is much wider than I thought and it's a beautiful turquoise precisely as you said it would be,

Yorkin."

"Gorgeous isn't it?" Yorkin said.

"We will land on that ridge, GreeHee." Said Boldor pointing with his nose to a wide flat green ledge at the top of the gigantic mountain to their right. "Now I'll tell you where we're going and a little of what to expect. Look to the south, does everyone see the gold tipped-mountain?" he asked.

"That one," Loni pointed, "that's shining brighter than all the rest?"

"Yes! Does everyone see it?" Boldor repeated.

"Yes!"

"That's known as 'The Point of Gold.' It sits above the tunnels of Wizards' Web. It's called Wizards' Web because it is a labyrinth designed to keep anyone out who does not belong. It is said to have the final number of treacherous traps!"

"You mean ninety-nine?" asked Yorkin his aquamarine eyes widened

"Yes!"

Potemkin frowned, "Why, we'll spend the rest of our lives trying to get through that many traps. How are we to accomplish this mission? Had I known this beforehand I would have never come! What--"

"Please, Potemkin," Boldor said shaking his head, "have a little faith in the Ancients and me! Now would be a good time for you to use the oil Eulool gave you. He definitely pegged you right!" Boldor's shrill whinny took the company by surprise.

Without hesitation, Potemkin put on the oil.

"Now I will continue," Boldor said. "The secret to the labyrinth is to stay centered. We must unify with the power of love and keep each other centered. So as soon as anyone needs their oil, we'll stop and wait for them to put it on. We need to consider each other as we move just as we might consider the placement of one of our own limbs." The unicorn took a breath and surveyed the group's response to his words. "Yorkin, you have a question. Ask it."

"Well, will we," he hesitated.

Boldor cleared his throat waiting for the prince to continue.

"Will we have to go through all ninety-nine? Uh, all the traps?"

"No. Even as the firmament has loopholes so does the web. If you doubt what I say, please recall the Tunnel of Passage. That is a loophole in the firmament. Understand?"

Everyone sighed and relaxed.

"Good! Now that that is out of the way, I will continue. The traps are activated by thought, word, and action. A centered being can walk past all of them directly to the Seat of Stars. This I could do alone, but it would be without merit. We must do it, as <u>one</u>," Boldor stated, "We must enter the

Seat of Stars and convert five stars into one much the same as we will convert our individual minds into one. The power of the new star will destroy Tana and the war will end. Is this clear?"

"I guess," GreeHee said, scratching his scaly green cheek.

"I don't know but I feel we can do it!" said the now optimistic giant.

"I think we only need to trust you Boldor." Yorkin stood, arms extended, blonde hair blowing, "You took us through the Crystal Mountains and past Tana, I'm sure we can do this with your help."

"You need to understand something about me," said the unicorn. "I'm not a physical being. Because I vibrate at a higher frequency I can surround you with love and raise your vibrations but unless you work with me, I will not survive the web. I'm constantly fighting the lower vibrations here in Tamoor and I cannot be expected to carry you through the web. I will die unless you each contribute by controlling your thoughts, words, and actions. Eulool understood this and that is why he gave each of you magic oil. We must do this together. My life is in your hands. We must tether our consciousness together or we will not win and some of us may die. I am very serious." Boldor's ears flattened and his body flashed sharp tones of blue and violet.

"Can we sit and strategize the situation?" asked Potemkin.

"Right before we reach the web, we will do that. In the meantime, you may think about how to keep centered and I will give you a key technique. Think of the happiest sound you have ever heard and imitate it for a moment."

GreeHee looked at Potemkin, both clueless. But Loni sang a note that sounded like, "Ooosh, ooosh, ooosh."

"Excellent, Loni, that is the sound that balances your vibrations. What made you think of it?"

"I thought of the sound the trees make as the wind rushes through them. It feels good to me."

"Exactly!" said the unicorn. "Anyone else want to test a sound?"

"Uh, we giants have an ancient chant we use, would that sound be aligned with my vibrations?" Potemkin asked.

"How do you feel when you sing it?"

Potemkin, hand on chin, head nodding said, "In peace. It washes away all thoughts and I feel peaceful."

"Then it is the perfect sound for your vibratory rate," said Boldor. "I think you're getting the idea. We are going to make it."

"I think I know what to sing," said Yorkin, jumping up, eyebrows raised, "For the first three soars of my life, Eulool used to sound a bell in the evening. I don't recall what happened to it but I loved that sound. It went dooooou dooooou." He sang the sound until he ran out of breath.

"How do you feel when you sing that?" asked Boldor.

"In harmony with life."

"Excellent, then it sings to your vibration. And you, GreeHee, is there a sound you love?" asked Boldor telekinetically lifting the dragon's big chin.

"This is going to sound really strange but when I sleep in my cave, Tamoor sings to me. It's a very deep low resonating sound that makes me feel warm and comfortable. It sounds like, soooouhl, soooouhl."

"Yes! Yes! You each have your vibratory sounds. These will align you and carry you through any experience with balance and grace. They will keep you centered. Now it's up to you to use them. If at any time I feel we're out of alignment, I will stop and say; 'Sing' and we will come into balance again. Will you do this?" Boldor asked, his coat flashing gold and pink.

"Yes!"

"One last word of caution. When Tana appears, and she will appear, do not let surprise or fear throw you out of balance. Sing instead. Got it?"

They agreed.

Chapter 28

THE MYSTIC MOUNTAINS

Boldor led the way. GreeHee and Potemkin followed.

"Where are you going?" asked a crow appearing next to Potemkin.

"Uh, to that mountain." Potemkin pointed.

"Oh, you're headed to Wizards' Web. All five of you?" continued the shiny big-eyed black crow.

"Yes, why do you ask?" said Potemkin.

"Simply curious. We crows are a curious species you know. And besides you five are a most unusual group."

"Yes, I suppose we are," answered Potemkin.

"Why are you going there? Stories say no one ever comes back out. So why are you going there?" Crow continued.

"Well, that is not for me to say," answered Potemkin.

"I know something that might interest you and I would tell you if you would do something for me," said Crow.

"I can't imagine what you might know that would be of interest to me," said Potemkin his eyebrows knitted. "After all you don't even know me."

"I know you are a giant and I know this is a dragon," said Crow. "And I know that both giants and dragons seek treasures. Wouldn't a treasure be of interest to you?"

"Well, most beedites I guess it would be. What do you think of this crow, GreeHee?" asked Potemkin, shaking his head.

"Very odd indeed," said GreeHee. "I'm curious why Crow is offering us treasure and what he might need from us."

"Quite my question as well. So what is it, Crow? Why have you approached us with your tales of treasure."

"Well," said Crow, "My friend is stuck under a bridge and I cannot free him. Then I look up at the sky and Creator has answered my prayer. There you and this mighty dragon fly. Both of you could easily save my friend, but then I thought to myself, why would you. And I remembered the treasure I discovered soars ago. So I thought I might be able to trade with you. You help me and I will help you. Do we have a deal?"

Potemkin pointed to Boldor and the fairies, "As you can see we don't travel alone, and I would have to confer with my companions before giving you my word. So let me see what they think. Boldor!" shouted Potemkin. GreeHee flew closer to the unicorn. "Boldor!" Potemkin repeated. "I have a question. This crow has asked us for help. It seems his friend is stuck under a bridge and he would like us to help him. Could we take a few moments to do this for him?"

"How far away is your friend?" asked the unicorn.

"Not far at all," said Crow pointing to the wide valley below them. "My friend is down there. And I have promised the dragon and giant a treasure for doing this deed for me."

"We are on a mission but a few moments to free your friend should not endanger that," said Boldor. "How do you feel about it, Loni? Yorkin?"

"I'm happy to help," said Loni smiling.

"I would love to see what the valley looks like," said Yorkin. "And besides I am starting to feel hungry."

"Yorkin, you're speaking my language!" GreeHee added.

"Thank you so much," said Crow as he led the way down into the valley to one of the few bridges on the Mystic River.

The shiny bridge stood high above the river connecting two rocky mountain ledges, narrow and not very long but exquisite in detail and workmanship. The bridge had thick polished wooden planks and an intricately carved railing of walnut, overlaid with silver, gold and pierced in places with colorful glass cabochons that threw playful rainbows. At the West end of the bridge, the railing hung precariously, the walnut piers snapped at the base.

Surveying the damage, Potemkin said, "How did this happen?"

Crow said, "We were sitting under the bridge like we do every morning when we heard a terrible noise. It sounded like the roar of an angry troll, but it had an enormous tail like a dragon and as it went over us the tail lashed downward and broke the railing on the bridge. When it collapsed it swung fast and trapped Doder," said Crow. "Doder, how are you doing?'"

"I would like to be free. I'm not hurt, but trapped I am. Yes, trapped. Please free me." Doder cocked his blue-black head, peering from behind the carved wooden railing.

"Well, I think we can free you easily," said Potemkin. "GreeHee, fly closer and I'll pull the railing."

GreeHee flew under the the bridge and positioned himself so Potemkin could grip the railing. Potemkin loosened it enough for Doder to escape.

"Yes, I am free! Thanking you, I am. Thanking you!" shouted Doder, bowing profusely.

"And what is your name, Crow?" asked Potemkin.

"I am Hydous," said the first crow, bowing in mid air. "We are beholden to you and would be happy to show you the treasure."

"Excuse me, Hydous," Yorkin said, "Did you say the beast who did this damage sounded like a troll but had the tail of a dragon?"

"Yes, well kind of. I looked at it after it broke the bridge. It definitely wasn't a troll or a dragon. It was a very strange-looking creature. I have never seen any like it before," said Hydous scratching his head.

"Doesn't that sound like Tana?" Yorkin questioned his companions.

"Tana!" said both crows, their eyes bulging, staring at each other.

"Yes, that definitely sounds like Tana!" said Potemkin. GreeHee and Loni nodded.

"Why would Tana walk across a bridge when she can fly?" Yorkin asked.

"Because she knows we're here and we would see her if she flew," replied Boldor. "This means she is on her way to Wizards' Web and she must have some plan to foil us. We need to stay calm and keep a watchful eye for anything that looks the least bit suspicious."

"Loni," Yorkin said, "do continue to ask Beauty for guidance."

"Yes, especially if we see something unusual," Potemkin added.

"Okay." Loni replied checking her enchantment band. .

"So is Tana after the five of you?" asked Hydous.

"Hum, yes," answered Potemkin.

"Then you are very fortunate to still be alive. We have never heard of anyone surviving the pursuit of Tana. Have we, Doder?" said Hydous.

"Nope, nope we haven't heard of anyone living to tell the tale. Definitely not. Are you magicians?" asked Doder.

"No," Potemkin said, frowning and shaking his head.

"We need to get going," Boldor pointed his nose toward The Point of Gold. "We have stood still long enough. We now know the road Tana has taken, let us fly past her and get to the web before she arrives there."

"But don't you want to see the treasure?" asked Hydous.

"We may have no need for it, if we don't get through the web. However if we do, where can we find you to retrieve this bounty?" asked Potemkin.

"We are here at this bridge every sun rise. You can always find us here."

"Then let it be so! We'll meet you here in another beedite," said Potemkin raising his right hand in the salute of giants.

"Do you mind if we fly with you until you get to the web?" asked Hydous.

"We know interesting shortcuts and could be of assistance if you needed someone small to do something? We would enjoy the adventure and would feel we are of some service for the help you have given us."

"Come along, Crows. Let's get going," replied the unicorn.

Once in the air, GreeHee asked the crows, "Is there an area around here where a dragon might find something to eat?"

"Hey, I heard that," said Yorkin, "I'm hungry too. Perhaps a grove of fruit trees?"

"Well yes, there is a place not far from here and it is on the way to the web. We can show you," Hydous said.

"Yes, yes, we can show you! I know where it is. Can I show them Hydous?" asked Doder.

"Certainly Doder, be my guest," said Hydous.

The crows led the way downward through the purple mountains along the swirling mystic river until they came to a foggy misty area where all the colors muted into blues.

"This feels eerie," said GreeHee. "I don't like it."

"I agree," said Loni. "But Beauty is silent. I guess it's okay."

"I don't like this," said Boldor. "It doesn't feel right. Ask Beauty again."

"Beauty isn't saying anything. She isn't shining at all. It's a little unusual for her when I ask but she does that sometimes. If we were in danger, she would be gleaming red. So it must be all right, Boldor?"

They continued following the crows and the fog got thicker.

"Hydous, can you see clearly?" asked Potemkin.

"Oh yes, we know this place like the back of our talons," replied Hydous.

"Yes we do, yes we do!" said Doder.

"Does this place always look like this?" asked Boldor. "The sunlight has totally disappeared here."

"Oh yes, it's always like this," said Doder. "Right Hydous?"

"Yes, it's perfect for catching that meal. The treasure we promised is down here too. When we land we will be very close to it."

"Really?" said Yorkin. "Could we look at it then, Boldor?"

"If we're right there, I don't see the harm in that and then we would know where it is for later. Certainly that sounds reasonable."

"Oh, this is exciting," Yorkin smiled.

"I think it's rather creepy," said GreeHee. "How much further, Hydous?"

"About another ten elides and we'll land," Hydrous answered. "You'll love this place, GreeHee, there's lots of food and it's very easy to catch here."

"Yes, yes, it's an easy catch! We will love it. It's an easy catch!" said Doder.

"You have to forgive Doder, he is a highly excitable crow. He loves the chase. I think you understand don't you, GreeHee?"

"I guess."

"Loni, is Beauty still silent?" asked Boldor.

"Yes, but I think we should get out of here. My skin is starting to crawl. I don't like this a bit. I would rather go without food than--"

"Here we are!" Hydous said landing on a piece of driftwood.

"Where exactly are the trees?" asked Yorkin.

"The trees are over that ridge to my right, the treasure is down this path in a cave, and there are lots of wild things for GreeHee in the rocks at the foot of the mountain to my left."

"Very interesting," said Boldor. "Potemkin stick with GreeHee and I will stay with the fairies. We will meet back here in twenty elides, is that enough time for you GreeHee?"

"I think so." Replied the dragon.

"What about the treasure?" asked Yorkin.

"Let's eat first and then check the treasure," said GreeHee.

"What about you crows?" asked Potemkin. "Do you want to come with us or wait?"

"We'll go with you and GreeHee. It's so much fun to watch a dragon," said Hydous

"Yes, I like to watch the dragon. A big strong dragon," said Doder.

"Okay, we'll meet in twenty elides, whoever gets here first will wait until the other arrives." said Boldor.

They went in opposite directions through the eerie dark blue foggy mist.

Boldor trotted over the ridge.

"I guess you could call this a grove of fruit trees but what do you make of blue fruit?" asked Yorkin.

"I'm not eating it," said Loni, looking once more at Beauty. "I'm not getting off Boldor's back. I don't trust this place at all even if Beauty is silent."

"Boldor could you trot over to the right a little. I noticed something over there I want to take a closer look at," Yorkin said.

"All right, but I have to agree with Loni, I'm ready to fly out of here. I wouldn't eat anything in this grove."

"Right there!" said Yorkin pointing. "Look at that Loni, it's a tree in the shape of a hanging giant. Isn't that what we saw in Eulool's gazing ball?"

"Oh no, Yorkin, it's the 'Tree of Death!' Boldor, let's get out of here right now! We need to find the others and get away from this place."

"What are you two looking at?" asked Boldor as he continued to walk toward the tree.

"Boldor, no!" Loni shouted. "Turn around. Yorkin help me get through to him. Beauty, why are you silent?"

"Boldor your oil! Use your oil!" Yorkin shouted, leaping off the unicorn and standing in front of him, forcing him to stop. Yorkin grabbed the oil out of Boldor's pouch and poured some on his horn. "Look now Boldor and you will see 'The Tree of Death.'"

"Boldor, any closer and we'll die. Eulool warned us," Loni shouted. "Closer than twenty leets and we'll die! We must go! No! It's moving towards us!" "Boldor can you see now?" shouted Yorkin.

"I…I…Oh my, let's get out of here. That's not a tree, it's a death siren!" Boldor cried. Yorkin flew onto his back. The siren leapt toward them but Boldor flew out of its reach. "I knew this was a trap. We'd better find GreeHee and Potemkin before something else happens."

"What's happened to Beauty? I don't understand?" Loni asked, staring at her enchantment band.

"Do you know where you're going?" asked Yorkin.

"Yes. That oil has made this place crystal clear for me. Everything you're seeing is magic, it's not real. Put some of my oil on your foreheads. And Loni, try placing a drop on Beauty, I think she has some kind of cover over her. Look there, can you see GreeHee?"

"Oh this oil is amazing. The blue disappeared and the sun is back. Incredible! Yorkin grinned. "Here Loni, try this you won't believe it. Yes, I see GreeHee. Oh no, it looks like he's pinned under those rocks! Where is Potemkin? Oh, this looks bad. Boldor, why are you slowing down? Let's get in there and help GreeHee!"

"No. We need to survey this place first. It may be a trap to get us too. Tana is behind this and I need to know exactly where she is. Sing, Yorkin! Sing, Loni! Please sing your sounds and I'll look around before we dive into that crevice to help GreeHee."

"Holy Ancients! Boldor, you're right! Beauty is streaming red. We're in danger just being here!" Loni shouted.

Chapter 29

TANA

"**B**oldor, we've been looking for you," said Hydous.

"Hydous, what has happened here? How did GreeHee get pinned under those rocks, is he still alive?"

"I don't know what happened to GreeHee. He said we were annoying him and so he told us to take Potemkin to the treasure."

"Well, where is Potemkin?"

"He's in the cave and may be hurt. He fell and is stuck in a thing he called a system? I don't know what it is?" said Hydous. "I left Doder with him. We need to help him."

"Well, first let's see what we can do for GreeHee."

"Why are the fairies singing? Are they happy?"

"No, they're helping. Hydous go back to the cave and tell Potemkin we'll be there as soon as possible. In the meantime, we'll help GreeHee."

"Boldor, Beauty is no longer red. She's gleaming white again. I think the danger is over."

"Well, that is curious. Right now we need to concentrate on helping GreeHee." Boldor flew down into the crevice.

"GreeHee, are you all right?" asked Loni, hopping down next to GreeHee's smiling face.

"Thank Tamoor you're here, Loni. I think I'm fine. But I can't get all these rocks off of me. Can you help?"

"GreeHee," Boldor said, "I may be able to use my energy to move the boulders. Loni, Yorkin, I need all the support you can give because this will take a lot of energy, so please sing with all your hearts."

Loni and Yorkin stood next to the unicorn and sang.

Boldor focused on the huge rocks that covered the dragon. One by one the little ones lifted into the air and then landed on the opposite side of the crevice. Now the unicorn concentrated on the gigantic boulder that pinned the dragon. Furrows formed on Boldor's forehead, his horn turned a deep gold, but nothing moved. The fairies sang louder. Then slowly the enormous boulder lifted. It rolled back away from the dragon.

GreeHee, fists clenched, face strained, pushed the rest of the rocks off his chest. "Boldor I couldn't have done that without you. You are incredible!" The dragon shook his big scaly body and snapped his tail. "I'm one lucky dragon!" GreeHee said. "If it hadn't been for this crevice, the rocks would have crushed me. Thanks so much for freeing me. What about Potemkin? Have you seen him?"

"According to Hydous, Potemkin needs our help. I think he has fallen into a cistern. At least that is what I understood from the crow," said Boldor, "GreeHee, can you fly?"

"I think so," said the dragon, shaking out his wings and springing into the air." Rocks started crashing. Boldor and the fairies flew, dodging them. They flew toward Hydous.

"Come this way and I will show you where Potemkin is," said the crow.

"GreeHee, how are you seeing, is it still misty for you?" asked Yorkin.

"What do you mean? Isn't it misty for you?' asked the dragon.

"When we land we'll put some of Boldor's oil on your head and it will clear it up."

"Beauty is flashing red again, Boldor! I think we should stop and figure this out," said Loni.

"Can you understand what she is saying?" Boldor asked, landing.

"I think Beauty's saying there's danger in the direction we're facing. Now that we've stopped moving, she's white again."

"Point and ask her like you did in the forests of Oberlon," said Yorkin.

"Good idea." Loni pointed Beauty in each direction, asking if it was safe. "She is gleaming white until I point at the cave."

"Tana may be in the cave and that means Potemkin may be in a lot more danger then only being trapped in a cistern." Boldor's brow furrowed. "I have a plan, this is what we must do," Boldor began. "First, GreeHee needs the oil."

Yorkin took the oil from Boldor's pouch and placed a drop on GreeHee's forehead. "Now you will see through Tana's magic."

"Aren't you coming?' Hydous asked, shaking his head.

"Beauty is streaming red!" shouted Loni, holding out her hand.

"I thought so," said Boldor. "Sing! Everyone, now sing! Yorkin put a drop of oil an a piece of cloth."

"Uh, okay.' Yorkin said, eyebrows raised.

Boldor commanded, "Hydous, take us to the cave."

At the entrance of the cave, still singing, the unicorn asked, "Where exactly is Potemkin?"

"He is inside in a system. I will show you."

"No, if indeed you are our friend, you will give him this," the unicorn took the cloth from Yorkin and gave it to Hydous. "Drop this on his forehead and tell him I sent the oil for him."

"Don't you want to help him?" asked the crow, eyebrows raised, shaking his shiny black head.

"We are helping him if you do as I say. We'll wait here until you return."

Hydous left and Boldor joined the others singing his favorite sound.

"Boldor," said Loni, "Aren't we going to save Potemkin?"

"Loni what does Beauty say about this cave?"

"She gleams red."

"Then do you think it is safe for us to go?"

"No. But we have to help Potemkin, don't we?" Loni asked, shrugging her shoulders, her arms extended.

"We <u>are</u> helping him. We must surround him with love by singing loud so Potemkin can hear us. Then listen."

Voices came from the cave.

"Potemkin, this is from Boldor," said, the high-pitched Hydous.

Tana's icy voice curdled, "Release the cloth, bird or die!"

Scuffling sounds.

Potemkin's deep voice shouted, "Your cruel magic is a reflection of your insensitive mind. You coward, come down here and fight."

Tana laughed, "You think you can fight me. You are a mouse and I am an owl. I will toy with you until I choose to kill you. And, that will be sooner than you think. Here, eat a little crow you fool!" The laugh continued.

"Oh no! Hydous, are you all right? I swear I will kill you, Tana!"

Tana's laughter rose from the cave. "You're losing the battle. Even now the sun has passed noon and your king is dying. You will kill me? Ha! You can't even get past my magic! Ha ha ha. I will see you later, my little fools" Tana flashed through the entrance of the cave and disappeared.

"Boldor, Beauty is shining white." Loni said.

Potemkin stood in the entrance of the cave, holding Hydous's body.

Chapter 30

WIZARDS' WEB

GreeHee said little as they flew. He thanked the Ancients that Boldor moved those rocks. But if Tana moved boulders so easily, and killed Hydous so effortlessly, maybe she really was toying with them. What strength could he possibly have against her? Was being true to his heart, enough? GreeHee shrugged.

The Point of Gold sparkled ahead. The mountain, no longer violet, clearly covered with trees in various shades of green, splattered with blossoms of white, pink and violet. "Let's eat here Yorkin, look at all the fruit!" Loni shouted, smiling.

"Yes, can we stop for a moment, Boldor?" asked Yorkin.

"Yes, but only for a few moments. In this terrain the sunlight will disappear fast."

Boldor and GreeHee landed in the small meadow.

"What a delightful place," said Potemkin. "I will have some of these fruits too, what about you GreeHee?"

"Yes, I'm hungry and fruit will be fine at this point."

Boldor waited, watching the sun.

In fifteen elides, the group continued the descent down the mountain.

"Is that the entrance, Boldor?" GreeHee pointed to the rusted sundial centered in a wide flat opening at the bottom of the mountain. The sundial stood about five leets high on a pedestal of stone. From the north corner of the square pedestal, an indentation began in the hard white ground. It curved around and around the sundial in an ever-widening circle with the spiral ending at the center of two enormous ornate bronze doors. On the doors in bas-relief were rune-like glyphs from an ancient language.

"Yes," replied Boldor landing in front of the sundial, "this is the entrance and we will need to walk the spiral to the doorway speaking as one the ancient code."

"What is the ancient code?" asked GreeHee, landing.

"These three words," said the unicorn pointing with his horn to the hieraglyphs on the doors, "are written in the original language called 'Wizard'. The web was created as the secret meeting place for wizards nearly a hundred and seventy linglorns ago."

Potemkin scratched his chin "I don't think our history contains any written references that old?"

"I have heard references to that time from Eulool, but I don't recall seeing anything written about it," said Yorkin.

"No most information about that time has been forgotten. The Unicorn Elders have access to the records through a doorway in time and they have prepared me for this journey." Boldor's shoulders sagged, his head hung low.

"Boldor, are you all right?" asked Loni.

"I'm tired," sighed Boldor.

"Would it help if we sang?" asked GreeHee.

"Yes, yes it would. It's time for us to start singing again. Once we are inside you must remember to sing in your mind even if you're speaking out loud. This will help us stay aligned no matter what is happening. Also, this is a good time for each of us to put on our oil. We need to use all the help we have." Then he added, "Loni, this is a perfect time to speak with Draydel. Let's see if he has any more wisdom for us."

They rested on the spiral facing the doors. Loni pulled the indigo book out of a pocket. "Draydel, is there anything else we should know before entering Wizards' Web?" She opened the book and the wizard smiled at her from the first page. Then he appeared before the group, aquamarine eyes sparkling, long honey blonde hair and beard flowing over his white silk robes reflecting orange in the setting sun.

"Boldor, you have done a wonderful job getting this little group to Wizards' Web. GreeHee, I am proud of you and how you continue to grow in trust and love. Potemkin, you stood against Tana but need to remember she is wielding illusions at you, and has no power she can use against you if you stand firm in your own power and love. Do not let your emotion dictate your action. Yorkin, you need to stay centered on your mission. Don't let distractions like treasures take your attention. The web contains many distractions and, as Boldor has already stated, you must tether your minds and hearts to pass through it to the Seat of Stars. Loni, you have done well tethering to Boldor, continue to do this and your love will carry you through. Finally, you will meet Tana again and you already have the clues necessary to defeat her, use them! All Tamoor is depending on you." Draydel faded in an emerald glow.

"I thought he would give us important advice but I'm not sure he has," said Yorkin shaking his head.

"Nor I," said Potemkin his great arms crossed over his armored chest.

"He has given us each what we need. Let us take it and move forward. Remember to sing in your head," Boldor said, gazing from face to face. "The words to enter Wizards' Web are: <u>Nazitor distora majicoh</u>!"

"What does that mean?" asked Loni.

"It means, 'Walls of illusion, open!'"

Boldor instructed the group, "We must each start at the beginning point by the sundial and continue until we reach the doors. While walking, repeat the words: <u>Nazitor distora majicoh</u>. I will go first, then Loni, Yorkin, GreeHee, and Potemkin. Are you ready?" asked the unicorn.

"Could you repeat those words one more time?" asked GreeHee.

"<u>Nazitor distora majicoh</u>. I will speak them out loud as we go so you will continue to hear them."

The group repeated the words.

They walked the spiral from the sundial to the entrance doors, repeating the code like a mantra. "<u>Nazitor distora majicoh</u>." By the time Boldor reached the entrance, the sun had slipped past the mountain casting long cold shadows across the labyrinth. Loni shivered as she stopped behind Boldor in front of the doors. The doors creaked and opened to a dark cavern.

Once Potemkin entered, Boldor said, "Sing!"

"I can't see," said Yorkin as the doors closed behind them in a stony thud.

"Sing and think light, then put out your right hand and reach for your light," Boldor said.

Following Boldor's instructions, a light of some type appeared.

"Unbelievable!" shouted Potemkin as a torch appeared in his right hand.

"Yes!" GreeHee said, showing Potemkin his star. Loni held a crystal and Yorkin a wand. "Boldor, where is your light?" asked the dragon.

"At the tip of my horn." The unicorn turned to show GreeHee.

"Please, sing," said the unicorn as they came to a set of stairs that led upward to a long narrow rail-less bridge that crossed an unfathomable depth. This is the bridge of Sarran, the ancient wizard word for sorrow; it will pull the saddest memories from your heart. If you allow it, it will weigh you down so heavily, the bridge will break and we will all fall to our deaths. So sing and think the happiest thoughts you can."

"But Boldor, all of us except Potemkin can fly, why don't we fly across?" asked Yorkin, wings flapping.

"Because your natural abilities will deceive you in the web and you will find yourself at the bottom. Take my word for these things -- if I could fly across I assure you I would. The bridge is the safest way to go."

As they approached the middle of the bridge, GreeHee sighed.

"GreeHee are you all right?" asked Yorkin.

"I see my mother. I wish…" he said, sighing again, "she hadn't died."

"GreeHee, think about us. We love you!" Loni said.

"Sing louder, GreeHee. So loud that you burn everything from your mind," said Boldor.

The bridge began to crack.

"Sing!" Boldor repeated.

"What's the matter GreeHee?" taunted the voice of Tana as the group reached the middle of the bridge.

"It's an illusion!" Boldor said. "We must move faster. Keep your attention on the ledge at the other end and sing."

Tereem said, "You runtling son! You're an embarrassment to dragons, look at you with unicorns, giants and fairies. Disgusting! I will never call you my son, you're a disgrace!"

"But father, I…" GreeHee began and a tear rolled from his eye.

The bridge cracked apart in front of GreeHee's right foot. Stones crashed into the abyss. Potemkin stumbled and grabbed GreeHee's tail.

"Oh, Potemkin, are you all right?" asked the dragon.

"Please GreeHee help me, I'm afraid of falling," said the giant clutching GreeHee's tail.

"Would you feel safer on my back?" asked GreeHee stepping over the break in the bridge, his tail spanning the opening.

"Would you mind?" asked the giant.

"No, not at all," said GreeHee. "Climb up my tail and hang on to my spines. I will get you across in no time at all."

Loni, Yorkin, and Boldor kept singing. They were nearly across the bridge. GreeHee's moved faster, leaping over the wide breaks in the bridge.

A few elides later the five had crossed successfully. Yorkin took a deep breath saying, "Wow, that was close. That bridge started to come apart, look at it." He pointed.

Whole sections of the bridge were missing, cracked, shattered and broken in many places too wide for even a giant to leap across. Now only the stupendous foot of a dragon could traverse what remained of the overpass.

"Good work Potemkin!" Boldor, winked at the giant. "That is how we have to work through the web. Taking care of each other can save us from the traps. The love we have around us can protect us from harm here but we need to keep it tight. Well done, group!"

"Are you okay, GreeHee?" asked Loni.

"I was filled with sorrow when I thought of my mother, and then when my father started in on me, I wanted to break down and cry. If Potemkin hadn't needed my help I don't think I could have made it. Thank you, Potemkin, are you okay?"

"Absolutely, GreeHee, I was betting on your love and I was right. As they will write in our history books, you are the big-hearted dragon!"

Everyone smiled and Boldor led them onward up yet another staircase. "Sing," he said.

The small group sang. GreeHee felt something in the darkness pulling at him, so he concentrated on Loni's long blonde hair bouncing in the light of Yorkin's wand, and sang louder.

After a while they came to a wide ledge bordered by black water that appeared to go on forever. Driven by a cold wind, the waves lashed against the stones and every few tithes a wailing noise rose from its depths like a cry from a crypt. "What is that sound?" GreeHee asked, his spines shaking.

"I don't like this--" Loni said, rubbing her arms.

"It is the Centopod," said the unicorn.

"It is creepy," whispered Yorkin.

"What is a Centopod?" asked Potemkin, drawing his sword.

"The Centopod is a watchdog from the depths of the Azura Kah. It breeds on fear. The Centopod can hear fear in your voice, smell it on your breath, or feel it through your energy. If it senses this in any of us, one of its hundred tentacles will find us and take us to the bottom of the sea," the unicorn spoke barely loud enough to be heard above the wind.

"Can we fly here?" asked GreeHee.

"No, unfortunately," replied the unicorn. "But we must cross this sea and the less noise we make the better, so we will have to sing silently. But first I must call the night boats. The words are somewhere on the wall. Throw your lights toward it." Boldor turned to the wall behind him.

Not seeing anything on the cold, damp stones, Yorkin and Potemkin methodically touching the granite for clues.

"Here!" said Yorkin, "There is something here."

Everyone moved in closer.

"Yes, that's it," said Boldor. "'<u>Zedor tee et quay</u>', that means 'Boat come hither to me.' Those must be the call words. Everyone stand close to me while I say them."

"Zedor tee et quay!" commanded the unicorn in a confident voice that meshed with the wind.

As Loni sucked in a breath to speak, Boldor commanded telepathically, "Be silent and wait!"

After a few tithes a large boat appeared, Loni and Yorkin stared at each other, a boat large enough to fit a dragon. GreeHee grinned.

Boldor signaled with his horn, "GreeHee, you will get into the boat first. Stay balanced in the center, close your eyes and remember to sing in your head. No matter what you hear," he continued eyeing fairies and giant, "you must keep singing. You will know when the boat docks."

"Yes," said the dragon while the others nodded. GreeHee carefully stepped into the boat and sat down in the center. The boat had no oars and no one to steer it. Fascinated by its construction, GreeHee wondered how the boat answered the call and how it would know where to take them. It's magic of course. GreeHee closed his eyes and started to sing in his head, "Soooouhl, soooouhl, soooouhl..."

The others carefully positioned themselves around the dragon.

The boat began to move. The wailing of the Centopod grew louder, it pierced Potemkin's thoughts and he could not keep his eyes shut. He stared into the darkness.

After a few elides the shrill sound intensified. Yorkin's eyes flashed. Potemkin reached out to him, wanting to speak, then pulled back. Yorkin nodded.

The little lights held by the group lit the boat exposing the rune carvings along the inside of the hull. What do they mean? The more Potemkin looked at them the more they looked like winged beasts and snakes. The wailing Centopod, the waters lapping against the boat, rocking it back and forth, back and forth, wood creaking, Potemkin mesmerized, watched the glyphs begin to crawl. He readied his sword for a strike.

The snakes spread. Yorkin grasped his sword.

Eyes still closed, GreeHee, Loni and Boldor continued singing.

The snakes wriggled toward GreeHee's feet. Still optimistic, Potemkin struck at the snakes cutting them in two. Instead of dying, the snakes multiplied. Yorkin and Potemkin, mouths gapping, eyebrows raised, stared at each other.

Yorkin struck with his sword. The snakes continued to proliferate.

"Boldor," Potemkin whispered, "if one were to see snakes in this place would they be real?"

Boldor opened his eyes. "You have made them real," he said in a calm voice. Before he could continue, screeching winged beasts filled the air above them. "You have brought these to life as well, if you become frightened of them, you will wake the Centopod and we will all die."

"What should we do?" begged Yorkin, his eyes wide with terror.

"Send them love, close your eyes, and sing. That is all any of us can do. They will only multiply if you attempt to kill them because anger betrays power."

By now the snakes were crawling on GreeHee's tail and on Potemkin's feet. "Love them and sing or we are doomed." The unicorn closed his eyes and began to sing once more.

Yorkin took deep breaths, closed his eyes. Snakes wriggled up his legs. "Dear Draydel," he whispered. "Please help me. Draydel, please help me. Stand by me and guard me from these beasts."

Potemkin squeezed his eyes shut and chanted, oool…aaamm, oool…aaamm. But he still felt the snakes. Slithering up his legs, on his knees. What if they reach my waist? My neck? My face? Potemkin's blood ran cold. Blessed Ancients, help me, he prayed. As he pleaded, the boat pitched and rolled. A winged beast screeched past his face! Something touched his back! He pivoted, swinging his sword. A huge black tentacle flashed out of the water. Fear shot through him. He must scream.

"Hush!" a voice whispered in his ear and a smooth hand covered his gaping mouth. "Relax, you are perfectly safe. I am here. Together we will sing the song of giants until we reach the shore. Oool…aaamm." As Potemkin closed his eyes, he saw Queen Beetrea next to him singing and smiling.

At last the boat docked and the five climbed onto a strange blue ledge. "It is a miracle we made it to this point," said Potemkin, kneeling on the lapis blue stone. He bowed his head, "Thank you Queen Beetrea! Thank you!"

"Queen Beetrea helped you Potemkin?" asked Yorkin.

"Yes and you?" said Potemkin.

"Draydel came to my aid."

"Thank the ancients that GreeHee and Loni kept their concentration," said Boldor looking at the giant and fairy prince.

"Well, I almost lost it when Potemkin started playing with my tail. How could you tickle me like that?" asked the dragon.

"Tickle you? Did you hear that, Yorkin? GreeHee thinks I was tickling him, can you believe that?" Potemkin laughed.

"Oh, you were too tickling me," said GreeHee, grinning.

"Blessed Tamoor, that you thought so. You're such a fine dragon, GreeHee. Maybe when we get home I will tell you what really happened in the boat," Potemkin said laughing, and winking at Yorkin.

Chapter 31

MORE TRAPS

"Come now," said Boldor, "we must continue up these stairs to the next test. It's the Caverns of Ice. Here again we will be challenged to stay balanced or become frozen in place, still conscious, and forced to stand and watch for linglorns. You will see many such beings here. Beware not to touch anything you see because the ice will trigger feelings and you will follow the same path of those who you see imprisoned there."

"Could we rest before this next test, Boldor?" asked Loni. "I'm tired."

"Loni, it's not wise to linger anywhere in the web. We must keep moving. Would it help if you rode on my back for a while?" asked the unicorn.

"Yes, if you wouldn't mind. I'm so tired."

"All right then."

Where the Sea of Centopod was dark and filled with noise, the Ice Caverns were bright and still. Here the silence numbed one's sense of reality. The ceiling was high and stalactites dropped down like swords while the stalagmites rose like angry warriors out of the ground.

The lights carried by the five disappeared.

"Hey where did my wand go?" asked Yorkin.

"You won't need it any longer," said Boldor.

"But I really liked mine," said GreeHee.

"Sorry, but that is the last you will 'see' of it," Boldor, chuckled.

"Holy Tamoor, there are creatures in the ice!" exclaimed Loni.

At every turn, giants, dwarfs, ogres, trolls, and carrons stood frozen in blocks of ice. They shouted, screamed, cried. Their eyes followed the companions' every move.

"This is by far the eeriest place we have been yet," said Yorkin shivering.

"I could set these creatures free with a little fire. Boldor can I do this?" asked GreeHee.

"Absolutely not!" exclaimed the unicorn. "Freeing these beings will put us in danger beyond anything you could imagine."

"Boldor, I can't stand to look at this. It's too painful," said Loni burying her face in his mane.

"Loni, put on your oil. Send love to all the beings you see and we'll pass through this trap easily," said the unicorn.

"Oh no, there is Goran. I can't believe it! All these soars my father wondered what had happened to him!" said Potemkin, running toward a block of ice that held a giant. "I must free him, he is my uncle!" Potemkin unsheathed his sword.

Boldor jumped between Potemkin and his frozen uncle. "No! Potemkin, please put your sword away. If you free Goran, you will free the Giant Darkors and we will each be devoured, including your uncle."

"What? Giant Darkors? You mean the three mythical birds with ten leet beaks and sixty leet wingspans from our nursery rhymes? But they're not real, are they?" Potemkin asked, eyes widened, shifting his sword to his side.

"Yes! They are part of the magic of the Ice Caverns. We must not call them, even GreeHee would be an easy catch for them."

"I cannot look on this," Potemkin said, shaking his head. "I cannot leave my uncle here. Not like this. What will I tell my father? How can I face my kin?" He raised his hand in the salute of giants. Goran did the same. Tears welled in Potemkin's eyes and he leaned closer to the ice, moving his hand closer to Goran's. "Uncle, I--"

"Stop!" Yorkin, flew to catch Potemkin's hand. Startled Potemkin fell back. "Potemkin, if you touch the ice, you will join Goran!"

"Oh, I forgot," said the giant, wiping his cheek.

"Look," said Yorkin, "when we return home, we'll ask Eulool how to free Goran and we'll come back and get him. But if we do not finish our journey, all Tamoor will be lost to Tana and it will not matter if Goran is free."

"Yes, you're right," Potemkin frowned, his eyes still moist. To Goran, he added, "I promise on my mother's grave, I will return to free you Goran. I will return."

Goran nodded.

"Please sing in your minds and let us get through this cold place. The feelings of desperation are so strong here that I am getting weary. Think loving thoughts and sing," the unicorn said.

"Boldor, I can carry you, if you like," GreeHee offered, leveling his great emerald eyes to the unicorn's.

"No, I can make it, GreeHee, as long as we just stay close together and stop looking at the creatures here. Just remember they have each created their own fate and are responsible for it. It's not our responsibility to free them, even if we know them. We must go on to the Seat of Stars, that is our responsibility."

"Yes," said Loni rubbing her arms, teeth chattering. "We can do it, Boldor."

"Yes," said the rest of the companions.

GreeHee squeezed Potemkin's shoulder as The Commander looked back at his uncle.

After a while the air warmed and the ground changed from blue to reddish brown. Yorkin looked up saying, "Boldor, where are we now?"

"We're entering '"The Bode of Satiety', if we make it through, we will have renewed energy and should feel strong enough to complete the web."

Boldor came to a rushing stream and stopped. He turned to the group. "This is one of the hardest of all the tests of Wizards' Web. I cannot tell you what you will see here or who you may meet. But I will tell you this, not a single one of us will want to leave this place. All that you could ever want is here for you. You will face your greatest desires and they will seem real. You will feel totally content here and only if we concentrate together on our mission will we pass this place. It is very easy to forget everything here, especially anything that is a test. We must sing and ignore the offers we will receive or we'll all be lost."

"But this place sounds wonderful," said Loni.

"Yes, it does, but it is not what it seems, it is an eternity of comfort without challenge or growth, it is an illusion. It is much like sleeping forever and of course it will keep us from achieving our mission." Boldor gauged his companions. Their faces lit with smiles, eyes sparkled. They stared beyond the unicorn across the stream to the group of fairies, giants and dragons offering food and beautiful trinkets.

"Listen to me," Boldor said, rearing, jewel tones flashing across his coat, "I need your attention."

"Uh, Boldor did you say something?" said Loni, still staring.

"Yes, hear me now, each of you, turn around!" the unicorn shouted.

Slowly Loni turned about.

"GreeHee, turn around!" Boldor flew around the head of the dragon.

"Uh yes, yes Boldor," said the dragon in a stupor.

"Yorkin, Potemkin, turn around!" Boldor shook the pair.

"I don't want to," said Potemkin still staring.

"Nor I," said Yorkin.

"GreeHee, Loni, are you feeling clear?" asked the unicorn.

"Yes, I felt like I'd eaten Elysianberries," said GreeHee, shaking his head.

"Me, too," said Loni flapping her wings and taking deep breathes.

"We need to turn Yorkin and Potemkin around."

"No problem," said GreeHee, stretching, "I can do that."

"Wait," Boldor said touching GreeHee's arm, "look at the ground as you turn. Don't look across the creek."

GreeHee and Loni both did what Boldor said. "Now, GreeHee take Potemkin by the shoulders and turn him towards you."

"No!" shouted Potemkin, arms flailing. "Leave me alone!" GreeHee forced the Commander around holding him in an iron grip so he could not pull his sword. "Let me go, I want to see my mother. Let me go!" the giant shouted.

"Loni, try to move Yorkin, I will get in front of him and block his view."

As Loni reached for Yorkin's wings and Boldor stepped in front of the fairy, a bridge glittering with jewels formed across the stream beckoning the prince.

"Stop, I need to go. Out of my way!" Yorkin grasped his sword.

"No!" Screamed Loni. "Beauty, do something to make him see, what is real, Boldor and me."

Nothing happened.

"Get out of my way, unicorn!" hollered the prince. "Or I shall slay you."

"What is happening?" Potemkin asked shaking his head.

"Are you normal?" asked GreeHee.

"Yes, why are you holding me and what's going on?"

"Okay, just stand here Potemkin and do not turn around," said the dragon, vaulting to stop Yorkin.

GreeHee gripped Yorkin, pressing his arms to his body. He lifted the screaming prince, turning him away from the bridge.

"Let me go, you stupid dragon, can't you see the parade? They're waiting for me. Put me down. Stop! Put me down!" Yorkin kicked and hollered.

"Well done, GreeHee!" Boldor smiled. "Hold him till he comes to his senses."

"Where's the parade? GreeHee, where are we?" asked Yorkin.

"I will put you down, Yorkin, right next to Potemkin. But you must promise to keep facing in this direction, okay?" said the dragon.

"Yes, okay," said Yorkin, one eyebrow raised.

Boldor once more stood before the group, but this time he faced the stream and they faced him. "Does anyone here remember what I said about 'The Bode of Satiety'?"

"That it's the most difficult trap because we'll feel good here?" said Loni.

"Yes, everything you have ever wanted and ever dreamed of is here for you. There will be others real and unreal waiting for you, calling to you, offering you gifts of food and other wonderful things. If you take anything or eat anything offered, you will be lost here forever and we will not get through this trap. We haven't even crossed the stream yet and we nearly lost Yorkin and Potemkin. Any suggestions as to how we can get through this?" Boldor sighed.

"Could we be blindfolded?" asked Loni.

"Yes that's a good idea!" said Potemkin nodding

"You will need to have ear plugs too, unless you constantly sing out loud and in your heads, they will get inside your mind," said Boldor.

"We can do this, Boldor!" said Potemkin, putting on his Optimism Oil.

"Hey, what about your Illusion Oil, Boldor? Do you think that could help us here?" asked GreeHee.

"It couldn't hurt. Loni, why don't you test it first?"

"Okay." Loni took the oil and placed it on her forehead.

"Now Loni, close your eyes and turn around facing Yorkin."

Loni did as the unicorn suggested. "Yorkin, hold her, and turn her back around in case it doesn't work."

Yorkin nodded and held his little sister.

"Okay Loni, open your eyes and tell us what you see."

"The trees are beautiful and I see Mother and Eulool beckoning me. Oh look, there is Father! Oh wait, something is happening. The trees are turning old. Father is dying. Oh no, Father!" Loni cried.

"It's okay Loni, it's just an illusion. It's not real," said Yorkin.

"Yes, they are gone. The trees are dead except for a little sparkle that seems to pass across the landscape. It's very weird. But I can hear them as though they are there? It's very confusing, Yorkin. I feel pulled by what I hear and set back by what I see."

"Do you feel like you want to stay in this place, Loni?" asked Boldor.

"No, it's too confusing. I wouldn't feel comfortable sleeping there at all!"

"Okay then, let's all put on the oil and hope it lasts long enough for us to pass through this bode," Boldor said.

Chapter 32

THE DOORWAY OF TIME

"**I** feel strong!" smiled GreeHee, voice booming.

"Yes, me too," said Loni. "The energy is changing, I can feel it."

"Yes, it is changing. We've made it through the Bode of Satiety and will soon come to the staircase that leads to the Doorway of Time," Boldor said.

"I can't wait!" Potemkin smiled. "Can I let go of GreeHee's tail now?"

"Yes, I think we're safe. We've passed the trees and as you can see the ground is changing to stone," said Boldor pointing to the big gray stone floor in the wide corridor ahead.

"Thank the Ancients we have passed that test. I would have stayed there forever." Potemkin said, closing his eyes and licking his lips. "You should have seen the feast my mother had laid out for me. It was a warrior's banquet and it smelled so good."

"Wow, this looks like the entrance to a castle," said Yorkin, pointing to the expansive corridor of four leet square granite stones and flags of coats of arms ahead of them.

"There's the staircase!" exclaimed Boldor, coat flashing pink and lavender. He started to trot.

The staircase stood in the middle of an enormous stone wall. The colossal size and the exquisite embroidered silk banners that adorned the front, created a ceremonial entrance. Ten bottom steps protruded like a half moon and ascended to a wide landing bounded by a wall of two leet square silver stones decorated with stars. At either end of this massive wall were two more staircases with ornate silver railings imprinted with moons, stars and wizard's script. Rising thirty-three steps, they merged onto a wide balcony that appeared to overlook a vast space. It glowed with a the light of three gold stars that could be seen shining in the sky beyond. To the left and right of the balcony rose another set of stairs to a space that could not been seen from where the companions stood at the base.

"What does that say, Boldor?" asked Loni, pointing to the silver rune-like glyphs inlayed on the railings.

"It reads," said the unicorn, "Wizards of light enter here, the stars await you with glory and cheer. If you are not called and have made it thus far, now is the time to wish on a star."

"What does that mean, Boldor?" asked Yorkin tapping his cheek.

"This looks awfully nice but I think we're the ones who are not called and I don't think wishing on a star is going to help us now," said Potemkin, shaking his head.

"Right you are, my little fool!" the voice of Tana boomed. "I have been watching you and congratulate you on reaching the stairway. It will be such fun to play with each of you. She laughed and the voice faded.

"What should we do?" asked GreeHee shaking, the avalanche of rocks and death of Hydous flooding his mind.

"Stay centered, love each other and we will be fine," said the unicorn. "Tana is testing our strength and she is surprised we have made it here, but she knows if we make it through the doorway, she will have only one more chance to destroy us. You can bet she expected one of us to be lost before now. That is why we have not seen her."

"I can't wait to see what the landing overlooks," said Yorkin rushing up the stairs. "Let's get going, and teach Tana a lesson."

"Wait Yorkin, now is the time for you to put on your oil. The last thing we should do in this test is rush forward. This is a test of discernment and intelligence. We cannot afford to make even a small mistake here. The wizards planned this doorway very carefully and one slip can pull any of us or all of us through a time hole."

"A time hole?" asked Loni.

"A space much like the tunnel we came through from The Crystal Forest to the Mystic Mountains, only here we will have no control as to where it takes us." Boldor said, brows knitted, coat flashing dark blue. "However, the good news is that in this doorway, there is a tunnel that bypasses ninety three traps and will leave us in the Hall of Mirrors, which is the final entrance to the Seat of Stars."

"You mean if we miss that tunnel we'll have to go through ninety-three more traps? Dear Tamoor, I could not survive such a thing," said Potemkin, shaking his head, hand on his brow.

"Please Potemkin, put on your Optimism Oil, this is no time to worry about mistakes. We must take each step seriously and know we will make it through to the Hall of Mirrors."

"Boldor, what do we have to do?" asked GreeHee biting his lower lip.

"Exactly what we've been doing, only a little better. That is to say, we need to tether our minds together and take each step aligned with each other. Any voice you hear or vision you see, especially Tana, will be an illusion. You must stay centered in love. Listen to your sound and my voice only. Stay close and follow me." The unicorn began to climb the stairs to The Doorway of Time.

Stepping onto the balcony, Boldor turned to the others. "As you reach this point turn to your left, <u>do not</u> look over the railing or you will be pulled into a time tunnel." Then he added, swishing his tail, "Loni, hold my tail. Yorkin, hold Loni's hand. GreeHee, stay very close, and Potemkin, hold GreeHee's tail. We cannot afford to lose anyone!"

"GreeHee, put your hands over my eyes, please," said Yorkin, wings flicking. "I desperately want to look over the railing, I'm afraid I may do it."

The dragon placed one enormous hand over Yorkin's face.

"Oh, you're smothering me," came Yorkin's muffled voice.

"I think it would be better if I just carry you and force you to face away." GreeHee said, picking Yorkin up and accidentally lifting both fairies and part of Boldor too.

"Wait an elide, GreeHee!" exclaimed the unicorn.

"Oh, sorry." said the dragon as Yorkin let go of Loni. Once they reached the top of the staircase, GreeHee put Yorkin back on the floor.

"That was nearly excellent. As long as we each ask for help, we'll get through this. Only next time a little warning would be nice." The unicorn chuckled, winking at GreeHee.

"Gee what did I miss? You know it's not easy traveling behind the tail of a dragon," said Potemkin.

"We'll tell you the whole story later when we can rest. For now, let's keep moving," Boldor said.

The top of the staircase opened to a large rotunda. On the midnight blue, star sprinkled mosaic floor, spanned the solar system of ten planets around a brilliant sun, tiny Tamoor and her three moons clearly marked with a bright green wizard glyph. Plush velvet benches in deep purples, greens and blues lined the edge of the fifty-leet panoramic mural. Twenty leets further, bounding the perimeter of the rotunda stood seven colossal pearlescent engraved wood arched-doors, guarded by luminous jewel-toned statues of wizards holding books in their right hands and a magical tool in their left. Magnificent gold embellished scrolled columns braced the wondrous color-shifting walls that soared two hundred leets to a celestial vaulted ceiling, shimmering with rainbows.

"This place is breath-taking!" said Loni.

"Yes, this is the welcoming center for wizards. You can tell how powerful their magic is by the incredible beauty, which in no way has been diminished, in nearly a hundred and seventy linglorns."

"Is this our solar system?" asked Potemkin.

"Yes, see here," Boldor touched the bright green wizard glyph with his right hoof, "it says Tamoor. And here are our three little moons."

"I didn't realize there were so many other planets. I knew there were stars but I guess I never thought of them as other planets like ours," GreeHee said, extending his arms.

Pivoting about, Boldor pointed his horn at the seven doorways, "Okay, now is the test of choosing the correct door."

"I like the one with the fairy wizard there," Yorkin, pointed to a green doorway, guarded by a fairy dressed in a long emerald velvet robe studded with gold shooting stars, the face oval, gentle and feminine, aquamarine eyes, long glistening golden hair, and iridescent flittering wings. In her left hand she held a wand with a crystal point, lavender rays emanated from it.

"Yes she looks welcoming, but may not be the correct door," said Boldor.

"What about this one with the giant wizard?" asked Potemkin, pointing to a sky blue silky robed strong masculine giant, with a square jaw, thick eyebrows, piercing brown eyes, and enormous earthy hands. He held a knurled silver wand emitting a crescent moon.

"Also a good possibility but perhaps not correct," said the unicorn.

"How do we know which is the right doorway, Boldor?" asked GreeHee tapping his scaly cheek.

"Well, that is what I'm trying to figure out." The unicorn stood at the base of the mosaic facing all the doors. "The Elders told me to look for the constellation of Narties which in the spring appears from Tamoor's ecliptic to the northeast."

"What is Narties?" asked Loni, eyebrows raised.

"Oh, I know that constellation," Yorkin said, scanning the mosaic, "Eulool taught me Narties is the constellation of five fixed stars in a winged cup formation. Here it is." Yorkin pointed to a milky blue and pink area of the mosaic that looked like a set of wings.

"Yes that is it!" said Boldor, his coat flashing rainbows.

"Where? I don't see it?" asked GreeHee.

"Right here," said Yorkin, pointing to five stars that outlined a chalice. "You can always tell it because it has nebula on the outside of the stars that make it look like it has wings. See!"

"Oh, yes," said GreeHee.

"Yes, I see it too. Don't you, Potemkin?" Loni asked.

"Yes, but how does it show us the right door?" asked the giant.

"Well, once located, we must look to the center star, known as the Star of Wizards and proclaim ourselves."

"How do we do that?" asked Potemkin.

"We must follow a formula to find the proclamation. The formula says take the number of beings and multiply them by the number of stars in Narties, then divide that number by the number of planets in our solar system. Then walk that distance in benchmarks from left to right to find the inscription."

"Wow, that is confusing," said GreeHee, scratching his head and shaking his tail.

"Not that difficult," said Yorkin. "First the number of beings must refer to us, don't you think?"

"Yes, that would be my understanding."

"We are five," Yorkin said showing his right hand. "Then multiply that by the number of stars in Narties and that would be five. So five times five equals twenty-five. Then divide that by the number of planets in our solar system and that would be ten. Ten into twenty-five equals two and a half."

"Okay, that sounds correct but what are benchmarks?" asked Potemkin.

The five stared at each other, then started looking for clues.

"Maybe it is referring to the benches?" asked Loni, flying to the first bench on the left.

"Wait, I think you have the right idea," said Potemkin. "I remember on Tarktor's drawings, he noted benchmarks. They appeared at the base of a structure indicating the distance to the next structure, I think."

Potemkin kneeled on the floor and peered at the base of the first bench. "Here! This must be what they're referring to!" He pointed to a small mark at the bottom of the bench. "See, there's a little silver plate engraved with the number twenty-seven. The number is on an arrow pointing to that bench."

"Yes, that fits the formula," said Boldor.

"I'm going to take your word on this," GreeHee said, not wanting to even attempt to crawl under the bench to look at the number.

Boldor paced, "The formula says then you take that number and walk that distance in benchmarks from left to right."

"So," Yorkin pointed, "if this is the first benchmark and each subsequent one is likely located in the same place on each bench; we would walk to the second bench mark and go half that distance further to find the inscription."

Potemkin scrutinized the second bench, "There's no mark on this one?"

"Try the next one," said Yorkin.

"Yes!" exclaimed Loni. "There's a mark here just like the first one!"

"That means the next bench should have the proclamation." Yorkin said flying to the bench.

"Here it is!" shouted Potemkin, placing his big hand on the small inscription at the front base of the bench.

"What does it say?" asked GreeHee, snaking his head between the fairies.

"It's in Wizard. Boldor will have to read it." Potemkin said.

Everyone backed away.

Boldor knelt down, cocked his head to one side and read, "Dadork et vinkor partin olt tors, Ielt Amin!"

A loud rumbling shook the room. The companions turned to their left and there in an unmarked place on the wall between two well-marked doors, a white almost transparent portal opened.

"Hurry, we need to get in before they close!" said Yorkin, flying toward the opening.

"Wait!" shouted Boldor. "That is not the door!"

Yorkin reached the doorway. He was fading into the white light. The portal started to close.

"Come back now!" Boldor commanded.

"I can't! Something is pulling me!" cried Yorkin.

"I'll get him," said Potemkin leaping.

"I'll help you!" GreeHee vaulted over Potemkin.

"GreeHee, pull me free!" Shouted Yorkin.

GreeHee grabbed the fairy prince around the waist. The dragon felt the doorway's energy pulling on him and the best he could do was to stand still.

"I have your tail, GreeHee, and I won't let you go. Do you have Yorkin?" Potemkin hollered.

"Yes, and I am pulling as hard as I can, but I can't free him. And what's worse I feel myself slipping forward. Boldor, can you help?"

Boldor stood inside the edge of the mosaic and focused energetically to close the doors. Nothing happened.

"GreeHee is being pulled into the doorway! I can see him moving!" Cried Loni. "Please Boldor, try harder."

The unicorn closed his eyes, his coat flashing sharp dark colors. "Loni, tell me when you see something positive.

"Boldor!" screamed GreeHee, claws screeching against the marble floor.

Boldor shouted back, "Sing!" The companions sang their sounds loudly as the unicorn continued to concentrate on closing the doors.

"They're moving! Boldor, they're closing!" shouted Loni.

As the doors reached a halfway point, GreeHee fell backward, clutching Yorkin and nearly crushing Potemkin.

The portal vanished.

Loni flew to her brother shouting, "Yorkin, I thought you put on your oil before we came up the staircase?"

"Gee, I thought I had too," Yorkin's eyebrows raised and he reached into his pocket for the little blue bottle.

"Let me see that," Potemkin said, taking the potion. "This is my bottle, it's green! How in Tamoor did that happen?"

"Ahaaah," came the laugh of Tana, "a slight of hand, my little fools." Then in a stinging malevolent voice she added, "And my trick almost worked!"

A shiver ran through the companions.

"Shake it off," Boldor said, taking a deep breath and throwing his head.

Potemkin gave the blue bottle to Yorkin, "Here's the right oil."

Taking a deep sigh, GreeHee asked Boldor. "What did we do wrong? I thought we followed the formula correctly?"

"We didn't speak the proclamation from the right position," Boldor said, shaking his silky white head. "If everyone is ready, stand with me at the center of the mosaic and face the center door." The companions did as they were told crowding very close to Boldor. "Dadork et vinkor partin olt tors, Ielt Amin!"

Chapter 33

THE HALL OF MIRRORS

A roaring wind surrounded the five and lifted them into the air. As they floated upward the ceiling opened.

In another tithe they stood together at one end of a long corridor lined with towering white marble pillars. It appeared to go on forever.

"What is this place?" asked GreeHee.

"This is 'The Hall of Mirrors', corridor to 'The Seat of Stars'. We're almost home," said Boldor.

"I don't see any mirrors. Where are they Boldor?" asked Loni.

"They're everywhere. You may think this corridor goes on forever but it does not. The mirrors create the illusion of distance."

"What are we supposed to do here?" asked Yorkin.

"Step through the corridor without entering a mirror. So it is wise if we stand still for a moment so I can get my bearings. This Hall has many clues but you need to know how to see them." Boldor said.

The unicorn stood still and GreeHee wondered what part he would play here. Will I have the courage I need? Am I really the dragon of the prophecy? An icy voice interrupted his thoughts.

"What's the matter, unicorn, afraid to make a mistake?" taunted the voice of Tana, shattering the silence. "Here, let me help you." The blue troll face, curled lips, orange eyes and whipping dragon tail appeared at the end of the corridor. "I will move the pillars out of the way!"

In a tithe the infinite white colonnade slid back against the walls. The gigantic mirrors became obvious, equally stationed every twenty leets between the half round pillars. The five's reflection bounced from mirror to mirror infinitely into the distance.

"Now, isn't everything crystal clear!" Tana laughed, her swirling orange eyes, and writhing troll hands towered over them in every reflection.

"Boldor, what should we do?" Loni's voice cracked, blue eyes wide.

"Loni, put on your oil and everyone, sing in your heads while I figure out this maze of mirrors. Stay very close to me. I'm putting a telepathic rope of love around us and you should be able to feel it. Stay inside that rope."

"You think your telepathic commands can save these little fools! Ha! This is going to be fun devouring each of you. Why not step here? This is the entrance, unicorn," Tana called, forming a doorway filled with the night sky in a mirror not far from where the group stood.

"No, I think we need to consider awhile before stepping into your game," replied Boldor in a calm even voice.

"Look at the floor, Boldor." whispered Yorkin.

"Excellent!" said Boldor.

The floor, like the pillars, was white marble and there were subtle changes in color as it reflected light back from the mirrors.

"Look here, unicorn!" Tana flung an image of the Crystal Forest across the boundless mirrors, trees uprooted, ground burnt, dead unicorns charred and burning like embers in a dying fireplace. "I've broken your code and destroyed your Elders but you will never break my code!" She laughed again.

GreeHee closed his eyes, he touched Boldor's back. "Boldor, --"

"Are you all right?" asked Loni leaning against his silky neck.

"It's just an illusion, Loni. The Elders are fine. Tana is taunting us hoping we will miss the clues. Keep looking at the floor and for anything that appears to be stable, not wavering, as light on a mirror surface."

"You, Potemkin!" Images of dead giants flashed along the reflective corridor and then it focused on one body, the King, as Tana spoke. "Your King Narsor is in his grave and your castle has been leveled by my trolls. Nadeckador's castle looks better!"

"I only know you are evil, Tana, and that your game is filled with lies," Potemkin said, voice steady but body shaking.

"Boldor, could we ask Draydel for help?" asked Yorkin.

"Draydel is dead. He died the last time we met," Tana said. But her voice cracked.

"Oh, he may be dead but you are worried about him aren't you, Tana?" coaxed Boldor.

"Don't be such a fool, unicorn, I am afraid of no one! I am more powerful than anyone has ever been or ever will be on Tamoor."

"Loni, take out the book," Boldor said.

"You wanted to go to your father's four hundredth birth party, little Loni, but your father had a seizure when my trolls murdered your mother and sisters and now he is dead!" Tana shouted, images filled the mirrors with the crumbling Castle Farion, hundreds of trolls crushing fairies, and ripping wings from the bodies of the King and Queen.

"You lie! You lying coward!" screamed Yorkin and he began to break through the rope.

"Hold him, GreeHee!" shouted Potemkin as he grabbed the fairy prince's arm.

GreeHee quickly placed his hand in front of Yorkin, forcing him back inside the rope. "Don't give her what she wants. She is taunting you because she cannot touch us here, don't you see that," said GreeHee.

"You are correct, GreeHee. As long as we stay close and act as one Tana cannot hurt us," Boldor stated.

"I will destroy you, all of you. You cannot stay close for much longer and soon you will be mine." Tana laughed her terrifying laugh. An enormous image of Tana's orange eyes filled the corridor, then her hand came forward holding the five, her eyes swirled red-orange, blue mouth dripped blood. Screams and sounds of bones breaking echoed as she crushed the five bodies, blood oozing down her blue arm.

GreeHee's body twitched. He felt the others trembling. "Shake it off! It's an illusion," Boldor said shaking his mane. "Loni, the book!"

Shaking out her wings, blonde hair flying, Loni said, "Here's it is."

"Fine, let's face each other with Loni in the center and see if Draydel can give us a clue." Boldor turned to face the others. Loni and Yorkin stood beneath GreeHee. Potemkin to his left and Boldor faced him.

As Loni held the book before the group, together they said, "Draydel, please, give us clue."

Loni opened the book and Draydel sparkled like an emerald waterfall.

"I wish I could open the door for you and so does Queen Beetrea,"

The Queen appeared in a soft lavender light, auburn hair flowing. "We have been with you all the way and we are very proud of you," said the Queen in a melodic voice. "Combine what you learned at the Pool of Reckoning and Tana will step back so you can see. Then look for light and sound. The Seat of Stars has a blue light just like the star in GreeHee's hand. The sound is the wind and if you hear it, you will feel it. Then follow it and you will be there."

Draydel and the Queen disappeared. Tana was absent.

"She knows," said Boldor. "She knows she is no match for Draydel, the Queen, and us."

"But what did we each learn at the Pool of Reckoning?" asked GreeHee.

"I learned that though Tana's heart is cold, it can be warmed by love," said Loni. "So instead of fearing her we need to send her love. But I am not sure how to do this?"

"I know how," said Yorkin. "By sending her pictures. At the pool Eulool told me that I could send Tana images just as she creates images for us. All

I could think of was sending Tana images that would destroy her and I had been warned that this would be dangerous. But if we combine what I learned with Loni's understanding we should send Tana pictures of love!"

"Oh, that is so perfect!" said Potemkin. "I learned that time is not real and therefore we always have time to be wise before taking action. So we do not have to rush in our search for the Seat of Stars, instead we can practice loving Tana and looking for the light and sound as Queen Beetrea suggested."

"Exactly," said Boldor, flashing pink and green. "I feel us tethering closer as each one speaks. We are becoming centered in our gathered power." And to the dragon he asked, "GreeHee, you have been silent. What did you learn at the Pool of Reckoning?"

"I didn't understand what I learned until now. My experience at the Pool was filled with pain. I felt my parents and ancestors were ashamed of me and that I should not continue the journey. But now in light of all we have experienced together and what each of you learned at the Pool, I realize love is at the core of joy, and friendship is at the core of love. To commit oneself to another or to others as we have done is by far the purest form of love and its reward is both joy and friendship. The bond we have created cannot be broken by Tana's evil because we love each other wholly without judgment or fear." GreeHee paused a tithe, then added, "Each of you have taught me to trust myself because you each have put your trust in me. Trust that is reciprocated breeds love, not only of each other but of ourselves."

"GreeHee, you are one deep-thinking dragon!" said Potemkin, smiling. "I feel empowered to face Tana and finish our task."

"Me too!" said Yorkin and Loni together.

"I am very proud of all of you," said Boldor, smiling. "We are centered and ready to enter the Seat of Stars. Let's focus on the light and sound."

The group closed their eyes.

"I can hear the wind," GreeHee said, "It is coming from our right."

The group moved toward what appeared to be their own reflection.

"Look at the floor," said Yorkin. "It has a different cast in the reflection. Doesn't it look blue to everyone?"

The highly polished marble shone white along the corridor, but a few leets on the right, a hint of blue like the shadow of a fairy wing, almost imperceptible.

The group crept carefully, in tiny fairy steps.

"Yes, and I can feel the wind now," said Loni.

"I can smell it," said GreeHee.

"I don't like this," said Potemkin.

"Why?" asked Boldor.

"Tana is too silent and it looks like we are going into a mirror."

"Potemkin, your optimism oil has worn off. Trust us," said Yorkin. "And look at the floor, it's turning blue!"

"Yes, that does look good," said the giant as the others chuckled.

"Boldor, my hand is itching. Right where the Star of Knowing is, what do you think that means?" asked the dragon.

"I don't know GreeHee, but I think we're about to enter the Seat of Stars."

"Maybe it wants to join the other stars, GreeHee. Maybe this is its home," said Loni.

"I feel the wind getting stronger," said Boldor.

"It is getting very loud too," said Yorkin.

"Look to the right and to the left!" shouted Potemkin.

"We're moving through the space like light on water. Our images are rippling. This is the door!" Boldor exclaimed.

A loud popping filled the air and GreeHee felt as though they had burst from a bottle into a new place. An enormous circular room, the ceiling looked like the solar system they had seen in the mosaic except now it was real.

"It's as though we have a room in the stars and can watch the solar system at work," said Potemkin.

In the center of the room stood a big round carved golden table.

"Look, there are five places set at the table, it's as though someone is expecting us," said Loni.

"Right! I am expecting you!" Tana appeared in her hideous fleshy form. "Take this, you little love bugs!" she threw lightening bolts at them.

Boldor said, "Sing and love." He held the light rope tight around the five.

Their voices rose as one and formed a mirror of blinding light.

The lightening bolts turned back on Tana. She screamed dodging them.

Tana moved closer. "I will set fire to each of you. Who wants to be first?"

The five kept singing, eyes closed, their voices grew louder as she spoke.

"The little fairy princess should be first. Barbequed, she will make a tasty appetizer," Tana said, now close enough to touch Loni.

The group continued to sing. GreeHee opened one eye. He watched Tana, still singing but waiting for her to strike.

Tana grabbed for Loni's head. "Aaagh, my hand is on fire!"

GreeHee smiled as he sang and watched. The others seemed in a trance.

Tana said, "So, you think it's funny. Well try this you runtling wimp of a dragon." Tana fired upon GreeHee.

"Aagh!" GreeHee screamed, raising his right hand to cover his face.

Instinctually he inhaled to blow fire, but nothing came out. The pain had disappeared and he felt calm.

"Ha, I guess I will just destroy you, GreeHee. You're powerless to attack me, bound in your little mirror with your chanting friends. But you will slowly be burnt alive, then I will take them one by one and Tamoor will be mine." Tana drew in a deep breath and fired on the dragon.

GreeHee's right hand turned palm out covering his face. The Star of Knowing flew from his palm turning the flame directly at Tana.

"Aaagh!" Tana screamed.

"What's happening?" Loni and Yorkin asked, waking from the trance.

The Star flew into Tana, bursting into a brilliant blue light. It lifted her shrieking into the night sky.

"It's the Star of Knowing!" Loni shouted.

"Ancient Tamoor, the Star has trapped Tana!" shouted Potemkin.

"GreeHee, you had the key all the time and Draydel knew it!" Yorkin grinned, slapping the dragon's shoulder.

"I didn't know it," said GreeHee, mouth agape, staring at Tana.

"What do we do now?" asked Potemkin.

"We need to take our places at the table and complete the journey," Boldor released a long breath, as he watched the Star of Knowing begin to shoot through the solar system carrying Tana. "Come to the table and let's see what the Wizards have for us."

Five gold and silver place settings dressed the big circular table, instead of place cards, the unusual lights suggested seating.

"Look!" said Loni "There's my crystal and Yorkin's wand."

"And my star and Boldor's horn." Added GreeHee.

"And my torch!" exclaimed Potemkin. "No question those wizards knew we were coming." Potemkin sat in a big gold velvet chair.

They gathered around the table, the giant and fairies sat in comfortable chairs, the dragon sat on a bed of soft down, and the unicorn stood in soothing sea foam.

After a moment a whirring sound began. The Star of Knowing had entered the constellation of Narties. The winged cup merged in a great ball of light engulfing Tana and the Star. The nebula swirled around it and a powerful light struck the table filling it with food and music. The light circled the five, five times and then pulled back into the sky claiming The Star of Knowing for it's own and thrusting a black star filled with Tana further into the solar system.

"Where are they sending Tana?" asked Loni.

"It looks like she is being transported to the far side of the galaxy to the constellation of Sakorst," said Yorkin.

"Is that the constellation of the Night Riders?" asked Potemkin.

"Yes, but the correct name is the Horsemen of Death," Boldor said.

"Why would they take her there instead of killing her?" asked GreeHee.

Boldor, flicked his ears, saying, "Because you cannot kill a merged star such as Tana. She is an immortal and that is why she toyed with us. She thought mere mortals could not win against her power."

"How did we win?" asked Yorkin.

"By acting as one," said Boldor.

"Look at Narties!" exclaimed Loni.

In deep space, the tiny five star chalice merged into a single brilliant star, it's milky nebula closed around it creating a wondrous blue glow in the heavens.

"Holy Mother of Tamoor, it is as the prophecy stated!" said Potemkin.

"Yes, the merging of five stars!" said Yorkin. "What do you think they will call Narties now?"

"Maybe it should be called, GreeHee's Star," said Boldor, winking at the dragon. "Since it took the Star of Knowing to bind the five."

"Yes I will drink to that!" Potemkin held out his glass.

Four goblets were raised to honor the dragon. GreeHee's eyes filled and he said in a near whisper, "I am honored."

"Here! Here! To GreeHee's Star!"

Chapter 34

WARRIORS' WELCOME

When the sun threw her rosy fingers over the horizon, GreeHee awoke no longer in the Seat of Stars. Instead he and his companions slept under the golden canopy, known as 'The Point of Gold' at the top of Wizards' Web. He sat up, breathed deeply the fresh mountain air and listened to the gentle voices from the far side of the cupola.

"What a wonderful beedite this is!" said Loni flying next to Boldor, who stood looking out over the Mystic Mountains.

Mountain peaks shimmered in the brilliant orange glow of dawn. Far below the Mystic River still cloaked in violet shadows, rushed cold and swirling to the distant teal blue Azura Kah.

"Yes, finally we can go home without fear of Tana," said the unicorn.

"I didn't realize there was so much water around this mountain," Loni said, looking down the mountainside.

Hundreds of leets below, past the evergreens patched with magnolias, cherry blossoms and violets, swirled the Mystic Wizard tributary, a magical moat of blue water a hundred leets wide flowing around Wizards' Web.

"Ah, the illusions we have been dealt. But the good news is Tana is gone and we may go home and deal with the reality she has left behind." Boldor said, his coat muted colors of lavender, pink, and gold.

"Do you think my father is dead?" asked the little fairy.

"What do you think, Loni?"

Loni smiled, "I think Castle Farion stands and we will have a parade when we get home."

"Then let it be so," said the unicorn.

"Wow, look at the water!" said Yorkin stretching. "Can we go for a swim?"

"I think that would be delightful," said Boldor.

"I have had such strange dreams. What about you two?" Yorkin asked.

"Yes, prophetic and lucid," said the unicorn.

"Well, if it's prophetic, I'm going to get that parade after all," Yorkin smiled.

"No doubt," Loni said, "and I think there will be lots of room in Oberlon for the Commander and GreeHee."

"Hm. I hadn't really considered where I might go when we finished this journey," said GreeHee joining them. "Oberlon is a beautiful place."

"There's Narsor too, you know. You will always have friends in Narsor." Potemkin yawned, slapping GreeHee's shoulder.

"Thank you, Potemkin, I will consider that. You know I prefer mountains and this is a beautiful place. I wonder how Doder is doing?"

"If we're all awake, let's go down to the Mystic River and take a dip. After that we'll find Doder," Boldor said to his companions, their faces warm with the glow of dawn.

The five left the mountaintop Potemkin on GreeHee's back and the fairies with Boldor. After an energizing dip in the icy river they headed to the bridge where they had first met Doder.

"Isn't this great!" said Loni as they landed. "Doder has lots of new friends."

Under the silver railing, seven crows chatted away watching the sunrise.

"Oh these are my friends, they are. They are!" Doder greeted the five.

"Doder you look well!" said GreeHee, smiling.

"And you have new friends," said Loni.

"Yes, yes I do, I do!" said Doder, beaming, his chest puffed. "And all of you are well too! I am so happy, I am happy to see all of you again. Then Tana is dead? Is she dead, Tana?" asked the crow, eyebrows raised, flapping.

"Not exactly dead," said Boldor.

"But no longer in Tamoor," said Potemkin.

"And I don't think she will ever bother us again," said Yorkin.

"Then we should celebrate! We will celebrate." Doder stuttered.

Boldor began, "Actually we are on our way home and--"

"But you will get the treasure? Remember the treasure? You will get the treasure, won't you?" asked Doder.

"What about it, Boldor?" asked Yorkin.

"It'll only take us a few moments," Potemkin added.

"Yes, let's go," said the unicorn.

The five and Doder flew to the cave where Hydous had died.

"Oh my! Oh my!" exclaimed Doder. "It's so clear and pretty. Very pretty."

The green grassy meadow dotted with delicate posies sparkled with light, abundant with flowering fruits serenaded by bees, finches and jays.

"Yes Doder, Tana's magic is gone and the valley is alive with fragrant flowers and song." Potemkin said.

Inside the cave stretched fifty leets wide, little shafts of light filtered through cracks in the sandstone ceiling. Barrels of gold coins and trunks of shiny jewels glistened throughout the uneven brown and red rock floor.

"Potemkin, where is the cistern that you fell into? asked GreeHee.

"Huh?" Potemkin said eyebrows raised, holding a sack of gold coins.

"As I suspected," said Boldor, "There was no cistern, was there, Potemkin?"

"I don't know what you're talking about," said the giant.

"I suspected Tana might be using Hydous, the dear sweet crow," Boldor said, "to lure us into this cave."

"What do you mean, Boldor?" questioned Loni.

"If you remember Loni, while we were helping GreeHee, Hydous approached and Beauty streamed red."

"Yes, I remember."

"That is when I deduced Tana must be using Hydous, much the same way she used General Maltor when we were in the Crystal Mountains. She wanted to get us into this cave."

"You mean you were not trapped in a cistern, Potemkin?" asked Yorkin standing on top of a trunk.

"No. I was trapped by Tana!" said Potemkin, brows knitted, hands on hips.

"Well, now it makes sense to me," said Loni flying over to Boldor. "That's why you had us wait outside - because Tana wanted to trap us all in here."

"Holy Tamoor!" GreeHee said, shaking his head and looking at the entrance. " She could have crashed this opening and we'ld have never gotten out."

"Thank you Boldor," Loni said hugging the unicorn's neck.

Boldor beamed, his coat flashing gold and pink.

Yorkin and Potemkin filled their packs with gold coins and jewels.

"Look, Yorkin!" said Loni, holding a fabulous double tiered gold and emerald necklace up for him to see. "Don't you think mother will love this?"

"That is gorgeous and yes, mother will love it."

Loni placed it in her pocket.

They found a pack filled with gold and gave it to GreeHee.

As they reached the bridge, Doder asked, "Will I see you again? Sometime? Soon?"

"Yes, I don't know when but we'll return at sometime to collect more of the treasure," said Yorkin.

"Who can say when?" said GreeHee. "I too am sure we will return but I'm not sure how soon. Do take care of yourself, Doder, and thanks for all the help."

"Take care, Doder," said Loni, giving the crow a hug.

"May the ancients bless you, Doder," Boldor said.

The sun shone high above them, the Mystic Mountains resplendent in lavenders, purples, and blues. At their feet, trees in every shade of green danced in the breeze, birds sang and the Mystic River rushed and swirled, crashing over rocks in frothy kisses.

As they landed on the grassy knoll at the opening of the tunnel to the Crystal Forest, Potemkin asked, "How much will we forget, Boldor, once we go through the mirror?"

"I'm not certain how much you need to forget now that Tana is gone. Perhaps the Elders will have a plan when we get to the Crystal Forest. I will be saddened if I'm the only one who can remember this incredible journey."

"I hope we will remember," said Loni, touching Boldor's shoulder.

As they entered the Crystal Forest, there in the rainbow mist at the bottom of the waterfall, waited hundreds of jubilant unicorns. The Elders stood in front and greeted Boldor as he emerged from behind the falls.

"Welcome home, Boldor!" said Majesic, the Merlin of the Elders. "And welcome to each of you!" he added, sending a wave of love to embrace Loni, Yorkin, GreeHee, and Potemkin.

The unicorns cheered in their unique way, telepathically sending lily and rose petals into the air and making musical high-pitched sounds, much like notes on a piccolo.

"We cannot thank each of you enough for your courage and wisdom. You have saved Tamoor and we wish to honor you," the Merlin said, energetically raising five beautiful gold medals into the air and suspending them in front of each of the five. The medals had the word 'Honor' above a picture of Wizen, the ancient unicorn on one side and a picture of the Crystal Forest surrounded by the phrase, 'Gratitude For Courage & Wisdom' on the other. Each medal was strung on wide emerald green ribbon.

"Oh, this is beautiful!" exclaimed Loni, reaching for the one in front of her.

"Thank you this means so much to me!" exclaimed Potemkin.

"Thank you!" said Yorkin, mouth gaping.

"I am so grateful, I cannot believe this is happening," said GreeHee, touching the gold to his heart.

The unicorns escorted the companions to the Sacred Mirror of Time, an enormous white energy field that vibrated, shimmered, and gleamed reflecting images like a looking-glass.

"Majesic," said Boldor bowing to the Elder, "Is it possible that my friends may remember everything except the coded secrets of the Crystal Mountains?"

"We have already considered this, Boldor," replied Majesic, the other six Elders nodded. "It will be so! And," he said to the fairies, giant, and dragon, "We have decided to let you pass through the mirror directly to Oberlon, so you will not tarry in the Crystal Mountains. It is a small gift for you."

"Your Highest Elder," said Potemkin, bowing to Majesic, "could I go directly home to Narsor?"

"If you wish, Potemkin, but your giants are waiting for you at Castle Farion, are they not?" said Majesic.

"Oh, yes, I totally forgot about them, I have been so worried about my king," Potemkin said, looking down. Then turning again to the Merlin, he implored. "Has there been any word from Narsor? Can you tell me anything?"

"We have watched and seen many devastating events take place in your homeland. Your King is dying and I do not believe he will last much longer."

"Then please, Your Highest, send me directly home. I must see him before he dies."

"As you wish," the Elder Unicorn replied.

Turning to Yorkin, Potemkin said, "Yorkin, tell Tyron it is my command that he lead the troop home to Narsor."

"Yes, Potemkin I shall," the fairy replied locking hands with the giant.

Loni hugged Boldor's neck, tears flowing, "goodbye."

"Let us not say goodbye," Boldor said to his friends. "Let us plan to meet again in Oberlon one moontide from now and then together we can delve into a deeper understanding of the events of our journey."

"Oh that would be wonderful!" said Loni brightening.

"I agree!" said Yorkin and GreeHee.

"Excellent!" said Potemkin, face strained, fingers twitching.

"Then let us say, until then!" Boldor smiled, telepathically embracing the four as they entered the Mirror.

In a tithe Yorkin, Loni, and GreeHee found themselves at the entrance to Castle Farion.

"They're here! They're here!" shouted Doctor Paychente and Sarolla, both standing in the courtyard. Voices inside and around the castle picked up their words, echoing them everywhere. Fairies and giants poured into the courtyard to greet the threesome.

"Father! Mother!" shouted Loni as her parents came running toward her.

"We're so proud of you!" said King Allielt, embracing his children.

GreeHee smiled watching them. He felt a longing inside for the love of family he had never known. Then something touched his tail and he spun around to see Eulool.

"I am so proud of you!" said the Wizard. "We have seen much of the journey in the gazing ball and you are truly a "Master of the Heart", GreeHee! This is for you from me and all of us in Oberlon," Eulool said, throwing an embrace of light and love around the dragon. Hundreds of fairies flew about him giving the dragon fairy kisses and tiny hugs. The warmth, the love, the joy, I will remember this all my life.

The next beedite GreeHee watched and waved, as Tyron followed Potemkin's orders and left with Sarolla, Pazard, and the others. GreeHee and Paychente stayed behind in Oberlon.

Feelings mixed with joy and sadness. GreeHee pondered the vast distruction that Tana had generated, thousands had died, property and homes had been destroyed, and now one leedite after his return, word arrived from the land of Narsor, that Potemkin's beloved King had died.

In the midst of all this, GreeHee watched as Oberlon made plans for a parade to honor him and his companions at the next moontide when Boldor would arrive. No one knew for sure if Potemkin would make it for the parade. Rumor had it a change in kingship was stirring in Narsor.

GreeHee settled into Oberlon to ponder, to rest and to wonder, how this journey had changed his life and what destiny or wizards might have in store for him next.

About the Author

Michele Avanti
www.MicheleAvanti.com

Michele Avanti is a lover of other worlds. She has been traveling to the inner planes, as she calls them, since birth. To her Tamoor is a real place and GreeHee and Loni are real beings. No, not on earth, as she will tell you, but in Tamoor, a land before men, in a time that must be reached by inner travel - through dreams, daydreams, meditation, or conscious travel.

What was your greatest difficulty in writing the Tales of Tamoor?
"To convey to the reader all I experience. I don't only see, hear and feel GreeHee or Loni, but all the characters, their thoughts and emotions in every scene. The rules of fiction preclude my telling all!"

What are your aspirations for Tamoor?
"Well, I have quite a few. First, I'ld like fantasy lovers to visit and experience the wonder and beauty of Tamoor and the precocious nature of innocence.

We, humans, are a wonderous species at birth, but too easily filled with fear, depleted of wonder and robbed of love. If I could give anything to every person on this planet, I would toss my fairy dust and give each one the freedom to love themselves. I'm not speaking ego, but innocent joyous love. When anyone is filled with love, they're like a helium balloon, lifting everything and everyone in their path.

I hope many readers will make their vision of Tamoor into a physical form. I can see Tamoor as a video game, much like The Legend of Zelda. I have been told by my personal guides that it will be a film, and some years back, one of my dear artist friends who was a Disney animator at the time felt it was perfect material for a Disney film. I don't know if I will write the screenplay or if someone else will.

Right now, I'm developing a set of forty-eight or fifty trading cards. My fabulous artist Jane Starr Weils is gathering a group of artists to create the paintings. There are forty-six characters in the original manuscript, though some have been deleted from the book, but they will all appear in the cards. I plan to have the first run of twelve available at Faeireworlds Festival in Eugene, Oregon, July 2007.

I'm also working on the Tales of Tamoor website. There will be a section titled 'Characters' and there you will be able to click on a character's name and learn more about them. What I cannot put in a book, I will be putting on the website. I also plan to add art for each character as the paintings are available.

The website will also have a section for artists to present their Tamooran artwork for sale and I have plans to offer other licensed items there as well.

I'm also planning a blog where readers can ask questions regarding the book or other items.

Finally, my dream is to make the website interactive where a reader can actually travel through Tamoor to visit GreeHee's cave or Castle Farion or Wizards' Web and even fly along the Crystal River or the Mystic River. I want to make Tamoor real for everyone to visit and rediscover their personal passion and love of self.

Oh, and I'm also working on a theatrical Mp3 version of the book.

You're amazing! I look forward to seeing what you create.
Why did you decide to write this tale?

"Over the decades, I've worked with literally thousands of people. I have witnessed their pain, their desire for good and the burden of their souls. This book, hopefully will give them a place to visit, to refresh their energy and to remember that a divine hand weaves all our imperfections into a magnificent tapestry. Each of us needs so desperately to learn the lesson that GreeHee learns in this book - to love yourself and in so doing - to follow your heart."

You're passionate about this issue, why is it so important to you?

"I believe that when we are born, we are clearly driven by our soul's desire and soul is passionate. The majority of adults I see today are living to pay bills, not waking each morning vibrant with a passion for life, excited to experience the wonder and joy of being here in this amazing world. I love what I do and have lived a life filled with fascinating experiences and incredible people. I wish this for eveyone and hope that GreeHee's awakening might help some to re-align themselves with their passion."

In the book you talk about evil, do you believe what Boldor says?

"Yes. I was raised on the inner planes (a place most people only go to in their dreamtime) to see this world as a playpen, that Creator made for us, It's beloved creations. In this safe environment we can in time, master the art of creation (or as many people call it, manifestation). Here we all have the freedom to create whatever we want, be it good or evil. But we as soul will always remain pure and protected at the highest level of creation. Does that mean that I sanction evil, no. But I realize that souls sometimes need to experience it in order to understand it. I also realize that karma is the Creator's way of teaching us - over lifetimes the value of good and the value of love."

You have created five characters, what do they represent to you?

"Great question! Most people will not notice the thread behind these characters but they actually represent the five bodies of man. Physical, Astral, Mental, Etheric and Soul. Potemkin embodies the Physical, Yorkin, the Astral, GreeHee, the Mental, Loni the Etheric and Boldor, Soul. Each character vibrates in and out of all the levels during the story but carries a preponderance in the area I have designated. This is how we develop consciousness and self-mastery by vibrating at higher levels in each lifetime and eventually sustaining the vibration of the one above. This is the true journey of soul, so when we read about this journey it resonates with our soul, calling us home."

I understand this is the first of five books, can you tell us more about the next one?

"The next book is titled, *Potemkin In Search of The Manuscript*. In it Potemkin travels with his companions to the City of Teeth to find the Manuscript hidden by Tana that reveals how to create a star. It is filled with adventure, mystery and mystical insights."

Why are you donating a portion of the book sales to the SPCA?

"Because we need to realize that all life forms are blessed and that we - the ones with the thumbs, written language and computers - are the designated guardians for all life on our planet. The Society for the Prevention of Cruelty to Animals is a no-kill shelter that cares for animals that have been neglected, abandoned or abused by their guardians. I pray more people will realize how important our job of steward is."

Original Art
by
Jane Starr Weils

Water Spirits

Rose Fairy

Rose Maident

Monarch Butterfly Queen

About the Artist

Jane Starr Weils
www.JaneStarrWeils.com

Jane Starr Weils is a painter of intoxicating beauty and the hypnotic myth of bygone days. Inspired by ancient cultures and the romantic drama of the Pre-Raphaelites, Jane draws the viewer into her world of legend and magick with mesmerizing color and the thread of symbolism woven into every painting.

Through multiple layers of watercolor, colored pencils, and sometimes gouache and ink, Jane explores the depth and richness of color evoking the enchanting dance of shadow and light.

Self-taught for the most part, some wonderful people have influenced and inspired her. Outstanding high school art teachers imbued her with their passion and talent. During one semestar at a local college in Arizona, a brilliant art history teacher challenged and inspired Jane to take the next step in becoming the artist.

Jane's romance with the Medieval Era - it's art, peoples and legends, influence not only her painting but also her daily life. She is Celtic in blood and a fiery red- haired Lady in appearance. Jane is a member of two re-enactment clubs - *Norseland,* and *The Society for Creative Anachronism* (SCA).

Born in New Hampshire, Jane lived most of her adult life in the Western United States, owning and operating art galleries in Jerome and Sedona Arizona, as well as, in Silver City, New Mexico. All enchanting and inspiring places! Eventually she relocated to an idyllic setting in upstate New York. There Jane currently lives, with her three kitties and wonderful husband in a charming, hundred year old farm house by a beautiful river.

GreeHee Publishng

GreeHee Publishing will release Three Books in 2006

Secrets of Wisdom - *A Toolkit For Living*

No matter what path you are on, what your belief system, this book will give you keys to live life to the fullest, understand how to honor and work with others and how to avoid the traps to enjoying each moment of your life.
In minutes you will learn how to tabulate your real nature, the traps and talents you were born with and how to figure that for everyone you know. This book is easy reading and filled with simple techniques.

    Pocketsize Softcover $7.95
    ISBN   978-0-9779590-1-3

Learn The Tarot - *Beginner to Professional*

In Mp3 format, you will be able to take one of the most complete classes available on how to read tarot cards. This class is over thirteen hours, includes a small booklet and online assistance. You will have access to online materials as well as the teacher for questions. Visit www.GreeHee.com to see chapter titles.

    Mp3 coded on CD plus booklet   **$98.00**
    ISBN   **978-0-9779590-2-0**

Place an order at: www.GreeHee.com or call: 775-673-6568
Also available at: Borders Books & www.Amazon.com

Potemkin
In Search of The Manuscript

by
Michele Avanti

Coming in 2008

Tales of Tamoor
Book Two

Register now for a First Edition of
Tales of Tamoor Book Two. And you will recieve a pre-order form as soon as the book goes to press, this will assure you of getting one of the Limited First Editions.

Each book in the series of **Tales of Tamoor**
will first be printed in a Limited First Edition,
signed and numbered by the author.

To Register, go to **www.GreeHee.com** or write to:
GreeHee Publishing - Potemkin Registration
125 Susan Street Myrtle Creek, OR 97457

City of Teeth

Wolfking Mountains

DORCOR FOREST

TROLL

OGRES HOLLOW

Home of GREEHEE

BRYN SERES

YEASTIN? MARSH

BLOOD BARRENS

FAIRINS ROUND

PLAINS OF SASSO

RIVER RYON

VERDANT VALLEY

BRENTIPPEES RIVER

LAND OF NARSOR

CRYSTAL RIV

JEWELED MOUNTAINS

SADO SWAMP

VALLEY OF BORTERLEEN

MYSTIC MOUNTA

WIZARD'S WEB